DARK ENERGY

by

S.W. Ahmed

BRANE Science Fiction

DARK ENERGY

Published by
Brane Science Fiction

ISBN: 0-9815263-7-3
ISBN-13: 978-0-9815263-7-9

PRINTED IN THE UNITED STATES OF AMERICA

Sequel to the book DARK MATTER, published in 2008.

To my parents,
for the gift of a life full of blessings
beyond the reach of far too many.

TABLE OF CONTENTS

AUTHOR'S NOTE

String theory is currently the leading framework in modern physics with the lofty goal of unifying the four fundamental forces of nature – electromagnetism, gravity, and the strong and weak nuclear forces. It also attempts to unify the two most established, conflicting theories of nature – general relativity which deals with the very large, and quantum mechanics which deals with the very small. In essence, string theory postulates that all subatomic particles are actually composed of tiny strings that vibrate in different ways, giving rise to the possibility of many different dimensions beyond our own. Raised to the macroscopic level, this has led to the coining of a whole new branch of science known as brane cosmology, whose central tenet is that our entire universe, as unfathomably big as it is, is nothing but a three-dimensional "brane" in a much larger, multi-dimensional "bulk." It also implies the possible existence of countless other branes in the bulk, some of them existing in other dimensions of which we have no perception or understanding.

Over the past few decades, scientists have become increasingly convinced that the empty space in our universe actually isn't empty. Rather, it's filled with a hypothetical form of energy that has the opposite effect of gravity and is causing the universe to expand at an ever-increasing rate. Not only is this energy invisible to us, the knowledge of its composition and how it came into existence continues to evade us. Hence why it's been given the name "dark energy." Of the total mass-energy density in the universe, it is estimated that all visible atoms make up only 4.6%, dark matter constitutes 23% and dark energy takes all the rest at a whopping 72%.

While neither the existence of branes in a multi-dimensional bulk nor of dark energy has so far been proven with any direct, empirical evidence, both theories are gaining momentum as their effects continue to be indirectly observed and made sense of by the world's leading scientists. The story in this book, a sequel to my first book Dark Matter, offers one possible explanation for these two great scientific theories of our time.

Chapter 1

The view from the podium was bare. All Marc could see were the bright lights pointed at his face. Beyond lay nothing but a dark, empty auditorium. Perhaps it was all he wanted to see, or perhaps it didn't matter one way or the other. The hundreds of people who sat there quietly, listening intently to every word he uttered, could just as well not have been there at all.

His eyes drifted briefly to his laptop. The contents of the slide deck he knew by heart. Over the past few months, he had delivered the same speech to audiences all over the country.

"The latest projections serve as clear evidence of the importance of our work," he said softly, pointing to images of statistics charts on the projector screen. "Assuming that the current economic growth trends continue, China's GDP will overtake ours by as early as 2025. Other emerging economies like India, Brazil, Russia and Indonesia will also continue to grow rapidly. Together, the share these countries hold of the global GDP will rise from 35% in 2014 to 58% in 2060. Today's mature economies, which include the European Union, Canada, Japan and of course the United States, will shrink in comparison. There is very little any of us can do to halt or change this trend.

"It's becoming increasingly clear that the world is changing more rapidly than ever before. In the coming decades, we will see subtle, perhaps even dramatic, shifts in the balance of power and prosperity across the globe. In the West and particularly here in the United States, we have enjoyed political, military and economic dominance over the rest of the world for as long as I have lived. I dare say, however, that our relative position in the years ahead will not be as clear-cut.

"The paths we have to tread will not be as black-and-white either. We should never forego our principles or our values, or our commitment to the spread of freedom and democracy. We should always champion the sanctity of human rights and individual dignity. But we should also understand that other countries have not evolved in the same way that we have. They have their own histories, their own events and their own interpretations that have shaped their culture and world outlook.

"Many of us have often argued that our way is the best way because it is the most successful. As China continues to rise in power over the coming years, I'm not sure we'll be able to maintain that view with the same amount of conviction."

Marc paused habitually, before adding, "and I'm not just saying that because I'm half Chinese."

The expected laughter and customary applause came almost immediately.

He went on. "Does that mean we should now embrace communism, or switch to an authoritarian system of government? Of course not. But it does mean that we may need to view the rest of the world with a slightly greater degree of humility, with a better understanding of where others are coming from. At the same time, we need to stand strong by our own values. In short, we need to be grounded in our roots but be more knowledgeable and open minded about the roots of others. And we should expect nothing less from others either, especially as the world continues to become smaller by the day."

Marc looked down at the edge of the podium. "This bridging of cultural divides is what some of us have been on about for the past decade," he said, letting out a big sigh. The sigh always helped to hold back the rising lump in his throat, to dry up the tears before they could even take shape.

He wouldn't remember when exactly the speech ended – it was quite often that he didn't. He wouldn't remember how loud the applause was, or how many people came to congratulate him as he stepped down from the podium and slowly walked toward the exit.

"Nice job, Mr. Zemin!" he thought he heard one person say.

"Very timely presentation, Professor!" said another. "Keep up the good work."

The rest of the voices just faded away as he walked out of the hall and into the warm sunlight.

The drive from the UCLA Conference Center to the W Hotel in Westwood was short. Marc had asked his assistant to find a hotel as close to the university campus as possible, and she had done her job. Although he placed no emphasis on the amount of luxury, Stanford did have a minimum standard of accommodation for traveling professors, especially one of the up and coming ones. The W, a four-star hotel in a trendy part of Los Angeles, easily met and surpassed the mark.

He walked through the plush corridors to his room on the seventh floor. Stepping right away into the bathroom, he turned on the tap and splashed some cool water on his face. Then he stared in the mirror. The past couple of years had not been kind to him. Dark, wrinkled circles had permanently formed under his eyes, only partially concealed by his rectangular metal frame eyeglasses. His forehead had developed creases, and his once shiny brown hair now had strands of gray. The smile he was once known for hardly ever appeared – even when he tried he couldn't bend his mouth into one anymore. He looked almost forty years old, he thought, a good five years older than his actual age. His mixed Asian and Caucasian genes, the Asian half of which was once a source of his youthful appearance, no longer seemed to help.

His mobile phone buzzed. A new email had just arrived. He walked over to the desk where he had placed the device and read the message:

From: Doug Berger
To: Marc Zemin
Subject: UCLA

Sent: Fri 9/12/2014 11:29AM

Marc,

Regarding your presentation this morning. Please call me ASAP.

Regards,
Doug

Doug Berger
Ray Lyman Wilbur Professor
Department of Sociology
Stanford University
www.stanford.edu/dept/soc

The contents of the message were no surprise. Marc ignored it and instead called the front desk to extend his checkout time to 3 pm. Then he turned on the TV to get the latest news. There was growing belligerence between Japan and China on the ownership of the Senkaku islands in the Pacific. Anti-Japanese protests were erupting across China due to the recent inflammatory remarks by Tokyo's governor about buying the disputed territory and claiming it once and for all for Japan.

Better for Japan to be careful, he thought. Their heyday was over, and as an economy they were now becoming increasingly dependent on China. A trade war in this day and age would hurt Japan much more than it would hurt its larger neighbor.

He changed the channel to find something interesting to watch, quickly flipping through soap operas and reality shows. He finally stopped at a program about Bollywood, where the latest movie releases were being talked about and a few songs were flashed across the screen.

He was stunned by the beauty of some of the actresses. The show's hosts covered all the latest gossip about who they were currently dating, showing photos of them appearing with their hunky boyfriends at parties and other social events. They also mentioned how it was becoming increasingly common for Indian movie stars to come to the US and sign contracts to appear in Hollywood movies.

Marc watched some of the young couples, wondering if they were in love or if they even knew what true love meant. Who knows if they'll ever know, he thought. The track record of lasting relationships in the entertainment industry was far from spectacular.

For a rare moment, he caught himself asking the question what it might be like to love again, or if he ever could. He was thankful for the phone call that abruptly ended that thought.

He checked the caller name displayed on his phone before answering. "Hello, Doug."

"Thanks for responding to my message."

"I was busy."

"Of course."

"What's up?" Marc asked.

"I got a call from the conference organizers, from the Vice Provost over at the UCLA International Institute. General feedback to your presentation was positive, but they expected you to stay and mingle with the crowd afterwards."

"I had things to do."

"I want you to go back there and meet the Vice Provost. Needless to say, he wasn't too happy with your abrupt exit."

"I don't have time. I'm checking out of the hotel soon, and then I'm driving home. Takes a while, you know."

"This isn't a request, Marc. This time we're really going to look bad if you don't make it up."

"I didn't suggest that it was a request. But I'm not going."

"Why not?"

"I gave the presentation."

"That's very nice. But you also need to mingle and socialize, make yourself popular. You chose this line of work."

Marc stepped to the window. The midday sky was cloudless. From his room, he had a clear view of the UCLA campus. He could see students busily walking and biking on the paths between the various buildings.

"Those were different times, different circumstances," he said.

"So why remain in this job? Do something you really want to do."

"I don't want to do anything."

"You'd rather waste all your talent?"

"What's it all good for anyway?"

Marc could hear Doug sigh. "Look, it's been over two years now. It's high time you started getting your act together. I'm not trying to belittle what happened, but at the rate you're going your candidacy for tenure will undoubtedly be put into question. I may be the head of the department, but I'm still only one voice."

"I couldn't care less about tenure."

"The institution you work for..."

"I couldn't care less about Stanford either."

"Careful what you wish for."

"I can always go back to the UN."

Doug laughed. "Funny."

"I'd rather not trivialize the only world body we have."

"It was your wife who pushed you to get your PhD in sociology and to come here. She had her reasons."

"That was then. Now, as far as I'm concerned, she's my only reason. I'm doing this for her. I promised her I would."

"I'm not saying it's..."

"Spare me all your mingling and socializing crap," Marc said, cutting him off. "I'm doing my job and I'm getting the word out."

"That's not enough."

"More than enough for me. To expect me to put my heart back into it... it ain't happening."

Doug was silent for a moment and sighed again. "This is a critical time, Marc. Never before has there been this much interest in our work. Your work, to be precise. You can't take the credit for the rise in interest – that goes to what's happening on the world stage. But you can sure as hell take advantage of it, because a chance like this may not come again in our lifetime.

"There's a growing realization that within fifty years the world's center of gravity will have shifted west over the Pacific. You know what this means. Right now, China is focused internally on economic development. Do you honestly think they won't start building up their military and begin flexing their political muscle on the world stage once they become the richest country on Earth? You think they're going to see eye-to-eye with us on everything? Do we really want another arms race, another Cold War?

"You did a lot of great work with your wife on bridging the cultural gap between the West and the Middle East. You can reuse some of the things you learned from that. You can also take advantage of your own mixed heritage to offer a unique view of how we should deal with China in the future. We're reaching a critical juncture. Now is the time to reach out and offer guidance on the best way forward before it's too late.

"You said the only reason you're doing this is for your wife. I'm asking you to put in the extra effort for her sake. Think about what she dedicated her life to, about what she would have wanted you to do. Think about your daughter and how proud she would one day have been of her dad, if you stood up to the occasion during this momentous period in history and made a real difference."

Marc felt the lump rising in his throat again, only this time he couldn't hold back the tears.

"You might not care about your job or about Stanford, but I do," Doug added. "You are a valuable asset to our department, and I'm not ashamed to admit it. I'm not prepared to give up on you, not yet anyway. So, whatever it takes, call on faith, on God or whatever you believe in, if you have to. But find it in your heart to go and meet the Vice Provost, now."

"Faith," Marc scoffed. "That's a laugh."

"Laugh if you want. I'm expecting an update after your meeting, before you hit the road. A short email is sufficient. Cheers."

Chapter 2

The i8, BMW's first plug-in hybrid sports car, went into production in the middle of 2014. Beating all the odds and ignoring the discouraging remarks of many a naysayer, BMW was able to produce a beautiful, fast and highly fuel-efficient automobile within the span of just a few years. To many who saw the car for the first time, the combination of its sleek styling, groundbreaking technology and overall sophistication suggested a product worthy of futuristic sci-fi movies, a real trendsetter for the auto industry in the earlier part of the 21st century.

Whether or not the i8 would one day nab the "coolest yet greenest" car throne from the Tesla Model S was still very much an open question in 2014. With a two-year head start, Tesla Motors had already taken the world by storm with its revolutionary electric cars, and in some parts of the world the Model S was already as commonplace as a Honda Accord. The i8, both due to its relative novelty and its hefty price tag, was a far rarer sighting.

Marc walked up to his prized possession, a proton blue metallic, brand new i8, parked in a campus lot near the International Institute. Sliding into the driver's seat, he breathed in deeply. This car was now the one thing in his life that offered him any relief, any sense of satisfaction.

That was the reason for his recent $140k purchase, even with the hefty bite it had taken out of his bank account and the crushing debt he would remain in for the next five years. He no longer had any other purpose for whatever money he had, nobody to share it with or save it for.

He pressed a button and the vehicle sprang to life. With its ability to generate over 357 hp and of reaching 60 mph from a standstill in 4.4 seconds, one may have expected a deafening roar from under the hood. Instead, all that could be heard was a soft whine, thanks to the electric motor serving as the sole source of initial power for the wheels. The car did have a gasoline engine as well, but it would only kick in once the 7.1 kWh lithium-ion battery pack reached the end of its charge. That is, unless, the driver pushed the car hard from the get-go and both sources of power were needed right away to thrust the vehicle forward.

The conversations with the Vice Provost and others wanting to meet Marc had been long and tedious, but at least they were over now. The supply of numerous hors d'oeuvres during the meetings would also eliminate the need to stop for dinner en route. The sun was already low in the sky, perhaps no more than two hours away from setting. Although that did mean hitting rush hour traffic in Los Angeles, the traffic would be much lighter once he reached the Pacific coastline, his favorite part of the journey back up to the San Francisco Bay Area.

After edging up north through a long traffic jam on Interstate 405, he crossed over to Highway 101, the long road that stretched all the way up from downtown LA to the northern tip of Washington State. The traffic lightened up as he passed Calabasas and was flowing freely by the time he reached Thousand Oaks. After Oxnard came the first stretch where Highway 101 merged with Highway 1, California's famous coastal highway.

Marc glanced out at the Pacific Ocean. The sun was now starting to set over the horizon, leaving behind a gorgeous orange hue over a cloudless sky. He moved to the left lane and pressed on the accelerator, passing other cars as if they were just standing still as he watched the speedometer gauge rise to 100 mph, then 110, then 120. In this car, he couldn't feel the speed at all.

What's life without risks, he thought, slowing down as his radar detector spotted a police car ahead. After he had passed out of range, he quickly sped up again. He gazed proudly at the car's dashboard and command center. It felt much like the cockpit of a simple spaceship, which, of course, was one of his reasons for getting the i8.

I wonder what the Mendoken would think of this car, he thought. Would it be one of those revolutionary breakthroughs in technological advancement that would lead humans one step closer to the dropping of the shroud, to the ultimate revelation of what actually lay beyond the doorstep of their tiny solar system?

The Mendoken, the Aftar, the Volona, the Phyrax. The Unghans, the Starguzzlers... Almost eleven years had passed since his fateful journey through space, yet sometimes it still felt as if even a day hadn't gone by. For all those years, he had kept this astounding secret entirely to himself. There were times when it had almost reached the tip of his tongue, especially during heated confrontations about global affairs with others. He had meant to warn them of the consequences for humanity if nations and cultures the world over didn't set aside their petty differences for a greater, common good.

But his solemn promise to the aliens had always gotten the better of him. He hadn't even ever told Iman, his wife, his soulmate, his best friend. The one person he had truly loved, the one person his galactic adventure had brought him back to. The one person with whom he had pledged to work to unite the human race, to prepare them for their first encounter with alien civilizations far more advanced than anything they could imagine, aliens who were quietly waiting for them to reach a minimum level of technological and social advancement before revealing themselves. Iman had never known his true motivation for abandoning the physical sciences and joining her line of work, and now she never would.

It was nearing 9 pm by the time Marc reached the split of Highways 1 and 101 at San Luis Obispo. From here on, he would follow the coastal route all the way up to the Bay Area. It would undoubtedly take longer this way than to continue on the inland route, but there was no substitute for the smooth, winding road atop cliffs overlooking the ocean. Especially not in an i8.

He was driving 95 mph on an undivided two-lane stretch past San Simeon, when he noticed bright white lights rapidly approaching in his rear mirror. He tensed up right away. Rarely did he come across anybody driving faster than him. It could only mean one thing.

He wondered how the radar detector could have missed it, as he gradually let the car slow down. From experience, he knew that slamming on the brakes would only further inflame the situation. The cop had surely already clocked him, either with a radar gun or by comparing relative speeds, and he or she would take him to task for assuming that an abrupt slowdown upon seeing the approaching police car would cause his speeding to remain unnoticed. As it was, a ticket for 95 in a 55 zone wouldn't be pretty and could even involve the suspension of his license.

The telltale flashing blue and red lights didn't come on, however. Instead, the mystery car moved into the opposite lane and zoomed past him, roughly swerving back into his lane just in time to avoid hitting an oncoming car. In the darkness, it took him a little longer than usual to figure out the make of the vehicle. Unless the California Highway Patrol had received an enormous budget increase and could suddenly afford Ferrari 458's in its fleet, it was unlikely to be a police car.

That driver is just asking for trouble, Marc thought, pressing on the accelerator again to see if he could keep up. The car was moving recklessly, taking some of the sharp curves over the cliffs at unmanageable speeds. Even with the i8's superb handling, Marc wasn't able to maintain the same pace. As superb as it was, when it came to handling it was no match for a Ferrari 458. With time, he found himself trailing further and further behind.

He was about to give up the chase, when he noticed the Ferrari abruptly lose control over a bend and shoot over the edge of the road. Luckily at that spot the edge of the cliff was at least a couple of hundred yards away. The car hurtled through patches of grass and brushy terrain, kicking up a huge cloud of dust, before coming to a stop not too far from the edge.

Marc slowed his car down and got off the highway at the same spot. No other cars were about – it seemed nobody else was privy to what had just happened. He turned off the headlights and slowly edged the BMW forward over the rough ground. There was enough light from the half-moon up in the sky to at least let him see where he was going. He wasn't sure what kind of people were inside the Ferrari or what state they were in, but he decided to take no chances. Calling 911 was a little premature – there was no indication yet that anybody needed help. There was only one way to find out.

He turned off the engine and quietly got out of the car, about seventy yards from the edge. Crouching, he waded through the thick brush until he came close to the Ferrari.

The car's headlights were off, but the interior lamp was on. Peering from behind a bush, he could see two silhouettes inside. They seemed to be arguing heatedly with each other – through the closed windows, he could hear muffled shouting. Then he noticed the driver's fist flying toward the passenger, accompanied by a thud and a scream. Then another punch, and another, then more screams.

Marc hesitated only for a few seconds. Then he jumped up and opened the driver side door.

"What the...!" was all he heard as he grabbed the man by the shirt, pulled him out of the car and threw him onto the ground.

Priceless, Marc thought, the man's expression of bewilderment. He instinctively moved one of his legs back and lifted his arms into fighting position. His Kung Fu training would hopefully come to good use – as long as his opponent didn't have similar credentials, at any rate, or wasn't carrying a gun.

By his reaction, it was evident he didn't and wasn't. He got up and bellowed in rage, then charged toward Marc. He lunged his fist in the direction of Marc's face, giving Marc plenty of time to move out of the way and land a crushing blow on his torso. The man fell to his knees and howled in pain, only to get up again to exact his revenge. He was about six feet tall, no more than an inch taller than Marc, and of a stockier, more muscular build. Not that his muscle mass was offering him much of an advantage at that moment over Marc's slender body.

He struck at Marc again, this time at his chest. Marc moved away just in time and swerved his arm toward the man's head, hitting his ear with a sharp punch. He stumbled and shook his head for a few seconds to regain his composure. Turning again, he charged with both his fists toward Marc's stomach. Marc blocked both strikes with one fast sweep and tripped him. As he came crashing to the ground, Marc pinned him on the chest with his knee and dealt the final, carefully aimed spearhand blow to the jaw. His eyes rolled as he fell unconscious.

Marc sat back and heaved a sigh. Sparring he had done plenty of in the training center, but this was his first real-life fight. He could easily have died if the man had been armed.

Having nothing to live for seems to have its uses, he thought, as he got up and turned to the car. He knelt down and peeked past the open driver's side door at the person sitting in the passenger's seat. The first things he noticed were the bruised eye and the bleeding ear, and the faint sobs he could hear above the sound of the waves splashing against the edge of the cliff. Nothing could have prepared him for the stunning element of surprise, though, once he recognized the battered face. Even with the bruises, there was no mistaking it.

"Alisha," he said in disbelief. "The actress?"

"Yes," she whispered, her voice quivering. Her lower lip was broken, and a small amount of blood oozed out as she spoke.

"Are... are you alright?"

She didn't answer. He noticed a tear trickling down from her left eye.

Some chance, he thought. If he hadn't seen that TV show about Bollywood earlier in the day, he would have no idea who she was. The sheer coincidence was unthinkable.

He stepped back to examine the face of the man he had knocked out. As he had guessed, it was her boyfriend, the same guy he had seen standing next to her on the show. If he recalled correctly, this individual was also a movie actor.

What a swine, he thought, holding back the urge to kick the unconscious man in the groin. He walked over to the passenger side of the car and opened the door, only to hear her gasp in fright.

"It's ok," he said reassuringly. "I'm not going to hurt you."

Alisha looked up at him, seemingly unconvinced.

"Honestly, I swear, it's ok," he said. "Are you hurt anywhere else? Other than the face?"

She shook her head.

"Why don't you step out? Let me take a closer look at your eye and ear."

She got out slowly, evidently trusting him enough to take the step. He saw that she wasn't wearing much – a very short skirt and a tight tank top, most unbecoming for the cold coastal night. It didn't take long for her to start shivering.

Marc took off his jacket and placed it around her shoulders. "I'll be right back," he said, and sprinted back to his car. He returned with a first aid kit and a bottle of water.

"He's not... dead?" she asked, pointing at the still body nearby.

"No, no, just out cold," Marc replied. "Here, come in front of the car." He turned on the Ferrari's headlamps.

She came forward and sat down on the ground, in the path of the bright light. He cleaned up the eye and ear with an antiseptic, and placed bandages on the cuts. Then he dabbed out the blood from her lip. He couldn't help noticing how the wounds did little to hide her striking beauty.

"I'm going to call the police," he said. "Is that ok?"

She hesitated first, but then nodded.

He took out his phone, dialed 911 and spoke briefly to the operator. "They'll be here in a few minutes," he announced after hanging up.

"Thank you," she said, taking a few sips of water. Her voice was starting to sound a little stronger.

"Glad to be of help."

"What's your name?"

"Marc. Marc Zemin."

"Where did you learn to fight like that?"

"Martial arts. Been doing it for five years. Helps me stay sane. Also keeps me in touch with my roots, on my Dad's side anyway."

"My lucky day," she said. The expression of shock on her face slowly gave way to a sweet smile. She sounded sweet too, with a distinct pronunciation that seemed to elegantly blend both British and Indian accents.

Marc grinned. "Hardly, given what you've just been through."

"Lucky that it was you who found me. Vinod takes great pride in his strength, and he would easily have beaten up anyone else who didn't know how to fight."

"Don't tell me he's done this before?"

Alisha shook her head. "Not to me. Others did warn me, but I didn't listen." She looked down at the ground. "He was so charming."

His charm is about to make news headlines, Marc thought. Vinod should have thought twice before pouncing on such a public figure.

"Charm is often only skin deep," he said.

"I've just learned my lesson."

"You're quite far from LA."

She looked surprised. "How did you know we came from LA?"

"Showbiz India. All the latest Bollywood gossip."

"You don't seem like the type to watch Showbiz India."

"Jumping to conclusions?"

"I'm just flattered you know who I am."

"I did run across you for the first time today while flipping channels. I'm not a regular."

"That's quite a coincidence."

"No kidding. Have you started shooting yet?"

"Shooting?"

"Your new movie. In Hollywood. That's why you're here in the US, isn't it?"

"Wow, Showbiz India is doing its homework. Yes, we've already started, although it's still in the early stages."

"What brought you up north?"

"We didn't plan to come this far," she replied. "It was a spur of the moment thing. Vinod just rented this car. He wanted to drive it up the famous California coastline. This evening was my one free timeslot since we arrived in LA, so I indulged. I thought it would be a good opportunity to get away from all the media spotlight and hubbub for a short while. Little did I know we'd get into such a heated argument along the way. We lost track of the time. And when he lost his temper, I got too scared to say or do anything. He just kept driving like a maniac. I've never seen him like that before."

"How long have you been dating?"

"A couple of months."

"Maybe that's why."

She nodded slowly. "And you?"

"Driving back home to the Bay Area. I was racing with you guys for a bit. Wasn't much of a race, I have to admit. But I got suspicious when your car flung off the road here."

"Where are you coming from?"

"LA. I was attending a conference there."

"What about?"

"Sociology."

"Are you an academic?"

He nodded.

"A professor who knows how to fight."

"I didn't say I was a professor."

"My intuition. Are you?"

"Actually, yes."

"Where?"

"Stanford University."

She smiled. "Smart too, as I guessed."

*   *   *

The police arrived within a few minutes, in a procession of three cars with their lights flashing and sirens wailing. They took custody of Vinod, who was slowly regaining consciousness, and took statements from both Marc and Alisha. They were astonished to learn of Alisha's identity. It wasn't often that law enforcement officers in these parts ran into movie stars, and that too of so exotic an origin and appearance. They offered to take her to the hospital for a checkup and then drive her back to LA, which she gladly accepted.

"Keep the jacket," Marc said, just as she was about to take it off and return it. "It won't be much warmer en route."

"I don't know how to ever thank you enough," she said, giving him a quick hug.

"Promise me you won't let this event put a scar on your life and your career. And that you'll only date decent men who respect women from now on."

"I promise."

Chapter 3

The moonlight glittered over the ocean. From a distance, it looked like a giant comet making its way over the waves toward the horizon, leaving behind a long, white cloud of dust across an otherwise dark expanse. As he stood at the very edge of the cliff, Marc listened to the sound of the waves splashing against the shore.

The police had already left with Alisha and Vinod. They had also confiscated the Ferrari, likely much to the delight of the officer fortunate enough to take the wheel. Marc was alone now, choosing to spend a few extra minutes savoring the serenity of the shoreline before getting back in his car and resuming the long drive up north.

He felt a sense of satisfaction in having saved an individual from what might have been severe mental and bodily injury. That it was such a famous and successful person was an added benefit, as was the general temperature of her appearance. He wished her well, and truly hoped she would quickly overcome the trauma of what had just happened to her. Somewhere deep down he also couldn't help hoping that she might always remember him in some small fashion. He certainly wouldn't forget her.

He gazed up at the sky. As always, it was filled with billions of stars, all close to each other, all twinkling brightly. The invisible lenses that his Mendoken friend Sibular had injected into his eyes eleven years ago were still working flawlessly to this day. His were the only eyes on Earth that could see such a crowded sky every clear night. He was the only individual on the planet who could see right through the filter that surrounded the entire solar system, blocking the view to all within of most of the star systems in the galaxy. Human scientists believed the Milky Way galaxy contained some 200 billion star systems, yet they couldn't explain why its gravitational characteristics indicated that the total mass of the galaxy was almost ten times that of the sum of those star systems. They attributed this difference to the existence of a mysterious, unknown substance called 'dark matter' that permeated across the galaxy and much of the universe. They had no idea that the galaxy actually contained ten times as many stars, most of them homes to planets filled with life of all shapes and sizes, all purposely hidden from view until humanity was deemed ready to face and interact with them. The only star systems visible to people on Earth were those devoid of any intelligent life, absent of any obvious traces of civilization or settlement.

"Silupsal," Marc said softly. That amazing self-replicating membrane the aliens had used to build something so colossal that it could encapsulate an entire solar system. That intelligent membrane that knew how to hide some things while exposing others, how to let natural objects pass unhindered but to block unauthorized ships. That one, thin, semi-transparent membrane that had hidden the true nature of the universe from humans since the very beginning of their existence.

The constellations meant nothing to him anymore. He couldn't see any of their shapes in the sky, not with so many additional stars in between all the ones familiar to everyone else. He would never again be able to share his enjoyment of the night sky with anyone else, at least not until the filter finally came down. And that was unlikely to happen anytime soon, especially given the rate at which human society was currently progressing.

He looked more closely at the area of the sky where the Summer Triangle was located, its vertices identifiable by the bright stars Altair, Deneb and Vega. Mendo-Zueger, the home star for the Mendoken civilization, was somewhere inside that triangle. He wasn't completely sure about this, as during his travels with the Mendoken eleven years ago he had not mapped out its exact location. But in the time since then, he had performed numerous calculations based on what he remembered, and that area seemed to be the most likely culprit.

If they would only come back, he thought. The Mendoken had left no way for him to communicate with them, and in the eleven years since he had last seen them, there had been no contact whatsoever. He had often wished for them to return, especially so during Iman's troubled pregnancy. With their advanced medical technology, saving her and her unborn child wouldn't just have been possible, it would have been easy.

But they wouldn't be back, probably not in his lifetime. They were always watching, and they would continue to wait until humanity was ready for them. He had once had grandiose ambitions to unite the human race to prepare it for that eventual, fateful encounter with the Mendoken. Together with Iman, he had been ready to take on the world, and he had actually believed that he would be able to pull it off. Now he longed for those days of blissful naivete.

As he watched the sky, he thought he noticed something moving inside the Summer Triangle. One of the stars, it seemed, had just shifted ever so slightly. He wasn't sure if he was just imagining it, so he blinked and stared again. That same star had just gotten a little bigger and brighter.

Again he blinked, looked down at the ocean for a moment, then up again. The star was still growing, without a doubt. That could only mean that it was moving in the direction of the Earth. It could also only mean that it wasn't a star, or a planet, for that matter. It couldn't even be a comet or a meteor. Nothing natural could possibly be moving that fast.

It could always be an airplane or something else man-made, he thought. But there were no blinking lights, no sounds of jets or rotors. A plane or helicopter would also be following some kind of trajectory in the sky. This mystery object, whatever it was, just seemed to keep growing. Soon it had surpassed the Moon in apparent size.

Marc realized that it was heading straight for the very spot he was standing on. That was why he couldn't see any trajectory. His curiosity soon turned to fear. The cliff, the ocean – everything was starting to brighten up, reflecting the brilliant light of the rapidly approaching ball of fire. He began hearing a sound that seemed to be an eerie combination of a high-pitched whine and a deep rumble. Even the air seemed to be warming up.

"Holy crap," he whispered. Whatever this thing was, it would meet its fate with a crash landing. If he didn't move out of the way, he probably wouldn't live to tell the tale. He turned and started running away from the cliff. He reached his car and opened the door. Before getting in, he looked back one more time. What he saw caused him to freeze in shock.

The fireball was huge now, and the noise deafening. Fortunately it looked like it was going to crash into the ocean and not the cliff, perhaps no more than a few hundred feet from the shore. In between the flames, he could make out a silhouette. It was something he hadn't seen in a long time, and it took a good several seconds for it to register in his memory.

A Mendoken scout ship, he realized, most likely of the Sil variety. A small ship, no larger than a Boeing 737, shaped more like a supersonic jetfighter. He remembered the many days and nights he had spent onboard a Sil-5 those eleven years ago.

They're back, he thought. Finally! The only problem was, this ship was clearly in trouble and its inhabitants likely wouldn't survive the crash. How a civilization as technologically advanced as the Mendoken could be in such a quagmire with one of their ships was anyone's guess. Engine trouble wasn't a term they were familiar with. The outer hulls of their ships were impervious to the heat generated during atmospheric entry. They would also surely have cloaked themselves from all the satellites and monitoring equipment around the Earth, making it impossible for their presence to be detected. They couldn't possibly have been targeted by manmade missiles.

Marc watched with horror as the ship slammed into the sea, sending out waves that shot high up into the sky. The ground shook with ferocity, causing him to lose his balance and fall to the ground. He couldn't hear the rumbling noise of the fireball anymore. It had been replaced by the roar of the raging sea.

He got up to see what was happening. The flames were trying their best to survive as they battled the towering waves, but they were hopelessly outnumbered. For a moment, he felt a rising fear about the imminent tsunami that would wash over the cliff and sweep him into the ocean. But as he watched the approaching flotilla of waves, he realized that his fear was unfounded. This was no earthquake. The waves soon began splashing with all their might against the cliff, but they couldn't make it anywhere close to the top.

It took several minutes for the high waves to begin subsiding. Marc stood at the cliff's edge, too dumbfounded to move. The ship had broken into pieces, some of them floating, others already submerged and probably on their way to the bottom of the ocean. He wasn't sure what to do. He couldn't swim out there to try to help any potential survivors – not in these cold, stormy waters. He would likely drown well before he reached what was left of the ship. He could call for help, but he wasn't sure the Mendoken on board wanted to be discovered by humans, even if it cost them their lives.

Which brought him to the inevitable question: what were the Mendoken doing here? That they had crashed right on the very spot where he was standing was too much of a coincidence. It could only mean that they were coming for him, or at least to meet him. They must have been watching him and his movements from outer space for a while, and they had decided to come down when they saw him hanging out in this secluded spot. But something had gone horribly awry during the descent.

He noticed something moving over the waves in between the wrecked pieces of the ship. It was heading in the direction of the shore. He wasn't sure what it was, but he wasted no time in looking for a way down to get a closer look. A short distance along the cliff's edge, he found a steep and narrow trail that led to the beach. Trying his best to keep his balance, he trudged down the trail as fast as he could. At one point, he tripped over a rock and almost fell over the edge, but luckily he was able to regain his foothold and keep walking.

After reaching the bottom, he ran over the sandy beach toward the ocean. The object had already reached the shore and seemed to have stopped moving. As he got closer, he could see it lying still in the wet sand. Every few seconds, a wave would calmly creep up around it and recede back into the ocean.

Marc reached the object, only to have his suspicions confirmed. It was no object. The large, round head with the single eye that went all around left little room for doubt, as did the metallic armor that encased most of the body. Only two of the robotic arms were there, the other two probably crushed or blown away during the crash. He couldn't tell whether it was a male or female. The hat on the head was blue in color, signifying that he or she was a commander of some sort. Every Mendoken wore a hat, as he well remembered, and the color was indicative of the position and rank in the grand hierarchy that encompassed the entire population. That was simply how they had chosen to run their highly advanced, structured and mechanized society.

"Are you alright?" Marc asked, kneeling to get a closer look at the lying Mendoken. He could only hope this individual was carrying a translator device.

"No, Mr. Zemin," a female voice said feebly in English. Evidently she was carrying one. Her head lifted ever so slightly to look at him. "I have... two minutes at most to live."

"Can I help you?"

"No. My internals are damaged. You would not know how."

"What happened?"

"No time to explain. You must..." She stopped.

"What?" he asked frantically. "I must what?"

"This... mission failed. You must be ready for next... window."

"Window?"

"Pickup window. In 48 hours."

"Why? And why do you need windows?"

"No... time to explain. 48 hours. Find an open, uninhabited space where ship can land."

"Like this?"

"More space is... better. Like desert. Ship will find you." She paused again. "Do not... do not reveal anything... to anyone on Earth. Principle of... non-interference. Understand?"

Marc nodded. "I do."

"Hurry out of here, Mr. Zemin."

"I will, but please tell me what's going on."

She didn't answer. Her head dropped to the sand. One of her limbs moved toward him, and the hand opened to reveal her translator device. That was the last movement she would ever make.

Marc sat back and closed his eyes. His nerves, on edge now for quite a while, began to give in. An entire Mendoken crew had just sacrificed their lives for his sake. He had no idea why. His could feel his heart pounding and his breathing turned shallow. He tried to counter it by inhaling and exhaling more slowly, more deeply. It took him a few minutes to regain even a little of his composure.

When he opened his eyes, he noticed the body of the Mendoken was gone. All he could see was the translator device in the sand. Looking out to sea, he could no longer spot any of the ship's wreckage.

No big surprise, he thought. The Mendoken wouldn't have wanted any of their remains to be found by humans. They must have activated some emergency mechanism to vaporize themselves and their possessions as they died. The fact that the translator was still there could only mean that he was supposed to keep it. So he picked it up and put it in his pocket.

However, some damage was already done. Gazing up toward the top of the cliff, he could see a number of people gathered, intently watching him. They had probably been driving on the highway when they saw the crash and had stopped to see what was going on. That could only mean the Mendoken had failed in cloaking their descent and the crash from everyone other than him. Something really must have gone terribly wrong onboard for the Mendoken to make so big a mistake. It also meant that he had minutes, at most, before some kind of authority arrived on the scene, be it Coast Guard, Navy, Air Force, whatever. Some of the onlookers had surely also called the police by now.

The dying Mendoken had explicitly warned him not to tell anyone on Earth what had just happened. The principle of non-interference was a key tenet followed by the four advanced civilizations in the galaxy. None of the less advanced species could ever know about the existence of aliens until they were advanced enough to join the galactic community of civilizations.

He realized he had only one choice. He got up and ran, like the wind, like he had never run before. He didn't know where his strength was coming from. Perhaps it was the adrenaline rushing through his body, every one of its molecules reminding him of his promise to the Mendoken commander. Knowing the Mendoken, they hadn't sacrificed their lives like this without good reason. He would not fail them.

The sand felt like solid pavement, his dress shoes like padded sneakers. He climbed up the steep, narrow trail to the top of the cliff like a sure-footed mountain lion. He covered his face as he sprinted past the curious onlookers, some of them trying their best to stop him and ask him what was going on. He dashed to his car, got in and sped off, just as he began hearing the whopping sound of helicopters approaching the coastline.

Chapter 4

Sunday September 14th, 10pm. That was when they would come again. Marc had two days left to prepare for the pickup. The amount of preparation, however, was not the issue. The issue was lying low, staying out of the limelight. From that perspective, two days were an eternity.

He had made it back to the Bay Area without any further incidents. The police cars he had passed on Highway 1 heading toward the crash site had ignored him, and nobody had followed him.

From his home in Palo Alto, he spent the next morning carefully combing the Internet and the news channels on TV for any information about the events from the night before. It didn't take him long to find articles on celebrity gossip websites about Alisha and the mishap with her boyfriend. Pictures were already circulating showing the bruises on her face, and numerous bloggers had posted lengthy opinions about how she should immediately dump him and file charges against him in court. Surprisingly, there was no mention of Marc by name or even of his intervention. Word was that she had somehow gotten out of the car and called the police.

She couldn't have forgotten me already, he thought. He certainly hoped not. The likelier scenario was that she had chosen to protect his identity from the media frenzy. If that was true, then it was very thoughtful of her. It was also especially opportune, given what else had happened to him that night.

He turned his attention to any news about the crash. He switched to CNN on the TV, which began covering it within a few minutes. A newscaster was reporting live from the scene, now in broad daylight, atop the cliff where Marc had stood several hours earlier.

"Behind me is the very spot where the impact seems to have occurred," he said, pointing to the ocean. "About 200 feet from the shore. Numerous eyewitness accounts state that a huge ball of fire slammed into the ocean at about 10 pm local time, sending out tsunami-like waves that splashed against these cliffs for several minutes. The strange thing is that no traces have so far been found of any meteorite, rock or any other object anywhere within a two-mile radius."

The camera zoomed in toward the ocean. There were a number of helicopters in the air, as well as Coast Guard boats circling the suspected crash site. Divers kept appearing on the surface of the water, none of them with anything newsworthy to report from the ocean floor. The newscaster then brought forth a couple of the witnesses, who presented their versions of what they had seen.

"It was the most amazing thing," one of them said. "The way the sky lit up. I could've sworn I saw something there, between the flames. I know for sure there were pieces of something flying out during the impact."

"What was that 'something'?" the newscaster asked.

"I don't know. I've no idea. I just know that I saw it."

So far, so good, Marc thought. These eyewitnesses had nothing tangible to report. Even with the accident, the Mendoken had been able to maintain their uninterrupted policy of concealment from humans. Perhaps things wouldn't be so bad after all, and he would be able to go about his normal life until the pickup time. His optimism, however, was about to be crushed.

"I saw a man, down there on the beach," said another eyewitness. "It looked like he was interacting with somebody or something from the craft that crashed in the ocean. Before everything disappeared. Then he ran up the cliff, got into a car and drove off."

"Are you certain it was a 'craft'?" the newscaster asked.

"As certain as the sky is blue. I don't care what the Coast Guard says. I saw a ship."

"A ship? Not an airplane or a missile?"

"A ship. Never seen anything like it before."

"A UFO, perhaps?"

"Hell, yeah! It wasn't anything manmade, that's for sure."

"Would you be able to identify the man that you saw?"

"No, can't say. It was too dark. He was driving some kind of fancy sports car, that's all I know."

Marc rushed to pack his bags. It was only a matter of time before they put two and two together. He kept looking out the window of his apartment at the street below, just to make sure no police cars were coming. He eyed his phone suspiciously, expecting a call at any moment. The police had his name, thanks to the incident with Alisha and her violent boyfriend. They also knew that he had stayed behind on the cliff after their departure, and now they had these eyewitness reports.

He sent an email to his assistant at Stanford, telling her that he was sick and wouldn't be in that day. He forwarded the message to Doug, the head of the Sociology department, and added a note that he might be out for a few more days the following week if he didn't recover over the weekend.

In truth, he didn't know for how long he would be gone. He didn't care either. If the Mendoken really needed him once again, it would be for a grand cause, something far greater than any of the menial stuff he was doing here on Earth. In hindsight, he thought, he should have just stayed with them the last time around. Granted, he wouldn't have found Iman again. But at least she would still be alive today, living her own life in peace.

He left the apartment briefly to get a sizeable amount of cash from the nearby ATM. Credit cards would leave trails. As he sprinted along the sidewalk, he felt a rising sense of excitement. They're coming for me, he kept saying to himself. Regardless of all the risks involved, both here on Earth until the pickup time and whatever awaited him out there afterwards, there was finally something worth living for again. Why they couldn't come right away he didn't know. This time window thing was a mystery. But it would also give him time to prepare himself, mentally and physically. He just had to somehow get by until the next window without getting caught.

Easier said than done, he realized. His phone rang as he stepped back into the apartment. He pulled it out of his pocket and checked the caller ID. The area code was 323. If he remembered correctly, that was Los Angeles.

Didn't take them long, he thought. Better to let it go to voicemail. He waited anxiously for the message and dialed in to listen to it as soon as he saw the voicemail notification on his phone.

"Hi Marc, this is Alisha Bedi. I wanted to thank you again for saving me last night. I'd like to speak to you when you have a moment." She left her number and then hung up.

He felt relieved, and strangely excited. She hadn't forgotten him at all. There was a certain sense of satisfaction in that.

He dialed the number and waited. She picked up after three rings.

"This is Alisha."

"Alisha, hi, this is Marc. Marc Zemin."

"Oh, hi, Marc! Thank you for calling me back."

"Of course. How are you doing?"

"Ok. Lots of activity this morning. It's a media circus."

"How are the wounds?"

"Getting better. They did a thorough job at the hospital last night."

"That's good. How did you get my number?"

"Let's see – Stanford University, Sociology Department, Professor Zemin. You aren't that hard to track down for my manager and his team. Your assistant provided your mobile number. She said you were sick."

"Yes, I am whenever I need some downtime."

He thought he heard a giggle. "I can relate to that," she said. "Marc, I'd like to thank you again for what you did for me last night."

"Gladly. Thanks for keeping my name a secret."

"I didn't think you were the type to enjoy the media spotlight. Believe me, they can be quite brutal."

"So I've heard."

"I also wanted to check that you're ok. I heard in the news that there was some kind of crash in the ocean, near the spot where we were."

Marc stumbled, at first unsure of what to say. "I'm... fine. Nothing happened to me."

"Did you see it? You stayed behind, right?"

"I, uh, saw it from a distance. While driving."

"Oh, ok. I wonder what it was. It seems nobody knows."

"Beats me. Thanks for checking on me, though. I really appreciate the thought."

"There's one other thing. I'd like to give you your jacket back."

He smiled. "Don't worry about the jacket, seriously."

"You know, it's a coincidence, but I'm going to be in San Francisco next week to shoot a scene for my movie. We could meet if you like. I could give it to you then. I would love to meet your family too."

Marc stumbled again. "I... don't have a family."

There was a brief pause. "Oh, ok. How about just you and me, then?"

"I, uh, would love to... to meet you," he stammered. "But... I can't. Not next week. Very busy."

There was another brief pause. "That's a shame," she said, sounding both surprised and disappointed. "Maybe next time."

"Yes, certainly."

Marc kicked himself as she hung up. Someone like her probably never got rejected, for anything. With good reason, and not just because of her gorgeous looks. He took a moment to read up on her on the Internet. According to Wikipedia, she was a highly talented and much sought-after movie actress in the Bollywood scene. A couple of mega box-office hits earlier in the year had largely contributed to her growing fame and success.

He stared at some of her pictures. Her brown eyes were very nicely shaped, somewhat like large, elongated teardrops. Her long, dark brown hair was straight, curling up a little at the ends where they rested on her shoulders. Her figure was slender and curved in the right places, and her skin smooth. There was something very alluring about her overall appearance that he just couldn't put a finger on. It wasn't just because of his state of mind, or because he had hardly set his eyes on any woman since Iman's death. No doubt, she had the same enchanting effect on many millions of her fans.

He couldn't imagine why someone like her would want to spend any time with someone like him. Had the circumstances been any different, he would have jumped on the opportunity, regardless what her intentions and regardless what the ultimate outcome. Not that he would have had any intentions or expectations of his own. Just enjoying her company, her presence for an hour or two would have been worth it. It would have made for interesting conversation with others in the future, finally an exotic encounter that he could actually have openly bragged about.

Nothing happens for years and then everything happens at once, he thought. Such was life.

Chapter 5

The dreaded calls did start coming, although a few hours later than Marc had anticipated. By then, he was already well on his way eastward, this time in his old Subaru Outback station wagon. The BMW i8 he had left in his garage. It was way too conspicuous, given how uncommon it was and especially since the police knew he had one. The Subaru was registered in Iman's younger brother's name, a graduate student at Stanford. Marc had given it to him after Iman's death, but he rarely drove it and just kept it parked at Marc's place.

The painful memories were the main reason why Marc had given the car away. It was the one he and Iman had used on many a long trip, including the one in the spring of 2012. It was their last vacation together, only two months away from her planned delivery date. It was also to be their last getaway as a couple before the long-awaited addition to their family.

He smirked as he recalled the name – Death Valley, the lowest, hottest and driest spot in North America. The name of this infamous valley in the Mojave Desert would always hold a special significance in his memory. He had so wanted to show it to her. It was the last place on Earth she would ever live to see.

Had he not planned that fateful vacation, she may have been alive today and his daughter would have been two years old. The expert doctors at Stanford Medical would have had a chance of saving both or at least one of them, at least a fairer chance than the folks at the Desert View Hospital in Pahrump, Nevada. No disrespect intended – they had tried their best. But there was only so much that could have been expected from doctors in so remote and secluded a location.

He had hesitated to revive this painful memory in so vivid a way by driving back there, and in the same car no less. All things considered, however, it was the most practical option available to him at that moment. The Mendoken commander had told him to make it to a desert. Death Valley was the only desert he had ever visited in North America. He knew his way around there, and he recalled a highly secluded spot that would make the perfect pickup point. The Subaru was the only car he had easy access to that wasn't registered in his name, which would make it all the more difficult for him to be tracked down. It also had no GPS or other communication equipment installed, given its age, a plus that would make it much harder to locate or track digitally.

At least by humans. He certainly hoped the Mendoken would have no trouble tracking him down. Given their level of technology and surveillance capability, they would likely find him anywhere in a heartbeat. The translator device they had given him would also make it much easier for them to locate him.

Marc nervously eyed any passing or standing Highway Patrol cars, and he took extra care to drive at or close to the speed limit for most of the way. Now wasn't the time to get pulled over by a cop, for any reason whatsoever. In hindsight, it was kind of silly that he had driven all the way back home, only to head down to Southern California again the next day. But there hadn't been any choice. He didn't know how long he would be gone for, and the necessary packing and preparation could only have been done from his home. The switching of cars had also been vital, as had been the downloading and printing out of a list of all payphones and their locations still in existence in the state of California.

Why? Because his mobile phone would be a liability. Mobile phones could easily be tracked using either GPS or cell tower triangulation, so every time he turned it on, he could instantly be located by the authorities if they were looking for him. The only option was to leave the phone at home and use payphones on the go as needed.

Every two hours, he stopped at a spot where there was a payphone and checked his voicemail messages. Thankfully he had plenty of quarters stocked up in his car. The first couple of times he checked, there was nothing of significance. But then, as he stopped in Bakersfield for another check, he was told he had three messages.

"Mr. Zemin, this is Lieutenant James Bradley at Station Morro Bay of the United States Coast Guard," a stern voice said. "I understand you may have been in the vicinity of an incident that occurred last night on the coast near San Simeon. We have some questions to ask you. Call us back or come by the Coast Guard station that is currently nearest to you. Please note that this is of the utmost importance."

The second message was from the Morro Bay Police Department, and the third from the police in Palo Alto. Both requested him to immediately get in touch with them.

At least they're all communicating with each other, he thought, smiling as he tried to make light of his predicament. Something was evidently working in the nation's law enforcement apparatus. He got back in the car and kept driving, and he tuned in to CNN on the satellite radio to shift his attention to something else. After the news headlines, a panel of experts began discussing the cause of the impact in the ocean from the night before.

"It couldn't have been a meteorite," one of the scientists said. "We would undoubtedly have found large fragments of rock on the ocean floor by now."

"The same could be said of a manmade object," another scientist chimed in. "We ought to have seen some traces of the destroyed machine."

"Not if it was a military maneuver gone wrong," the first scientist replied. "They would have cleaned up the whole area before any civilians got close enough to take a look. For that matter, I don't think they've let any civilians out into the water where that thing actually landed. Nobody from the news media has actually been allowed to dive underwater and take a look for themselves. Whatever information we're receiving is all from our armed forces."

The debate continued for a while. There was unanimous agreement that it couldn't have been something natural, and that it was either a failed secret military experiment of some kind or something extra-terrestrial. Most tended to think it was the former, especially due to the way the military was handling the situation so far. The eyewitness reports about an individual on the beach during the time of the impact also gave credence to that theory – possibly someone from the military coordinating or observing the experiment. If this was true, then it was unlikely that the public would be told anytime soon what had really happened.

Nevertheless, that wasn't preventing tons of alien conspiracy theories from exploding all over the world. CNN went on to report about numerous blogs and websites on the Internet, warning of impending doom from an alien invasion. Others spoke of a warning from God, that the end of the world was coming and that people should mend their ways to attain salvation before it was too late. Facebook pages discussing these topics already had millions of followers, and both Google searches and Twitter posts with keywords involving aliens and UFO's had multiplied by several orders of magnitude.

Too many nutcases on this Earth, Marc thought. If they only knew the truth. On reflection, however, all this activity and the generation of one crazy theory after another was probably a good thing. It would take the attention away from him, and maybe the police would eventually stop their search for him too. He began easing up a little as he exited the city of Bakersfield.

It wasn't until he had reached the payphone of a gas station at the starting point of the winding 178 state highway that the period of easing came to an abrupt end.

"This is Jay Mistry, Alisha Bedi's manager," said the voicemail message. "I need your help. Please call me back immediately. My US phone number is 301-555-4371."

The urgency in the man's voice clearly surpassed those of the police and Coast Guard officers that had already left voicemail messages. Marc suspected it could only mean one thing, and it wasn't a trick. He called back right away.

"Jay Mistry."

"Hi, this is Marc Zemin."

"Thank goodness! Mr. Zemin, Ms. Bedi has been taken by the authorities."

As I guessed, Marc thought. "When?"

"A half hour ago. They said they had some questions for her, in relation to her meeting you last night. They said they were actively looking for you. I thought you might know why, which is why I called you." There was genuine concern in his voice, something even his thick Indian accent and fast pace of talking couldn't hide. He sounded almost frantic.

"Did they arrest her?"

"No, but they just took her away, without giving her any preparation time. Ms. Bedi was shocked. What have you gotten her into? Do you realize how much turmoil she's been through in the past 24 hours? And now this, all in a foreign country. She's going to be devastated."

"Wait, they took her without arresting her? They can't do that."

"What a pity you weren't here to witness it, then. I thought everyone has rights in America. I don't know what to do now. They wouldn't let me go with her."

"Did they leave behind any contact info?"

"Yes, one of the people left me his mobile number. I tried to call it already, but it keeps going to voicemail."

"Have you called anyone else?"

"Yes, a couple of my contacts here, but they're in the movie business. They just told me to call a lawyer. Gave me a name too. What good is a lawyer going to do me? A bribe would work, if I knew who to offer it to."

"Ok, calm down. This isn't India. Tell me which police station they took her to."

"They didn't take her to a police station!"

"Coast Guard, then?"

"You still don't understand, do you? Do you have any idea what all this will do to her image once the public finds out? And the movie? Who's to say the producers won't pick someone else to replace her? With her wounded face and all? Do you know how vicious the movie industry can...?

"Not interested, Jay," Marc said, cutting him off. "Where did they take her?"

"The name they gave me was Vandan... Vandinbah...," he stammered.

"Say what?"

"I don't know how to pronounce it."

"Vandenberg?"

"Yes, that's it."

"Vandenberg Air Force Base? You serious?"

"Yes."

Chapter 6

The drive to Lompoc took almost four hours, most of it over the twisty 166 state highway that cut west over the mountains from Bakersfield. By the time Marc reached the main gate of Vandenberg Air Force Base, it was already 9 pm on Friday. There were 25 hours left until the pickup. If things here went as he hoped, he would still be able to get out in time to return to the desert or at least to some open space suitable enough for the pickup. Four hours in the car had given him enough time to cook up a story that he felt was believable enough to swallow and didn't contradict any of the eyewitness reports.

It hadn't been an easy decision to turn around, but there wasn't any alternative. Alisha had nothing to do with any of this. She was a victim of circumstance, a hostage of determination to get to the bottom of a mystery. It was a mystery which, if left unsolved, could have huge repercussions on both the Department of Homeland Security and the Department of Defense. Something unknown had crashed into the coastal waters of the United States. Not only had all the complex surveillance systems of the military been unable to stop it, they hadn't even detected it during its descent. That was the only explanation Marc had for why the Air Force had gotten involved. Clearly this was a bigger deal to the US government than he had initially anticipated.

In any case, the person the government was interested in was him, not Alisha. They may even have been using her as a bait to get him. He had instructed her manager Jay to once again call the mobile phone number obtained from the people who had taken her away, and to tell them that he was coming to the base. They were, however, to let her go as a precondition.

Marc pulled into a Burger King parking lot near the main entrance to the base and called Jay once more from a payphone. "Have they let her go yet?" he asked.

"They're not answering right now," Jay replied. "I've been trying to call again and again. They did agree to it earlier."

Marc got back in his car and drove up a mile to a deserted spot near the main gate. He would wait for a half hour and then return to the parking lot to call Jay once more to check if he had an update. He would keep doing that every half hour until he heard that Alisha was free.

Rolling down the windows, he decided to try to sit back and relax for a bit, if that was at all possible given the circumstances. But he knew he really needed to – the whole day had been more than exhausting, not to mention nerve-wrecking.

He wouldn't remember exactly how long he had been waiting before he passed out. All he would remember was that canister flying in from outside, diffusing gas the instant it landed on the front passenger seat. The reaction of his body was instantaneous, offering him no time to throw it out. The chilling numbness spread quickly from his chest out to his arms and legs. His head spun as his eyes forced themselves shut, leaving his thoughts to drift away into oblivion.

The room was small and bare, with no windows. Its only furnishings consisted of a table and three chairs, all made of cold, hard steel. The wall on one side was different from the others, covered almost entirely by huge glass doors. Their tint, however, was so dark that it was impossible to see through.

From this side anyway, Marc thought. He had just awoken to survey his surroundings. His head was aching and still spinning, and he had to swallow to hold back the vomit rising from his churning stomach. His eyes hurt too – it had taken a while to open them and even longer to get them to focus.

He shifted upright from the slouching position in his chair when he noticed the two men sitting on the other chairs. They were wearing Air Force uniforms, but his vision was still too blurry to help him discern how many stars or badges they were carrying. Not that he knew enough about military uniforms to determine their ranks anyway. He could see that one of them was gray haired and balding, while the other one looked younger by a decade at least.

"You should be feeling better in a few minutes," the older one said.

"Some welcoming ritual you have here," Marc said in a broken voice. "Got some aspirin?"

"You've given us enough of a headache tracking you down. We couldn't risk you changing your mind and trying to get away, right at our doorstep."

"Here," the other officer said, offering Marc a glass of water and a pair of tablets. "Tylenol. Should work just as well, and it's easier on the stomach."

Marc took them and drank the water.

"Before you try to spin any stories and waste our time, let's cut to the chase," the older man said. "We know you were there last night. We know you witnessed the crash, and we know you communicated with someone or something from the vessel before it disappeared."

"Not so fast," Marc said. "Where is she?"

"She is fine."

"Let her go first. She has nothing to do with any of this."

"We'll be the judges of that."

"Let her go, and then we can talk. You can't hold her like that."

The gray-haired officer shook his head. "National security. We'll hold her as long as we need to. The sooner you start talking, the higher the chances she'll be let go."

"You do realize who she is, don't you? Ready for the consequences?"

"We'll deal with the Indians if and when we have to. There are much greater issues at stake here that need to be dealt with first."

Marc could feel his head slowly starting to clear. "Then give me a guarantee that she's healthy and well."

"We're the Armed Forces of the United States, not ISIS."

"Then let's hope you're half as nice as the way you're portrayed on WikiLeaks."

The older man got up, his face starting to redden with anger. He was abruptly stopped by the other officer. "We don't have time for this, Sir."

The older officer reluctantly sat down again and nodded. The younger one then got up and left the room.

"Remember, no games," the older man said. He stared icily at Marc until the door opened again.

Marc turned to look at her as she walked in, followed closely by the officer who had left to fetch her. This time she was dressed more appropriately for the occasion, with a black blouse and tight blue jeans covering her body. The past several hours had taken their toll on her, for sure. But the wounds on her face appeared to be healing fast, no doubt thanks to the work of both the hospital doctors from the night before and her makeup artists from the morning after. Now that he was able to see her under proper light, he couldn't decide which of the pictures on the Internet she most resembled in real life, or whether she actually looked better than all of them.

She stared at him intently as she sat down, the expression on her face a combination of fear and utter bewilderment. He nodded and smiled at her with a sorrowful look, but she offered no acknowledgment in return.

"Now, start talking," the older officer said.

"What, in front of her?" Marc asked.

"Yes."

"I asked you to let her go."

"Not until we have the full picture. You have proof now that's she's fine. Start talking."

Marc realized he was out of options. At least she was alive and well, he reminded himself.

"I think it was an alien vessel," he said, clearing his throat.

"No kidding. Who are they and what do they want?"

"I don't know. But isn't it amazing? Now we know aliens exist."

"And I suppose you just happened to be there at that time of night. Some coincidence."

"I'd have to agree."

"Care to elaborate?"

Marc went on to describe how he had followed the Ferrari off the highway to the cliff, how he had intervened in the tiff between Alisha and Vinod, and how he had called the police right after. He knew they would have obtained an account from Alisha already, and he could only hope his version of the story matched hers exactly.

"What prompted you to stay after they all left?" the younger officer asked. He was standing in the room, having given up his seat to Alisha.

"To enjoy the night sky for a bit. It was crystal clear last night."

"A bit of a romantic, are we?" the older officer asked.

"Once upon a time. Anyway, as I watched the sky, I saw this fireball come hurtling down and crash into the ocean. I could see that it was a ship of some kind. I was so shocked that I just stood and watched. After the waves subsided, I could see pieces of the ship floating in the water. I went down to the beach to get a closer look. One of the pieces came up to the shore. It looked bizarre."

"Bizarre?"

"Yes, like nothing I had ever seen before. Like a weird machine with many long arms. Then, all of a sudden, it lunged at me. I thought it would eat me or something. I got scared, so I ran."

"You ran, yes," the younger officer said. "Past all the onlookers. You got in your car and sped off. Why didn't you stop and ask them for help?"

"I thought the machine was following me. Sure, in hindsight, I should have stopped and asked the other people there for help. Perhaps I would have noticed that the machine and all the other pieces of the ship had actually disappeared in the meantime. But I wasn't rational. I was terrified, too terrified to turn around and look. My only thought was my own survival, getting out of there as quickly as possible."

The older officer's mouth widened to reveal a smirk. "What kind of idiots do you take us for?"

"I'm not taking you for idiots. That's what happened." Marc began feeling his pockets, and he tensed up when he couldn't find it. Four hours of deliberating, yet he had forgotten about that one thing. But then, his plan had been to leave it in his car before entering the base. He hadn't counted on such a sudden, non-consensual method of entry.

"Looking for this?" The officer produced the Mendoken translator device and placed it on the table.

"Ah! Did you enjoy strip-searching an unconscious man?"

"Good thing we did. This isn't anything built by humans, is it?"

It certainly wasn't. It was much too solid, too sleek-looking an object. It had no openings and no creases. It was small and thin, oval in shape, completely transparent and slightly fluorescent.

"I was just going to tell you about it," Marc said, trying to recover from his blunder. "I did get to pick up that one thing on the shore, before the machine came toward me."

The older officer was starting to look increasingly frustrated. "Look here, this is your last chance," he said, leaning forward. "Tell us the truth."

"I just did."

The younger officer walked over to his older counterpart and whispered something into his ear. The older officer sat still for several seconds, and then got up. He walked over to the edge of the wall with the wide glass doors and pressed a button. The doors began moving apart automatically. Marc took advantage of the opportunity to slip the translator device back into his pocket while the two officers weren't looking. Alisha noticed the move, but she thankfully kept quiet.

"I am General Steve Robson, head of the Air Force Space Command," the older officer said, turning back to face Marc.

"And I'm Lieutenant General Larry Phelps, heading up the 14th Air Force and the Joint Functional Component Command for Space," said the other officer. "JFCC Space for short."

Marc felt a growing sense of uneasiness, at both the mention of the ranks of the two individuals he had just toyed with, and at what he could now clearly see through the widening gap between the doors. The hall beyond was in many ways the antithesis of the room they were in. To call it big would be an understatement. It was filled and crowded, filled with large screens covering the walls and computers atop multiple rows of desks, and crowded with uniformed people operating them. There was an air of frenzied activity about the place, almost like the way Marc imagined a busy stock exchange to be. Several individuals were moving from desk to desk, giving orders to others and constantly casting glances back at the screens on the walls.

"What's going on here?" Alisha asked in surprise.

"This, Ms. Bedi, is our command center for the JFCC," Lt. General Phelps said. "Our main directive is to ensure our freedom of action in space, and to ensure that nobody can use space against us in any way. What you see, what you hear from this point on, you must consider a hundred percent classified information. You do not have security clearance, you are not even a US citizen, but desperate times call for desperate actions. We have no choice, thanks to your friend here." He pointed at Marc. "Please do not ever disclose any of it to anybody outside these walls. This is especially critical given what a public figure you are."

Alisha nodded.

"The same goes for you," General Robson said to Marc.

"You have my word."

"Step in, please."

Marc and Alisha followed the two men into the hall. Many of the people turned to look at the newcomers, mostly at Alisha, and a hush fell over the entire room.

A number of individuals came forward, and General Robson introduced them to Marc and Alisha. Among other Air Force officers, there were representatives from the Office of Naval Intelligence, the Coast Guard and even a number of scientists from NASA.

"I mentioned that we don't have much time," Phelps said to Marc. "I wasn't joking." He pointed at one of the screens on the wall that showed an image of the night sky filled with stars, and he asked one of the computer operators to zoom in on it. A bright red spot appeared in the center.

"What's this?" Marc asked.

"Actually, we're not sure," one of the NASA scientists said. "It's nothing natural – no comet, asteroid, anything like that. We first observed it three months ago, at a distance of 4 astronomical units. That's about as far as Jupiter's orbit. Then it disappeared after a month, only to reappear just over an hour later. But this time, it was at a distance of 2.5 AU's, and it had moved to our line of vision on the other side of the Earth. We have no idea how it was able to traverse such a huge distance so quickly. Then, it disappeared again after 21 days for just over an hour. When it reappeared, it had moved back to our line of vision on this side of the Earth, but at a distance of 1.5 AU's. It's been disappearing and reappearing since, but after shorter and shorter intervals. Every time, it disappears for a little over an hour only, and every time it reappears, it's moved closer."

The scientist pressed a key on one of the computers near him, and a graph plotting the object's trajectory to date appeared on the screen. It looked like an inward traveling spiral. He pressed another key, and the time intervals between the disappearances were superimposed on the screen.

Marc did some calculations in his head. "A spiral based on the Fibonacci sequence?"

"Good call," the scientist said. "In reverse anyway. And it's doing so both in time and in distance. As the intervals get shorter, so does the distance it travels during each disappearance after the interval. Right now, it's already closer to us than Mars. Here's what you get if this thing completes the sequence, down to 0." He pressed another key, and the spiral completed its inward path, with an end point right next to the position of the Earth.

"Holy crap," Marc whispered.

"Our sentiments exactly. According to our calculations, we've got four more intervals after the current one before it arrives here. But each of those intervals should be no more than 24 hours long, corresponding to the differences between the very first few numbers in the Fibonacci sequence. The last disappearance began last night close to 10 pm, just before the reported crash. The next one should occur tomorrow at the same time."

The time windows, Marc realized. Now it made sense. Whatever this thing was, it was only when it disappeared for an hour between each interval that a Mendoken ship could come to Earth to get him.

"Needless to say," another NASA scientist said, "we've kept this information completely hidden from the public to avoid panic. At least until we know what the intentions are of whoever sent it. It hasn't been a problem so far because it hasn't emitted any light in the visible range, so most people using telescopes won't have spotted it. The images you see are all captured by our X-ray observatory."

"Chandra?" Marc asked.

"Yes."

"I see you know your NASA missions," General Robson said. "Kind of surprising for a sociologist."

"I was an astrophysicist in my past life."

"So I've heard. And you wonder why we're suspicious?"

Alisha's eyebrows lifted a little, but she chose to say nothing.

"In the beginning, it was emitting only X-rays," the second NASA scientist said. "But it's constantly been moving up the electromagnetic spectrum as it draws closer. It's been emitting fully in the ultraviolet now for several days, and as of last night it's started moving up to visible light. It's only a matter of hours now, maybe minutes before other people see it with their telescopes and reporting their findings to the media."

"How big is it?" Marc asked.

"According to our calculations, about a thousand miles across at most. But it's emitting way more light than its size would imply. By tomorrow night, it should be visible to the naked eye. By Sunday night, it will be the brightest object in the sky other than the moon. By the time it arrives here, well, I dread to think what it'll look like then."

"Any idea what it's made of?"

"No. We did the spectral analysis, of course, but none of the patterns amount to anything we can identify."

"Does it pulsate?"

"Every three seconds. Plus the wavelengths are increasing over time. There's good news in that, since it means we won't be blasted with radioactivity when it gets here. That's assuming it isn't concealing anything more sinister inside."

"How far from us is the end point?"

"About half way between us and the Moon's orbit," the scientist said, zooming the image in on the end of the object's trajectory.

"Well, at least it isn't colliding with the Earth."

"Very amusing," Robson said. "The clock is ticking. It will be here in five days. We're assuming the aliens who crashed last night are the ones operating this thing. We need to know what their intentions are, if they're hostile or not. We need to know what to prepare for, and we need to know what we should tell the public."

"We need you to tell us the truth," Phelps said. "Now you know what's at stake, for all of us. This isn't just about national security, it's security for the whole world. We have never before faced a threat of this kind, and we don't even know what kind it really is."

"So, again, what kind of contact did you have with the aliens?" Robson asked. "What did they tell you? And can you reestablish contact with them?"

Marc's uneasiness was rising further. It was unlikely the Mendoken were operating this object, or they wouldn't be held hostage to those time windows. The more probable scenario was that the Mendoken were worried about it too, and that was why they had attempted to contact him. He wondered if it could be a lone Starguzzler that had somehow survived the galactic war from eleven years prior, but quickly brushed that thought aside. This was no Starguzzler. The composition of those massive, hydrogen and helium filled weapons of mass destruction would easily have been identified by spectral analysis. Plus, Starguzzlers couldn't instantly disappear and reappear like that across vast expanses of space, nor did they pulsate. This was something else altogether, but possibly no less terrifying.

He hesitated, trying to calculate all the possible scenarios in his mind and what the best next step would be. If this thing really was a threat to Earth, then there was no country better equipped than the United States and no authority better prepared than the US government to deal with an imminent global disaster or a hostile alien invasion. It wasn't very likely they would believe him if he told them what he knew, and very little of what he knew would actually help them prepare for the threat anyway. He still felt a moral obligation to tell them, but the only thing he could hear repeating itself in his head was the voice of that dying Mendoken commander, saying, "Do not reveal anything... to anyone on Earth."

Chapter 7

"I'm sorry you got pulled into this," Marc said.

"So am I." Alisha's response was swift, and she did little to hide her irritation. "This is absurd. They can't do this to me. Who do they think they're dealing with?"

The room they were in had a twin bunk bed on one side, a TV on the other and a window on the wall in between. A door next to the TV led the way to a tiny bathroom. A table with a single chair took up the remaining space in the center of the room.

"They won't get away with this," she added. "They've taken away my phone, so I can't call anyone. And how can they hole both of us up in a single room? What kind of decency do these people have, demeaning me like this? Very chivalrous, your government."

"It's on purpose," Marc said. "By keeping us together, they're hoping you'll convince me to talk to them."

"Much effect I'm having. What is it with you anyway? Why won't you tell them? And why did you lie to me about what you saw last night? You told me you saw the crash from your car, while you were driving."

He kept quiet.

"See what I mean?" she went on. "This is all thanks to you. The sooner you open your mouth, the sooner they'll let me go."

"I wouldn't count on it."

"Excuse me?"

"Somehow they think we're inextricably linked – you, me, the alien crash, the approaching object. Even if I tell them what they want to hear, they'll keep both of us here until they figure out how to deal with that thing. I'm sure they discovered that you called me this morning, and that must have further raised their level of suspicion. Now trying to convince them it was all a coincidence won't get us anywhere."

"How do you know?"

"They said so already – national security. Under coverage of that term, they can pretty much do anything they want to. Can't say I totally blame them, given what appears to be at stake. They've even allowed you, a non-US citizen, to witness classified things. Because this affects the whole world, not just this country. They will do anything to more quickly get to the answers they're looking for. That it sucks for you and me in the process is of no concern to them at the moment."

She threw her hands up in the air and sighed. "I can't believe this is happening to me." She went on to complain about the quality of the food and the bedding as she lay down on the upper bed, and once more about Marc's stubborn refusal to cooperate with the people holding them in confinement.

Marc sat quietly and listened for a while from the lower bed. Then, to divert his attention, he turned on the TV to catch the latest news. Reports were already coming in from various parts of the world – astronomers had sighted this bizarre new object in the night sky and were in the process of analyzing it. Some thought it was a meteor or possibly a comet that hadn't been noticed before, but many dismissed those theories and admitted it was a UFO. Whether it was intelligent and operated by aliens or not was a different question they weren't yet in a position to address. Questions were being raised whether the US or any other government had known about it for some time and purposely kept quiet.

Several religious figures were already claiming it for their own, with a few Christian groups openly declaring that it was Jesus returning from Heaven to Earth. The End Times had finally come – only the faithful would be spared, and all others would perish in the anticipated Rapture that would soon engulf the Earth. Ironically, some Muslims were in agreement that it was Jesus returning, but claimed he was coming for the Muslims and not the Christians. Doomsday theorists pointed to the end of some ancient calendar or the other and the much anticipated apocalypse, suggesting it was a hidden planet that had finally appeared. It would soon collide with the Earth, just as they had predicted.

Unbelievable, Marc thought. He cringed as he recalled the futile, idealistic vision he had once held to unite the human race.

"Whatever it is you're hiding," he heard Alisha say from above, "I hope they raise the pressure on you tomorrow to talk. I don't know what's going on, but I just want this over with. I want to get out of here."

"I don't think they'll have to," he replied.

"Meaning?"

"That object is able to travel at unimaginable speeds, it's emitting almost as much energy as a brown dwarf star, and it seems to be defying all the laws of gravity as it approaches us. There's absolutely no need for it to be following a slow Fibonacci spiral like that. If it wanted to, it could have come straight here in no time."

Alisha's head appeared over the edge of the upper bed. "Then... why is it following that pattern?"

"Because it's playing with us, trying to scare us as much and for as long as possible. It isn't concerned about our preparations in the meantime, because it knows we're no match for it. That thing is not benign. It's going to launch some kind of attack on us, and it will do so before the end of the spiral. Maybe even tomorrow. That way, it will surprise us and freak us out even more, just when we're starting to think we've figured things out. And once that happens, our buddies in the Air Force will have more pressing things to worry about than my confession."

"How do you know all this?"

"I don't. It's just a hunch. We'll see."

The ground shook with ferocity, jolting Marc awake. The tremor was so severe that he almost fell off the bed. He waited for the earthquake to stop before he opened his eyes and sat up. The sunlight coming in through the window was lighting up the whole room.

The time on his watch only showed 5 am, which made no sense. It couldn't possibly be so bright this early. He got up and walked over to the window to locate the position of the Sun.

"Holy smokes!" he uttered.

"What's happening?" Alisha asked sleepily from the upper bed.

"Looks like my hunch was right."

The ground shook again, more violently than the last time. Alisha lost her balance and fell from the upper bed. Were it not for the lightning reaction of Marc's arms, she would have hit the floor with a loud thud.

"Goodness!" she exclaimed in shock. "Thanks."

"Sure," he said, helping her steady herself. "Here, take a look."

Her eyes opened wide as she looked out the window. "It can't be!"

The object had arrived, and it was glowing brightly in the sky. It looked like a red giant star, appearing both redder and larger than the Sun. Like the Sun, it was too bright to look at directly. It was pulsating, as expected. Every three seconds, it dimmed slightly and then brightened up again right after. As they watched out of the corners of their eyes, the object seemed to be slowly changing shape by growing sideways.

"My God, it's replicating," Marc whispered. "At an amazing speed for something that big."

Several minutes passed before the second, newly formed object dislodged itself from the original and began gliding away in a direction perpendicular to their line of vision. The first object seemed to have lost no size or brightness in the process, and the second one looked identical to its parent. They were both pulsating at the same rate, in unison.

A short while later, both objects shot something simultaneously in the direction of the Earth. The flashes of light raced through the sky and entered the atmosphere within a few minutes. Tails of white smoke formed behind them as they forced themselves through the air. Seconds later, they disappeared from view behind the roofs of the neighboring buildings at the base. Lightning-like bursts appeared in the distance, followed by the shattering sound of mighty explosions. Then the ground shook again, even more violently.

The attack has begun, Marc thought. He had been right. NASA and the Air Force had been wrong. For that matter, even the Mendoken had been wrong. They had told him the next time window would occur on Saturday night. But there had evidently been a window on Friday night, which the object had used to bypass the rest of the spiral path and head straight to the end point. Clearly things were unraveling more quickly than the Mendoken had anticipated. He could only hope they would still be able to keep their word and somehow come to get him the following night. He wasn't aware of any Plan B.

Voices could be heard yelling in the corridors, and sirens began wailing across the base.

"No!" Marc exclaimed.

"What?" Alisha asked, her voice filled with alarm.

"The sirens – it's a tsunami warning. This base is located on the Pacific coast."

"You've got to be joking."

"I wish I was."

She stepped to the heavy metal door, locked from the outside, and began banging on it with her fists. "Can anyone hear us? Let us out! Please!"

There was no response. Through the window, soldiers could be seen rushing out of the buildings, just as the noise of rising helicopters filled the air. Soon after, Marc thought he could also hear jet fighters taking off from the base.

He turned on the TV to find out what the news stations were saying, but there was no reception on any channel. Alisha kept banging on the door, but nobody came by.

"It's no use," Marc said. "Nobody's going to pay any attention to us right now."

"Then what do we do?"

"I don't know. We've got to get out of here."

Alisha was staring at him.

"What?" he asked.

"What's that in your pants?" She pointed at his crotch.

"Huh? Now is not the..." He looked down before saying anything more that he might end up regretting, and he noticed the right pocket area of his jeans was glowing. He reached into his pocket and pulled out the Mendoken translator device. The whole thing was gleaming in a brilliant red color, and it felt warm to the touch.

"What is that thing?"

Marc didn't answer. He wasn't sure why it was glowing like that – he had never seen a translator do that before. He could only assume that it wanted to draw attention to itself, and the reason for that he discovered within a few seconds. As he held it, it began to change shape, growing longer and bending at the edges into the shape of a horseshoe magnet. A virtual visor appeared in front of his eyes. It took him a few more seconds to recognize what the device was changing into – a ganvex.

Amazing, he thought. The Mendoken gun that allowed its operator to blast invisible shock rays simultaneously at any number of targets. He remembered using one only once those eleven years ago, during that fateful battle at the Bara Dilshai asteroid. The translator the Mendoken had given him this time apparently had more than one purpose. It could automatically sense danger and convert itself into a weapon for the benefit of its carrier. It certainly was a good thing the people holding them at the base had forgotten about it amongst all the other activity from the night before.

"Stand back," he told Alisha. He pointed the ganvex at the door, but then changed his mind and pointed it at the window instead. That would be an easier exit, he realized. They were on the ground floor.

He blinked his eyes to activate the visor. The whole wall instantly began shaking and crumbled quickly to pieces, sending plumes of dust into the air. A gaping hole to the outside slowly became visible as the dust cleared.

"Who... what are you?" she asked in horror.

"I'm as much a human being as you," he replied. "I just happen to have some very advanced, powerful friends who aren't."

The dawn hours on the Central Coast were always a cold affair, regardless of the season. On this particular morning, however, the air was considerably warmer than usual. Marc had little doubt it was because of those bright objects. Now that he was out in the open, he could see several of them up in the sky. They were continuing to replicate, spewing out more and more of themselves in a grid-like fashion across his entire field of vision. Every few minutes, flashes of light shot out from all of them at the same time, hitting the surface of the Earth several minutes later. Every time, loud explosions could be heard in the distance, soon to be followed by clouds of smoke rising into the air. The ground shook every time as well, forcing him and Alisha to stop running and take cover under something, under anything they could find along the way.

Only a matter of time before one of them hits us, he thought.

The going was tough, especially trying to stay out of sight of all the personnel running or driving around on the grounds of the base. Fortunately the attention of everybody was focused either upwards or in the direction of the shore. The sirens were still blaring – the tsunami threat was real, it seemed, probably due to many of those flashes slamming into the ocean. The raging sea could be heard in the distance. Any minute now, a giant wave would come splashing over the cliffs. Everybody was evidently too concerned about saving his or her own behind, not about the jailbreak of two individuals they didn't know and couldn't care less about.

Crouching behind a parked vehicle, Marc scanned the parking lot between several adjacent buildings for his car, but he couldn't see it anywhere.

"I don't suppose you know how to hotwire a car?" he asked Alisha.

She scowled at him. "I don't suppose your pants are on fire again?"

He glanced at his pocket. The ganvex, which had automatically transformed itself back into its original translator device shape, was quiet and dark. He shook his head.

"So what's the plan?" she asked nervously.

"Don't know." He watched as several cars pulled out of the parking lot, followed by trucks, buses and vans carrying cohorts of people. Those who weren't taking to the skies in planes and helicopters were apparently abandoning the base en masse.

"What kind of car did you say you have again?" she asked abruptly.

"A Subaru Outback."

"Is that it?" She pointed toward a spot at the far end of the parking lot that had just been cleared by a van, revealing a gray Subaru behind.

Marc nodded approvingly.

They quietly made their way to the car, stopping every few meters to hide behind something and looking out to wait for the coast to clear. Just as they finally reached it, Marc heard a voice.

"Hey! Stop!"

He turned around to see a couple of uniformed men running toward them.

"Quick!" he said to Alisha. "Get in and buckle up."

The doors were unlocked, and the key was in the ignition. A stroke of luck, he thought. He sprang the engine to life and floored the gas pedal.

Under different circumstances, there would have been no chance for escape. But the place was in chaos, with hundreds of vehicles of all shapes and sizes scrambling to leave the base. With good reason too – the first wave had made it over the cliffs and had already crashed into the nearest buildings, just a few hundred feet from where Marc and Alisha had just stood.

Marc maneuvered the car skillfully, continuously swerving off the path onto the grass to bypass all the vehicles jamming up the exit road. Luckily the only things to hit him were the loads of honks and profane insults from the angry drivers he was passing by.

He glanced briefly at Alisha, who was grabbing the armrest on the door with both her hands. Her face was ashen with fear. "Don't worry," he said reassuringly as he patted the dashboard. "Might not look like much, but this car's a sturdy beast."

She didn't answer. She didn't have to – the icy stare she gave him at that moment left little doubt who she thought the real beast was.

The gate to the base was abandoned. Not surprising, Marc thought. He raced past it and turned the car right onto Highway 1 South. Casting a glance back at the base, he could see another wave, this one much higher than the previous ones, rising over the cliffs. Missiles were being fired from the ground and from some of the fighter planes in the sky, trying to hit the barrage of oncoming flashes. The majority were able to hit their targets and explode. But not only were the flashes not destroyed, they didn't even slow down.

Alisha was shaking her head in disbelief. "Why is this all happening? What's going to happen to us?"

"I don't know," Marc said. "I'm not sure if I can do anything to stop it. But regardless what happens, I promise to get you back to your people."

Chapter 8

Under normal conditions, the drive from Lompoc to Beverly Hills usually took about two and a half hours. On Sunday September 14th, 2014, it took Marc and Alisha over 15 hours to travel that distance of 145 miles. The traffic flowed at a snail's pace for most of the way, thanks to the large number of people frantically trying to flee from their homes along the coastal areas. Tsunami warnings were in effect up and down the entire coast, and it seemed that most had chosen to take heed.

People were also trying to flee the devastation being caused by the steady torrent of flashes from the sky, soon realizing to their chagrin that there were no safe havens further inland. The projectiles or meteorites, whatever they were, were falling everywhere, setting off loud explosions that caused the ground to shake violently. Entire buildings and roads were being reduced to rubble, woodlands and grass fields were set ablaze, and clouds of smoke and dust could be seen rising into the air. People with bloodied faces and hands limped out into the streets from their destroyed homes, screaming and calling for help to save their loved ones still trapped underneath all the debris.

But there was nobody available to help. Everybody was only looking out for his or her own, for at any moment another explosion could occur anywhere and more would die. With so much death and devastation all around, it was impossible for any coordinated relief effort to take shape. Sirens could be heard in the distance, but Marc would rarely spot a fire truck or ambulance nearby. Helicopters and planes were continuously flying overhead, but they were mostly military and their sole objective seemed to be to engage the enemy. With no knowledge of its vulnerabilities and no way to fight back, however, they were little more than sitting ducks. Many of them were hit by the incoming flashes and instantly blown up.

The scene reminded Marc of some of the apocalyptic movies he had seen. Sitting behind the wheel of his car, he felt helpless, powerless to do anything for all the panic-stricken people. There were too many of them, even the ones stumbling onto the sides of the freeway to stop passing cars. He noticed how other drivers who had stopped to help were forced out of their own cars by the hordes of desperate people. Whoever reached the driver's seat first was the one to drive off, leaving the rest behind. As guilty as he felt about not stopping to help, there was no way he was going to put Alisha and himself at risk like that. He had a goal to reach – to get Alisha back to her people and to still make it in time to a spot where the Mendoken could pick him up. That was the only hope he had to somehow stop this vicious attack on Earth, if that was at all possible.

There were several close calls along the way when flashes hit the ground nearby. Many sections of the freeway were blown up, sending large chunks of asphalt high up into the sky and causing even more traffic mayhem as drivers tried to navigate their cars around the newly formed craters. Every time he drove off the road, he was more thankful than ever to be driving the rugged Subaru Outback. It was just made for rough conditions like this.

As the hours passed, the sky turned gray and hazy with all the rising smoke and ash. A burning smell began to pervade the warming air. The traffic finally began to lighten a little once they reached Ventura, at which point Marc decided to take a chance and get off the highway to stop for food and gas. It was already mid-afternoon, and they hadn't eaten or drunk anything all day. Neither of them had spoken much the entire time either – they were both in a state of shock with all that was happening around them.

They found an abandoned gas station near the highway exit. Incoming flashes had already destroyed much of the neighborhood. The pumps were still working, however, so Marc filled up the car and went to pick up some food and drinks from the small convenience store inside the station.

"Hurry, Marc!" Alisha called out from the car, casting nervous glances to the left and right as he walked into the store.

Her concerns were not unfounded. A group of people emerged from the street corner, holding signs and large crosses. Some were singing, others shouting.

"The Rapture is at hand, the Great Tribulation is at hand!" they chanted. "All you sinners, your time is over! The Lord Jesus is coming back for us!"

When they noticed the car at the gas station, they turned toward it and quickened their pace. Their chanting grew louder.

"Marc, run!" Alisha shouted.

Marc needed no second warning. Holding whatever he had picked up from the store, he sprinted back to the car, got in and started the engine, just as the first few from the crowd reached the station.

"Ours is the world now!" they yelled as they surrounded the car, their faces brimming with a combination of excitement and rage. Some of them looked as if they were almost in a trance-like state. They began banging on the hood and sides of the car with their doomsday signs. Then they began rocking the car from side to side.

"Do something!" Alisha said fearfully.

Marc pressed lightly on the gas, trying to edge the car forward through the crowd. That seemed to further enrage some of the individuals, who began banging their signs against the car's windows. One of the rear windows shattered into pieces.

Marc realized there was no way to break out of this tough spot without inflicting physical harm. He pressed harder on the gas pedal, slamming the front bumper into the people standing in front of the car. There were shrieks of pain, and a few people fell to the ground. He honked the horn as a warning to them to get up and move out of the way or risk being run over, and he moved the car further forward to show he wasn't joking. Those still standing pulled away the ones who had fallen, opening the way just enough for the car to move out. They cursed at Marc and warned how the Lord would show him no mercy when He finally arrived.

Marc wasted no time in pressing full force on the gas. The tires screeched, and the car zoomed out onto the street.

LA was in total chaos. It was a marked contrast from the way it had been just two days earlier, when Marc had left it under such different circumstances. Many parts of the city were in ruins and people were out on the streets in large numbers, seeking food, shelter and medical help from anyone who bothered to lend a hand. Others were trying to get out of the city, others still were taking advantage of the situation to raid abandoned shops and restaurants. The only good news was that the devastating flashes had finally stopped falling from the sky as the evening hours rolled in, making it easier for emergency personnel to move around the city to reach those in the direst of need. The sources of the flashes were still there, spread apart in a grid-like fashion across the entire sky. They were barely visible, however, with all the thick dust and smoke in the air.

Creeping along at a snail's pace, Marc and Alisha finally made it to their destination well after 9 pm – the luxurious Beverly Wilshire Hotel in the heart of Beverly Hills, adjacent to Rodeo Drive. It was the hotel where Alisha and her entourage were staying, and the spot where she had asked Marc to drop her off. There had been no means for her to get in touch with her assistants or her manager en route – her mobile phone had been taken away back at the Air Force Base, and Marc wasn't carrying his. Not that having it would have helped anyway, as all phone lines, both wired and wireless, were dead.

Neither Marc nor Alisha knew, therefore, that the entire western half of the hotel had been demolished by a series of descending flashes from the sky earlier in the day. Many nearby buildings had fared much worse – they had been completely destroyed.

"Oh, my God," Alisha whispered in horror. "Are they all...?" Her words trailed off.

"I don't know," Marc replied. He brought the car to a halt in front of the building. "Which side were you staying at?"

She pointed at the side that was reduced to rubble.

"Don't give up hope yet," he said. "Come on."

They got out of the car and walked into the hotel through the main entrance. The streets were filled with people, many of them looting the fancy stores lining Rodeo Drive, but the hotel lobby was deserted. Everyone had fled, it seemed, probably as soon as the first flash had hit the building.

They turned to the right and walked over to the destroyed wing, treading carefully over the dust and blocks of broken concrete. The roof was gone, leaving a clear view of the dark, ash-filled sky above. Alisha gasped when she noticed a dead body lying nearby. Luckily it wasn't anyone she knew. It was, however, only the first of many bodies they would end up finding. Further ahead in the ruins, they did discover the bodies of her manager and one of her assistants. It was hardly a stretch to imagine that most other members of her team were buried deep in the rubble.

Alisha was crestfallen. She shook her head in disbelief and closed her eyes. Marc noticed her stumble. He quickly placed his hands on the sides of her arms to hold her upright.

"I'm very sorry," he said.

Distressed as he was with all the death and destruction around him, Marc was also beginning to feel a rising anxiety. The clock was ticking. He needed to find an open space for the Mendoken pickup at 10 pm, assuming it was still happening, and he needed to get Alisha into safe hands before that. But now he had no idea whose hands they could be.

He walked with her into a clearing in the midst of all the rubble and found a slab of concrete for her to sit on. Given her state of mind, he thought about how best to ask her what she wanted to do now. Before he could open his mouth, however, he heard a voice behind him.

"I knew you'd come back here, Alisha. I've been waiting." That was a male voice with a slight Indian accent.

Marc turned around to face the man. It was Vinod, Alisha's boyfriend. Ex-boyfriend, he corrected himself. Somehow this individual had managed to give the police the slip, or maybe the police just had bigger issues to worry about at that moment. Either way, he was here, and free.

Alisha slowly lifted her face to look at Vinod. Her teary eyes widened at first to indicate her surprise, but they narrowed soon after in a show of anger and disdain.

"I thought you might bring him too," Vinod added, pointing a finger at Marc. "I'm prepared this time."

"Now isn't the time, Vinod," Alisha said.

Vinod stepped forward and stood in front of Marc. The bruises on his face from the skirmish with Marc two days earlier were still clearly visible. "Not so fast, my dear. This man poked his nose into..."

"He didn't poke his nose, he intervened because you were hitting me."

Vinod smirked. "He just happened to be there, right? Tell me, did he follow us all the way from LA? For that matter, how long have you two been hitting the sack?"

Alisha looked dumbfounded. "What are you talking about?"

"At least it's clear now why you were so insolent with me that night. How long has this been going on?"

She shook her head. "It's nothing of the sort, you imbecile! He..."

"You could have had anyone," Vinod said, cutting her off. "You picked him, of all people? A Chinese guy?" He proceeded to hurl a series of insults in Hindi that the Mendoken translator device in Marc's pocket happily translated into English for him. Evidently it was also adept in translating between various human languages.

"What's wrong with being Chinese?" Marc asked. "Technically I'm only half Chinese, if that makes any difference."

"Shut up, pig!"

"Stop it, Vinod," Alisha said in a broken voice. "I can't deal with you right now." She dropped her face into her hands.

"No more games, Alisha," Vinod said. "This man has insulted me and he has attacked me. Now he'll pay the price."

Marc instinctively began pushing his right leg back to get into a fighting position.

"That won't help you this time," Vinod said, laughing. "And no, I don't have a gun. That would be too instantaneous."

A figure walked into the clearing behind him. Then came another, and another. Then came five more. They were all big men with tough appearances, almost certainly mercenaries for hire. A couple were brandishing baseball bats, another held a knife. They moved quickly and formed a circle around Marc.

"What is this?" Alisha demanded. "He did nothing wrong!"

"I'll be the judge of that," Vinod replied quietly.

She got up and stood in front of Marc in a protective manner, facing Vinod. "Leave him out of this. This is between you and me."

Vinod grabbed her to pull her aside.

Marc immediately reached out to stop Vinod, but he felt a sharp pain on his back before his hand could reach its destination. He stumbled and almost fell, but instantly turned around to face the mercenary who had just attacked him. He landed a sharp blow on the man's chest and tripped him over. He was about to strike at him again, but he was hit by another of the men on his head. Dazed, he turned again to face the second attacker before a third lunged toward him.

Marc's Kung Fu training proved far superior to the individual fighting techniques of his opponents. He fought valiantly, dealing numerous injuries to the towering men. But he was vastly outnumbered, and blow after blow to his head and stomach weakened him to the point of no return. The last straw was a knife stab on his shoulder, causing his knees to buckle and making him fall to the ground. He could feel the sharp pain and the blood gushing out from the deep wound. He tried to gather the strength to get up again, but in vain. He could hear Alisha sobbing, and out of the corner of his eye he saw Vinod firmly holding her back.

Two of the men held him pinned to the ground. The apparent leader of the group spoke to Vinod. "What now?"

"Well, I don't think we need to worry about police or prison in this new world out there." A big, sly grin appeared across his face.

"No!" Alisha screamed. "You can't do..."

Vinod clasped his hand over her mouth, reducing her voice to a mere muffle. A big mistake on his part, as almost immediately she raised her elbow and brought it crashing down on his groin with full force. Letting her go, he howled in pain and stumbled backward.

She ran toward Marc to help him, pushing aside one of the men standing in her way and punching another in the face. But before she could reach him, two other men grabbed her and pulled her back. They took extra care to pin her arms behind her, in order to have their private parts avoid the same fate as Vinod's. Unable to make another step forward, she gnashed her teeth in frustration and spit on the face of the man on her left.

In between the pangs of pain emanating from various parts of his body, Marc could feel something moving in his pocket. It was the translator device. Sensing danger, it was probably transforming itself into a ganvex again. A little late, he thought. It was impossible to reach it now with his own arms rendered completely immobile. There was no way out this time, he realized. He had finally reached the end of the road.

"Cut his throat," the leader of the mercenaries said.

The man with the knife stepped forward and leaned over Marc's head. "Sorry buddy, nothing personal," he said. "Any last words?"

Marc felt too weak, too dejected to move. He barely had enough energy left to open his mouth. "What... time is it?" he stammered.

The men began laughing. "If you must know, 10:14 pm," the leader said, glancing at his watch. "How's that gonna help?"

"This is how," a deep, booming voice suddenly said.

The men jumped in surprise and turned around to see who had just spoken. A figure had appeared out of thin air in front of them. Two others appeared behind. They were incredibly tall, almost eight feet in height, and dressed in loose brown robes. Their heads were covered and their faces veiled, revealing only their large, round brown eyes. They were not human.

"Let him go," the figure in front said.

The men didn't budge, probably too stunned to move.

"Who are you?" the leader demanded, his voice quivering.

"Last warning," the figure said. "Let him go."

"We'll... kill him if you hurt us."

"Just try."

The leader seemed unsure what to do, perhaps trying to figure out where to draw the line between bravery and foolishness. Then he nodded at his men, and together they charged at the three newcomers.

The figure in front raised and spread out his long arms, and then in a sweeping motion brought them together until his hands were clasped tightly. A brilliant streak of light appeared above his hands and spread out toward the attacking men. It struck them with a vicious force, knocking them all down and leaving them dazed.

A couple of them got up after a few seconds and charged again. This time, one of the other newcomers stepped forward and effortlessly picked them both up by their necks, one in each hand.

"Surely the Creator watches over us in life and in death," he said, slowly tightening the grip on their necks. Both of them began choking, frantically waving their arms and legs with whatever energy they had left in their bodies.

"No need for that," the figure in front said.

The figure holding the two men let them go. They fell to the ground like large bags of sand.

Marc had raised his head and was watching the whole spectacle with exhilaration. Help had arrived in the nick of time, saving him from imminent death. He tried to open his mouth and warn that Vinod was escaping while the others weren't looking, hands still holding on to his crotch. But Marc couldn't manage anything more than a hoarse whisper. Nobody heard him. Alisha was still standing there, too shocked to speak or move.

The figure in front made another sweeping motion with his arms. Another streak of light appeared and struck at all eight of the mercenaries. This time, they were instantly rendered unconscious. The figure then walked up to Marc, knelt in front of him and removed his veil.

It took Marc several seconds to recognize the Aftaran's owl-like, feathery face. "Dumyan!" he whispered in surprise.

"Good to see you again, my friend."

"You... have no idea." Marc managed a weak smile.

Dumyan closed his eyes and uttered a short prayer, then waved his hand over Marc's body. Marc could feel a little strength returning to his muscles, and the pain in his wounds began subsiding. The bleeding from the knife cut stopped immediately.

"You've picked up quite a few spiritual enchantments since we last met," Marc said, finding his voice again as he slowly sat up.

"I've had time to master the art."

"Are you carrying your own translator device?" Marc could feel his shifting back to its original shape again in his pocket.

"No, we were told you would have one."

"I do. Seems to be working flawlessly too, for everyone here."

They heard some commotion from behind the clearing. Vinod appeared again, this time with reinforcements. There were many individuals, perhaps between thirty and forty. Marc surmised these weren't mercenaries but some of the more violent looters from the street, likely brought here with the promise that they could strike back at the aliens who had launched this vicious attack on Earth. They filed quickly into the clearing. Some of them were carrying guns, others had knives.

Dumyan stood up. "I suppose it doesn't matter anymore," he said to the other two Aftarans. "We've already had to expose ourselves to these humans, so the principle of non-interference no longer applies." He raised his hands to the sky, closed his eyes and uttered something quietly.

A monstrous shadow appeared high above their heads, covering the full view of the sky from the clearing. Marc realized it was a spaceship, submarine-shaped like most Aftaran ships, but much bigger than any he remembered traveling on all those years ago. Bright blue and red lights, the lights of battle, were flowing all over the surface of the ship.

"If you value your lives," Dumyan rumbled, "then step back and disappear."

Some turned immediately and ran away in fright.

"Now!" Dumyan roared, raising his hands again in a threatening gesture. The span of his outstretched arms had to be almost seven feet, which, with the layers of robe that hung loose all over his tall body, made for a formidable and intimidating sight. The backdrop of the colossal spaceship in the sky only helped to hit the point home.

The rest of the crowd quickly dispersed. Vinod followed suit, after one last, longing look at his lost girlfriend.

"No Gyra class ship, eh?" Marc asked.

"Maura, a new class altogether," Dumyan replied, turning around to face him. "Three times the size and much faster. We've significantly upped our defense and travel capabilities since you last saw us, with the help of the Mendoken. Nowhere near on par with them, of course, but way better than before. After what happened with the Starguzzler conspiracy, we decided to take no more chances."

"A wise choice."

Alisha, who had so far been watching everything from the sidelines, came up to Marc. "I'm so sorry," she said in a shaky voice, "for what those cowards did to you."

"Don't worry about it."

"Who is this?" Dumyan asked.

"This is Alisha," Marc said. "She's a famous movie actress."

"Good for her," Dumyan said. "Ready, Marc?"

Alisha looked both frightened and worried. She instinctively slithered her hand under Marc's arm.

Marc looked at her and shook his head. "You have no idea what you're getting into."

"You've seen what's left for me here," she said.

"It's going to be anything but fun and games out there."

"I'll take my chances."

"What about your family?"

"They're in India, if they're still alive."

"Can we check?" Marc asked Dumyan.

"What's India?"

"Country on the other side of the planet."

"We don't have time. We must pass the location of the enemy blockade before the window closes. Only during the window do they disappear and give us a chance to move."

Marc looked up, past the shadow of the Aftaran ship. Through all the smoke and ash in the air, he noticed for the first time that the bright objects in the sky were no longer there.

"If all goes as planned," Dumyan added, "we can return later, find her family and drop her off. But we can't vouch for her safety while she's with us."

Alisha nodded hastily. "Just don't leave me here alone."

"Very well." Dumyan uttered a prayer and blew a whiff of air over Marc, Alisha and the other two Aftarans.

Marc felt his surroundings evaporate in a whirlwind.

Chapter 9

The Aftaran Maura class vessel lifted effortlessly into the sky, its powerful, anti-matter driven kilasic engines springing to life as it cleared the Earth's atmosphere and headed for deep space. Within minutes, it passed the location of the blockade unhindered. The bright objects that had surrounded the planet and caused so much devastation were nowhere to be seen. They were projected to reappear only in another twenty minutes.

"This has got to be a dream," Alisha said, gazing out the rear window of a small cabin in the upper section of the ship. The Earth was quickly shrinking from a massive sphere to a small speck in the black sky.

"I wish it was." Marc winced in pain as she tended to his wounds. A supply of sanitized cloths and a tray carrying food and drinks had been provided in a corner of the cabin.

He took a sip of the yellow, strength-giving Aftaran drink known as rauka, and urged her to do the same. "It does wonders," he said.

Alisha took a sip. "Bah... bitter!"

"Yes, but I guarantee you'll feel better, and quickly. Especially after the exhausting day."

Her face seemed to perk up. "Feels like a shot of pure energy seeping down my throat. And... now it's tingling all over my body."

"Feels good, eh?

She nodded.

"You should eat something too," he added. "You'll be surprised how similar their food is to yours."

"Meaning?"

"Take a look."

She reached over and lifted the lid of one of the bowls. "You're joking."

"Curry, all vegetarian," he said.

The look of disgust on her face left little doubt about her feelings on the matter. Curry or not, the unfamiliar shapes, colors and pungent smells of the assorted Aftaran vegetables were unlikely to instill nostalgic feelings of her mom's cooking.

"Try it," he said. "Trust me, you'll like it."

"Not in my lifetime."

"Your lifetime won't be very long if you don't eat."

She lifted the handle again and peered cautiously inside.

"You had a choice back on Earth, and you decided to stay with me," he added. "Now you have none. We may be out here for days, weeks, or longer."

She reluctantly transferred some food onto a plate. Closing her eyes, she took a bite. The look of disgust on her face slowly disappeared.

"Well?" he asked.

"Spicy, very. But good." She gulped down some more rauka.

"Told you. Certainly beats our hottest chilies." Marc helped himself to some food as well.

"Who are these creatures?" she asked between mouthfuls.

"They're called Aftarans. They are a very old, highly advanced civilization that occupies much of the core of our galaxy. As you may have noticed, they're deeply religious. They also have magical powers, which they somehow attribute to spiritual strength from their holy scriptures. That's how they instantly transported us from the surface of the Earth to this ship, and how they placed you and me directly in this room. The funny thing is, they weren't the ones I was expecting."

"Who were you expecting?"

"We actually live in a region inhabited and controlled by another alien species - the Mendoken. They are the most technologically advanced civilization in our galaxy, and they live largely by logic and reason. Our solar system is under their watch. They call it the Mendo-Biesel system. You remember the crash off the coast where you and I met? That was one of their smaller scout ships. I was expecting them to come again."

"Under their watch? What does that mean? Mendoken, Aftarans... how many of these civilizations are there?"

Marc smiled, mostly in remembrance of his own reaction upon discovering these same facts for the first time. He also felt relieved to finally be able to talk to another human about it. The promise he had made to the dying Mendoken commander clearly didn't apply to Alisha – she had already witnessed too many inexplicable things firsthand, and she was about to witness a whole lot more.

"Space isn't as empty as we humans think it is," he said. "It's just made to appear to us that way."

"What? How?"

"There's a... well, you'll see for yourself soon enough. But to answer your question, there are two other major civilizations in the Glaessan galaxy..."

"The what?" she asked, cutting him off.

"The Glaessan. That's the actual name of our galaxy. 'Milky Way' isn't widely used beyond Earth's surface. Actually, it isn't used at all. Anyway, there are two other major civilizations - the Volona and the Phyrax. The Volona live in virtual worlds where they live out their fantasies and desires, while the Phyrax are eccentric loners who love a good adventure. Then there are millions of other, less advanced species, most of whom are as oblivious to the rest of what's out there as we on Earth are."

"You've done this before?"

"Eleven years ago, but the circumstances were different. Earth wasn't under attack then. There was a big intragalactic war going on fueled by an external conspiracy, and I just happened to be working on something on Earth that caught the eye of the Mendoken. I got pulled into the whole conflict and ended up traveling from one end of the galaxy to the other and beyond. It's a long story. Fortunately it ended well and I eventually came back home."

"How do these aliens travel such large distances? I'm no scientist, but I thought nothing can travel faster than the speed of light. Wouldn't it take years just to travel even to the nearest stars?"

"Turns out that isn't true. You just need enough thrust and a way to shell the ship as it accelerates, reaches and exceeds the light speed limit in order to prevent the time dilation effects of relativity. There's a technology called bosian layering that's used to do it. Mendoken ships can reach up to half a million times the speed of light, from what I remember."

She shook her head, dumbfounded. "How do they even reach so much thrust?"

"Matter and anti-matter collisions, if I remember correctly. The ships are able to pick up anti-matter as they travel through space and pass it through their engines, where it collides with regular matter. The result – complete annihilation of the matter and generation of huge amounts of energy."

"So... what do these aliens want this time?"

Marc nodded at the cabin door that was sliding open. "I think we're about to find out."

An Aftaran crewmember led Marc and Alisha through two corridors to the main deck of the ship, where Dumyan and a number of other Aftarans were seated on the floor with their faces unveiled. The pilot was sitting in front of a number of screens. There were no instrument panels, no gauges. As with all Aftaran ships, the pilot was controlling everything solely with her thoughts.

"This is how they choose to live," Marc whispered to Alisha, pointing out the contrast between the austere garments of the Aftarans and their spartan choice of furniture on the one hand, and the ornately decorated walls and spotless white stone floors of the ship on the other.

Alisha nodded in bewilderment but stayed silent.

"May the Creator protect you from harm, Marc," one of the Aftarans said.

"Raiha!" Marc exclaimed. It didn't take him long to recognize her soft, warm owl-like eyes. He would never forget those eyes – the very last things he had once seen upon staring death in the face back on the Aftaran planet Meenjaza. Taking the place of his real executioner, she had saved him in the nick of time.

Raiha stood up and came forward to embrace Marc.

"How have you been?" Marc asked her.

"Well, with the help of the Creator. Time heals all wounds."

Marc introduced Raiha to Alisha. "Raiha's love, Sharjam, was the big hero in the war that I told you about," he said. "Sharjam sacrificed himself to save all of us. There was nobody who was better versed in the powers of the Scriptures than he was."

"Don't let Marc sell himself short," Raiha said. "He was just as much a hero. Without him, there is no way we could have prevailed."

"Dumyan here is Sharjam's older brother," Marc said to Alisha. "Their father, Autamrin…" He stopped and turned to Dumyan.

"He is still the ruler of the Aftaran Dominion," Dumyan said. "Now come sit, both of you."

As Marc and Alisha sat down on the floor, Dumyan took out a silver coin-like object from inside his robe and placed it on his thin, long palm. He then ran his finger gently along the edge of the coin. Once he had completed the full circle, the coin turned golden in color and began to glow brightly.

"A scripture coin," Marc whispered to Alisha. "It contains sacred verses of the Aftaran religion."

Beautiful calligraphy in bright golden letters appeared in the air, about three feet above the coin and in full view of everybody.

"What does it say?" Alisha asked Marc quietly.

"No idea. It's written in their Altareezyan script."

"I'll read it aloud," Dumyan said. Your translator device will automatically translate the words for you." He began chanting:

"Live on your worlds with free reign,
Pass through your skies without limits,
They were created for none other than you.
Stray not from righteousness or justice,
And no harm shall ever befall you.

Stray neither from your worlds or skies,
Venture not into depths you cannot sense.
They are there all around and even inside you,
But they are meant for others, not you.

Pay heed, pay heed,
Venture not into the depths of others.
Never awaken forces you do not understand,
Against which you have no power,
For naught shall save you from their terrible wrath."

The golden letters slowly faded away after Dumyan had finished chanting. Nobody else spoke.

Marc could feel a dryness spreading down his throat, causing him to swallow inadvertently. "These verses...?"

"There are various ways to interpret these verses," Dumyan said. "But our High Clerics never had any doubt. They say the depths refer to dimensions, so these verses in the Scripture of Societies warn against traveling into other dimensions that we don't live in. There may be other forms of life in those dimensions that we shouldn't interfere with, because they don't wish to be disturbed and they are far more powerful than we are. This is the very reason we Aftarans have always insisted on banning consar travel in our galaxy."

"Sorry, what's a consar?" Alisha asked.

"Essentially a wormhole, one that isn't just hypothetical," Marc said. "It allows you to traverse great distances in space through a shortcut in other dimensions, orders of magnitude faster than through bosian layering in conventional space. A consar is more than just a wormhole, though, in that it doesn't require negative energy density to be opened or remain stable. It also doesn't allow you to travel in time. For that matter, nothing does, as I discovered the hard way. I was experimenting with this stuff as an astrophysicist back in the day, and what caused the Mendoken to take notice of me."

"Consar travel, even any research about it, was always banned in our galaxy," Raiha said. "But an alien race known as the Unghans from a faraway galaxy used consars to travel here and infiltrate the major civilizations of our galaxy, all with the goal of destroying us by instigating us to fight each other. With Marc's help, we all united several years ago and had to use consars to uncover the conspiracy and defeat them. There wouldn't have been any other way to do it."

"Hasn't the ban been upheld since then, though?" Marc asked.

"It has, but it seems the damage was already done," Dumyan replied. "The ironic thing is, all the consars the Unghans used over all those years to travel between their galaxy and ours never bothered anybody or anything in the other dimensions. Nor did all the consars we used to transport the Phyrax homeships to all corners of the galaxy to fight the Starguzzlers. There was, however, one consar, just one, that stirred them up."

"Them?"

"For lack of a better word. We have no idea who *they* are. All we know is that the warning in the Scripture has come true. Their wrath has indeed been terrible, and nobody has the power to stop them. Not us or the Mendoken, or the Volona or Phyrax."

"Not even with the military might you all have combined?"

"Not even. And not even with all the spiritual power we Aftarans hold, although our enchantments have made it somewhat easier for us to move around relatively unscathed. That's why we are the ones who ultimately had to come for you. Despite their technological prowess and all their huge, fast ships, the Mendoken are completely paralyzed at the moment."

"Which consar was this?"

"You remember when some of us traveled in the small Mendoken scout ship from the Afta-Raushan system to the Unghan galaxy?"

"The consar that took several days? Where we destroyed the Unghans?"

"Yes. Apparently it was only the consar we took coming back, not the one going there. We don't know how much damage it caused in the other dimensions the consar passed through, but their inhabitants have taken no prisoners in expressing their rage."

"And when did they start expressing themselves?" Marc asked.

"Five Earth years ago. Reports began coming in of these bright anomalies appearing across the galaxy. They were usually concentrated in or near heavily populated star systems. They didn't do much initially, other than periodically disappearing and reappearing, every time moving a fair distance. But then they began multiplying and attacking."

"Like what just happened on Earth?"

"Yes, although many of the attacks were on much larger scales, especially the ones on the fortified inner sections of entire Mendoken star systems. All of us struck back with force, of course, but we discovered to our dismay that none of our firepower had any effect whatsoever. The objects seemed to effortlessly absorb whatever came toward them. They weren't the slightest bit weakened, let alone destroyed. Even the devastating rays of Mendoken planet destroyers amounted to nothing. The freezer weapons of the Phyraxes, so effective against the Starguzzlers, melted into oblivion once they reached their targets.

"We fell back to a purely defensive strategy, mounting various types of shields and barriers to protect our worlds, but none of them worked either. The blasts from the anomalies passed through the shields as if they weren't there at all, always hitting their targets."

"Much luck we'll have on Earth, then," Marc said.

"It's no contest," Dumyan said. "The amount of destruction they have wreaked across the galaxy over the past few years is unfathomable. Their trademark has been to take their sweet time with every attack, surrounding a planet or moon and then slowly killing all forms of life on it with showers of these blasts. The intention always appears to be to inflict the maximum amount of pain, suffering and desperation on the victims, prolonged over as long a period of time as possible."

Marc shook his head in disbelief. "All this because of that one consar? Why? How did you find that out anyway?"

"As to why, I can't answer that. We don't even know who or what they are, so understanding what motivates them would be a stretch. Both the Mendoken and Phyrax tried launching probes into the anomalies to determine their nature and their source, but the probes all vanished, never to be heard from again. We only learned to communicate with them, as much as it can be called 'communication,' after they began sending us messages telling us what they wanted. That they only began sending the messages very recently, after five years of a unilaterally initiated and executed war on us, should give you an indication how different their nature is from anything we're familiar with. The same goes for the difficulty we've had in deciphering the messages."

"How did you do it?"

"A few Earth months ago, we noticed a sudden shift in the disappearance and reappearance patterns of some of the anomalies. Up until then, they usually followed a specific sequence of rising or dropping interval lengths as they traveled toward their targets, conforming to various spiral mathematical patterns found in nature. But it was anyone's guess which particular spiral an anomaly would choose to follow, as they had so many different ones to choose from."

"Why bother?" Alisha asked. "Why couldn't these things just show up directly in front of their targets?"

"They certainly could, given how they can apparently appear anywhere at will. And in some cases they have suddenly shown up in front of a particular world, taking all its inhabitants by surprise. My opinion is that they're just playing with us, making us guess and worry for as long as possible before each attack, well knowing there's nothing we can do to stop them. They choose predictable patterns in order to make us think we have some level of control of the situation, but then they sometimes break the pattern before the end point, throwing us back into disarray and keeping us guessing."

Marc agreed. "That's what I thought too."

"There actually is another explanation which the Mendoken have proposed," Raiha said. "They may keep disappearing to return to wherever they came from, to replenish their energy supply or perform some other action before continuing the journey to the target."

"Possibly," Dumyan said. "But I do think they're playing with us at the same time. Think about it - the intervals when the anomalies disappear are the only times they allow us to travel to and from a target area. Otherwise, there's a complete movement ban – anything or anybody trying to pass them gets destroyed. Sometimes, they reappear at random before the expected end of the interval and destroy any ships that may be passing by. Or they might leave behind some kind of invisible sensor array that targets ships even during the interval. That's what happened to the Mendoken ship that tried to pick you up from Earth two days ago, as well as the others that tried to reach you before that. Luckily we Aftarans have ways of bypassing the arrays with our unique powers."

"There were other Mendoken ships?"

"They've been trying to reach you ever since the anomaly first appeared in your system. Many of their ships have been destroyed like this over the past few years, across the Republic."

Marc took a deep breath and nodded. "Isn't there any prophecy in your Scriptures about how to deal with all of this?"

"I'm afraid not, nothing the High Clerics have been able to find anyway. You're spared from any prophetic burden this time."

"I suppose that would have been too easy."

"Quite," Dumyan said. "Anyway, as I was saying, we recently noticed a shift in the patterns of some of the anomalies, where they seemed to follow a path of some sort through space and not the conventional inward spiral toward an inhabited region. The path was the same every time. At first, it made no sense to us, but then we noticed a residue emanated by the anomalies as they traversed the path."

"What kind of residue?" Marc asked.

"An energy signature. Bulk energy, to be precise."

"You mean 'dark energy'?"

"Is that what you humans call it?"

"You're referring to the invisible energy that is expanding our universe at an accelerating rate."

"Yes. The energy that controls the rate of expansion and contraction of individual branes within the wider multi-dimensional bulk, where our whole universe is one of those branes. And yes, our universe is currently in the expansion phase. It won't always be that way."

Marc recalled the discussions he had once had with his Mendoken friend Sibular about it. Quintessence, one of the theories proposed by human physicists about the true nature of dark energy, had been verified by the Mendoken eons ago. Dark energy, or bulk energy as it was evidently referred to by everyone other than humans, was not a constant force permeating linearly across all of space. Rather, it was a dynamic scalar field that varied with time and space, within and across branes. This variation was what caused individual branes to expand and contract over vast stretches of time. Our universe, currently in the expansion phase, was estimated to continue expanding for another 20 billion Earth years before it would begin contracting again, all the way back to the singularity it had once originated from over 13 billion years ago.

As to why bulk energy behaved this way, not even the Mendoken knew. The only thing they did know was that bulk energy flowed freely between branes in the wider bulk, keeping all the branes in check, causing some to expand and others to contract. Bulk energy was responsible for ensuring that branes never barged into or harmed each other. It was, in a sense, the sheepdog of branes that kept the flock together, ensuring everyone was a good citizen and followed the rules. Many branes existed in the same dimensions, while many others were in completely different dimensions. A brane could co-exist right in or around another with different dimensions, with neither brane having any perception or understanding of the other. There was, in a sense, no end of branes in the bulk, nor was there any end of dimensions.

"What's the context here?" Marc asked.

"The bulk energy is everywhere, all around us," Dumyan replied. "It has a very low density across space, which is why it's difficult to accurately measure. It turns out that matter interacts with the bulk energy when it passes through space, generating minute ripples in the energy density that usually last no longer than a millionth of a second. That basically means that we can't do much with these ripples to detect any movement or identify someone. But somehow these aliens have figured out how to do it.

"With consars, however, the story is quite different. When you open a consar, you are essentially tunneling through another brane in different dimensions around your brane. A consar will open up a dimensional rift between the branes, generating an unnatural movement of bulk energy from the brane the consar is tunneling through to the brane it originated from and is leading back to. This flow creates a different kind of bulk energy ripple that never disappears – it remains as a residue at the consar entry and exit points, long after the consar has closed up and disappeared."

Dumyan paused to clear his throat. "I'm no expert on this topic, as I'm not a scientist. If you want a more detailed technical explanation, you'll have to ask the Mendoken. What I do know is that this residue freezes in time all the minute bulk energy ripples generated by everybody and everything that passed through the consar. Because everything down to the atomic level generates its own unique ripple, an individual like you or me generates a unique combination of ripples that nobody else does. This combination can be treated as a signature, a way of identifying an individual."

"So that fateful consar that we traveled through still has our energy signatures floating around its exit point?" Marc asked.

"Yes. And it's the same set of signatures that kept emanating from the anomalies. The Mendoken eventually figured it out, after running tons of simulations and analyses. What's more, further analysis revealed that the new path the anomalies were following matched the general shape of that consar's trajectory.

"The next thing provided the final clue as to what these aliens were after. Somehow they were able to sweep across our galaxy and identify the closest matches to each of the energy signatures they had captured from the consar's residue. Once they had a list of individuals, their attacks then began to center on the home worlds where those individuals lived. First came the attacks on two Aftaran planets where the six Aftaran soldiers who had accompanied us on that journey lived, and then the attack on the planet Meenjaza where I was. That was followed by attacks on the Mendoken worlds that hosted the six Mendoken troopers who had also come with us, and also on the moon Ailen where our friend Sibular was. They even found Zorina deep inside the Volonan Empire and launched an attack on her home world."

"Were any of them hurt?" Marc asked.

"No, fortunately not. But many others were. Many died too."

"Seems like they left Earth for last."

"We were actually hoping they'd leave you out of it altogether, and that your silupsal filter would keep you hidden. Our plan was simply to amass the rest of us at the assembly point."

"Assembly point?"

"We figured what the aliens really wanted was us – just those of us who traveled on that consar. To what end, we don't know, but we expect it's to exact some kind of revenge or punishment on us."

"As if all these attacks aren't punishment enough?"

Dumyan smiled. "We further figured they'd be waiting for us at the very spot where the consar exit point once had been, near Meenjaza in the Afta-Raushan system. Taking all things into account, it was a reasonable assumption. And it turned out to be correct, at least the part about where they were expecting us. We arrived there, all fifteen of us, and waited. An anomaly appeared right in front of us within a few days. It grew and appeared to want to engulf us, only to eventually shrink and wither away. Soon after, reports came in of the emergence of an anomaly right here in your solar system."

"Three months ago?"

"Yes. The Mendoken plan was to come get you out and take you to the assembly point before the attack on Earth could even begin. Nobody on Earth would notice a thing, and we'd continue to keep humans in ignorance about all of us. You've seen what happened to that plan."

Marc swallowed hard. "Well, I suppose I know now why you came for me."

"If it's any consolation, the attacks on all our worlds, including yours, should stop once the aliens have us."

"How do you know?"

"Actually, we don't. But it's the only thing we have to work toward at the moment."

Chapter 10

The passing through the silupsal filter at the edge of the solar system was uneventful for Marc, quite unlike the first time he had traveled through it. Thanks to the invisible Mendoken lenses implanted in his eyes, he couldn't even see the filter this time or the monstrous, square-shaped gate opening up in space to let the Aftaran Maura-class ship through.

For Alisha, however, it was a different story altogether. For the first time in her life, she was finally witnessing the universe as it really was. Beyond the gate lay a night sky far brighter than anything she had ever seen before, almost as if she was staring right into the very center of the Milky Way galaxy. Her mouth was agape with wonder as the ship passed through the gate, and it took Marc a while to explain the existence of the filter and the myth about dark matter.

"Two trillion stars in our galaxy?" she blurted after Marc had finished.

"Ten times as many as what our scientists on Earth would have you believe. The shape of the galaxy is actually much fuller and rounder than the flat spiral we're used to seeing. The same is true for the other visible galaxies in the sky – they're all made to look like that through the filter to keep things consistent."

"And all of this just to hide the existence of life from us?"

"Intelligent life anyway, yes."

"Will the filter ever be removed?"

"Who knows. A lot of taboos have already been broken in the past couple of days. Given what's happening right now, anything is possible. But if these attacks don't stop soon, it won't make a difference anyway."

The ship soon arrived at Selcher-44328, the giant Mendoken space station responsible for monitoring the silupsal filter around Earth's solar system. It appeared to have grown, at least compared to the way Marc remembered it.

As if it isn't big enough already, he thought, gazing through one of the cockpit windows. He remembered it being comparable to the size of a whole moon, sliced in half with a major thruway between the two hemispheres for passing ships. Now it was an array of sliced moons, spread apart around a wide circle. Hundreds of ships were docked at ports on each hemisphere. He could see the familiar inverted mushroom shapes of Mendoken battlecruisers and research vessels, each one easily dwarfing the Aftaran ship he was on but dwarfed themselves by the looming shadows of the space station's hemispheres. He noticed a few of the mighty sunflower-shaped planet destroyers as well, so ineffective against the enemy they were now up against.

"Seems like you Aftarans aren't the only ones who have beefed things up in the last few years," Marc said.

"Yes," Dumyan acknowledged. "But much good it's done any of us."

The Aftaran ship approached one of the hemispheres. Marc noticed several other Aftaran ships docked nearby, and further away he saw a number of Volonan warships, easily distinguishable by their flat shapes and bright colors. A few cloud-shaped Phyrax homeships could also be spotted in their midst. It was clear Dumyan wasn't joking about the scale of the enemy onslaught and the determination of all four major civilizations to work together this time, from the outset.

A series of large clamps took shape on the surface of the hemisphere and surrounded the ship as it slowed down to a standstill, slowly coming closer until they almost touched the ship. Walkways appeared next, slithering forward and docking with the ship's doors. After the doors opened, Marc and Alisha followed Dumyan, Raiha and several other Aftarans down one of the walkways into the space station.

The arrival hall was grand, easily the size of a football stadium. The walls running along the edge of the space station were transparent, offering breathtaking views of the other hemispheres and the starlit sky beyond. Marc noticed a number of individuals at the end of the walkway, waiting for him and the rest of the landing party. Most of them were clearly Mendoken, with their floating, greenish metal-encased bodies, four robotic arms and single eyes that went all around their hat-covered heads. But there were also a few Aftarans and Volonans among them. It didn't take him long to make out two familiar figures in the crowd.

"Sibular!" he exclaimed. "Zorina!" He hugged them both. "I never thought I'd see either of you again."

"Nor did we, old friend," Zorina said. The crouching Volonan flapped her large, elephant-like ears with excitement.

"It is a pleasure to see you again, Marc," Sibular added. "I only wish the circumstances were different." The tall, slim Mendoken's robotic style of talking hadn't changed at all.

As Marc introduced an awestruck Alisha to his friends, he saw a gray cloud taking shape a short distance away. It soon rose to a towering twenty feet in height, and it developed a head and a few limbs. Then it suddenly lunged toward them. Both Marc and Alisha jumped in fright.

Zorina laughed. "Relax, Marc. Don't you remember Jinser-Shosa?"

The gender-neutral Phyrax spoke with its loud, raspy voice. "Forgotten me? That is an insult!" An object shaped like a weapon of some sort took shape on one of its limbs.

"No, no, I remember," Marc said hastily, recalling the Phyrax's erratic behavior and incredibly short temper. "A very, uh, pleasant surprise to meet again."

Jinser-Shosa let out an unintelligible grumble as the weapon disappeared. Then it flew off toward the other end of the hall without another word.

Marc turned to Zorina. "What's it doing here? It didn't come with us on that consar."

"That's the Phyrax for you. It wouldn't have missed an opportunity for an adventure like this for anything in the galaxy. Its biggest complaint is that it won't be able to accompany us."

"I'd gladly trade my place if I could."

"Wouldn't we all, my friend, wouldn't we all."

A Mendoken Kril-3 battlecruiser was ready and waiting to take the designated individuals to the assumed assembly point in the heart of the Afta-Raushan system. The only problem was that Afta-Raushan was a good ten days journey away, even with the fastest Mendoken ships. Consar travel would have cut the journey down to a couple of hours, but that was obviously out of the question. There wasn't a moment left to lose.

Marc attended a preparatory meeting along with Sibular, Zorina, Dumyan and the six Mendoken troopers and six Aftaran soldiers who had traveled on that one consar. The meeting was held in the arrival hall next to the waiting ship.

"Let's be clear," Dumyan was saying to the select group, "we are going into this with no idea of the ultimate outcome. We don't know what fate awaits us in the other realm, whether we will have to endure harsh punishment or insufferable amounts of pain, whether they will let us live or cut our heads off the moment we arrive. We don't even know if they will really leave our worlds and peoples alone once they have us. We have no idea if or how our bodies will handle a universe composed of other dimensions, with laws of physics that may be quite different from our own. No matter what the circumstances, it's a tall order for anyone to swallow, and especially for us who only traveled on that consar to protect and defend our galaxy from annihilation. We had no idea it would lead to such disastrous consequences years later.

"All that said, the question I pose is whether each of us is ready to accept the sacrifice we are about to make with our lives for the sake of our worlds and our peoples, for our homes and especially our loved ones.

I know most of us have already answered that question. There hasn't been time to ask the rest."

Dumyan's large, owl-like eyes shifted their focus from one individual to the other, eventually stopping once they reached Marc. Everyone else also turned to face him.

Marc glanced nervously at the others. "It's, uh, a lot to absorb. There isn't any guarantee either that our actions will stop the attacks. But I see no other option at the moment."

"That wasn't what I asked," Dumyan said.

Marc tried to force a grin. "It's kind of late to turn back now, isn't it?"

"We're wasting time, Marc."

"Ok, yes, I'm ready."

"You'll be alright?" Marc asked.

Alisha looked surprised. "Are you seriously asking?"

"I, uh, just want to make sure."

"Stranded billions of miles from home, with no knowledge if my family is ok or even alive. Many of the people I used to work with are dead. Now I'm stuck with strange aliens I don't know or understand. You want me to continue?"

"I know, I'm sorry. I did warn you about coming with me though."

"What was I supposed to do? It was either that or be fed to the wolves prowling the streets of LA. I had no choice."

"Yeah, I get it."

"Now you're leaving too," she said, shaking her head.

"If it's any consolation, the Mendoken are very trustworthy. They will take care of and protect you until they feel it's safe for you to return to Earth."

"If there's any Earth to go back to."

"There will be. The attacks will stop once we're gone."

"There's no guarantee of that."

"It's my hunch."

She scoffed. "That's what I'm supposed to go by?"

Marc kept quiet, not knowing what else to say. They watched from the arrival hall as Sibular, Zorina and the others disappeared into the walkway leading up to the waiting ship. Jinser-Shosa could be seen flying around the entrance to the walkway, cursing everyone for not allowing it to come along.

"They have put me up in surprisingly comfortable quarters, though," Alisha said, changing her tone. "They seem to know a great deal about human preferences."

"That they do. They've had eons to watch us, since the time we lived in caves and hunted mammoths."

"I still can't believe it, any of it."

"It's a lot to digest."

"You seem excited. I can't understand why."

Marc nodded. "I am."

"Aren't you afraid? Of what lies ahead? Of death?"

"Somewhat, but truthfully not a lot."

"Of leaving behind your family, your loved ones?"

"I don't have any, not anymore. It might sound crazy, but I've been waiting for a moment like this for a long time."

"Why?"

"I finally have a purpose in my life again. I'm not proud of all the lives lost and damage caused due to something I seem to be partially responsible for, but now I have the opportunity to help put a stop to the continuing carnage. If I end up paying with my life, well, I'd rather save the lives of those who have a lot more to live for than worry too much about my own."

Alisha was silent for a moment. "I wish we'd met under different circumstances."

"Under any other circumstances, I doubt someone like you would ever have taken notice of someone like me."

"You are crazy, I'll give you that. But don't sell yourself short."

"I don't know about that."

"You should."

"Says Ms. Relationship Expert?"

"My recent track record might not be great, but in my line of work I've met all kinds of men."

"No other man would have dragged you into an alien quagmire out in space. For that, I apologize."

"Just come back alive," she said.

"I promise I'll try."

She gave him a hug. Her touch was tender and warm. It triggered the inkling of a sensation he hadn't felt in a very long time. He stepped back to look at her, wondering once again what unbelievable twist of fate had crossed his path with someone of her beauty and stature. But the path intertwinement, as bizarre as it had been, was about to end.

Better that way anyway, he thought, much better. He began walking toward the gateway, turning once in the middle to wave goodbye to her. She was still standing there, watching him go.

His gaze shifted from her to the transparent wall behind her, offering a wide view beyond the hemisphere they were on to the circle of sliced spheres that comprised the entire space station. What he saw, however, caused him to stop dead in his tracks.

It didn't take long for the alarm sirens to begin blaring through the arrival hall. Mendoken soon began rushing out of the Kril-3 ship through the numerous connected walkways into the hall. Marc ran back to Alisha.

"What's happening?" she asked.

"Turn around and look."

Her eyes followed the direction his finger was pointing, out the transparent wall to the center of the circle of spheres. She gasped in shock.

A bright object had suddenly appeared, looking awfully similar to a glowing red star, awfully similar to the alien entities that had all too recently surrounded and attacked Earth. It seemed smaller than each of the sliced spheres of the space station, but unless his eyes were deceiving him, Marc was fairly certain it was growing in size. Its brilliant light pulsated every three seconds, the peaks so bright that they blinded his view of everything else in sight.

"Will it... attack?" she asked.

"I don't know," Marc replied. "Evidently these aliens aren't quiet as patient as we thought. They're not going to wait until we get to the assembly point."

A series of three-dimensional screens descended from above, spaced out to offer visual range to individuals anywhere in the hall. They began displaying close-up views of the entity, along with sets of data in Mendoken script.

The sirens were replaced by the voice of an announcer. "Alien anomaly has appeared at coordinates 142-764-903," it said in the typical composed, robotic tone of the Mendoken, the words echoing across the expanses of the hall. "Currently at stage 2 evolution but rapidly progressing. The consar contingent should exit the Kril-3 vessel and wait for a smaller scout ship to travel in the direction of the anomaly. The scout ship will only carry the contingent, no other crew members."

There was a short pause, after which the announcer continued. "Never before has an anomaly appeared this close to any of our structures. There is no use in engaging it with any of the weapons at our disposal. Doing so will only increase its power. Instead, we will generate a recently upgraded force field in an attempt to contain it until the contingent is on its way. The operating assumption should be that the anomaly will cease any hostile intentions once it notices the contingent and that it is finally complete."

"What should we do?" Alisha asked nervously.

Marc watched as Sibular and Zorina came out of one of the gateways and headed in his direction. "Well, it looks like I'm going to meet my fate a little sooner than expected," he said.

The screens showed how the force field was quickly put in place around the growing anomaly by an array of tiny drone ships, at a radius four times the size of the anomaly at that very point in time. The field flashed once brilliantly as it was activated, then rendered itself invisible to the naked eye.

A Sil-5 scout ship arrived and docked at the same arrival hall where Marc and the others were waiting, adjacent to the far larger Kril vessel. The pilot and other crew members exited the craft through the single gateway it was latched on to, making way for the consar contingent to board.

Marc eyed the sleek, supersonic jetfighter-like shape of the scout ship. Ironic, he thought, recalling that they had also traveled through that one consar onboard a Sil-5. He said goodbye to Alisha once more, and then followed the others toward the gateway. He hadn't taken any more than five steps when the sirens wailed again.

He looked out to see what was happening. The alien anomaly now looked quite different. It had more than doubled in size, and no longer did it boast a uniform red. There was a whirlwind of colors, spreading across its surface like a collection of violent storms competing for regional dominance.

Perhaps it's annoyed by the placement of the force field around it, Marc thought. He turned to look around him. The others in the contingent had also stopped to stare at the raging entity.

The Mendoken announcer's voice could be heard again, and the screens began flashing warning messages. "Alien anomaly has progressed beyond stage 5 evolution. Normal progression is for it to multiply at stage 4 and commence an attack. This has never before been recorded. Uncertain what to expect next. Consar contingent should wait until additional information available or anomaly stabilizes."

"That's a great help," Zorina said, flapping her ears.

"This is not good," Sibular added.

No kidding, Marc thought. He motioned to Alisha, standing further away, to come join him. She ran up to him and grabbed his arm.

Jinser-Shosa flew over from the other end of the hall. "I'd really like to show that blob of gas who's boss!" it said angrily.

It was almost as if the anomaly had heard the Phyrax's words. Its variable brightness gave way to a different kind of pulsation – one that looked a lot more frightening.

Like a beating heart, Marc thought. He had no idea how an object that big could suddenly start growing and shrinking in size so rapidly, and that repeatedly every minute. With every pulsation, it seemed to shrink to a smaller size and then grow even larger.

"Uh-oh," Jinser-Shosa wheezed, now sounding more worried than angry.

Marc could feel the familiar sensation of rising alarm, of inevitable imminence. In the distance, he could see Dumyan and the other Aftarans raising their hands in prayer. His own hand instinctively found itself holding Alisha's. Her other hand, in turn, squeezed tighter against his arm.

"What about the force field?" Zorina asked, her voice quivering.

"I highly doubt it," Sibular replied. "Even with repeated applications and subsequent upgrades, our force fields have never succeeded in containing an anomaly. Even if this one stood a chance, it was only designed to do so up to a stage 4 evolution."

The announcer's voice came on again, and simply said, "Everyone take cover."

But there was no time for that. The anomaly had already shrunk once more, this time to its smallest size yet, before finally bursting. The solid colossus split apart into billions of bits, all spreading every which way with tremendous force. Just as Sibular had predicted, the force field instantly succumbed to the outward pressure, quickly crumbling and disappearing into nothingness.

Marc couldn't help letting out a long shriek. The blinding light emanating from the massive explosion forced him to close his eyes. He began counting the seconds, trying his best to sort out all his thoughts with the time he had left. He didn't understand why it was all going to end like this. It seemed the alien entities weren't interested in recovering the selected individuals from the consar contingent, at least not alive. Perhaps that had been their intention all along – to ascertain the death of every member of the consar contingent. That they had no concern for the additional carnage of the millions of innocents on the space station would hardly be a surprise to anyone, given their track record. But it was also no surprise that he couldn't find any solace in that thought. The only surprise, in fact, was the one he and everyone else on the space station had been taken by, the latest yet in a series of surprises enacted by these mysterious, unpredictable aliens. And, it seemed, the last surprise he would ever live to encounter. His sole hope was that the attacks on Earth and the rest of the galaxy would cease after this, once and for all. Otherwise, the sacrifice about to be made by such a large number of individuals would be entirely in vain.

The shockwave reached all the sliced spheres of the space station at the same time, less than a minute after the explosion. Marc expected the outward facing walls of the hall to shatter into pieces, causing the air and everything inside to be sucked out into the vacuum of space. The sudden drop in pressure would swiftly bloat and kill everyone, if the impact of the blast didn't do the job first.

He felt the huge jolt that threw him and the others off balance, causing everyone to fall to the floor with a thud. But he felt nothing else thereafter. He was still breathing, still in one piece. There was no shattering of glass, or whatever spaceworthy equivalent the station's transparent walls were made of. He didn't understand what was going on. Daring to open his eyes, he cast a glance in the direction of the wall. It took him a moment to digest what he saw, to realize that there was yet one more surprise in store for him.

Chapter 11

It was the largest consar opening Marc had ever seen. For that matter, he wasn't sure that it was a consar. Perhaps it was just a gateway into a universe of different dimensions, not a tunnel through it – a gateway that led through the bulk from one brane to another. All he knew for sure was that it was an opening, and one that looked far from inviting.

The shockwave that had blasted outward from the exploding anomaly was somehow frozen in time and space, surrounding all of the space station's split spheres without smashing through them. From a distance, the whole spectacle probably looked like a monstrous doughnut, a ring of fire engulfing the entire circumference of the station. From inside, all Marc could see were two burning, brilliant awnings, one above and one below. They led off into the distance, converging into the mysterious opening at the very center of the wide circle where the anomaly had just stood.

The opening itself had slowly turned completely dark, now looking awfully similar to a gaping black hole. Marc found himself shuddering as he realized what was about to happen. He looked to his left and right – everyone was staring at the same spectacle, speechless and awestruck. The faces which displayed emotions that he could discern, like those of

Alisha and Zorina, were riddled with fear. The Mendoken were expressionless as usual, and the Aftarans had their faces veiled. Jinser-Shosa was nowhere to be seen, probably retreated into a thinly spread gas cloud somewhere to avoid the shame of imminent defeat.

It was almost as if time had come to a standstill. Nobody else was moving, nothing was happening. But Marc knew better. This was only the eye of the storm, and it wouldn't last long.

It probably lasted no longer than a few seconds, in fact. The first thing he felt was the pull, the pull that he would never forget. He had never felt such a pull in all his life, not even during the times he had entered consars before. His feet pulled first, then his legs, then his hips, arms, chest, neck and finally his head.

The pain should have been unbearable. And it was, at least initially. But he couldn't understand why it subsided so quickly. There was also no explanation for the fact that he hadn't died right away. He felt numb all over. He wasn't sure, but he wondered if perhaps his mind had separated from his body, allowing the sentient part of him to become a passive, unaffected observer to the agonizing demise of his body. Or perhaps he was already dead, and this was how his soul would start its journey into eternity. All he knew for sure was that his thoughts and his consciousness were fading away, and he was powerless to do anything about it.

His last sensation was the sight of being rushed forward with unimaginable speed toward the opening. All the occupants of the hall, the entire hemisphere, the other split spheres of the space station surrounding the opening, everything was suddenly sucked into the opening like layers of dust into the bowels of a powerful vacuum cleaner.

Everything was a haze. Marc couldn't open his eyes. He didn't even know if he had eyes anymore. He didn't know if he had a body anymore. He could feel nothing, just the vague notion that he was moving, that everything around him was also moving.

Something swished around him. Then came another swish, and another. Trickles of light began to appear, blurred beyond any form of recognition. Slowly they allowed his vision to come into focus. He began to see that he was indeed moving, through a tunnel of some sort at high speed. The walls, filled with random outlines of different colors that constantly changed shape and size, reminded him of a consar. But this was far wider than any consar he had ever been in, and the bands of thin matter so typical of the interior of consars were nowhere to be seen.

As his vision regained more strength, he began to see what the interior of this tunnel was actually filled with. The structure in front of him wasn't like anything he had ever seen before. It was more like an array of structures, almost like a crystalline lattice. It was beautiful. He felt as if he was staring at a monstrous snowflake with a highly complex design, and that too bathed in all the colors of the rainbow.

The structure seemed to observe him for a moment, and then it split into two, then four, then sixteen. The smaller structures kept on dividing until there were hundreds of them, perhaps thousands. They surrounded him and began touching him all over his body.

At least I still have my body, he thought. It was spread-eagled, with his arms and legs pulled apart to their limits by some invisible force. But he could feel no part of it. He couldn't hear or smell. He wasn't breathing. All he had was his vision. He didn't know how he could possibly still be alive.

He watched with horror as the tiny structures burst open his hands and arms, his feet and legs. The tiny bits of flesh and bone that began spreading out were quickly caught, and then further split apart into even smaller bits. Even his blood, clumped together into small blobs in this zero-gravity environment, was captured and handled in the same way. The process continued until he could no longer see the individual bits. Then the structures seemed to perform some kind of operation on them, before clumping the pieces together and building up the tissue again.

Down to the molecular level, Marc thought, or perhaps even lower. Evidently the matter in his body was somehow being reconfigured, perhaps to prepare for a different universe with different dimensions, different laws of nature. He didn't know how that was even scientifically possible. Further away, he noticed more structures hard at work, doing the same thing to other bodies. He couldn't recognize any of them, not even Alisha. He could only hope that she was ok, that she was somehow coping with all that was happening. Further still, he could see his surroundings, probably what was left of the space station, also being broken down and similarly reworked.

The entire space station was in for the ride, he realized, the entire space station that was responsible for maintaining the silupsal filter around Earth's solar system. Without the station, the filter would likely begin deteriorating with time. Still, Earth would have much bigger issues to worry about in the days ahead.

His thoughts wandered as he felt his consciousness fading away once more. The structures operating on him were working their way up the rest of his body and to his head.

When he awoke again, his senses seemed to have returned. He felt pain everywhere – his head, shoulders, back, arms and legs. It was accompanied by a strong urge to throw up, but thankfully he didn't and the feeling soon subsided. The pain also began to wither away within a few moments.

As his eyes slowly opened and brought his vision into focus, he noticed that the tunnel was gone. The crystalline structures working on his body were also gone. Dark space surrounded him. There wasn't a single star in sight. It took him a while to adjust and focus his vision, to realize the space wasn't so dark after all. There was opaqueness all around, a consistent haze that made it difficult to see anything clearly. As his eyes continued to adjust, he began to slowly make out distinct formations in the distance. They were everywhere, spread thinly across the vast expanse.

Gas clouds, most likely, he thought. Or whatever the equivalent of gas was in this universe. He had little doubt that he was in the realm of another universe, another brane, for it looked nothing like his own. There was nothing he could compare it to, not even in the array of unique, striking images still stored in his memory from all his travels across the Milky Way galaxy.

This was, he surmised, a universe in a very different state than the one he had just come from. The haze could very likely be attributed to the abundance of high energy plasma, filled with electrons or their corresponding equivalents in this universe. With no atomic nuclei to serve, the electrons were free to roam about in space, blocking and scattering the energy of any photons trying to transmit light from their sources to any observers.

Not just a different state but also a different age, he guessed. The conditions here were perhaps not too different from his own universe in the first few hundred thousand years after the Big Bang.

On a cosmological timescale, this was possibly a universe in its infancy, or perhaps it just had very different laws of physics that had always prevented it from evolving further than its current state. Either way, all it probably had were very simple, basic gases coupled with tremendous amounts of concentrated, high energy. At least, that was all he could deduce from the view he currently had.

As awestruck as he was, it didn't take Marc long to reach the obvious question why the mind-blowingly high temperatures and lethal doses of radiation that came with such a territory weren't instantly rendering his body to ashes and dust. It was only at that moment that he noticed how his body had grown in size.

Actually, it wasn't that his body had grown. It was just puffed up with layers of what had to be some kind of shielding. His arms and legs looked like they were covered by solid armor.

The next thing he noticed was the boundary set on the periphery of his vision, leading him to realize that he was also wearing some kind of shielding over and around his head. Just enough of the shield was transparent in front of his eyes, or whatever equivalent of human eyes he now had, to allow him to survey his surroundings.

Hence the reason why I haven't been converted to ashes, he thought. He was sealed within an impervious shell. It was a terrifying thought.

There wouldn't be much time to wallow in terror and fear, however. Things were changing fast. He noticed the crystalline objects again – hundreds, maybe thousands of them, whichever way he looked. They were incredibly bright. He surmised they were the only nearby source of light, allowing him to see anything at all around him. They were also hard at work, gliding back and forth, building at an unimaginable pace.

Walls, he realized. They were building walls, possibly by restructuring some of the matter from the Mendoken space station. It was a massive undertaking. Construction was underway all around him, as far as he could see. The walls were growing upwards, downwards, sideways. Some sections were transparent, others solid. A floor came into existence out of nowhere and shot past him beneath his legs. A ceiling above soon followed.

As the entire structure began to take shape over time, he thought he could identify the layout of what appeared to be a large arena. He also noticed that he was right in its center. Along the edges, layers of what had to be spectator rows quickly rose to towering heights. Through the transparent sections of the walls, he could see lots more construction beyond the arena, though for what he had no idea.

In the distance, he could see more of the crystalline objects pushing and prodding groups of objects. There were hundreds, no, thousands of them, floating every which way across the arena's expanse. As some of them came closer, he began to realize what they were.

At least they're not dead, he thought. It was impossible to recognize any of them individually, inflated as they all were with layers of protective shielding. There was no other explanation, however – they had to be the occupants of the space station, the vast majority of them Mendoken, but also a sizeable cohort of Aftarans and the few Volonan visitors who had the classic misfortune of having been at the wrong place at the wrong time when the anomaly had struck. He didn't know if the few Phyrax on the station had also been sealed into shells – it would be hard to imagine how gaseous lifeforms could be confined like that. Perhaps they didn't need to be.

Somewhere among all those individuals was Alisha, or so he hoped. If she was, then at least she had a chance of still being in one piece and alive.

They all looked helpless in their oversized suits, their motion dictated solely by the crystalline objects in their midst sending them sprawling in different directions. They had about as much power to resist as a collection of stationary pins did to a large bowling ball hurtling mercilessly down the alley toward them. Apart from their flagrant obesity, the shapes were familiar for the most part – he thought he could make out where the heads, arms and legs were supposed to be.

The other bodies soon began passing him on all sides. He noticed a cloudy haze following their motion, almost like plumes of magical pixie dust. He strived to look past the visors covering their faces, the only irregularities in their otherwise solid, heavy helmets. But all he could see were gaping holes of darkness.

The crystalline objects started to clear the space around him, pushing the bodies out toward the spectator rows at the edge of the arena. He could sense the familiar mix of fear and uncertainty rising quickly again. He also began to feel a pull on his body toward the floor. His muscles begin to weigh down, as if a series of clamps had grabbed hold of every one of them and begun yanking them to the ground.

Gravity, he realized. He had been weightless for a long enough period of time that the effects of its sudden onset felt distinctly uncomfortable. He shifted his gaze upward, to the transparent sections of the walls and the ceiling. There were massive beams in place outside now, spaced apart along the perimeter of the ceiling. All of them led from the ceiling to a bright sphere far away. Then he noticed that the ceiling was curved, in a wide circle around that sphere.

The entire structure around the sphere had started moving, coinciding perfectly with the start of the gravitational pull. He discerned that the structure was shaped like a monstrous ring with the sphere at its center. The arena took up just one section of this ring, with the ceiling facing inward and the floor outward. Artificial gravity toward the floor was being generated by the centrifugal force of the ring's rotation.

This is what they've done with the Mendoken space station, he thought. They had broken up all of its matter, adapted it to be able to exist in this universe, and had then built a new space station out of it. All at an unimaginable pace. If only he knew why.

He was standing on the floor now, his body slowly getting used to the gravity. It seemed much lighter than the gravity he was used to, but it still required adjustment from the weightlessness he was coming out of. He tried to move his legs, but it felt impossible under the sheer weight of the body armor. It seemed like his desire to move had been noticed, however, for at that very moment his armor began to slowly fade away. All of it appeared to just fold up and wither into nothingness, starting with his feet and moving its way up. The helmet on his head and the visor in front of his eyes also disappeared.

He choked in fear, worried that he wouldn't be able to survive without the protective suit. But his fear appeared unfounded. His body didn't instantly vaporize from high doses of radiation, nor did any vacuum suck his innards out. He was able to breathe. Air had somehow been pumped into the arena in the meantime, or maybe it had all just been generated in place. At this point, nothing seemed beyond the realm of impossibility.

He noticed he was still wearing the same clothes, although they appeared cleaner and crisper. Looking around, he noticed that the armor was coming off all the others as well. Most of them were up in the spectator rows by now, too far away for their faces to be recognizable. Their familiar Mendoken physiques, however, were unmistakable. Among them were a number of Aftarans and a few Volonans, as well as a couple of cloudy shapes that could only be attributed to the Phyrax. Alisha remained elusive. A search for her in between so many thousands of non-humans, at least from where he was standing, would be about as effective as looking for a needle in a haystack.

The air was cold but fresh, and evidently filled with oxygen. The magnitude of the low gravity seemed to vary ever so slightly with time, and it would definitely take some getting used to. He felt a tide of nausea too, but it soon cleared. Or maybe he just forgot all about it when he saw what was approaching him.

Chapter 12

Franzek Treital 00000001. That was the name of the Imgoerin, holder of the topmost position in the Mendoken government and elected leader of the Mendoken Republic. The numeric suffix stood for the rank of the individual in the expansive Mendoken hierarchy, a requirement for every single Mendoken. Marc's friend Sibular, for example, had a rank of 44383532.

The Mendoken Republic spanned across 350 billion star systems, a fifth of the galaxy in its entirety. 50 billion of those systems were actively inhabited by Mendoken. The Mendoken were the most populous, most technologically advanced and militarily the mightiest society in the galaxy. The power and authority commanded by the Imgoerin were beyond the wildest dreams of most living things, including all humans on the one small planet in the one star system they called home.

Not that having power or authority were things Mendoken were generally concerned with. Their approach to life was strictly based on reason and logic. Petty things such as emotions or desires, positive or negative, had no place in their behavior or daily interactions. Even the most powerful individual in the Mendoken hierarchy was no exception to this rule.

And yet, as he floated among numerous three-dimensional screens, the Imgoerin knew that he had feelings. Feelings, however minute they were compared to those of humans, of dismay and helplessness, of anger and regret. Nothing in his long tenure as the head of the Republic could be considered comparable to the current state of his people. Never had they been as weakened or as paralyzed, as repeatedly caught off guard with no means to react. Even the Unghan conspiracy and the battles with the Starguzzlers didn't come close. This most recent incident was just the latest in a series of devastating blows to the Mendoken morale and reputation.

He moved to the window to stare out at the endless rows of massive, black towers that made up the heart of the Mendoken capital city, spread across the flatlands of the planet Lind in the Mendo-Zueger star system. His palace, if that was what it could be called, was nothing more than a small apartment atop one of these towers.

Miraculously, Lind had been spared by the attacking anomalies. They had concentrated all their attention on Ailen, one of its moons. Ailen, the most advanced hub of scientific research and technology for the Mendoken, was home to none other than Sibular. As they had done across the galaxy for each individual who had traveled on that one fateful consar, the anomalies had successfully located him and focused their efforts on destroying his home world.

Another Mendoken floated into the room and to the Imgoerin's side. It was Osalya Heyfass 00000663, his trusted aide who had been with him throughout his tenure as the Imgoerin. To the human eye, the only real way to distinguish between them would be by the color of their hats. The Imgoerin's was black, Osalya's white. The hats, mandatory for all Mendoken to wear, were color-coded to signify the ranks of their wearers in the Mendoken hierarchy.

"What news?" Osalya asked. Without the presence of a translator device, her utterance of words would sound like nothing more than a quiet, monotonous hum to the human ear.

"I just received a report from the commander of the armada that just arrived on site at Mendo-Biesel," the Imgoerin hummed back. "They see no trace of anything unusual yet."

"Any bulk energy ripples?"

"I am still waiting for the scan results."

"Was it an anomaly?"

"That is the most likely candidate. But there are no traces of any destruction, which means this would be the first time that one of them took the target back instead of destroying it. Not exactly a small target either."

"Given the circumstances, that would be the best scenario."

The Imgoerin had to agree. At least that would mean everyone on board the space station still had a trickle of a chance of being alive. He gazed at the giant Mendo-Zueger sun, getting ready to set over the distant horizon. As always, air traffic was busy at this time of day, with many rows of vehicles zipping by between the towers.

"The attacks have stopped completely and the anomalies have all disappeared," Osalya added. "Reports have come in from across the Republic and beyond. It is quiet everywhere in the galaxy."

"It would appear the anomalies have finally gotten what they wanted," the Imgoerin replied. "The Aftarans predicted this would happen."

"Yes, but only after we Mendoken discovered the bulk energy signatures the anomalies were emanating and determined what it was they were after."

"Regardless, Autamrin will be far from happy. It was our responsibility to transport the group of sixteen to the meeting point and to be ready with our probes, ready to follow them wherever they went if an anomaly appeared to take them away. Now we have no idea what happened to them and if they are still alive."

"We were ready," she countered. "At least where we all expected the anomaly to appear."

"Except the anomaly had other plans," the Imgoerin said. "Instead of appearing where we expected it to, it took us by surprise by showing up right in our own region of space. The first time around, the anomaly did appear at the original consar entry point in the Afta-Raushan system. We had amassed the fifteen individuals there, hoping it would not notice that one of them was missing."

"The human from the Mendo-Biesel system."

"Yes."

"It did notice."

"Yes," the Imgoerin admitted. "And it disappeared. It was therefore only logical that the anomaly would appear again at the same spot when the complete sixteen arrived this time."

"These anomalies are not driven by logic," Osalya replied. "If we had the capacity to understand their devious nature, then we would have had a higher chance of predicting their actions."

"Autamrin did warn us not to be too certain with our conclusions," the Imgoerin said. "We did not listen."

"When do you see him?"

"He is on his way from Meenjaza. The ship arrives in three days."

Maginder Kloiden 52110984, commander of the 357th Mendoken Armada, used to have a total of ten ships at his disposal. By human standards, that was not a large number for a naval fleet. Humans, however, would be simply awestruck if they ever saw the sizes of the ships in this fleet. The four Euma exploration vessels were each the size of an entire city, shaped like inverted mushrooms and housing many tens of thousands of individuals. Indeed, the ships had actual cities with buildings, parks and rivers carved into their interiors. The four Kril military vessels were even larger, similar in shape but with many more extensions and their insides stocked with smaller battleships and heavy weaponry. Largest of all was the one planet destroyer, a sunflower-shaped monstrosity that dwarfed all the other ships by an order of magnitude.

The planet destroyer, the ultimate Mendoken weapon, was a part of every armada. Not a single one had ever actually been used on any planet, but one was always there in every battle to act as a deterrent. Its very sight was usually more than enough to frighten any enemy into backing off from conflict. But not so with the anomalies – not only had they not been intimidated into submission, they had totally vaporized every planet destroyer crossing their paths. In all, the anomalies had faced about as much resistance from the Mendoken planet destroyers as a nuclear missile racing through the sky would have from a flock of geese. They had simply absorbed every deadly ray from the destroyers without as much as a hiccup. It had been the biggest, most humiliating defeat for the Mendoken in the entire history of their advanced civilization.

Commander Maginder's armada now was less than half the size of what it used to be. The planet destroyer, one Euma ship and three Kril vessels had been annihilated by a single anomaly, the same anomaly that had subsequently attacked Earth. Ironically, it was the fact that this armada had been attacked that had ultimately saved what was left of it. Maginder was assigned with protecting the region of space that the Mendo-Biesel system was a part of, including the space station that maintained and watched over the silupsal filter surrounding that very system. Had his fleet not been attacked and left stranded in empty space, his ships would very likely have been docked at the doomed space station when it vanished in its entirety.

Here he now was with his fleet, at the very spot where the space station once used to be. He had just finished filing a report to his superiors, describing what he had discovered so far. It was a very short report, for as of yet he had discovered absolutely nothing. On the third level of the massive control deck of the lead Kril-4 ship, he floated from panel to panel, monitoring the activities of his pilots and other crewmembers. He stopped in front of a collection of three-dimensional screens, around which a group of Mendoken scientists were already huddled.

One of them turned to Maginder and spoke. "Commander, the silupsal filter surrounding the Mendo-Biesel system is starting to disintegrate."

"That is expected, Sautal," Maginder said. "With the space station now gone, there is nothing in place to maintain the filter."

Sautal pointed to a screen displaying the filter. It was ovoid in shape and monstrous, large enough to encompass an entire solar system. It already had a number of holes spread over its surface, and they seemed to be slowly growing in size even as Maginder stared at the screen.

"This is the first time we have ever seen this happening to a silupsal filter," Sautal said.

"This is also the first time that one of our space stations has suddenly vanished without a trace," Maginder replied. "The inhabitants of the Earth planet will soon be able to see through the holes. They will be perplexed, beyond the state of disarray they are already facing after the anomaly attack on their world."

"They will need our help," Sautal said.

"I will need approval first. It would be the first time that we Mendoken break the principle of non-interference before a species is ready."

Sautal hummed in agreement. "At least with the anomalies now gone, we can finally move about freely again without the risk of being destroyed."

Another scientist by the name of Hansa spoke. "Commander, we have once again surveyed the entire perimeter where the Selcher-44328 space station used to be, now for the tenth time."

"And?"

"The first five scans were run across band ranges of the electromagnetic spectrum," she replied. "The sixth scan was used to search for unexpected graviton fluctuations. For the seventh scan, we sent drones back and forth inside the perimeter searching for any signs of quark transmutation."

"To locate any unusual weak force activity?"

"Yes. We found nothing. The eighth and ninth were run to look for bulk energy ripples. For the ninth, we concentrated on the area at the very center of the space station array."

"Why?"

Hansa pulled up some graphs with a sweeping gesture of her hand and spread them across the screens. She then pointed at one of the screens, showing a detailed wave pattern superimposed on top of a seemingly empty region of space.

"This is the result of the eighth scan, Commander," she said. "What you see is the complete zone of the space station array. There were seven pairs of hemispheres in total, spread apart in a circle around the empty center."

Maginder peered at the screen. At first, all he could see were the typical random patterns of bulk energy, the result of billions of free-flowing, massless particles permeating everywhere across space. It took him a moment to begin making out the thin streaks that reached from the points where each of the hemisphere pairs used to be to the very center of the circle.

"Are those ripples?" he asked, pointing at the streaks.

"Yes."

"Left behind by the anomaly?"

"By the hemisphere pairs. The inevitable result of sudden, forced, high-speed motion."

"The anomaly was in the center?"

Instead of answering right away, Hansa used one of the screens to zoom in on the focal point of the circle.

"The trajectories of the ripples led us to the ninth scan," she said. "Of the center only."

What the screen showed was awfully similar to what would be left behind if a bullet had ripped through the middle of a canvas, tearing a big piece away and leaving nothing but a gaping hole behind.

"The signature of a departing anomaly," Hansa added. "Unless they choose to leave a specific pattern behind, they just tear the residual bulk energy around them away when they vanish."

"And it always stays that way after they are gone?" Maginder asked.

"Yes."

"Have we figured out why this happens?"

"Not yet," Hansa said. "Research is still underway. All we know is that the anomalies disappear into consar-like gateways. We have no information where those gateways may lead, however, as they close up as soon as the anomalies have passed through them. One can only assume it is into another brane in a different set of dimensions."

Maginder hummed a short note of acknowledgment. "So the anomaly appeared in the center, somehow pulled all the hemisphere pairs toward it and absorbed them, and then disappeared again."

"That is our conclusion," Sautal agreed.

Maginder glanced at the other screens, showing different graphs of analysis results. "And we are left with no trace whatsoever. Nothing to follow up on."

"Not quite," Hansa replied. "There was one more scan, which we just finished before you arrived. Since this was the first time an anomaly actually absorbed material before departing, we decided to also test for neutrino and antineutrino emissions."

"Why?" Maginder asked. "Are they not too small to matter?"

"Neutrinos and antineutrinos are generated when elementary particles such as protons and neutrons are converted into other particles. We wanted to determine if any elementary particles from the atoms of the space station and its inhabitants were converted during the absorption. If we could further identify the reasons for the conversion, then perhaps we could get a better idea of where they went."

"And what did you find?"

"See for yourself, Commander. Not at all what we expected." Hansa pushed the screens away with a gesture of her hand. They floated off and slowly faded away. Then, with a sweep of the same hand, she expanded a new screen in their place. It showed a fairly high concentration of both neutrinos and antineutrinos around the entire perimeter of the bulk energy hole that the anomaly had left behind.

Maginder was puzzled. "This just verifies what you were expecting to find."

"The presence of the neutrinos and antineutrinos, yes," Hansa said. "But not their oscillations." She poked the screen, after which another series of images superimposed themselves on top of the original one. "This image progression shows the oscillations between the various flavors the neutrinos are allowed to have. It is color coded to make it easier to decipher."

Maginder hissed softly, the controlled, Mendoken equivalent of a human dropping his or her jaw in total shock and involuntarily uttering a series of profanities. He had to slowly float around the screen to make sure he wasn't imagining things.

"You are right," he said in as composed a tone as he could. "Not at all what we expected."

Chapter 13

It is often said that the first of anything new is the most memorable, even if subsequent events of the same kind are actually more noteworthy. As far as the pain was concerned, Marc would probably agree.

The pain he hadn't felt when his body was pulled and stretched during the tunnel entry, or even when his body was restructured atom by atom by the crystalline objects as he traveled through the tunnel into this other universe – he had no explanation for why he hadn't felt it then, but what he felt now seemed to more than make up for that apparent oversight.

The alien structure that had come forward and now stood in front of him was much bigger than any of the others he had seen so far, the result of a conglomeration of several of the more regularly sized crystalline lattices. It rose to a towering height above him, and it began to change shape by spreading its body into long arms – at least, if that was what those gauzy, translucent extensions could be called. The arms reached out and soon encircled him. He was trapped, and before he had any idea what to make of the situation, the first strike from one of the arms slammed into his head with a burst of bright light.

The injury wasn't just local to his head. It seared through his whole body like an electric shock, causing him to lose balance and fall flat on the floor. His eyes closed involuntarily, and he felt his strength draining away. The alien, however, left him no time to gather his wits. Two of its arms lifted him effortlessly and brought him to his feet, before another arm struck into his chest in another burst of light.

He screeched in agony and fell again. As his head hit the floor with a thud, he thought he could hear the semblance of rising commotion in the distance. He turned to look, and out of the corner of his eye he saw the Mendoken and Aftarans in the spectator rows trying their best to come to his aid. But the crystalline aliens had arranged themselves in lines along the perimeter of the arena, creating a series of formidable barriers for anyone attempting to enter from the spectator rows.

Much good their protests will do, Marc thought between pangs of pain. The alien picked him up once more and hit him in the stomach. Again, he fell over backwards. It repeated this process several times, each time hitting him in a different part of his body.

To call the suffering unbearable would have been as much of an understatement as calling a stab right through the heart a simple flesh wound. With each thrash, he grew weaker, and every time it felt as if he had finally breathed his last breath. Yet every time he was raised back from the dead to receive another blow. Each successive strike seemed harder, more painful than the last.

It may well have been fifty, maybe even a hundred strikes before the alien finally moved away, letting him lie still on the cold, hard floor. By then, his mind had lost almost all cognizance of his surroundings. He was no longer able to distinguish reality from oblivion, or the past from the present.

The town of Indian Wells in California was home to no more than 5000 residents. Marc and his wife Iman would never have picked so remote a location to spend a night, were it not for its proximity to Joshua Tree National Park. On their itinerary, that was the second stop on their weeklong vacation before finishing it off further north in the heart of the Mojave Desert. Indian Wells did have one attraction that both of them were interested in – the Indian Wells Resort Hotel. Founded by Hollywood legends Desi Arnaz and Lucille Ball in 1957, it offered a unique combination of contemporary flair with the charm of a glorious past.

The Lucy Show had certainly aired long before their time, but both Marc and Iman had often heard their parents speak of the show with much nostalgia. They had only found it fitting, therefore, to spend a night in this hotel before braving the desert. It was to be their last outing as a couple before the birth of their daughter. The due date was only a month away, and ample warning had been given by friends and family about how their lives would completely change after her arrival.

Marc had further surprised Iman by reserving the Presidential Suite, a dazzling 4500 square foot luxury extravaganza with four bedrooms, five marble baths and a full kitchen. It was the same suite the Hollywood couple had often used for many a getaway all those years ago.

"You are nuts!" Iman exclaimed as they walked into the suite, her eyes wide with surprise. "How much did you spend?"

Marc shrugged. "Doesn't matter."

"It does. Why do this?"

"For you. For us. Why else?"

She turned to look at him. Seven months of pregnancy had certainly taken its toll on her appearance, for it hadn't been an easy one. But there was no hiding her sublime beauty, with her long auburn hair and big brown eyes, with that striking blend of sweet and sharp features that so many women of the Middle East were blessed with.

"Do we even have the money?" she asked.

"It's not like we do this every day." He gently patted her bulging belly. "And we surely won't again for a while. I want this to be a memorable occasion."

"It already is for me. I'd actually have been fine with a Motel 6. I'm just excited about the next two days."

He smiled.

"Hey, you chose to marry a girl from the desert," she said.

"I did."

"Joshua Tree and Death Valley both have famous landmarks and features. I've always wanted to see them."

"I'm not complaining. We've already had our share of California's beaches and mountains. No better way to end our outdoors adventures than with something truly different."

She came forward and gave him a warm hug. "Thank you for this, Marc."

"You are welcome." He embraced her tightly and gave her a tender kiss. "I'd be happy to do a lot more for you, a whole lot more. For you and for the little one." He placed his hand on her belly again. "It's weird, but I feel like a proud dad already."

"You will make a great dad, just as you've made a great husband."

Marc shook his head. "Only because I'm lucky enough to have you by my side. Not just because of what you mean to me, but because there's nobody else alive who means anything to me. I remember what my life was like without you, and I don't ever want to have to go back to that."

"Don't worry," she said, smiling and patting her own belly. "Not that I ever had any intention of leaving you, but now it's totally out of the question."

The beautiful memory faded away, as abruptly as it had begun. The time shifted forward by two days, in the blink of an eye. The peaceful, comfortable setting of the luxurious hotel suite in Indian Wells was replaced by the chaos of one of the operating rooms at the Desert View Hospital in Pahrump, Nevada, 280 miles away.

There were three doctors around her, with an array of nurses rushing back and forth from the bed. She was already unconscious – she had been so for hours. Marc wasn't allowed near the bed. He had to keep a fair distance to give the doctors and nurses the space they needed to try to revive her and get the baby out. All he could do was stand there, desperate and helpless.

He didn't understand how it had all happened. Maybe it was the extreme heat of the desert, maybe she hadn't been drinking enough water, or perhaps she had been overwhelmed with too much activity and excitement. Granted, the pregnancy had been tough. Her gynecologist had warned her that she was at risk for developing pre-eclampsia that could eventually grow into full-blown eclampsia, a serious complication of pregnancy that often resulted in violent seizures and even comas. It could also be extremely harmful to the fetus, and in some cases fatal.

During her last exam, however, her doctor had told her she was still ok. Only if some of the symptoms, such as high blood pressure, foot swelling or weight gain were to suddenly worsen, then she would have to come in right away for an induced premature delivery. That would be the only way to protect both her and the baby.

Fortunately none of those symptoms seemed to have manifested themselves over the past couple of weeks, which is why Marc and Iman had taken the chance to make the trip. He had had his doubts, but she had been insistent on this one last vacation. In hindsight, he now realized, it had been extremely foolish. He should have stood his ground and gone with his intuition that something could go wrong.

It certainly had. The eclampsia had struck with full force without any of the early warning signs, right in the heart of Death Valley. There had been no choice but for him to drive like a madman to the nearest hospital, which happened to be across the state border in Nevada.

Now all he could was pray for her recovery. The doctors had already begun a Caesarean section to get the baby out. He clenched his fists and closed his eyes as they lifted her out of her mother's womb, uttering yet another solemn request to the Almighty Creator, the same Creator the Aftarans believed in, the Creator he had developed faith in after learning of the powers of their mighty religion in his last adventure through space. Then he opened them again, only to stare at the comatose lump of a tiny body, a beautiful baby girl who would never get to open her eyes to this world.

He would have been ready to collapse at that very moment, but there was one more thing he was destined to witness. He didn't have to wait long, for it began almost instantaneously after the delivery – a gradual slowing down of the beep frequency emanating from the monitor linked to Iman's heart.

The flurry of activity around her sped up correspondingly, with several different attempts to revive her. Marc had no idea what the doctors were doing, and he didn't care. The level of shock to his system had already reached its threshold. Time seemed to have come to a stop, and everything happening around him was nothing more than a blur. All he could see were the stillborn baby and Iman's lifeless face. All he could hear was the beeps slowing down until all that was left a solid, steady flat line. And it was at that moment that he finally collapsed.

Marc felt like he was being dragged along the floor. That was the first sensation that came to him as his consciousness slowly returned. Then came the moving lights, causing him to slowly open his eyes. A bright, crystalline structure loomed over him, pulling him away from the center of the arena with a couple of its long arms.

The flashbacks were gone – the pleasant, happy one, followed by the horrifying, devastating one. Harsh, painful reality was back, with the added pain of just having relived the most agonizing moment of his life in excruciating detail. He felt his heart pounding, his mouth dry, the tears beginning to squeeze out of the ducts in his eyes.

He lay helpless on the ground after the alien let him go at the lowest level of the spectator rows. Crowds of Mendoken and Aftarans soon gathered around him, finally able to reach his side. Many touched him and spoke to him, asking him if he was ok and how they could help him. But he hardly noticed any of that. All he could think of was that hospital room in Pahrump, Nevada.

He thought he yelled out in agony at some point, perhaps several times. Then all he could do was sob softly to himself. He had watched the love of his life die, and he had been unable to prevent it. He should never have taken her on that vacation. Even if she had gotten a similar eclampsia attack at home, the world-renowned doctors at Stanford Medical may very well have been to save both her and the baby.

He was responsible for her passing, as he was for his daughter's doomed fate. That little angel who had done nobody any harm, who had had her one chance at life taken away from her before it had even begun. He had finally lost everybody and everything he had ever held dear.

Now, here he was, in an impossible situation in an impossible place, paying the price for something he was once again responsible for. As for the millions, if not billions of innocents who had already lost their lives for the mistakes he and a mere handful of others had made – he had no idea how to even begin seeking retribution for that.

With time, most of the individuals crowded around him began to move away. They seemed to have turned their attention to the arena. He lifted his head to look that way as well, toward the multiple line barriers of crystalline aliens blocking the way to the center. He felt the strong urge to call out to them, to beg them to come get him again and to strike him harder, to finish the job and finally put him out of his misery once and for all.

It seemed, however, that another had just taken his place of misfortune. Beyond the barrier, he noticed the extraordinarily large crystalline alien again in the center of the arena, the same one that had so effortlessly thrashed him about earlier. It was doing the same thing to another individual now. Straining his eyes, he could barely make out the silhouette of an Aftaran.

"Not Dumyan?" he whispered.

"I'm afraid so," said a voice behind him.

He sighed in exasperation and shook his head. "But why? Why?"

"I don't know, my friend."

Marc felt himself being lifted up by strong hands. The dizziness came quickly. He felt weak, unable to sit up. But the hands holding him remained steady.

"Zorina," he whispered, turning around slowly to face the elephant-like Volonan crouching behind him. He felt his pocket – the Mendoken translator device was still there, evidently reconfigured to work just fine in this universe. The only issue – it wasn't helping him at all otherwise. No automatic sensing of danger, no conversion into a weapon to help him defend himself. Perhaps the physical laws of this universe didn't allow it.

"How are you feeling?" she asked.

"I've been better. I don't wish what I just went through on anybody else, not even my worst enemy."

"Well, at least you don't seem to have any visible injuries. I fear I may be up next, or soon anyway. Not looking forward to it." Zorina flapped her large ears.

Marc sighed. "What the hell is going on here?"

"Our punishment, it seems. For whatever those crystals think we did to them."

Crystals, Marc thought. A fitting name for these bizarre creatures.

"Some punishment alright," he said. "It's not just the physical pain. I was reminded... of painful events in my life. As if they just happened again."

"Figures. They want us to break us down completely – mentally and physically."

"They seem to have a way of reading our minds. They've totally figured us out."

"Don't know. At the very least, they've figured out how to push our buttons. Either way, this is not going to be fun. My guess is they're going to punish only those few of us who were on that consar. The rest are here for the ride. Call it collateral damage if you like."

"Have you seen Alisha?" Marc asked.

"Your girlfriend? Yes, she's around here somewhere. Saw her a short while ago. She's alright, I think."

"She's not my... Never mind." She was fine, and that was all that mattered.

Sibular came forward through the crowd and inquired about Marc's health, to which Marc responded with the same answer that he had given Zorina. They watched Dumyan getting battered in the distance.

"Why doesn't he do something?" Marc asked, frustrated. "Use an enchantment, for heaven's sake!"

"He may not be able to," Sibular replied. "The Aftarans' magic may not even work here. We do not yet know what does and does not work in this universe."

"Well, at least we can communicate," Zorina said. "Plus we're each still in one piece."

"I just don't get it," Marc said. "All those attacks across our galaxy, all the destruction, the mass killings, all the effort to bring us here to their universe and create this huge structure – all just to beat a few of us around in an unbalanced show of kicks and punches?"

Zorina shrugged.

"Their method of thought is clearly quite different from ours," Sibular said. "But I would be cautious of jumping to conclusions. There may be more happening here than meets the eye."

"Meaning?"

"That they may have more than one reason for bringing us here and doing this to us. Hopefully time will tell."

Marc gnashed his teeth in frustration. "How are we ever going to get out of here?"

"I don't know, my friend," Zorina said. "I'm not sure we ever will. I have a nasty feeling that we're going to be in this for the long haul."

Chapter 14

Aftarans were generally able to withstand hardships unimaginable to humans, largely thanks to a combination of their rugged bodies and supernatural abilities. They could survive for hours with very little air to breathe, water to drink or food to eat, and the versatile robes they wore also offered them layers of protection from extreme heat or cold.

The mightier they are, the harder they fall, Marc thought, as he studied Dumyan's unconscious face. He looked in worse shape than Marc had been after his punishment ordeal, as if the Aftaran had been stripped of his life and all his reasons to exist. Fellow Aftarans had rushed to his aid as soon as he had been dragged by a crystal past the last barrier to the spectator rows. Marc had also walked over from where he had been sitting.

"Let him be," Marc said to Raiha and the other Aftarans crowded around him, trying their best to revive him and praying to the Creator for help. "He just needs time."

He did. It took a long while for him to regain enough consciousness to begin the wailing and sobbing routine, and when he finally did, that lasted even longer. There was nothing anybody could do but wait for him to fully awaken. Like Marc, he had no visible, physical injuries that needed attention. In the meantime, a couple of the crystals came and dragged Sibular away for his punishment. Many of his fellow Mendoken tried to hold him back, but the crystals easily brushed them aside with repeated sweeps of their many long arms.

As Dumyan slowly came to, he began recounting the vivid memory of his brother Sharjam's death.

"It was all... all my fault," he stammered between cries of agony. "I was the one who, the one who kept looking at him. I was expecting him to do something in front of those Unghans."

"There was no way you could have known what he had in mind," Marc said. "He was the one with the knowledge of your Scriptures, of all the possible enchantments."

"But... I was expecting him to do... *something*. Anything."

"He was the only one who could have done something," Raiha said.

Dumyan cried again. "Because I never learned. I never learned. Because I resisted our ways all my life. I should have been as versed in the Scriptures as he was. Then he would still be alive today."

"And you would be dead," Marc said. "If you had the ability, then you would have done the same thing in that situation that he did."

"He was my younger brother. That's how it should have been."

"He was an adult," Raiha said reassuringly. "Adult enough to make his own decisions. He saved all of you who were with him, and all of you came back to save the rest of us. *All* of us. Think about what would have happened to our galaxy had the Starguzzler invasion succeeded."

"No different from what's happening now," Dumyan said. "What's it all been good for, tell me?" He went back to his sobbing, which no amount of comforting from those around him was able to bring to a stop.

Raiha and a couple of other Aftarans slowly lifted him to a sitting position. They all watched Sibular in the distance, getting his beating in the center of the arena.

The Mendoken mind, with all its emphasis on logic and the shunning of unnecessary emotions, surprisingly proved to fare little better than its

Aftaran counterpart. The only major difference, perhaps, was the lack of audible weeping. Sibular lay perfectly still after the crystals dragged him over to the spectator rows, oblivious to his surroundings and to all those who tried to help him. He remained in that state long after Zorina was dragged away, and even after he should have begun verbalizing the sorrows of his memories as Marc and Dumyan had.

Numerous attempts by other Mendoken to revive him failed. Marc tried as well, but to no avail. Only after a long time did he slowly open the one, long eye that went all around his head.

"I took too long," he said quietly. "Too long."

He repeated that statement several times, and every time he was asked by those around him what he meant.

"The consar research," he finally said. "I should have figured it out a long time ago, without needing Marc to show us how to do it. We could have stopped that war a lot sooner and avoided all those casualties."

"There were reasons for that," one of the Mendoken at his side said. "Consar research was banned, and the Unghans kept sabotaging our attempts to make progress. You cannot blame yourself for that."

"Plus that would have just meant an accelerated war between the Mendoken and the Volona, which is exactly what the Unghans wanted," Marc added. "That would actually have made things worse, not better. They would probably have gotten their way with the Starguzzler invasion."

The logic, as sound as it was, offered no solace to Sibular. He remained in his vegetative state throughout Zorina's ordeal and beyond.

Zorina turned out to be a total mess, even though she had known exactly what to expect after seeing Marc, Dumyan and Sibular already suffer through it. She was screeching loudly in pain as a crystal dragged her into the spectator rows and left her there. Her ears, arms and legs were all flapping wildly about, and it took several individuals to hold her down and try to steady her.

"Why, oh why?" she yelled. "Why did it have to be him?"

"Who?" was the question repeatedly asked.

But she paid no attention to those around her and continued to writhe in pain.

"Rudoso," she eventually whispered.

"Your man?" Marc asked.

"Yes."

"I thought you two got back together. Didn't the Empress pardon you after the Starguzzler war was over?"

"Yes."

"Then what happened?"

"Too much time had passed," she sobbed. "He was already in love with someone else. I lost him."

"But what happened wasn't your fault. Didn't your virtual Grid mix things up?"

"Yes, a glitch. Both my sister and I fell in love with him in our own virtual worlds. He thought he was with only one of us, while each of us thought he was ours alone. Then, when she found out, she accused me of orchestrating the whole thing and put both him and me in separate, virtual prisons. I broke out, and after six years of living as a hermit, met you on the planet Nopelio. The rest is history."

"Why didn't he wait for you?" Marc asked.

"He thought we'd never see each other again. He had no idea I had broken out and he definitely had no idea I'd be instrumental in ending the war. He didn't expect we'd ever be pardoned. He met somebody else while in prison."

"In prison?"

"Yes. Don't ask. Not sure how." Zorina broke down again. "Why, oh why couldn't I just have fallen in love with someone else?"

"It could have been someone else, but a glitch could still have happened. You'd be in the same boat. The problem is not the glitch itself, but rather that you have royalty in your blood and a very powerful sister who doesn't like glitches. At least not ones that affect her personally. Hopefully she's done something about fixing the Grid in the meantime, so that these glitches don't happen again."

"That she has. But it doesn't help me much anymore."

"There's nothing you can do about it," Marc said. "You have to pick up the strength to move on."

"I've tried, I have tried," she replied as her large, round eyes welled up with tears. "I just... can't."

"I know the feeling, my friend," Marc had to pause and swallow, to hold back the rising lump in his throat. "But I assure you it will get better with time."

For Zorina, it didn't, as it didn't for Marc. "The long haul," as she had earlier predicted, proved to be an exceptionally mild way of describing the timeline. There were no clocks, no day or night by which to measure the passage of time. The only thing for certain was that it felt endless, at least to all those who were not natives of this strange, hostile universe.

Zorina's predictions had otherwise been accurate – the punishments were reserved only for those who had traveled on that one fateful consar. Everybody else was spared, although they were forced to helplessly witness the continuous, savage infliction of pain on each of those sixteen individuals in the arena.

The pattern was surprisingly consistent. Every day, however long a day actually was, every one of the sixteen was subject to the same physical and mental abuse. The succession was always the same, starting with Marc, then Dumyan, Sibular, Zorina, then each of the six Aftaran soldiers followed by the six Mendoken troopers. All others were made to watch from the spectator rows, securely cordoned off from the rest of the arena. At the end of the day, there was a period of rest, when everyone was shoved into living quarters beside the arena.

The period of rest included nourishment, sleep and bathroom breaks. The basic needs of all the captives were evidently known by the crystals, even the subtle differences between the various species. The small, individual cells that they were all shoved into for the night, while bare, were correspondingly equipped based on the breeds of their occupants.

The food, if it could be called as such, was forcefully delivered as a pasty, tasteless substance via tubes into the captives' mouths in each of their cells. This was presumably to ensure that nobody voluntarily starved him or herself to death. Instead, they were all to stay alive and continue enduring or witnessing the punishments.

Mendoken needed no rest or food, of course, given their hybrid organic-robotic bodies and their ability to continuously replenish themselves from the surrounding electromagnetic radiation. They were treated no differently, however. Although they weren't offered any food in their cells, they were confined to cells at night nonetheless.

This was how the days passed, the number of which Marc slowly lost count. The sixteen individuals who received the daily punishment grew increasingly demoralized over time, everyday having to endure unbearable pain and reliving the most painful memories of their lives. It seemed to make no difference which species the individuals belonged to – they all broke down with the same speed and with the same intensity. Mendoken technical prowess fared no better than Aftaran austerity or Volonan creativity, and none of them fared any better than the one human from planet Earth. None of them stood a chance against the power and resolve of these unknown, perplexing crystalline entities.

Marc had to repeatedly witness his mother's battle with cancer in excruciating detail, watching her gradually wither away until that one rainy Spring morning in Vancouver when she passed away. He had to recall his father's fatal car accident again and again, the father whom fate had taken away from him before he had even had a chance to come into this world. The same repetitive pattern was applied to his breakup with Iman in college, the subsequent lonely years in graduate school and, of course, her more recent death and the loss of their baby. Over time, images of death and destruction back on Earth began to take shape as well, as he was repeatedly reminded of the havoc wreaked on his home planet by the alien anomaly assault. And all because of the actions of him and his fifteen conspirators, he was further reminded.

The nights were the worst. Exhaustion from the day's torment brought about sleep, but it was no restful sleep. The dreams always took him back to those same memories, with periodic awakenings amidst groans of anguish. The feeling of anguish only worsened as the morning approached, as he well knew what awaited him when the crystals would unfailingly arrive to drag him to the arena.

There was no hope for reprieve, nothing at all to hope for. There was no way to know when all the agony would end, or if it ever would. The demoralization grew steadily. The only wish Marc had was to die, a wish that grew with each passing day. But even that was not an option, for there were no means at his disposal to take his own life. He was to continuously wallow in his own guilt and misery. If he only knew why.

There was, however, one short moment every day that offered him a glimmer of anticipation. Initially it was nothing more than an ephemeral opportunity to appreciate beauty in as close to perfect a form as he knew it. Over time, however, it morphed itself into the only thing he had left to look forward to each day.

Whenever the crystals grabbed him from the spectator ranks to lead him to his daily punishment, he was always able to catch a short glimpse of Alisha in the distance. She would invariably try to reach him before they dragged him away, but she would usually fail to do so in time. The crystals would always wade through the crowds of prisoners and forcefully push everyone apart with their many long arms as easily as brooms sweeping dust away, possibly in order to control any form of dissent.

After that, he would generally lose track of her among all the commotion for the rest of the day. If he was lucky, he would catch sight of her again at some point before they were all taken to their quarters. Whenever he saw her, his eyes opened just a tad wider and his mind relaxed for a fleeting moment. The highest amount of anticipation was held for those days when they actually managed to get near enough to each other to talk, even if only for a few minutes. The conversations didn't always go smoothly, but often her words of consolation helped even if they changed nothing.

"I am so sorry," Marc said one time, not too long before one of the crystals would come to get him for his punishment. "I'm the one who got you into this mess."

"That you did," she replied. "I still can't believe where I've ended up. My life – all it is now is sitting around every day, waiting and watching you and your friends get beaten up." She shook her head in frustration.

"Like I said, I'm sorry. Nothing I can do now to help you. Can't even help myself."

"It's ok."

"At least we're alive."

"Yeah, but much of a life this is." She sighed. "I wish I could help you somehow."

"You already are."

"How?"

"By being here. By talking to me. I... have nothing else anymore." He buried his face in his hands.

"You have to be strong."

"You don't know what it's like. The pain... it's unbearable. My arms, legs, back, chest, stomach – every part of my body hurts from the daily torment. And my mind, my mind... I wish I could just switch my brain off and die."

"You have to try."

"What for? Will it convince them to stop?"

"Hardly."

"Then?"

Alisha didn't answer.

"I feel so... helpless," Marc said slowly. "I just don't know what to do."

"I don't really know you too well," she finally said. "But I feel like I've known you forever."

"How so?"

"I know very little about you or your background. And since I met you, you've continuously surprised me with one unbelievable thing after the next. You also got me into this mess. But I still feel like I can trust you."

"Just because I rescued you from that oaf of a boyfriend?"

"Maybe, but it's not just that. You went out of your way to help me out and to make sure I was taken care of. You had no reason to and there was nothing for you to gain from it. My immediate family aside, nobody has ever done that for me. Everybody else has always tried to exploit me, one way or the other."

"Two reasons – your looks and the industry you're in."

"Maybe. My point is that you clearly had... you still have... much bigger problems to deal with than me. But you kept looking out for me."

"You are not a problem, trust me."

"I became one when I took the chance to come out into space with you."

"Then why did you?"

"I don't know. I just feel... safe around you. As crazy as it sounds given our current situation, I know."

Marc sighed, watching the crystal in the distance. It had started its approach toward him from the far end of the arena, ready to take him for his beating. Trying to run away never did any good. He had done a lot of that in the beginning, but the crystals were much faster and always caught up with him.

"Your faith in me is misplaced," he finally said. "Look at me now – I am totally useless and helpless."

"Maybe you're right," Alisha said. "I don't know what will happen. I also don't know about all the things in your past that those monsters are haunting you with. All I know is that there isn't much point wallowing in the past. You can't change it anyway."

"Easy for you to say. You don't have to keep reliving it."

"I'm not pretending to understand what you're going through right now. But things that have happened in the past haunt all of us in one way or the other. You have to be strong enough to overcome the painful memories. You can't shut them out, but you can reach the realization that they've already happened and you've already done your due mourning for the ones who suffered or died. You shouldn't have to mourn again, even if you're reminded of the events in excruciating detail. Remembering and mourning are two different things – remembering allows you to keep living your life, mourning does not."

Marc was starting to feel irritated. "What's ever happened to you? How much more perfect a life would you have wanted?"

"Perfect?" Alisha sneered. "Because I'm a movie star? Because I'm too dainty for you?"

"I didn't suggest you..."

"Maybe you aren't as different from other men as I thought." She rolled her eyes and got up, ready to walk away.

"That is not what I meant, trust me," Marc said hastily.

"Ever been to Mumbai?" she asked, turning back to face him.

He was startled by the sudden question. "Mumbai?"

"Bombay, as it used to be known."

"I've never been to India at all."

"Ever been to a developing country?"

He shook his head.

"Mumbai, India's wealthiest city. Almost half of the city's 18 million people live in fancy, modern high rises. The other half live in the world's biggest pile of slums, spread like a web among the high rises."

"So I've heard. And?"

"You might think I have a privileged background, but you couldn't be more wrong."

Marc shrugged. "I don't know, I guess I just assumed, uh..."

"I grew up in Dharavi," she said. "One of Mumbai's largest slums."

He raised his eyebrows in surprise. "How did..."

"I end up in Bollywood? I got lucky. It's a long story. You have no idea how tough life can be in a slum."

"I've seen pictures, a couple of movies, that's about it."

"Slumdog Millionaire?"

"Yes."

"Overly dramatized, but the depiction of the slums wasn't too far off from reality. My father died when I was a child, and my mother had no choice but to marry again for security. My little brother I lost when he was three years old. He disappeared one day without a trace. We never found him again. My sister was kidnapped by traffickers when she was thirteen. When she refused to become a prostitute, she was tortured and killed. They dumped her body in front of our living quarters, in broad daylight. Nobody helped us out. No police ever came, nobody was brought to justice."

"I'm sorry," Marc said.

"To me, it still feels as if those horrible events happened yesterday," she went on. "But they didn't, they happened a long time ago. There's no point living in those memories, even if you see them again – in dreams, in visions, whatever. It helps nobody, not those who suffered or died, nor you. In fact, you owe it to those who suffered and died to live your life to the fullest, to be as successful and as accomplished as you can be so that you are in a position to help others avoid the same kind of pain. There is no greater way to honor them, no better way to remember them."

"Is that why you became an actress?"

"I try to give my dues to those who haven't been as fortunate as me, as much as I'm able to anyway. Of course, right now I'm able to do nothing at all."

There was no time left to continue the conversation. The crystal was in close proximity now, already having crossed the full length of the arena's wide expanse.

"Without you," Alisha said hurriedly, "I have no idea what I'll do here. I have no idea how I'll survive or ever get back home. I just need you to be strong. If you give up, I have nothing left."

The crystal reached out with its long arms to push Alisha away, as it began dragging Marc toward the center of the arena.

"From what I've heard so far," she called out as she moved away in the nick of time, "you and your friends have done some amazing things in the past. You guys need to be amazing again."

Chapter 15

The unveiled face looked old and withered. The large, owl-like eyes were droopy and worn, leaving no shadow of doubt that their owner had recently been through much sadness and pain.

The Aftaran spoke, his voice crackling and quivering. "You didn't listen, Franzek."

"We should have been better prepared," the Imgoerin admitted. "Hindsight always leaves room for doubt."

"We did have the foresight to warn you. We told you these alien anomalies were not the kind to follow any path of reason or logic. I don't know how much more evidence of that you needed."

The Imgoerin kept quiet. It was probably the best thing to do. There was no point trying to once again explain to the Aftarans how the Mendoken mind worked, that it simply wasn't wired to think through things any other way. They would never understand. And, frankly, this wiring had been nothing but a detriment since the anomalies had begun appearing. It was hardly a forgotten thing that an Aftaran ship had eventually been needed to pick up the sixteenth individual from the planet Earth. Every single Mendoken ship sent earlier had failed, every single one falling prey to the deceptive actions of the anomalies.

There had been no fanfare surrounding the meeting of the leaders of two of the galaxy's mightiest civilizations. There was little reason to have any. Autamrin's Maura class ship had docked safely at one of the many space stations orbiting the planet Lind. He had then boarded a small shuttle with his tiny contingent of five Aftaran dignitaries, which had transported them to the surface of the planet. Only the Imgoerin and a few of his aides had come to meet them on the landing pad, followed by a brief escort to a large conference room in the same tower where the Imgoerin's office was located.

They all stood in a wide circle around an empty center. There were no chairs or tables in the room. The Mendoken never sat down – their floating, metal-encased bodies would neither allow it nor require it. Aftarans usually sat on the floor, but here they chose to stand to keep level eye contact with their Mendoken counterparts.

"You should have had the probes ready," Autamrin said. "You should have had the probes accompanying the sixteen at all times, from the moment they all got together for the first time. If you'd had the probes in the space station, they would have departed with the anomaly to the other universe or wherever they went. We could have had a link, and maybe we could have determined where they went. Now we have nothing. And I..."

Autamrin's words trailed off as his voice broke. He needed a moment to regain his composure. "I... have just lost the only son I had left."

"I am truly sorry for that," the Imgoerin said. "We were certain the anomalies wanted us to gather the sixteen at the original consar exit point, just as we had gathered fifteen of them there last time. An anomaly did appear, if you remember."

"But you were missing the last individual, which was why the anomaly disappeared again and the attacks continued."

"Yes. We took a chance, because we did not want to interfere again in a silupsal-covered world. We wanted to leave the Mendo-Biesel system and its planet Earth alone. Obviously, it did not work."

"Marc Zemin," Autamrin said slowly. "We Aftarans remain heavily indebted to him."

"Not just you Aftarans."

"It was our High Clerics who picked him to carry the Hidden Scripture coin, to carry the enormous burden of unveiling the Unghan conspiracy."

"If your High Clerics hadn't done that, this galaxy would be infested with Starguzzlers right now and we would all be nothing more than stardust."

"Now he is gone too," Autamrin said.

"We must find him, as we must your son," the Imgoerin replied. "And everyone else who was on that space station if they are still alive. I am increasingly confident we will."

"The probes were our only hope."

"We did think so. Given how the anomaly absorbed the entire space station and vanished, however, it is unlikely any probes onboard would have remained intact or been able to leave any trail behind that we could have followed."

"Then we had no hope to begin with."

"Perhaps not, until this." The Imgoerin lifted his hand, and the empty center of the room was immediately filled with a large three-dimensional screen. The larger-than-life-sized image of a Mendoken that appeared within was vivid in clarity and brightness.

"This is Maginder Kloiden 52110984, commander of the fleet onsite," the Imgoerin said. "And here is his message."

Maginder's mouth lit up as he spoke. The sound of his voice was crystal clear, as if he was physically there in the room.

"We have completed the scans of the region where the Selcher-44328 space station used to be," he said. "We have also completed our initial analysis of the findings. We are certain at this point that it was an anomaly that appeared in the center of the ring and absorbed all of the station hemispheres before disappearing. Nine of our ten scans revealed no useful clues about where it may have gone. The last scan, however, was a different story altogether."

The image of Maginder's head shrank in size to give way to another image of space that correspondingly expanded to fill the screen. It was awash with dots of different colors, spread around a dark hole in the center. The distribution was random, not too different from a heap of colored sprinkles.

"What you see here are the flavors at a specific moment of time, of neutrinos and antineutrinos around the bulk energy hole left behind by the anomaly," he said. "And here is the progression of the flavors over a period of time as they oscillate."

The image changed dramatically. The spotty, random distribution of colors coalesced into a series of concentric rings around the bulk energy hole. The smaller rings appeared further away than the larger ones, leaving the illusion of a tunnel leading off into the distance.

Autamrin looked stunned. "What... is this?"

Maginder couldn't hear him, of course. The message he was relaying was pre-recorded, transmitted in tiny packets at hundreds of thousands of times the speed of light from his location to this conference room.

"A clue," the Imgoerin said, momentarily pausing the recording. "Left behind by someone, or something."

"Who? Those on board the space station?"

"Unlikely. They would have had no time to construct it once the anomaly struck. Or the knowledge."

The recording continued. "This progression, of apparent randomness to concentric rings and then back to randomness, continuously repeats itself," Maginder said. The image correspondingly began showing the cyclic pattern, with each cycle lasting no more than a few seconds.

"The oscillations of the neutrinos and antineutrinos are clearly being controlled," he added. "Yet careful scanning of the entire surrounding area has shown nothing nearby that could be held responsible. This leads us to conclude that a form of quantum entanglement is at play, where the flavors of other neutrinos and antineutrinos in a remote location are being manipulated to produce the corresponding, opposite result here. The particles were once together when they became entangled, then separated. We can only assume the other particles were transported away by the anomaly along with the space station. Distance is never an issue with entanglement - the effects are immediate even across millions of light years of space. But how it would work across universes in different dimensions is a mystery."

"I think the bigger mystery is who did this and why," Autamrin said.

"Somebody who wants to be found," the Imgoerin replied. "Keep watching."

"It appears what you have seen till now was merely meant to catch our attention," Maginder added. "The real information only reveals itself upon closer scrutiny."

The screen zoomed in on one of the concentric rings, revealing tiny variations in the uniform blue color. The variations themselves were uniform, grouped into rows of different shapes that stretched all across and around the ring.

"What is this?" Autamrin asked, looking dumbfounded. "It looks like..."

"Text," Maginder said, as if he could hear the Aftaran leader. "Millions of lines of text, coded into the neutrino and antineutrino oscillations. To our surprise, we found Mendoken characters and numerals, letters of the Aftaran Altareezyan script, and even some symbols of the Volonan language. They are intermixed in most places, making it somewhat difficult to decipher. We are, however, in the process of doing so.

"Preliminary results indicate the abundant presence of mathematical equations and descriptions of physical laws. Most seem to point to string level particle physics, and how to adapt matter in our brane at the fundamental string level to exist in a different brane with another set of dimensions. There is also a fair amount of information on consars, except that it seems restricted to those that do not return back to our brane but open into another. More of a gateway than a consar, a gateway through the bulk into a different brane altogether."

The Imgoerin paused the recording again as he heard the Aftarans gasp. "A set of detailed instructions, telling us how to follow the anomalies into their universe," he said.

"Incredible," Autamrin whispered. "All praise to the Creator for giving us a way. But... why? Who?"

"Nobody who was on the space station, unless they are somehow remotely controlling particle oscillations from the other universe they were taken to. But somehow I doubt they have the freedom to do so, wherever they are."

"The anomalies themselves, perhaps?"

"Based on all their behavior to-date, it would seem totally antithetical for them to want to be followed into their domain."

"Yet that may be precisely why," Autamrin countered. "You're once again forgetting that they don't practice any form of logic you Mendoken are familiar with."

"Perhaps, but there are reasons why we do not think it is the anomalies."

"What reasons?"

"Commander Maginder has sent us all the data already. Our scientists here are sifting through all of it as we speak, trying to decipher it and figure out a way to construct a stable opening to the other universe. The data apparently also contains details of the energy composition of the anomalies. Why would the anomalies themselves want us to know this?"

The Aftaran leader shrugged.

"Furthermore, the anomalies always used bulk energy ripples to communicate with us," the Imgoerin added. "It was the telltale signatures in the energy ripples they kept leaving behind that eventually led us to what they were after. Whoever left us this information, on the other hand, used a completely different mechanism. I would not be surprised if they did so on purpose, possibly to evade detection by the anomalies."

"What if it is a trap?"

"Do we have a choice but to find out?"

"I suppose not."

"We now need to pursue things on two fronts – finding a way to the other universe to bring our people back, and finding a way to fight the anomalies and defeat them." The Imgoerin then unpaused the recording.

The sound of Maginder's voice filled the room again. "There is something else I need to mention," he said. "With the space station that maintained it now gone, the silupsal filter surrounding the Mendo-Biesel solar system is quickly disintegrating. We have already spotted several holes forming over the surface. Inhabitants of the planet Earth will now be able to see parts of the universe unfiltered through those holes. That, in addition to the fact that their planet has been devastated by the anomalies, begs the question whether we should for once overlook our policy of non-interference. This is a unique case."

The image of Maginder's face slowly faded away. It was the end of the recording.

The Imgoerin eyed the Aftaran leader inquisitively.

"Thanks to us, they have suffered more than enough," Autamrin said after a brief pause.

"We have broken too many non-interference rules with them already. But we should wait and observe them for a while before we actually intervene."

"Yes."

"Several more fleets are preparing to head to the Mendo-Biesel system as we speak to assist Maginder and his crew," the Imgoerin added. "Do you want to send Aftaran representation to accompany them?"

"Most certainly."

Chapter 16

"Not a single enchantment works?" Marc asked.

"Nope," Dumyan replied, sighing. "I've tried all kinds from all the Scriptures. I can't initiate a single one. I close my eyes and start praying. I should be hearing the sounds, feeling the energy coming together. But I hear nothing. I feel nothing. Stone dead silence."

"I guess it only works in our universe. Something about the laws of physics in this one."

"Probably. It's incredible. I have never felt so utterly lost, so hopeless. I keep praying to the Creator, but nothing happens. Nothing changes."

Both of them had already received their daily punishment. Many days had passed since Marc's last conversation with Alisha. It was a rare moment for him amidst all the chaos to find the time to sit and talk with any of his friends, before one of the crystals came by and spread them apart. The crystals were everywhere now, watching the prisoners like hawks. They seemed to be increasingly averse to any of the prisoners mingling, perhaps because they feared the prisoners would devise a way to escape if they talked to each other. If their level of precautionary activity was anything to go by, this fear seemed to be growing with time. It was almost as if they were becoming more agitated with the prisoners, with more and more of them starting to sift through the crowds and thrashing everyone about with their long arms. Why that was the case remained a mystery, for the prisoners had no means to escape.

"A lot of us are here together in this," Dumyan added. "Yet I have never felt more alone."

"Same here. But this can't go on. We have to do something. We owe it to all the others who came with us involuntarily on this journey."

"Sorry, my friend. If you've come to me for ideas, I have none."

"We have to figure out a way. We need to understand what's motivating these crystals, from where they get their strength."

Dumyan sighed again. "I don't know. It seems they just want to extract their revenge on us."

"If it's revenge they seek, why not just kill us?"

"Too quick, perhaps? They want us to die a slow death."

"But they're not even slowly killing us. They're not making the punishments any harder, or reducing our food rations or amount of rest. The only thing that's been changing is that there's many more of them around us now."

Dumyan slowly blinked his large, owl-like eyes. It was the Aftaran equivalent of a shrug.

"Your mighty Aftaran religion has nothing to say about situations like this?" Marc asked.

"I told you. The silence of my mighty religion is deafening at the moment." Dumyan paused. "I have wondered, though, if this is all a test of some sort."

"A test?"

"Our Scriptures teach us that everything that happens in our lives, including all tragedies, accidents, even joyous occasions, are all part of a test. A test by the Creator to see how we react, to see if we are truly righteous, if we are worthy of eternal bliss after our deaths. Call it a way for us to deal with painful events if you like, but it's a central part of our faith."

"I'm not judging," Marc said.

"Alright. But I wonder if these crystals are testing us too."

"What for?"

"No idea. Maybe to determine what our limits are."

"Then what will prompt them to finally decide if we've passed the test?"

"I don't know. Maybe they're expecting us to do something. It could actually be one of the reasons we're seeing more and more of them pushing us about, with greater intensity. They're starting to get frustrated that we aren't passing the test. Although I have no idea what they expect us to do, or how they expect us to do it when they won't give us any opportunity to do anything at all."

Marc stared at the nearest of the crystals, no more than a hundred feet away. "Hmm... interesting idea."

The punishments over the next few days were the same as all the preceding ones. The only thing different was that Marc tried extra hard to keep his wits together, to try to observe the crystal more closely as it picked him up and thrashed him about. He was only able to observe a little every day, thanks to the sheer difficulty in keeping his eyes open amidst the explosive pangs of pain. Each successive blow always grew harder, bringing him closer to the inevitable unconsciousness that would force him to once again relive his most painful memories.

On the first day, he noticed how the main body was shaped like the wide trunk of a tall tree. The many arms, singlehandedly responsible for so much damage to his states of health and mind, looked like long, sweeping branches jutting out every which way along the full span of the trunk.

On the second day, he observed that the arms were composed of the same crystal lattice pattern that the main body was made up of. The "nodes" of the lattice, if that was what they could be called, were oval in shape and extremely bright.

Like blobs of brilliant light, he thought. The nodes were all roughly the same size, a little over a foot in diameter. Their light varied in color, however, with all the colors of the rainbow seemingly well represented across the entire structure. Unless his eyes were deceiving his mind, the consistency of the colors seemed to change with time, slowly shifting from light to dark and back. There was no uniformity in these variations, though. Different nodes across the body seemed to lighten or darken at different times and with different rates. The nodes in the arms also lightened up whenever they moved, especially every time they struck him.

In the very center of the main body, there was one extra-large node, more than twice as large as the others. It also appeared different, a little brighter and redder, fierier in its texture and the impression it gave. Marc wondered if that node represented the core, perhaps the "brain" or "heart" of the entire creature.

On the third and fourth days, he focused on the links between the nodes. They were quite thin in comparison to the nodes, presumably to allow maximum flexibility of motion. He noticed for the first time that they were almost transparent. Small flashes of light seemed to pass in pulses through them between the nodes.

Passing of information, he thought. As he tried to keep his wits together through the agony of each strike, he wondered if the structure resembled a neural network of sorts. There were, however, no more than forty or fifty nodes in total in the whole structure, a far cry from the many billions of neurons in a typical human brain. Then again, it was probably wrong to assume that each node represented only one neuron. There were likely many more layers of sophistication hidden beneath the visible surface. Perhaps all of the creatures were somehow connected with each other, representing a kind of collective intelligence. Either way, there was no doubt that this was a living organism, even if it resembled nothing close to any form of life he had ever seen before.

The next few days were spent in deep thought. Marc had no idea what to make of the composition of the crystals or how to combat them. He continuously searched for someone to talk to, even if only for a minute. Dumyan was invariably out of reach, always pushed away by one of the crystals before he could get close. Eventually he found Sibular late one day, dazed and totally demoralized after so many days of relentless agony. Even his robotic Mendoken heritage hadn't been able to shield him from the continuous mental and physical abuse.

"I do not know how much longer I can keep up with this, Marc," Sibular said slowly. His voice, though still monotonous, was broken. Marc could hear the strain, the bitter emotion between the words. He had never heard a Mendoken speak that way before.

"I know," Marc said reassuringly. "Can we fight them?"

"I would not know how. They are much bigger and stronger than any of us, and we are hopelessly outnumbered. We have no weapons either. All the matter from our space station appears to have been regenerated to create this prison. Perhaps there are more things outside beyond our current field of vision, I do not know. But we have nothing to fight these crystals with in here."

"What if they just want us to react when they're hitting us?"

"Every time I have tried to move any of my limbs even a little when they are holding and hitting me, I have felt twice as much pain. Trying to strike back is not an option, trust me. I cannot imagine the consequences for us if we try something like that."

Marc realized he had never tried to move while receiving his daily punishment. He had always felt way too helpless, too powerless to even try. To his agonizing chagrin, on the very next day he was able to personally verify Sibular's findings. As if the pain from each of the crystal's strikes wasn't high enough, the sheer shock that seared through his entire body whenever he as much as tried to shift his arm or leg was beyond unimaginable.

Utter defeat, he thought as he slowly regained consciousness after the habitual trance that always followed the physical blows. The recovery took much longer this time, thanks to his foolish efforts to test Sibular's words. Any hope he had gathered after the last conversation with Dumyan had just been eradicated. His wish to take his own life returned to the forefront of his thoughts. If he had any means at his disposal to do so, he would undoubtedly do himself the favor to end the suffering.

He didn't know how long he lay there on the cold, hard ground, right at the spot the crystal had dragged him to after beating him up. The days had long passed when others would come to his aid after his punishment. The increased crowd-dispersing activity of the crystals had made it much more difficult for groups of the prisoners to mingle or help each other out for any reasonable amount of time. For that reason, everyone just stayed away from each other to the best of his or her abilities. It had all become predictably routine anyway. It was common knowledge that nobody would die, that the punished ones would always recover even if left alone.

Hence the surprise when Marc noticed an elephant-like shadow looming over him as he recovered. But it was a welcome sight.

"How are you, my friend?" Zorina asked.

"Been better, definitely. Even by our current living standards."

"I noticed. That's why I thought I'd try to get to you today."

"How about you?"

Zorina flapped her big ears. "It was really tough in the beginning. For us Volonans, the norm is to be surrounded by pleasurable, virtual environments. Such suffering is likely much better handled by Aftarans who are used to hardship... by choice, mind you."

"It's their religion," Marc said. "But I can't say that the Aftarans are faring any better than the rest of us at the moment."

"No, they aren't. I am actually the one who is faring a little better at the moment. I've been able to turn my Volonan handicap into an advantage."

Marc slowly sat up, his eyes widening. "I'm listening."

"It's so simple, really, though it took me a while to realize it. Then again, when you're getting beaten up like that, it's almost impossible to think straight or act logically."

"Tell me about it."

"It seems the crystals are using our own minds against us. It's our fear, our anticipation of what's about to happen that they prey on to paralyze us, mentally and physically. It's how they subdue us into believing that we're powerless against them."

Marc shook his head. "You mean it's my fear of the punishment that punishes me all the more?"

"In a sense, yes. That's why each successive strike is always more painful than the last. It's a compounding effect. The only way to break out of it is to overcome your fear of the punishment when you're getting punished. Not only does the physical pain become more bearable, you won't have to endure as much of the traumatic memories afterwards either."

"How are we supposed to do that?"

"As I said, it's so simple in concept, but hard to put into practice. It comes much more naturally to a Volonan like yours truly, thanks to our, shall we say, lofty imaginations."

"And that is?"

"Just think of something else. Immerse yourself in an alternate reality."

It did work, though not as well as it had for Zorina and only after numerous attempts over several days. At first, Marc tried focusing his thoughts on good memories, usually involving happy times with Iman. But those thoughts quickly vanished with the shock of the very first blow each day. He soon realized he would have to lower his mind to a deeper dreamlike state, a kind of trance, if this was to work. That would be closer to the state of a mind connected to the Volonan Virtual Translation Grid.

He rummaged through his memories to revive his experiences with meditation. It didn't take him long to recall the teachings of his Kung Fu teacher, Wing Chun master Sam Gong. Wing Chun, the fighting style taught by legends such as Yip Man and his famous pupil Bruce Lee, was one of the most highly acclaimed styles of Kung Fu taught in Hong Kong and the wider region of southern China. Out of all the martial arts schools close to his home in the San Francisco Bay Area, Marc had chosen one that taught Wing Chun. It wasn't just because of his Hong Kong heritage or the immense popularity of Wing Chun, but also because of its emphasis on balance. Not just balance of the body's structure or stance, but between the mind and the body as a whole. It was the perfect combination of self-defense skills he had been looking for, and a meaningful way for him to connect with his long-lost heritage.

Every Wing Chun class had always started with ten minutes of deep breathing exercises that relaxed and cleared the mind, allowing it to focus on the self-defense training that would follow right after. Marc had had lots of trouble with this in his first year of training, trying to calm and bring his naturally busy, constantly wandering mind into line. But Master Gong, a true expert in the ways of Wing Chun, had offered him a steady hand and had patiently guided him past every hurdle until he eventually reached proficiency in the art of meditation.

Slowly but surely, Marc began using his meditation skills effectively during his daily punishments. It was hard in the beginning, just as it had been in his very first few Wing Chun classes, but recalling the wise words of his master always helped him:

"A calm mind is not disturbed by unwanted thoughts or feelings. Let them all fade away one by one, till all that remains is the awareness of your own being."

The awareness of his own being meant shutting off the five senses, one by one. It meant relying on a higher state of consciousness that kept him well aware of his surroundings, yet oblivious to how they physically affected him. It wouldn't matter anymore how painful each of the crystal's strikes were, for he would no longer be able to feel them.

With time, he got better and better with the meditation. As the days passed, the daily beatings soon ceased to feel like punishments. They became nothing more than his daily meditation ritual. Even the vicious memory flashbacks that used to follow the physical thrashings slowly diminished in intensity until they evaporated completely. The brutal imprisonment in this strange universe by these even stranger crystals had finally become bearable.

*   *   *

"Get a move on," a raspy voice said quietly.

"Huh?" Marc asked sleepily, opening his eyes. The dream he had just been awoken from was a good one, the frequency of which had increased from none to at least one a night since the successful implementation of his meditation techniques.

He got up slowly to survey the room in the dim light. Nobody was there. Nobody was ever there. Other than his interaction with the crystal that shoved him in every evening and the one that dragged him out the following morning, his confinement throughout the night in his tiny cell was always completely solitary.

That grating voice, however, had a distinct, unforgettable tone, one that was neither male nor female but somewhere in between. And although it took him a moment to recall its owner, once he did he had little doubt it could be anybody else.

"Where... are you?" he asked. "Show yourself."

The fluffy cloud seemed to come together from thin air from all the corners of the room, slowly shaping up into a head resting on a body with two long, wavy limbs. It was tall and wide, barely fitting within the dimensions of the small room. The head had no eyes, nose, ears or mouth. It was perfectly expressionless.

"Jinser-Shosa," Marc whispered. "How did you get in here? Nobody can."

"Harrrumpphhh!" the Phyrax growled. "You think I'm as useless as the lot of you? Forgotten what I'm made of?"

"Gas? So you..."

"These solid walls and doors mean nothing to me," Jinser-Shosa said, cutting Marc off. "I can gather and disperse at will."

"Through the cracks?"

"Quite so!" it said triumphantly, pointing to the small gap between the floor and the cell's only door.

"Hmm, interesting," Marc said. "I forgot that you were also on the Mendoken space station when the anomaly struck. Where have you been all this time?"

"Are you saying I've been hiding, like a coward?" Jinser-Shosa exclaimed. "How dare you!" It raised one of its limbs to hit him.

Marc didn't take long to recall the volatile temperament and the "shoot first, ask later" attitude of the typical Phyrax. "No, no, not at all!" he quickly said. "I apologize if it came across that way."

"Hmph!" Jinser-Shosa rasped, reluctantly lowering its arm.

"So you can, uh, go visit anybody's cell, then?" Marc asked. "You'd be the only one I know who can."

"I am!"

"Do you happen to know which cells are occupied by Zorina, Dumyan, Sibular – all fifteen of them?"

"I do!"

"That's great, because I was wondering if it wouldn't be too much trouble to ask you to convey a message to the other punishment recipients. You see, I've figured out a way to lessen the pain during the daily punishment. It..."

"What!" the Phyrax bellowed, momentarily inflating its head in anger. "If it wasn't too much trouble, I'd love to punish you myself right now. Your moronic behavior is the reason we're still stuck here!"

Marc sat back in surprise. "Huh? How so?"

"How so? The nerve! You think your stupid dreams will save you?"

"You mean my meditation? It's the only way to cope with the..."

"Pain? Hah! Who cares about pain? Pain is a worthy sacrifice for freedom. What have you got to lose anyway? You call this a life?"

"Do you have any idea what it's like to face those crystals every day?"

Jinser-Shosa's whole cloudy body shook, possibly in exasperation. "I would gladly trade your position for mine. I'd show those dratted aliens a thing or two, instead of sitting around like a loser. But they have no interest in me. You, on the other hand..."

"But it's not just me."

"Yes, and you're all good for nothing, all sixteen of you! Not even Zorina, my old friend. I tried so hard to convince her. Nobody has the guts."

"It's not lack of guts, it's lack of ability," Marc said, shaking his head. "I want to get out. I need to get out. But... I just... can't."

Jinser-Shosa laughed. "Loser! Where there's a will, there's always a way. And you are the closest to finding the way."

"Meaning?"

"I've been watching all of you. That's one advantage I have – my composition allows me to stretch myself thin and fly around the arena without the crystals noticing. I can tell you, the others have completely given up. But you, you're still the only one with any spark left. And that's why I'm here."

"What do you want me to do?"

"I want action, I want change. I want to go home, damn it! So does everybody else out there. You owe it to them, and to everyone we've left behind in our own universe. Who knows what's happened to them in the meantime? We've got to get back to help rebuild our worlds after all the devastation the anomalies have caused."

"What do you want me to do?" Marc repeated.

"You've found some kind of way to deal with the pain, now use it to your advantage. Do you understand?"

"No."

"Then I'm just going to keep coming back every night and yell at you, until you do. You need to get a move on."

Chapter 17

Offut Air Force Base near Omaha, Nebraska was the center of the United States Strategic Command, or USSTRATCOM for short. One of the nine Unified Combatant Commands of the Department of Defense, USSTRATCOM was responsible for all military operations in space, in addition to many other strategic initiatives such as information warfare, military intelligence, missile defense and the entire United States nuclear arsenal. The current head of USSTRATCOM, a Navy admiral, reported directly to the Secretary of Defense. Both the Air Force Space Command (AFSPC) and the Joint Functional Component Command for Space (JFCC Space) fell under the jurisdiction of USSTRATCOM.

It was no surprise to General Steve Robson of AFSPC, therefore, that both he and Lieutenant General Larry Phelps of JFCC Space had been summoned to Offutt. The situation was dire enough that an in-person meeting was required. With all the devastation that had recently been caused across the country from coast to coast, however, it had been no easy trek from California. The entire nation, with all its sophisticated infrastructure, transportation systems and communication networks, had come to a complete standstill. It had taken hours to locate a transport plane that had not been damaged and to prepare it for flight, and longer still to navigate across vast stretches of airspace without the support of fully operational radar systems. At least the commercial flight ban in effect over US airspace had reduced the chances of collision with another aircraft.

Landing at Offutt had also been a challenge, thanks to the heavy damage most of its runways had endured. They had finally made it, and yet they both knew that their biggest challenge still lay ahead. As they sat in one of the base's many bunkers deep underground, they waited tensely for the door to open. All they could do was watch the numerous video screens on the wall, awash with newsfeeds from all corners of the globe. Each announcement was gloomier than the last. General Robson wasn't sure whether to keep watching or to cover his eyes with his hands. He felt like he just couldn't take it anymore.

The door did eventually open. Both Robson and Phelps stood up immediately. In walked an entourage of four individuals in single file. The first person was Admiral Carter, head of USSTRATCOM, and he was followed by his boss, the Secretary of Defense. It took Robson a few seconds to register who the man was that came in right after. The face was certainly familiar to him, but only because it was the face of a highly public figure. He was surprised – he had been expecting the Secretary of Defense for sure, but he had no idea that this individual would also make an appearance. Then again, it was not uncommon for the President of the United States to take shelter in a military base during times of crisis. Perhaps he had already been here for a while.

The last person to walk in was General Schwartz, Chairman of the Joint Chiefs of Staff. As the door closed, Robson could see black-suited Secret Service agents taking position outside.

Everyone looked highly perturbed. Admiral Carter spoke first as they all sat down around the table in the center of the bunker. "Sir, we've just gotten word that the North Koreans have crossed the border. They've got hundreds of tanks headed toward Seoul. We don't have the ability to coordinate a defense against them with the diminished forces and equipment we still have in place over there, especially without any functioning bases of operations back here."

President Alan Tucker, a tall, middle-aged man and the first-ever African-American president of the United States, was always known for his calm demeanor and highly logical approach to solving problems. But it seemed the events of the past few weeks had brought even a person of his stature and composure to wit's end. He looked exhausted, as if he literally hadn't slept a wink in many nights. The deep, dark circles under his eyes seemed to have found a permanent home, as did the wrinkles that had now spread across much of his forehead. Not that any of the other five men in the room appeared any more rested.

"Fantastic," he uttered softly, shaking his head.

"I'm afraid that's not all, Sir," the admiral said. "Russian forces are amassing to cross into Ukraine. Chances are that more of the other former Soviet republics will be next."

"They're trying to rebuild their lost empire. No better time than now."

"The NSA, or what's left of it, has picked up increased chatter among various Al Qaeda and ISIS cells," General Schwartz added. "There's talk of launching an assault on our homeland. They're trying their best to get hold of one or more nuclear warheads, possibly with the help of the Russians."

"The Russians are becoming bigger foes of ours by the day," Tucker said.

He got up, walked to the TV screens and peered at the screen showing CNN. He had seen the images and footage dozens of times already – completely destroyed infrastructure across the United States – military bases, naval fleets, fighter planes, missile depots, federal and state government buildings, airports, highways, city streets, railway lines, trains, ships, commercial planes, houses, apartment buildings, corporate offices, stores, restaurants, etc. The number of dead was countless, the amount of damage unfathomable.

It was only the landmass of the North American continent that had specifically been targeted by the alien attack. Canada and Mexico had been affected too, although only in the areas close to the US border. The rest of the world, to every single human's sheer amazement, had been completely spared.

"We are powerless, so powerless," Tucker said. "In front of our eyes, terrorists and dictators will seize control bit by bit and take over. Everyone will finally realize the role our nation played in maintaining peace, order and prosperity around the globe for decades. Despite all our faults and all the bad things we've done, everyone will long for those golden years as the world descends into pure chaos."

The President slid his fingers through his short, curly graying hair and stared intently at each of the men in the room. "Everything our founding fathers envisioned, everything all the generations that followed did to build up this country to what it eventually became, all obliterated in the span of a few hours. And none of you can tell me who... what did this and why."

Steven Yates, the Secretary of Defense, was an older man, in his sixties like General Robson. He always spoke slowly, but with focus. "We had no chance, Sir. The bright objects in the sky disappeared abruptly, after relentlessly bombarding us for almost 24 hours."

"They left no trace of themselves for us to analyze or identify," General Schwartz added.

"And there's absolutely no chance this was done by another country?" Tucker asked. "The Russians? The Chinese?"

Schwartz shook his head. "The parent object first appeared months ago at the very outer edges of the solar system. We kept observing as it made its way toward us, following a unique mathematical pattern in its trajectory - we have no idea why. There's no way any power on Earth could have mustered that kind of destructive capability on so massive a scale and from so far away in space. We also have numerous eyewitness accounts of an alien spaceship crashing into the ocean off the California coast. All the debris abruptly disappeared soon after the crash. Another ship appeared two days later for a few minutes over downtown Los Angeles."

The President frowned. "Why would aliens target just us? And why the hell Canada and Mexico too? What have the Canadians ever done to anybody?"

"They clearly just targeted the North American continent," General Robson said. "And yes, given the focus of the attacks the US was undoubtedly the primary target. Parts of Canada and Mexico were, well, collateral damage. I doubt the aliens bothered to figure out where the borders between the three countries lay."

"Then why us?"

"We have a theory, Sir," General Robson said. "Although I have to admit it's going to sound a lot crazier than any of the other ones you may have already heard."

"I'm listening."

"It has to do with one man." Robson typed on his laptop keyboard, and a couple of seconds later an image of a face came into shape on one of the TV screens behind him. "Marc Zemin, professor of sociology at Stanford University. We have reason to believe he was in contact with the aliens."

"What would they want with a sociology professor? He looks quite ordinary."

"He used to be an astrophysicist. Eleven years ago, he was experimenting with wormholes and time travel at Cornell University. Then he vanished one day without a trace, only to emerge months later in Austria."

"Aus... Austria?"

"He supposedly had a change of heart and abandoned his field of study to pursue world peace with the UN."

"In Vienna?"

"Yes. Years later, he returned to this country and ended up at Stanford."

"And you think he was abducted by aliens."

"Given the circumstances, we believe it to be highly probable."

The President shook his head. "This is nuts."

"We do have some evidence, Sir," Lt. General Phelps said. "He was spotted at the site of the spaceship crash. We brought him in for questioning at Vandenberg Air Force Base, and his answers were highly suspect at best. He was also in possession of a device that most certainly wasn't anything built on Earth. What's more, a person matching his facial features was spotted by eyewitnesses near the location where the second spaceship appeared in LA."

"So let's bring him here for questioning. Where is he now?"

Secretary Yates looked a little nervous as he spoke. "That's the thing, Sir. We don't know."

"Didn't you just say you brought him in?"

"Vandenberg was pretty much leveled to the ground during the alien attack. In the chaos that ensued, he, uh, got away. The last recorded sighting of him after that was at the spot where the second spaceship appeared."

"The one lead we had, and you let him walk out." Tucker snorted. "What about the device?"

"He, uh, took it with him."

The room fell silent. The President looked exasperated. He walked to the TV screen and studied Marc's picture. "He's... half Asian, isn't he?"

"Half Chinese and half Canadian by heritage," Admiral Carter said. "He became a US citizen two years ago."

Tucker shook his head again. "Why would somebody want to destroy an entire country, an entire continent, just to get at one individual?"

"Evidently somebody who has a deep grudge against that one individual," Carter said.

"And somebody who has very little regard for any form of life on our planet," Schwartz added. "But what they want from this one individual is anybody's guess."

General Robson cringed at the thought of what the aliens might do with that individual once he was in their possession. "We do think the aliens eventually got him," he said after a brief moment of silence. "It would certainly explain why the attacks stopped abruptly and the bright objects vanished. They have not been back."

Tucker nodded. "Here's to hoping it stays that way. We need to focus first on defending our country against those who will take advantage of our vulnerability, then on rebuilding our infrastructure and basic services for the people. First identify any and all threats to the homeland,

and then assemble whatever resources we have still intact to tackle them. I want initial drafts of plans within 48 hours. Then and only then do we start worrying about our allies and the rest of the world."

"Yes, Sir," everyone said in unison.

"There's one more thing, Mr. President," Lt. General Phelps said, just as Tucker was getting up to leave.

"Something good, please."

"I'm afraid not. We've gotten reports from several observatories around the world that have spotted the same thing."

"What?"

Phelps proceeded to type on Robson's laptop. Seconds later, an image appeared on another of the TV screens.

Tucker looked dumbfounded. He was staring at a picture of a region of space, filled with stars as the sky normally looked at night from Earth. In the middle, however, was a small section containing many, many more stars than the rest of the image, all closely huddled together. It appeared as if that section was offering a peek into a different, much more crowded sky.

"What the hell is that?" he whispered.

"I wish we knew," Phelps replied. "A number of these have appeared in different parts of the sky. Some NASA astronomers are saying they think it's some kind of fracture in spacetime offering a glimpse of a different part of the universe, but that wouldn't explain why there's more than one. There is an alternate opinion already making the rounds at some research institutions."

"What?"

"That may actually be what real space is like. All this time, our view of space may have been covered by some kind of wall, or filter, preventing us from seeing most of the stars in our galaxy. What you're seeing could be a hole in the wall. Some astronomers are already trying to estimate how far away this wall might be."

"And for some reason this wall is starting to break up," Robson said.

President Tucker and Secretary Yates glanced at each other in bewilderment.

"An alien cover-up, preventing us from witnessing the true grandeur of the galaxy," Robson added. "For what reasons, we don't know. But it certainly explains one thing that has puzzled cosmologists for a long time – where all that missing matter is whose gravity keeps our galaxy from flying apart."

"You mean dark matter?" Tucker asked.

"Evidently it's not so dark."

"This is insane," Yates said, shaking his head. "What in heaven's name is going on? What does this all mean?"

Silence filled the room.

"One thing is clear," the President said after a while. "We're in for some unprecedented times. I'm a fairly imaginative person, and I dare say, what happens next may well be beyond anything I can imagine."

You're not the only one, Robson thought.

Chapter 18

"The essence of Wing Chun is to follow one's shadow, not one's hand. Focus on what you feel rather than what you see."

Marc kept repeating these words. The prospect of Jinser-Shosa nightly haunting him aside, the extra push from the temperamental Phyrax was all he needed to finally reach the determination to act against the crystals that had agonized him daily for so long.

What he needed to do, as he recalled from the teachings of his master, was to take the meditation techniques a step further. It was about clearing his mind completely to build a razor-sharp focus on his surroundings. He would no longer need his eyes or ears, or his nose. He would just need his thoughts and feelings to sense everything happening around him. And then maybe, just maybe, he would be able to strike without feeling any pain. What would happen after that was anyone's guess, but at least it would probably break the status quo.

This kind of capability was reserved for a level beyond that which Marc had reached in his Wing Chun training, so he had never attained the ability to fight without his basic senses. He had mastered reaching a meditative state, but not using the meditative state to fight. All he had for reference were his master's words and periodic demonstrations by higher level students in class, fighting each other with blindfolds over their eyes and plugs in their ears. It had always been a spectacle to watch, and often the combatants had fought better that way than with their eyes and ears open. The only choice, therefore, was to recall as much as he could and to practice, practice, practice. The low, variable gravity environment he was currently living in would undoubtedly make this task all the more difficult.

He began using the daily punishments as a starting point. Upon reaching his meditative state, he would begin trying to sense the motion of the crystal's long limbs just before they struck his body. As the days passed, his abilities improved. He continued to practice at night, as much as he could within the confines of his tiny cell. As promised, Jinser-Shosa showed up every night to pester him. Marc eventually learned to take advantage of the Phyrax's presence by occasionally provoking it to hit him, while he turned off his senses, tried to feel its movements and sometimes struck back. He also convinced Jinser-Shosa to spread the word to the other fifteen, to have them train in the same way to the best of their abilities. The Aftarans, given their rigid spiritual training, would likely learn the quickest.

"Tomorrow's the day," Jinser-Shosa said one night to Marc, after many such days had passed. "You've practiced enough. I want no more excuses."

"What about the others?"

"Hah! Ready or not, tomorrow we move."

Marc sighed. "Thanks for the support."

It was a day in the arena like any other. As the crystal dragged him to the center for his morning beating, Marc began dropping his mind into a deep state of meditation. It took longer than usual, thanks to his added nervousness. But by the time the punishment session began, he had cleared his mind and shut down his basic senses. As had become routine, by doing this he would avoid the pain of each strike.

He could sense the strikes coming toward him before they hit, one after the other. He waited for the next, and then the next. And then, just as he felt the next one about to come crashing down on him, he shot out his right fist with all his might into the stem of the crystal's long arm.

He felt no pain. Seizing the moment, he struck with his other fist. Then he struck again and again at the arm, wherever he could sense its presence. Slowly he allowed his senses to regain consciousness. He opened his eyes, and he couldn't believe what he was seeing.

The crystal's arm was shattered, severed from the rest of the body and broken into pieces. The creature had stopped in its tracks, as if it was dumbfounded and unsure what to do. The other arms were swaying back and forth, but they didn't move toward him. As towering as the entire body was compared to his own, it was the very first time Marc saw one of these crystals looking even the slightest bit vulnerable.

Time seemed to slow down. He turned around to look at all the other prisoners in the distance, intently watching the scene. He thought he saw Dumyan in the crowd, with his large, round eyes gleaming with pleasant surprise. Further to the right, he noticed Zorina, her elephant-sized ears flapping wildly with delight. Sibular was standing still as usual, and further behind he thought he caught a glimpse of Alisha. She was staring at him intently, her gorgeous face expressing a mix of glee and concern.

The other crystals, normally busy keeping the prisoners at bay, had stopped moving and had turned to face him. He blinked once, twice, before he noticed a cloud flying toward him. It was Jinser-Shosa, angrily edging him on to finish the job.

He turned back to face his punisher. He drew a deep breath, recalling all the suffering and frustration he had faced at the hands of these beasts for the past, now uncountable number of days. He closed his eyes to clear his mind again, and then jumped up high to deliver a classic hand strike to another of the crystal's arms. The arm broke apart. He followed up with a sharp cry and a rotating kick to the rest of the arm still clinging to the body, further cracking it into pieces.

The crystal, still flabbergasted by this prisoner's sudden courage and ability to fight, took a while to react and begin moving again. Raising one of its remaining arms, it brought the arm crashing down toward his torso. He shifted away just in time and dropped a sharp chop onto the middle of the arm. It split right away into two.

Then he targeted the other arms and eventually the rest of the body, repeatedly jumping high and delivering a rapid volley of strikes and kicks to the thin links between the nodes. He was careful to always avoid the nodes themselves, unsure how much energy they contained and whether he could actually do them any harm.

The crystal fought back, continuously flapping the rest of its arms about him, trying to hit him wherever it could. But he was always a step ahead, sensing the motions as they occurred and moving away in time. He continued to dance over and around the creature, dismantling the entire crystalline structure bit by bit. Each strike felt like a vindication for a single day's punishment. With each strike, he felt stronger, freer. It was an invigorating experience. The consequences, whatever they'd turn out to be, seemed so irrelevant.

By the time he was done, what was left of the crystal was nothing more than a litter of nodes and broken links, spread out all across the floor. Standing triumphant in their midst, he raised his arms up high and screamed at the top of his lungs. He made no effort to control his emotions – all the rage, all the desperation over so many days of torment, everything came out in one long, deafening yell. He had finally struck back.

The screams were repeated, not by him but by the other prisoners. By the Aftarans anyway, as Mendoken never made sounds amounting to anything more than a soft hum. The sound grew to a mighty roar that echoed from one corner of the arena to the other. It was a rallying cry. Emboldened by Marc's victory, the prisoners were readying themselves for battle. An assortment of Mendoken and Aftarans in the front began charging at the crystals. The crystals, now awakened from their state of shock, moved to meet them head-on with their arms swaying. The two sides clashed in the middle of the arena, not too far from where Marc was standing.

The prisoners jumped onto the arms and bodies of the crystals, trying to strike at the links between the nodes to mimic what Marc had just done. But all of them failed, writhing in pain and falling to the floor before they could even get near. The crystals swatted them about like flies and angrily pushed them back toward the spectator rows.

Marc watched the spectacle with horror. They're missing the training, he thought. The prisoners' attempts to strike at the crystals were being met with the same resistance he used to face before beginning his meditation routine. His triumph would be extremely short-lived. This was going to be a disaster on a large scale.

He was about to drop his head into his hands in disappointment, when he noticed a single figure standing strong in front of one of the crystals. It was a Mendoken.

"Sibular," he whispered.

Sibular seemed impervious to the crystal's swaying arms and completely unaffected by each strike on his body. He made straight for the crystal's core, using his four mechanical limbs to simultaneously slice through multiple links between neighboring nodes. The crystal collapsed, giving him free reign to tear the rest of its structure apart as Marc had just done. The other crystals stopped for a moment to take stock of this development, before resuming their vindictive onslaught against the rest of the prisoners.

Jinser-Shosa did its job, Marc thought as he heaved a sigh of relief. It had passed his message on to at least one other individual, one who had taken the time to learn his meditation technique. It was a Mendoken, no less. It couldn't have been easy for such a robotic creature to learn and master a human method of mind control. It certainly said something about how advanced the Mendoken mind was.

For that matter, the Aftaran mind too, for Sibular was soon followed by Dumyan and a number of Aftarans. Marc thought he saw Raiha among them as well. Each of them first broke up a crystal's arms, followed by a complete dismantling of the entire body. He also saw Zorina in action, as well as more Mendoken, Aftarans and a few Volonans. There were many more than the fifteen punishment recipients who had mastered his meditation techniques. Evidently his message had spread further than he had anticipated.

Feeling a renewed vigor, he sprinted off to take down another one of the crystals.

The entire arena was a mess, littered with fragments of broken crystalline links and orphaned nodes. Not a single one of the crystals was left standing. The prisoners were finally the masters of the arena, free to roam about and survey the carnage. It hadn't been easy and it had taken a long time, but it was finally over.

"We did it," Zorina said as she stooped to pick up a single crystal node. Its light had dimmed – now it was nothing more than a dark, lifeless sphere.

"Thanks to you, Marc," Sibular said, as he floated toward them with his levitated, metal-encased body. "And to Jinser-Shosa. The question is, now what?"

"Now we wait," Dumyan said. "For the reprisal."

"There is nothing else we can do," Raiha added. "We have no way to go back home."

Marc wasn't sure what to say. He felt greatly relieved to have won this battle, but he had no idea what lay ahead. The predictable daily routine was over.

He wandered around the arena to look for Alisha. As he did, he couldn't help sensing that somebody, or something, was following him. He wasn't sure what it was. Every time he turned to look, all he could see was crystalline rubble scattered across the floor around him.

He kept moving, and eventually spotted her lying on the floor between adjacent benches in the spectator rows. He ran to her, suspecting the worst. She was conscious, fortunately, but badly hurt. Her right arm and forehead were bleeding. He noticed blood oozing out onto the lower part of her blouse as well.

"What happened?" he asked frantically.

"I was... trying to help," she whispered weakly.

"What, you attacked a crystal?"

"Yes... Didn't go so well."

"Crap." Marc took off his top shirt, tore it into two pieces and tried his best to bandage her arm and her stomach. He then tore off a piece of his undershirt and gave it to her.

"Here, hold this to your forehead and apply pressure," he said. "This is all I've got right now."

She did as she was instructed. "How did you do it?"

"Do what?"

"Take down the crystals."

"I listened to you."

"Huh?

"Well, my other friends too, and to my own heart."

"I'm glad you..." She wheezed in pain before she could finish speaking.

Marc put his arm around her. "You'll be ok, don't worry."

He wasn't sure she would be, as she had already lost a lot of blood. He got up and turned around to go seek help – there were bound to be medical experts among the large Mendoken contingent. But he was forced to stop abruptly in his tracks.

"What is it?" Alisha raised her head to look.

It was one of the crystals, arisen from the dead. At least, a small fraction of one that was broken off from the rest of the body. It had no more than five nodes, but they were fully lit and rearranged with links in an uneven pentagram formation. And it was standing right in front of Marc.

My follower, Marc thought. He hadn't just been imagining the feeling. He heard Alisha gasp. He instinctively took a step forward to protect her, and he closed his eyes to drop into a meditative state. He would hit back as soon as he was ready.

But the crystal didn't strike. After a while, he opened his eyes again. This small creature seemed different. It wasn't menacing – for that matter, it didn't really have arms with which to strike. It was moving around a little, edging forward to get a closer look at the two humans. He peered at the glowing nodes. They were bright, but somehow unassuming. He didn't know what it was, but he didn't feel threatened by this particular crystal.

The crystal tried to move past Marc to get to Alisha. Again, he blocked the way. He stared even more closely at the nodes and raised his hand toward one of them. The crystal slowly dropped that node toward his hand.

"Careful!" Alisha hissed.

"I think it will be... ok," Marc replied. Taking a deep breath, he lowered his shield of caution and touched the node.

It was a warm, tingling sensation that started in his hand, moved up his arm and all over his body. It felt good, really good. Slowly he stepped aside, giving the crystal space to move toward Alisha.

She gaped in fear. "Marc, what...?"

"Let it," he said. "It wants to help you."

"How do you know?"

"I can sense it."

"You're crazy!"

"You just figured that out?"

She tried to get up, but the pain seared through her abdomen like a dagger. She yelped and lay back, helpless.

The crystal lifted its right node and gently brought it to rest over her bleeding stomach. The node began to glow brighter, and Marc could see some of the light creeping and spreading under Alisha's skin. Then it shifted its attention to her arm and her forehead, performing the same procedure each time. Finally, it moved back and turned its top node toward Marc, almost as if it was seeking his approval for its handiwork.

Some handiwork, he thought. The bleeding had stopped completely, everywhere. There weren't even any scars left. Her skin looked perfectly normal.

"How do you feel?" he asked.

She slowly sat up. "Good, good. I, uh... it's incredible. The pain is gone. I feel... alright. How is it...?"

"Well, it seems enough energy cures all ills. They certainly have no lack of it." Turning to the crystal, Marc nodded and smiled in acknowledgment.

Alisha looked perplexed. "But... how? Why help us? Change of heart?"

Marc shook his head. "I don't think so. This is a different creature. I'm guessing..." He raised his hand again to touch one of the nodes. The crystal obliged. Again, he felt the warm sensation tingle through all his veins.

"Trust," he whispered.

"What?"

"Trust. It wants us to trust it. And regret. As if it's, uh, sorry for everything that happened."

"You're joking."

He shook his head again. "I can feel it. Try yourself and see."

Alisha didn't budge. Marc gently grabbed her hand and lifted it to touch the node.

"No way," she retorted, pulling her hand back. "You may be crazy, but I'm not."

"It will be ok, I promise," he said reassuringly.

After much back and forth, she eventually gave up her resistance. Her eyes closed as her hand touched the node.

Marc raised his eyebrows. "Feel it too?"

She nodded.

"Communication," a voice said.

Marc turned around to see Sibular standing there. Dumyan and Zorina were not far behind.

"Not all life forms communicate in the same way," Sibular added. "We Mendoken have encountered all kinds across our galaxy alone. This kind is far from the strangest. It may be trying to communicate with you in the only way it can."

"Through touch?" Alisha asked.

"Yes, and by sharing emotions. With time, it could evolve to the transfer of thoughts and memories."

"Couldn't they just have done that from the start, instead of beating you guys around for so long?"

"Look around you," Sibular said.

Marc and Alisha raised their heads to gaze across the wider arena. It was astounding. While they had been busy with this one crystal, hundreds of others had emerged in the meantime from the remains of the ravaged, larger ones. They were all busily tending to the needs of the prisoners, in the arena and up in the spectator rows. Gone was all the violence, all the pushing and prodding. It was a completely transformed scene.

"What seems different about them?" Sibular asked.

"They're nicer now," Alisha said. "And smaller."

"Yes. What else?"

Marc scrutinized the crystals in the distance, then the one close by. "The cores. They're missing the core nodes in the center of their bodies. The big red ones."

"The cores were likely implants, connecting them to a network," Sibular said.

"So this is their natural state, the way they are now?" Alisha asked.

"Seems so," Dumyan said, joining the conversation. "When they were punishing us, they were not themselves. They were being controlled through those red cores. They actually seem to be helpful by nature. As they were when we were being transported here through that consar or whatever it was. If you remember, they transformed our bodies to adapt to the physics in this universe en route. At that time, they were similar in size and shape to the way they are now."

"Somebody, or something, has been using these crystals for its own ends," Sibular added.

"A higher power," Marc said as he laid his eyes on the nearby crystal. It stood quietly, watching them speaking to each other. Its demeanor seemed so calm, its aura so peaceful. It was amazing how different it was to the monster it had been a part of only an hour ago.

"A higher power controlling them," Dumyan said. "We have just broken that control."

Zorina flapped her ears. "That higher power is going to be pretty pissed. I dread to think what's in store for us now."

Chapter 19

Zorina didn't have to wait long to find out what lay in store for them. Minutes at most, or maybe it had already been there for a while or even all along. It only became visible, however, when the floor of the arena began to lose its opaqueness and slowly became transparent. The floor, of course, represented nothing less than the outer wall of the rotating space station that it was a part of.

What had initiated this transformation of the floor was a mystery, but the crystals seemed far from happy about it. They began to get fidgety, moving back and forth among the newly freed prisoners like busy ants looking for food. It would soon become clear why, for everyone in the arena could now begin peering into the depths of outer space by simply looking down.

"Holy crap," Marc whispered.

Alisha nodded slowly. "We're screwed."

What they all could see was an anomaly, like the ones that had attacked Earth and all the other worlds back in their home universe, like the one that had destroyed the Mendoken space station and transported all its occupants to this other, strange universe. The only difference was that this one looked bigger, although perhaps that was only because it was in such close proximity. It was huge and bulging bright red, blocking much of the view of anything beyond.

The anomaly remained still for a long time, like an angry parent staring at its disobedient kids, trying to decide how best to punish them for their transgressions. Eventually it began growing arms that quickly shot outward from the central body toward the rotating space station. From a distance, it was starting to resemble the shape of a gigantic squid, but with many more limbs. There had to be hundreds of them.

The ends of the limbs soon reached the outer edge of the space station, many of them hitting the floor of the arena from the outside with loud thuds and accompanying bursts of light. Then came the wind, the gale, forcefully sweeping across the whole arena.

Marc watched the spectacle around him, dazed and confused. The wind wasn't affecting him at all. He could certainly feel its presence with the gusts howling past him, but his body stood still. The same was true for Alisha and for all the other prisoners in the arena. The only ones affected, in fact, were the crystals. The wind was dragging them away toward the nearest spots where the anomaly's limbs were touching the floor. The ends of the limbs were acting like monstrous vacuum cleaners, sucking the crystals down toward them with relentless ferocity.

The one crystal that had tended to Alisha's wounds, the same one that Marc had touched a short while earlier, had just made its preferences clear. It was trying desperately to hold onto Marc by tangling its arms around his. He realized what was happening and spread his legs out, offering it more surface area over which to twist its body. But the wind grew stronger, tearing away at the creature and slowly causing it to loosen its grip on him.

"Alisha!" Marc shouted.

She was nearby, but her eyes had till then been focused on the anomaly outside. She jumped into action in the nick of time, just as the crystal was about to give up its last ounce of strength and finally surrender to the sucking force of the wind. She used her body to cover the exposed side of the crystal, locking her arms and legs onto Marc's. Together, they formed a complete protective shell around the creature.

The wind continued to blast away, but it found no room through which it could drag the crystal out from the entangled clutches of the two humans.

How long the whole storm lasted was anyone's guess. Marc certainly had no idea. The only thing he knew was that it felt like it was never going to end. He just kept his eyes closed and held tightly onto Alisha. That was all he could do.

Only when the howling noise finally ended was he able to summon the courage to open his eyes again. Alisha was fortunately still there, as was the little crystal they were protecting. The sight beyond, however, was far from appealing. All the other crystals had been reassembled to their original, large sizes, and the red cores were back in place in the hearts of their bodies. They were once again under the spell of whatever entity was controlling them, and it was quite clear that the culprits were the anomalies.

Worse yet, every one of the crystals now seemed to have a glowing shell around its structure. Marc guessed it was some kind of protective layer, designed to prevent any further attempts at breaking their limbs and reducing them to harmless, friendly companions.

The crystals had all lined up in a single row and had begun sweeping across the arena, leaving no gap across its entire span. They were moving fast, pushing the hundreds of individuals scattered across the grounds toward the far edge. There was only one direction to go – straight into a sky-high wall that covered the full length of the arena's edge. There was no escape.

"What the... what are we supposed to do?" Alisha asked in bewilderment. "They're going to smash us all against the wall?"

Marc scanned the arena frantically for his friends. Through all the commotion, he thought he spotted Dumyan, Sibular and Zorina in different parts of the arena, all of them fleeing as fast as they could from the advancing barricade. They certainly weren't in any position to help. And at the rate it was moving, the barricade would reach him and Alisha within a minute at most.

He felt a gentle pressure on his leg, and he looked down at the only crystal remaining in the entire arena that still had a free will. It was evidently seeking attention. He loosened his grip and lifted his hands, giving the little creature enough space to emerge from its hiding place. Its nodes sprang out as its limbs began stretching out to their fullest lengths. Wasting no time, it twisted one of its limbs around Marc's arm, and another around Alisha's.

"What's it...?" Alisha began.

The little crystal began pulling, softly at first but with progressively stronger tugs. Before either human had a chance to protest, they were both being dragged across the arena floor toward the far edge. Marc was astonished by the sheer strength of this creature. Had they waited even just a few more seconds, he realized, that rapidly moving barricade would have struck them with full force. His momentary state of indecision could have cost him his life, and Alisha's too.

But now they were racing toward a wall, a solid, high, insurmountable wall with no cracks or openings. He glanced at Alisha – she was as terrified as he was. Then he glanced back at the crystal barricade. It was only a few feet away now. The towering creatures looked menacing with their glowing protective coats, beating red cores, flashy nodes and swaying limbs. There were so many of them, all dancing to the same beat, all with the drive of an angry army eager for battle. This time, there would be no way to defeat them.

The area around the wall was already filled with Mendoken, Aftarans and Volonans, all pressed tightly against it. They were in panic, continuously shifting worried glances between the wall and the rapidly approaching barricade. Some of the Aftarans and Volonans began yelling out in fear of being crushed to their deaths. Many of the Mendoken began building a vertical structure by climbing on top of each other, thereby creating more space for everyone else. But there wasn't enough time or enough space to make a difference. They were all getting sandwiched between a rock and a hard place, almost literally.

The crystal dragging the two humans, however, seemed unperturbed. It crashed head-on into the crowd and pushed its way toward the wall.

Everyone in its path moved out of the way, either out of fear or because this little creature somehow gave the impression that it knew what it was doing. With a straight, open path now ahead, the crystal accelerated toward the wall with all its might.

"Hahhh!" Marc screamed, trying his best to untangle himself from the crystal's tight clench. Alisha's shrieks were barely audible above his own. As the wall drew ever closer, he gave in to the irresistible reflex to shut his eyes. He had no idea why it was all going to end like this – he just hoped it would be over so quickly that neither he nor her would feel a thing. Then came the deafening thud.

It was a different place, completely different. But Marc hadn't died and been resurrected. He knew that because Alisha was still there with him, as was the little crystal that had somehow pulled them right through that solid wall. Looking back into the darkness, he thought he could still make out the outlines of the wall. Out of that wall appeared one Mendoken, then two, then many more. Soon there were hundreds. Aftarans and Volonans were also in their midst. Everyone had evidently learned from the little crystal's example and had followed suit. Whiffs of gassy, cloudy substances floated by too, indicating that Jinser-Shosa and the few Phyrax among the total population had also made it. It seemed nobody had been left behind. They were all now in a different part of the rotating space station, a very dark part with no views of the outside or any discernible sources of light. A dim glow in the air offered the only means to see anything at all.

Marc looked down at the little crystal. It had finally let go of his arm. It stood there silently, its nodes glowing brightly. He touched one of the nodes and lowered his head toward it in a nod of gratitude. The crystal reciprocated by lowering its nodes toward him.

"This... thing just saved us," Alisha said, still visibly shaken.

"For sure." Marc stared at the creature. "I wish I knew why it's helping us, whether in their natural state these crystals are just helpful by nature or whether this one has some ulterior motive."

"At this point, does it matter?"

"I suppose not."

"Everyone seems to be moving away," Alisha observed, pointing at some of the individuals near them.

Marc turned to look. Everyone was indeed moving away, but the strange thing was that nobody was actually physically moving. They just seemed to be gaining distance from where he was standing, as if everyone was on an invisible conveyor belt leading away from his vantage point. This was the same no matter in which direction he looked. Then he noticed that Alisha and the little crystal were moving away too.

"Quick!" he exclaimed, lunging toward Alisha with his arms outstretched. She got the hint right away and grabbed onto him. The little crystal reached out with its long limbs and entangled itself with both of them again. The three of them stayed huddled together as everyone else slowly disappeared from view.

For a while, there was nothing around them but pure darkness. All they could do was shift their gazes from one side to the other, but the passing time did little to help their eyes adjust to the pitch-black surroundings. As frightening as it was to be in such an environment, it only got worse when the creaking noises began. They came from all sides and grew louder by the second.

Marc could feel Alisha's fingernails digging deeper into his arms. She was as terrified as he was, and with good reason. The little crystal, however, remained perfectly calm. Its glowing nodes were the only sources of light in this surrounding sea of darkness. To Marc, its confident demeanor also remained his only source of hope that things would eventually get better.

The only things that did improve were the gradual dampening of the loud noises and the corresponding rise of the level of ambient light. Soon Marc was able to make out the shapes of tall shadows, and it didn't take him long to realize that the three of them were complete encircled.

"What?" Alisha whispered, evidently sensing his unease.

"I... can't make out what they are."

"Who?"

"These shadows."

She looked perplexed. "What shadows?"

"The ones surrounding us."

"I see nothing."

"Huh? They're right here, all around us."

"Nonsense. There's nothing there."

"I'm telling you..."

"You're growing crazier by the minute. I'm telling you there's absolutely nothing there."

His eyes shifted their gaze from one shadow to the next. He tried his best to focus in the growing light. Slowly the shadows materialized into walls – tall, dark walls. They were everywhere, leading off in all directions into seemingly endless rows and columns.

"A maze," he whispered. "It's a maze. They must... they must have just built it. Their speed is incredible. That's why there was so much noise."

Alisha was starting to look annoyed. "What are you babbling about? It's empty all around us."

"Maybe I'm the only one who can see it."

"Huh."

"It's possible."

"But why? Are you...?"

"I really don't think I'm bonkers, if that's what you're suggesting."

"Then?"

"It's probably the next punishment," he said slowly, every word uttered with deep exasperation. "For us, the chosen sixteen."

Chapter 20

Construction was edging to completion. It was a massive undertaking, one that at times had pushed engineering prowess even as advanced as that of the Mendoken to its limits. There had been much to learn, much trial and error, and much delving into areas of science never before visited or even deemed possible.

Commander Maginder floated from station to station on the second level of the control deck on his lead Kril-4 ship, getting updates from various crewmembers monitoring the situation outside. Then he moved to the transparent walls at the edge of the deck to get a closer look himself.

The structure out there was big and hollow, a gigantic, shiny ring floating in empty space. Its diameter spanned well beyond the full width of the anomaly that had once appeared in its very center, the same anomaly that had sucked in an entire Mendoken space station and disappeared with it into an alternate universe. There were only a small number of ships left in position at various spots around the ring, finishing off the final touches of assembly with extensions protruding from their hulls. Most of the other ships had already finished their work and moved away to a safe distance. As Maginder watched, these last few vessels completed their remaining tasks, folded their extensions and sped off to join their counterparts.

He floated back to a group of stations around which a number of other Mendoken were huddled. Sautal and Hansa were among them.

"We are ready, Commander," Sautal said.

Maginder hummed in acknowledgment. "Light it up."

Sautal swept his hands along the screens of his station, and a few others followed suit with their own screens. It took no more than a few seconds for the view outside to begin changing. A light blue hue appeared around the surface of the ring, and it quickly spread inwards to fill up all of the hollow space inside. The entire circle was soon awash in a brilliant blue haze.

"All steady," Hansa reported. "As predicted by the instructions we were given. No leakage of matter or energy in either direction."

"Then open it," Maginder said.

Sautal swept his hands again, this time over a different set of screens. The blue circle outside began growing instantly, not in diameter or circumference, but in depth. It was as if a powerful, large projectile was plunging into its center, bulging it out to create a shape like a cone. From where Maginder and the others were watching, the tip of the cone was pushing away from them. Eventually it stopped, revealing nothing short of a gateway behind the circle with no end in sight, a gateway through a sea of dimensional no man's land in the bulk to another brane. The walls were awash with random outlines of different colors that seemed to constantly change shape and size. It very much resembled a consar opening, except that it was considerably larger and it was holding itself open in a stable way.

"The instructions appear correct," Hansa observed. "Whoever they are from."

Maginder hummed again in agreement.

They waited a while to watch for any instability in the formation of the gateway, carefully monitoring all measurements taken from the sensors along the circumference of the ring and from the ships stationed at a safe distance around it. There wasn't any.

"Send in the probe," Maginder instructed.

A streak of light could be seen in the distance, emanating from one of the ships facing the gateway. The unmanned probe was too small to be visible to the naked eye, but one of the screens on Hansa's station offered a magnified view of its slender body as it sped toward the gaping blue hole ahead. It looked like a torpedo, except with spikes spaced apart along its tough torso. Those spikes were equipped with sensors and powerful transmitters to send information back to its creators, even among the most adverse of anticipated conditions during this pioneering voyage into an unknown realm. Among those transmitters were cameras pointing in all directions around the probe, their views of space displayed on other screens at Hansa's station.

Maginder and the others watched the screens quietly, their Mendoken minds programmed since birth never to lose composure no matter how nerve-wrecking the situation. The probe passed through the ring and entered the depths of the gateway beyond. As expected, the visual displays of the probe's cameras on Hansa's screens soon faded away, their signals attenuated to nothingness in the dimensional morass they were trying to pass back through.

The only things left to indicate the probe's status and progress were the layered pulses from its bosian transmitters, a technique used to send messages across vast swathes of space at speeds far greater than that of light. Apart from the obvious advantage of relatively low transmission latency, bosian layering had the added benefit of being able to trudge through pretty much any known obstacle, including rifts in dimensions. It was an amazingly sturdy and reliable technology.

The data sent back through the bosian packets was continuously deconstructed, analyzed and modeled in real time to render a visual depiction on Hansa's screens of the probe's motion through the gateway. One of the screens showed a modeled rendition of the view ahead, another a depiction of the shape and structure of the probe itself, and yet another a mapping of the overall trajectory the probe had traversed through the gateway until that point in time.

"Is the probe holding?" Maginder asked.

"Yes, Commander," Sautal replied. "The matter transformation process for the probe to adapt to the physical conditions of the destination brane should begin shortly. We will lose bosian transmissions temporarily until the transformation is complete."

The trajectory mapping continued to grow as the probe moved further into the depths of the gateway. The rendition of the view ahead continued to show a consar tunnel-like environment, with the familiar changing shapes and colors on it walls.

"The transformation begins... now," Sautal announced.

All eyes focused on the screen showing the structure of the probe. The front part of the body began to open up into small pieces, each of which further split into even smaller pieces. The breaking up continued along the full length of the probe, all the way to the rear. The pieces would continue to split this way until they reached a subatomic level of granularity, after which they would align themselves to the dimensions of the new universe they were about to enter. Then they would merge again to reassemble the entire probe as it made its way along the trajectory.

At least, that had been the plan. Unfortunately that wasn't how it played out.

"Something is wrong with the trajectory," Hansa reported.

Maginder stared at the screen displaying the trajectory mapping. It had reached a fair distance beyond the entrance to the gateway, but it was no longer growing.

"Is it reaching the exit point?" he asked.

"Unlikely," Hansa replied. "There are no indications of an opening. It looks more like a dead end." She pointed at the screen showing the view in front of the probe – the rendition of a solid wall ahead was starting to take shape.

"Can you stop the probe?"

"Not in the middle of the transformation process," Sautal said.

"Slow it down?"

"No."

Maginder watched the probe hurtle toward the wall. The front part of its body had already broken up into miniscule pieces. Instead of coming back together, however, they began flying off in all directions. The rest of the body swiftly disintegrated in the same way, just as it was about to hit the wall. The bosian transmissions stopped abruptly, and all the screens went dark. The probe was no more.

Maginder couldn't help feeling a whiff of disappointment, but he quickly regained his composure. "What happened?"

"It is inexplicable," Sautal said as he shifted his gaze from the blank screens to the view outside. The cone shape inside the ring was shrinking back into a circle, before its blue hue began to fade away. Soon all that was left was an empty ring, just as it had all begun. The gateway was gone.

"We just followed the instructions on initiating the transformation," Hansa said.

"Did they mention anything about the trajectory?" Maginder asked.

"Just that it would eventually lead to the destination brane."

Maginder thought for a moment. "Alright, open the gateway again and send in another probe. This time at a lower speed. It appears we need more time to complete the transformation before the trajectory ends."

The second probe was sent within minutes, but it followed the same fate as the first. The lower speed did little other than to prolong the time it took to reach total annihilation. The third, sent at an ultra-high speed to see if it could reach the end before the gateway closed up, blew up in a majestic display of fireworks. The fourth was sent in slowly, then stopped and reversed direction for a while, then edged forward again before reversing once more. This process continued, all in the hopes of prolonging the probe's life inside the gateway until its subatomic transformation was complete.

"We appear to be doing something wrong," Sautal observed as the fourth probe also shattered into billions of tiny bits.

The Mendoken were not known for their sarcasm, or for having any sarcasm at all. Maginder simply hummed in agreement. "That we are."

*   *   *

The Mendoken Imgoerin stood still, puzzled. He and Autamrin were inside the same conference room they had met in a few days earlier, right after the Aftaran leader had arrived on the planet Lind. They had just finished watching the latest transmission from Commander Maginder.

"The instructions are clear," he said. "To open the gateway, enter it and initiate the matter transformation process as you proceed through it."

Autamrin didn't seem convinced. "Show me."

The Imgoerin motioned to his aide Osalya, who opened up a wide screen in front of the Aftaran leader. The data poured in right away, revealing a series of mathematical equations and diagrams, as well as simulations of gateway construction and subatomic transformation.

Autamrin's owl-like eyes widened as he studied the volumes of information. Then he closed them and thought deeply for a while.

"You're right," he finally said, opening his eyes again. "The instructions do seem clear enough, as much as I can grasp any of this technical jargon. But perhaps we're going about it the wrong way."

"Meaning?"

The Aftaran leader smiled. "You're looking at it too linearly, too literally."

"I do not understand."

"No offense, it's just the way you Mendoken are. To your credit, mind you. That's what has made you as great and advanced as you are. It's just that we Aftarans are, well, different. We tend to look at the spirit of things, rather than the letter. We read between the lines, if you will."

"If I will what?"

Autamrin smiled again. "We look for hidden meanings, what isn't said as much as what is. That's the only way we're able to interpret our holy scriptures."

"You think these instructions are holy?"

"No, no. What I mean is... may I?" Autamrin used his thin, long fingers to magnify a section of the screen displaying a model of the gateway entrance. "They're showing you how to build a gateway, how to send something into it and how to initiate its transformation. What they're not telling you is how to exit the gateway and enter the other universe."

"That should naturally follow," the Imgoerin said. "You saw how the trajectory kept growing as the probe moved through the gateway."

"Until it stopped growing, with no opening at the end. What that tells me is that the instructions weren't complete. The rest was to be inferred."

"Inferred?"

"Yes. They, whoever 'they' are, want you to enter the gateway, but then to wait once you've entered. They'll open the other side when they're ready, on their terms."

The Imgoerin was silent for a moment. "Interesting idea."

"It's not just an idea. I think it really is the case. They provided us the instructions, sure. But who knows what's happening on the other side? Maybe whoever is trying to help us is hiding in the other universe, waiting for the right opportunity to let us enter. Maybe if we enter right now, we'll get blown apart by those anomalies."

"Their progression of time may be quite different from ours, possibly slower," Osalya suggested. "That could also explain why we have to wait."

"There's no harm in trying, is there?" Autamrin said, shrugging. "It's just another probe."

"Send Commander Maginder a message," the Imgoerin instructed Osalya.

"How are things progressing on the other front?" Autamrin asked. "Figuring out how to fight the anomalies?"

"We have our best scientists working on that right here on Lind. The instructions have provided us some data about their composition, but we still have no real clue how to defeat them."

"Is there anything we can do in the meantime?"

"We can have Commander Maginder assemble a delegation to visit the planet Earth, as we discussed before," Osalya said. "The reinforcement fleets we sent from here should have arrived at his location by now."

The Imgoerin hummed in agreement. "Add that to the message."

Chapter 21

The little crystal lowered one of its nodes and pointed it in the direction of the nearest opening into the maze.

"It wants us to go in," Alisha said.

Marc eyed the looming structure that surrounded him. Its tall, dark walls looked anything but welcoming, with numerous dangers undoubtedly lurking in its shadows. "It wants *me* to go in. You're staying right here."

"Try and stop me."

"This doesn't scare you?"

She shrugged. "To me, there's nothing there at all."

"It seems the crystal can see it. Or sense its presence anyway."

"Well, I can't."

He hesitated, then gave in. "Hold my hand, I'll lead the way."

They treaded lightly toward the maze entrance, with the crystal following a few feet behind. As soon as they had passed through, he heard a loud thud behind him. He jumped in surprise and turned around to look. The opening had just sealed shut behind him. The crystal's nodes, which were now glowing quite dimly, were the only source of light in an otherwise pitch-black backdrop. He clenched Alisha's hand tightly.

"Oww!" she exclaimed, pulling her hand back.

"Sorry."

"What's wrong with you?"

"It's dark and scary."

"Seriously? You haven't gotten used to that by now?"

He reached out with his other hand toward the wall. It felt cold and very solid. "Here, try touching it," he said.

"There's nothing there to touch." Her hand went straight through. To demonstrate that she wasn't lying, she walked right through the wall and disappeared from his view.

Like a ghost, he thought. He tried to follow her, only to crash head-on against the hard surface. Seconds later, she reappeared through the wall, her face showing the expression of a mild giggle.

"Laugh away," he said sourly. He glanced at the crystal, hoping for an explanation of some sort. But it stood completely still.

"Just bear with me," he finally said to Alisha. "This is going to be weird for both of us."

"Twice as weird for me, believe me."

He slowly edged forward along the narrow trail, Alisha following right behind and the crystal taking up the rear. He glanced back nervously at the crystal every now and then, but it just prodded him to keep moving. The path twisted and turned for what felt to him like eons. Eventually it led to a small clearing, beyond which lay the entrances to two new paths stretching off in directions almost perpendicular to each other.

Marc looked at the crystal once again. It was already using one of its nodes to point to the left entrance. He eyed the left path carefully, as much as he could make anything out in the darkness. Then he stared down the right path. They both looked exactly the same.

He took a step forward through the left entrance, then another. The path was straight for a while, but then began twisting and turning. After many minutes of trekking, he began to feel afraid. He had no idea why. As he kept walking, the fear grew, slowly at first, then more and more quickly. It grew irrationally, soon to be coupled with a surge of anxiety. Every step he took, the more anxious he became. His body began shivering. He wasn't sure why, he just had a bad feeling that something was lurking in the shadows ahead.

"What is it?" Alisha asked as he stopped in his tracks and grabbed her arm.

"I don't know," he replied. The urge to turn around and run for his life rose quickly, but the crystal was blocking the way. Then he heard it – faint and distant at first, but growing louder and louder. It sounded like the thunder of a hundred hooves galloping over a hollow surface. Before long, it was deafening to his ears. The ground and the walls around him began to shake in unison.

"Can't you hear it?" he yelled in panic. "Can't you feel it?" He tried to bury his face in Alisha's shoulder.

"No, nothing," she said. "It's not real."

But her words did little to comfort him. He let go of her and tried once more to rush back to the path entrance. The crystal, however, had now spread its limbs and nodes across the full breadth of the narrow pathway, like a mesh with no room to wiggle past. Evidently it could perceive the pathways of the maze like he could, or perhaps it just knew really well how to estimate things. Either way, he was stuck.

He braced for its appearance, whatever it was. He didn't have to wait long. And, as he had already begun to suspect, it was an overgrown manifestation of one his biggest phobias.

The spider was monstrous, easily more than three times the size of an average human. Its abdomen, the rear and larger part of its two-segmented body, could barely fit in the narrow confines of the maze's pathways. Its long, hairy legs thrashed about as it lunged forward. As if the body wasn't ugly enough, its head was absolutely hideous and just plain terrifying to as much as cast a quick glance at.

Marc cringed with horror. A series of profanities came out of his mouth, much to Alisha's surprise. He cried as he held onto her with all his might, his eyes shut as tightly as they could ever be. Any sense of shame, any sense of self-control he once had in front of her was all gone.

The shrill hiss of the spider grew louder as it edged closer. Marc thought he felt the crystal prodding him with one of its nodes, but he ignored it.

"The crystal wants you to face your fear," Alisha said. "It's all in your head, remember that."

"I... can't," he yelped.

"I think it's part of the test." She grabbed his shoulders and slowly turned him around. "Open your eyes."

"No chance!"

"You have to."

"No!"

She slapped him on his cheek. "Get it together, Marc!"

The wind hit his face right after, the wind from the continuous flapping about of the spider's long legs. Gathering all the courage he had left, he opened his eyes just a little to face the monster.

The eyes, oh, those gigantic eyes – four pairs of them, round and completely black – staring him down. He couldn't bear the sight of it. Just below was the mouth, agape with sharp fangs sticking out. He had never seen such a horrendous looking creature in his whole life. He had to remind himself how fortunate he was to not have been born an insect, to have to face such dangers at this level of magnification on a daily basis.

The last thing he remembered was the sensation of those long legs feeling him up and down, followed by a slimy, sticky splash hitting his face. Venom, undoubtedly, meant to knock him out.

That was about as much as he could take. Letting go of Alisha, he scrambled to get away. He crashed into the crystal, which tried its best to push him back toward the giant spider. He writhed and wriggled with it, using all his might to push a few of its limbs out of the way. Then he crawled through the narrow opening he had just created and made a beeline back toward the path entrance, screaming at the top of his lungs as he ran the fastest he had probably ever run in his whole life. Several times he crashed against the walls, unable to see the upcoming turns clearly enough in the darkness. But nothing was going to stop him – no pain, no bruises, not even broken bones.

He was certain he could hear the spider on his heels, hissing away and ready to lash out at him again with a stream of its deadly poison. As he reached the path entrance, however, the fear began to subside. And, as he finally broke out into the clearing, he no longer felt afraid or anxious at all. He came to a standstill, panting and trying to regain his breath. Alisha and the crystal soon caught up with him.

"What happened?" she exclaimed, grabbing his arm.

"It's ok," he whispered. "It's gone now, back into the maze. We're safe."

"Safe from what?"

"A... spider. A giant one. Ugly as hell."

A hint of a giggle appeared across her mouth again. "You're afraid of spiders?"

He nodded. "Terrified. Of bugs in general, but particularly arachnids."

"All these theatrics because of a spider?"

"It was really big."

She sighed and shook her head in disbelief.

Food had appeared out of nowhere at the tunnel entrance, a pink, pasty substance packed into a collection of tubes. It was the same kind of food he had been forced to eat nightly in his cell during the earlier punishment. He didn't know what it was made of or why it had no taste. He did know, however, that it was edible to humans and provided both the necessary nourishment and fluids to stay alive. And, just by looking at it, he realized how long it had been since he had last eaten anything and how hungry he was.

He opened a couple of tubes and gulped down the paste. Then he glanced at the crystal. It was using one of its limbs to point back at the left entrance, to the path they had just come out of.

"No chance," he said right away. "I'm not going back in there."

"There must be a reason it wants you to go that way," Alisha said as she finished her own ration of the pink paste. "It wants you to face your fear."

"You don't know what it's like. There's absolutely no way."

"You have to. Otherwise we'll be stuck here forever."

He contemplated whether to try the other path or to walk back out of the maze altogether. Then he began to get a good feeling about this path to the right. Although the entrances appeared identical, this one just seemed more welcoming. He had no idea why. And despite the crystal's frantic efforts to get him to reenter the path to the left, he eventually stepped through the one to the right.

"Take the left path, Marc," Alisha said. "That's what the crystal wants."

But Marc paid no attention to her and continued down the path to the right.

"Did you hear me?" she called out. "Why aren't you listening?"

This path looked the same as the other – dark and narrow, with bends and curves aplenty. But it felt remarkably different. In fact, it just felt remarkable. Marc kept moving, confident and carefree, without a worry in the world. Alisha followed, cursing him for not paying attention to her, and the rear was taken begrudgingly by the little crystal. Every now and then, it tried to reach out with one of its limbs to stop Marc and pull him back, but to no avail. He was unstoppable.

He quickened his pace. The walking soon turned to slow running, then to sprinting. He thought he could sense something in the distance, something he cared for and so longed to see again. It became clearer as he drew nearer. It was a person, no two, an adult and a little child. He could make out the long brown hair on the adult, the smooth, tan skin and soft, brown eyes. She was beautiful, and so familiar. She turned to smile at him. Oh, that sweet smile. How he had missed it. How he had missed her. He had only one thought in his head – to reach her as quickly as possible.

The child, a girl, looked just like her. The resemblance was uncanny, like a smaller, two-year old rendition of her. And yet, Marc could have sworn he saw a faint resemblance of some of his own features in that cute little face. The eyes, the nose, even the cheeks were more like his, not hers – a genuine mix of both of them. He had no doubt anymore –

the little girl was his daughter, and the woman next to her his wife – Iman.

As he ran toward them, his surroundings began to change. The walls of the dark, narrow path faded and gave way to a bright, open space. The sun was starting to break through patches of clouds in the blue sky above, and the solid ground soon became a soft, sandy beach. To the left, ocean waves appeared and began crashing gently against a shore that had just taken shape. To the right, tall cliffs ran parallel to the coastline. Wife and daughter were still ahead, but they were standing there with arms outstretched toward him and with longing looks in their eyes. They were ecstatic to see him again.

He drew closer and closer. All his worries, his fears, sorrows and regrets, they were all gone. There was nothing left to hold him back anymore from his family, from the ones he so dearly loved. He reached out with his arms to touch them and to give both of them a tight hug. He had waited for this moment for so long.

And then, just like that, they were gone. Vanished, vaporized into thin air. His hands groped desperately for them, but in vain. The cliffs faded away, as did the ocean waves and the bright blue sky. The soft sand shifted back to hard ground, and darkness fell over all around him once again like a swiftly descending drape. Once his eyes had adjusted, he realized he was back in the maze, at the same entrance to the two paths he had started from earlier. This time, no more food had appeared.

"No!" he wailed in dismay, covering his face with his hands. "Noooo!" It had all been so real, so tangible. His wife, his daughter – the daughter he had never met, the daughter who had never been born, the daughter who could have been. He had lost both of them, as he had lost every single individual he had ever loved. His body shook in agony.

A warm hand landed on his shoulder, and then another on his arm. "Marc, are you ok?"

He turned around slowly to face Alisha. She was real at least, as unreal as the situation was that had intertwined their fates in so dramatic a way. Her big, tear-shaped eyes showed genuine concern.

"No," he said quietly. "I'm not. I saw... I saw my wife and daughter. They were... so real."

"Don't go into that path again," she said. "The crystal wasn't happy about it. It was lighting up in different colors and thrashing its limbs about."

Marc sighed in exasperation. "The other path is worse, way worse."

He noticed the crystal was standing in front of that other path again, pointing to the opening. "What the hell do you want from me?" he yelled. "I'm not going in there again! No chance."

The crystal was quiet, and just waved its limb in the direction of the path.

"I'm going back to my family," he said firmly. "I want to see them."

"Marc, no!" Alisha cried. She tried her best to hold him back, but he broke away and lunged toward the path to the right.

Before he was able to reach it, however, the crystal jumped over him and spread its limbs instantly to block the entrance.

"Out of the way!" he screeched, trying to tear its limbs off one by one from the walls of the opening. But the crystal wouldn't budge – it was obviously a lot stronger than it looked. Then he stepped back several yards to gain some distance, and then he sprinted forward to crash into the creature and take it down.

Crash into it he did, but what happened after that was far removed from anything he would have considered possible.

Chapter 22

The phone rang. It was a most unwelcome, shrill sound, and it woke up the President of the United States. He reluctantly opened his eyes, gave himself a few seconds to recall who and where he was, and then took note of the time on the bedside clock – 3:34 am. Then he picked up the phone.

"Yes?" he grunted.

"Sorry to wake you, Mr. President." It was Margaret Whisman, the White House Chief of Staff. She sounded shaken, most unlike her usual, composed self.

"What happened?"

"The worst possible."

President Tucker got up quietly and glanced at the other side of the bed. The First Lady was fortunately still fast asleep. They were both used to this kind of nighttime disturbance, after all. It was one of the downsides of being associated with so lofty and mission critical a job. After a quick wash and a change of clothes, he opened the door and stepped out. Two Secret Service agents were already standing there in the corridor.

"Sir," one of them said.

"I can walk by myself," Tucker said gruffly.

"It's protocol, Sir, given the situation."

Even they know more than me, he thought as he walked to the Oval Office.

Whisman was already there in the room, as were Steven Farthing, the Deputy Chief of Staff, and John Mimnaugh, the National Security Advisor. They were sitting on couches in front of the main desk, but they stood up right away as he entered.

"The Defense Secretary is on his way," Whisman announced. An elderly lady with white hair and wrinkly skin, she looked unusually tired and worn. Many believed she was past her prime and due for retirement, but her reputation as the iron lady of the Tucker administration was far from undeserved. She had a strong will and bouts of energy to match. The President relied on her like he did on no other.

Tucker sat down, after which the others followed suit. "I'm listening," he said.

"There's been an attack," Mimnaugh said.

"What kind of attack?"

"A... nuclear one."

"Where?"

"Your hometown, Sir. Boston."

Tucker's face sank. "What... how?"

"The bomb was planted on a boat in Boston Harbor, and probably set off by remote control," Mimnaugh said. "Judging by the latest reports, it appears to have been a two-stage thermonuclear device, and a fairly heavy one at that. The destruction is substantial. Downtown Boston has pretty much been leveled to the ground. It's been 30 minutes, and the radiation has already spread well beyond the Charles River. It's reached as far as Medford to the north and Dorchester to the south."

Whisman turned on the TV. CNN was showing live videos of the mayhem, with panic-strewn residents of the suburbs rushing out onto the streets, piling onto their cars and speeding off into the night. Sirens were constantly buzzing in the background, drowned out only by the screams of people frantically seeking help. The growing mushroom cloud over the city, glowing brightly in the dark sky, looked menacing. The downtown skyline, however much of a skyline Boston even had, was gone, leveled to the ground by the sheer pressure of the initial blast.

Tucker was aghast. "Natick," he said. "My brother, my nieces. They..."

"Natick is likely still outside the radiation perimeter," Farthing said. "But not for long. The Massachusetts Governor has declared a state of emergency and has summoned the local National Guard to evacuate all of Boston's suburbs as quickly as possible."

The President sat back and closed his eyes for a moment. "All those people, dead," he said quietly. "We've spent all the resources we had left to tighten our borders and focus on homeland security. We secured all our weapons of mass destruction."

"With the bulk of our surveillance systems still inoperable, there's only so much suspicious activity we could have monitored," Farthing replied. "It was just a matter of time before something like this happened."

"Frankly, Sir, we're lucky this has been the first attack on homeland soil," Mimnaugh added. "It's been almost a month since the alien attack that destroyed our infrastructure. Fortunately the aliens haven't been back. That's how we've been able to resume our lives and start rebuilding."

"I know, that's also why we're no longer in underground bunkers," Tucker said. "We've been safe, and with good reason. We've worked hard to protect ourselves."

"But given what's been happening in Europe and Asia since, and given the number of enemies we have in the world..."

"I get that," Tucker said, cutting him off. "But a nuclear attack. Oh, God."

"There could very well have been a nuclear attack elsewhere too, but it seems our enemies were leaving the big one for us," Mimnaugh replied. "They've been focusing on smaller scale, repeated strikes in Western Europe. Given the proximity to their bases, it's easier for them to plan, coordinate and infiltrate there than here."

"Eastern Europe has been awash with its own problems, with the Russians retaking the Ukraine and several other former Soviet republics," Whisman said. "It's back to the Cold War, except we're no match for the Russians anymore. They've got free reign to do whatever they want."

"So who did this, and... how?" Tucker asked.

Farthing shrugged. "As to how, they could easily have picked up a bomb from the Russians. The Russians are more than interested in seeing us further weakened, but they won't launch an attack on us directly because they don't want to be seen as the bad guys starting a war. They want to be the new superpower that rules and polices the world."

"And as to who, I think we're about to find out," Whisman said, pointing to the television.

CNN had breaking news, yet again. They had just received footage of a video recording made somewhere in Iraq or Syria, they weren't sure which. What they were sure of was that it was from ISIS and not Al Qaeda. Al Qaeda, once considered the biggest, worst enemy of the United States and the rest of the free world, had turned out to be a cuddly kitten compared to the likes of this spinoff of theirs. The tactics of subjugation and the brutality of ISIS were of a level well beyond that of Al Qaeda, possibly a level not witnessed by humanity at all since the Middle Ages. For Al Qaeda, violence was a means to an end. For ISIS, violence was an end in itself. ISIS was so brutal, in fact, that they had been kicked out of Al Qaeda for methods and ideology viewed as too extreme. Such a mentality coupled with the destructive capabilities of modern-day weaponry had led to one heck of a deadly force to reckon with.

ISIS had been active for years already, but had significantly upped both the frequency and intensity of its atrocities over the past couple of months since the alien attack that had essentially annihilated both the civilian infrastructure and the military capability of the United States. Not surprisingly, the terrorist group had taken full advantage of the situation to spread mayhem around the globe.

President Tucker therefore already had a fairly good hunch about the identity of the perpetrator of this latest attack, but in his job he knew never to jump to conclusions until the evidence was clear. As he glued his eyes to the TV, he expected that evidence was about to reveal itself. And it did.

The video recording showed a middle-aged, bearded man with a black turban and loose black clothing. His eyes looked soft and warm, a far cry from the glaring, piercing eyes of the stereotypical villain. And yet here he was, the undisputed leader of the most gruesome group of people in the world. Ali Abu Hashem Al-Suwari, or Abu Hashem for short, was a product of the US led invasion of Iraq and the ensuing chaos. He had lost both his mother and brother in a bombing run of his hometown, and he had spent several years in prison during the occupation. Word was that he had endured repeated, relentless torture at the hands of both US and Iraqi forces. His hatred of the US was not just based on the tenets of religious fanaticism, for him it was downright personal.

He was speaking softly as he always did, but with conviction. His hands were raised and repeatedly pointed at the camera. His Arabic words were translated to English by subtitles on the bottom of the screen, their clear meaning leaving no room for misinterpretation.

"Today we have avenged the blood of a million martyrs. Today we have unleashed the wrath of God on His enemies. Today the infidels and agents of Satan will experience the full weight of justice, of revenge. Let them see, I say. Let them hear, let them feel. Let them see their cities, their buildings and roads turn to rubble. Let them hear the deafening sound of scores of bombs exploding in their faces. Let them feel the pain of losing their loved ones, their friends and their own limbs.

"For decades, for centuries the West has ruled over us with pure tyranny. They have come and gone as they pleased, they have plundered, pillaged and murdered. They have killed our brothers and sisters, destroyed our lands and stolen our riches. To them, the only lives that matter are their own. To them, the life of one of their soldiers is worth the same as the lives of a hundred thousand of our children. They talk of freedom, of democracy and equal rights, and yet they conveniently ignore the double standard with which they apply the tenets – only for their own people and at the expense of ours.

"No more, I say. No more. God has heard our prayers, our calls for help, and God always stands with those who are righteous. God sent the fireballs from the heavens to punish them, to make them pay for their sins, to make them realize the erring of their evil ways. But have they learned? No, they have not. Even after all the havoc and destruction they've had to face, they still try to exert power over the rest of the world, they still try to rule over us and prevent us from following the path of God, from establishing God's kingdom on Earth and spreading His word to every one of its corners.

"So we've had no choice but to show them that times have changed for good. They can no longer do as they please, they are no longer the masters of this world or the human race. They must learn their place, they must succumb to the will of God. They have to experience the same pain, the same suffering they have inflicted on our people for so long.

"My brothers and sisters, what has happened today is only the first of many attacks against the apostates and infidels, against those who have wronged us and shunned all norms of human decency. God willing, we shall flatten all that's holy to them, we shall bomb them back to the Stone Age as they did to us. Let them die in the thousands, in the millions. Let them learn that their lives are no more important than ours. The time has finally come for justice and revenge."

CNN zoomed out of the video recording and back to the news reporter, who switched to updates on the unfolding situation in Boston.

President Tucker swallowed hard. His throat was dry, he felt hot and he could sense the moistening of his forehead and back. He had to keep his cool, he knew, he had to do all he could to avoid panicking or showing any weakness to his staff members.

"Well, I suppose that leaves little room for doubt about the identity of the perpetrators," he said, trying to break a smile.

"It's amazing that he can say all those things with a straight face," Whisman said, shaking her head. "Accusing us of atrocities? Forget what they've done to us, what have they been doing to their own people?

Suicide bombings, beheadings, burnings, drownings, mass shootings of anyone who doesn't submit to their authority or their narrow, extreme interpretation of their own religion. They've killed more of their own than anybody else has."

"The sheer majority of them innocent," Mimnaugh added. "That's the difference between us and them. We target the guilty, the perpetrators, and yes, sure, innocents often die in the process. But they, they purposely target the innocent, the helpless. The very definition of cowardice."

"And accusing us of driving them back to the Stone Age," Farthing added. "They've been doing that just fine by themselves since they took over power in parts of Syria and Iraq."

"Well, we can't expect anything less from a master manipulator and propagandist like Abu Hashem," Tucker said. "That something like this would happen was predictable. It's just surprising that they got their hands on a nuclear weapon so soon, and that they figured out how to transport and detonate it. I wouldn't take his warnings on what's to come next lightly either. Needless to say, we're in deep trouble."

"The Russians – unbelievable that they'd stoop to so low a level to collaborate with terrorists they once considered their own bitter enemy," Whisman said, shaking her head.

"The enemy of your enemy is your friend," Tucker said. "And, since the alien attack, we've become Russia's biggest enemy. They want us obliterated, with no chance ever of coming back."

"We're working as fast as we can to rebuild our defense and surveillance systems," Mimnaugh said. "But we're still a far cry from being able to launch strikes against ISIS. Our biggest issue is that our military and intelligence communications networks are still down. Even though our bases and equipment overseas were untouched by the alien attack, we can't coordinate with them to launch a meaningful attack anywhere. We're going to need help from the Europeans. Canada can't do much right now either – they're in almost as bad a shape as we are."

"The Europeans are dealing with enough troubles of their own," Tucker replied. "But yes, we'll have to reach out to them again."

There was a brief pause, during which Tucker cleared his throat and poured himself a glass of water.

"We may lack resources and infrastructure," he added after taking a sip. "But what we've never lacked is resolve. Let's redouble our efforts to secure our homeland, protect our people and fight back against this terror, this tyranny, this... this outrageous abomination of humanity and human nature."

Everyone else remained silent.

The President frowned. "For God's sake, please tell me there's nothing else."

"I wish I could," Whisman said. "The North Koreans have taken over all of South Korea. Reports from Seoul are not pleasant – there are mass executions of prominent figures underway, in public places. What's more, they are now amassing troops and boats for an invasion of Japan. Russia is no longer hiding their regional ambitions. Their president has openly declared that they intend to bring all the former Soviet Republics under their jurisdiction, as well as branch out west to raise the Iron Curtain again. The invasion of Ukraine, and the massacre of thousands of civilians in the process, was just the start."

"What about the Chinese?"

"Relatively speaking, they've been quiet. Everyone knows North Korea is no match for China militarily. I don't think the Chinese care too much about what happens to Japan. Too much historical animosity. South Korea taken out by the North only benefits their economy. They have made it clear, though, that Taiwan's days as an autonomous nation are numbered. It's only a matter of time before they invade that island. As far as Russia and China are concerned, we will likely see a peaceful rivalry there, at least for a while. It may turn into a new Cold War of sorts – that remains to be seen."

Tucker covered his face with his hands and rubbed his tired eyes. "I wish I was still in bed. Don't all these bastards know we have much bigger things to worry about? Haven't they seen how the night sky around us is changing? We've clearly been kept in the dark for all of human history. There are immensely powerful aliens out there, and they've been hiding the true nature of the universe from us. And now they're at war with us, or perhaps with each other and somehow we've been caught in the crossfire. Maybe that's how these holes got poked in the camouflage layer around us. And now the holes are growing. Who knows what's really going on? Our whole world could be wiped out in one instant, all of humanity obliterated. And all these... these shitheads can think of is how to acquire a few additional square miles of land and kill as many fellow humans as possible in the process."

"I'm afraid that's not all," Farthing said.

"You're kidding."

"There's another threat looming, this one of a more personal nature."

"Personal for whom?"

"Uh, for you, Sir."

Tucker's felt the dryness edging down his throat again. "What do you mean?"

"Your race," Farthing said. "As you know, there are elements in our society that haven't been able to accept a black president. It's sad that in this day and age we still have so many racists among..."

"Spare me," Tucker said, cutting him short. "I'm well aware of the racism that still permeates this country."

"Well, they've become increasingly vocal about their dissent since the alien attack. They've found a way to... dare I say it, blame it all on you."

"What?"

"Not the attack itself, but the chaos that's ensued in this country since."

"You are not to blame, Mr. President," Whisman interjected. "Given the incredible circumstances, you have done the best job any leader could have done. This has nothing to do with you individually. These people have a beef with black people, or anybody in general that doesn't look and think exactly like them. They've just been looking for an excuse and, as lame and unjustifiable as it is, now they've found one."

"Have you heard of the Aryan Nation, Sir?" Farthing asked.

"Yes, of course," Tucker replied. "White supremacists, neo-Nazis. The largest organization of its kind in this country. They've tripled in size since I took office. Their leader – he's a real nutjob."

"Steven Bane, yes. And he's been rallying all the racist nutjobs across the country into a frenzy, to take up arms and attack whatever civil order we have left, to fight and make life difficult for the government, and even to bring the fight to Washington. In short, they want to overthrow the government and take over. They are converging in cars, trucks and buses with their machine guns and rifles on this city. And I hate to say it, Sir, but they've made no secret of what they'd like to do you if they get their hands on you."

"We've deployed as much of the National Guard as we have left across the important sections of the city," Whisman said. "But I think it's in everyone's interest if you leave DC and go into hiding, Mr. President."

Tucker scoffed. "I will do no such thing."

"It's for your protection, Sir."

"I'm not afraid of those animals. Let them come. This country needs me here in the White House, now more than ever."

"Will you at least go down into the bunker with your family? Not just for this, but also in case of a nuclear attack."

"Yes. But first...."

"The press folks are already waiting," Whisman said. "For your statement on the Boston bombing."

"Do we have a choice?"

"I suppose not."

Chapter 23

Marc had crashed head-on into the crystal, hoping to take it down and gain access to the tunnel it didn't want him to go into. Not only had he failed in his mission, the crystal had now entangled its long, wavy limbs through his arms and legs, rendering him completely immobile.

"Let me... go!" he snorted as he struggled with all his might. "I need to get back to my family."

Alisha tried to put her hand on his shoulder. "Marc, stop fighting it. You need to..."

"Shut it!" he snarled, glowering at her.

She was taken aback by his outburst, the first time he had ever shown her such attitude, and she stepped back in fright.

He screamed with ferocity, the culmination of so much resentment after all those days of torture at the hands of these damned crystals. He could no longer distinguish this little friendly one from all the other, larger ones with the red cores that had beaten him every day for days on end, the ones that were being controlled by the anomalies. They were all the same, they were all responsible for his agony, his helplessness, his powerlessness to do all the things he wanted to do, all the things he absolutely needed to do.

He fought and fought, but to no avail. The crystal stood steady like a firmly planted tree. He couldn't move his arms or legs at all. He felt the strength slowly draining from his body and mind, and the will to keep resisting fading away. The screams gave way to sobs and tears. His head felt heavy, and he let it fall. It tilted forward until it hit one of the alien's nodes. And then it happened.

It was a sudden sensation, like a jolt of lightning that struck his head and flashed through his body. It wasn't painful, just startling. He pulled his head back in fright and stared at the crystal, but it just stood there silently.

"What is it?" Alisha asked.

"I don't know," he said, shaking his head. "I don't know. My mind is so... so muddled."

"It's ok." She came forward and put her hand on his shoulder again. "Pay attention to the crystal."

"I think it's trying to communicate. In the only way it can."

"You can trust it," she replied. "Remember how you touched it before. And how it healed me. It's trying to help us."

"Yeah." Marc sighed and breathed, trying to calm himself down. "I'm sorry, Alisha. I snapped at you. You've been nothing but supportive."

She ran her fingers through his hair. "It's ok."

He closed his eyes and gladly felt the warmth of her skin on his head. "My past is interfering with my present. I'm having a hard time keeping the two separate. My family – my wife, my daughter, they were so real in there." He pointed his head at the tunnel to the right. "But they're gone. I know they're gone. They'll never be back."

"Yes, they're gone. But your memory of them will always be there. Keep them as a memory, but keep them in the past. Don't give everything else up in the present for that past. The present is worth living for, and the past will never turn into the present again."

He sighed. "I'd be such a mess if you weren't here."

"Then listen to me. The crystal – it wants to communicate. With you, not me. So... communicate. Let's figure out why it wants to help and what it wants in return. It's the only chance we have right now of ever getting out of here."

He took another deep breath and lowered his head again toward the node he had touched earlier. It was the only node glowing brightly – the other nodes had dimmed. As soon as his forehead touched the surface of the node, the jolt came again. But this time he forced his head to stay there.

Marc couldn't see or hear anything. All he could do was feel. And the feelings, the heightened emotions, came one by one. He felt things not of his own memory, but of someone else's. And it wasn't just of one individual, but many. Thousands, millions, all with one voice. It was a collective consciousness.

He could sense helplessness, and pain. Not unlike his own, but amplified manifold by the collective. And it felt as if it were his own pain, his own memories. He couldn't visualize any particular memory, but the pain of the memories was there nonetheless. He was fully immersed in it. It was agonizing, all encompassing, and it stubbornly refused to go away. Eventually the helplessness gave way to despair. He felt like crying out loud, desperate enough to tear his heart out of his chest to end it. And if that meant ending his life, then so be it. He couldn't even remember anymore how he had ended up here or how he could possibly get out. It was all just too much to bear.

Then he felt a gentle tug on his head from behind, followed by a slightly stronger one, then followed by an even stronger pull. A sharp jolt of lightning struck through his whole body, and, before he knew it, he could see again. The crystal's glowing node was moving away from his face, and he could sense comforting hands steadying his head. Reality trickled back into his mind, allowing him to recall where he was.

"Easy," Alisha said.

He grunted and turned around to face her.

"What happened?" she asked. "You were shaking uncontrollably, so I pulled you back."

Marc clasped her hand and took deep breaths to try to calm down. He felt dizzy and nauseous.

"You're still shivering," she said.

He coughed. "My God, it was... unbearable. These aliens..." He pointed at the crystal, standing still and quietly observing the two humans. "They've suffered a lot, a hell of a lot."

"How? Why?"

"I don't know. I could only sense the pain, not its cause." He stared at the node his head had been touching. It was still glowing brightly, but now two adjacent nodes, one to the left and the other to the right, had come forward and were also glowing. They positioned themselves at the same height as the center node.

"What's it doing?" Alisha wondered.

"I think it wants to continue, to the next stage. It's figured out how to communicate with me."

"Touch with head *and* hands?"

"Yeah. To reveal more over multiple touchpoints. I think it's using its energy to pass thoughts, to pass feelings and memories."

"Well, that's what thoughts are made of, right? Energy."

"Yeah." Marc shook his head in exhaustion. "But I can't do this."

She placed her arms over his shoulders and looked him in the eye. "Take a break and then try again. You will learn more. You *can* do this, and you will. You have to, for the sake of all of us."

Marc's hands touched the nodes to the left and right first, and then his head touched the node in the middle. He was instantly transported back to the realm of collective pain and suffering. But this time he was better prepared. Instead of letting the feelings overcome his senses, he acknowledged their presence and tried his best to keep a certain level of aloofness to it all. That made the experience a lot less agonizing.

After some time, he wasn't sure how long, the next stage began as he had predicted. The raw emotions gave way to visions. They were blurry and fleeting at first, but gradually gained consistency and accuracy.

Images in front of him grew to create a three-dimensional immersion all around – he was soon experiencing the whole thing as if he was in the middle of it in real life. Virtual reality at its best.

At first, he saw an explosion, not unlike images he had so often seen depicting the Big Bang. Then he saw a rapidly expanding universe, filling up with a uniform haze everywhere and large numbers of clouds forming in the distance. He recalled the surroundings he had witnessed when he had first entered this universe through the gateway – this rendition appeared strikingly similar. The haze was likely due to high energy plasma everywhere, with freely roaming electrons that blocked and scattered the energy from any light source in all directions. The crystal was evidently giving him a history lesson of how its world and its life had come into existence.

The clouds in the distance seemed to be growing and changing shape over time. That is, as much as he could make out through the thick haze. It looked like they were dancing, spreading out thinly like a mesh, crashing into and merging with other clouds, then spiraling back into a single cloud before spreading out again. As this process continued, the thousands of smaller clouds coalesced over time into fewer, larger clouds. Eventually there was only one cloud left, a massive structure stretching across his entire field of vision.

Then came the explosions – one tiny explosion in the left half of the cloud followed by another in the right, followed by more in both halves. Soon explosions were taking place everywhere across the cloud. From Marc's vantage point, the entire cloud was alight with tiny blobs of light, almost like a galaxy of stars.

Except they weren't stars, he surmised. Each blob didn't last long in its initial state – it blew up, and other blobs blew up in the vicinity soon after. But instead of disappearing altogether, the blobs were still there after exploding. They were just a little dimmer than before. Then streaks of light began growing out from each blob that had already exploded. The streaks met with those growing from other blobs and began to connect. Before long, the entire cloud looked like a gigantic mesh of blobs linked to each other.

Life, Marc thought, although it wasn't a form of life even remotely resembling any of the kinds he was used to. A monstrous neural network of sorts, and composed primarily of pure energy coupled with very simple matter. He wondered what kind of energy it was and how it could possibly develop intelligence, but clearly the laws of physics in this universe were quite different from those of his own. Gravity here was comparatively non-existent, as was any heavy matter. Energy was king.

The unified cloud began to change shape, from an amorphous mass to a central, round base with hordes of spikes sticking out. Marc wasn't quite sure what to compare it to – it didn't look like anything he had ever seen before. Perhaps the closest thing was a supernova frozen in time – a super-bright core with millions of streaks of every color imaginable reaching out all in directions into empty space. The conditions that had led to the creation of something so huge and beautiful were likely one of a kind, the odds close to zero. A delicate balance of the physics in this universe.

It didn't take long for Marc to realize why this living entity, as unique as it was, seemed so eerily familiar. This network, perhaps neural in nature with its billions or trillions of blobs and connections, was composed of the same fundamental elements and structure as the crystals. It was just many, many orders of magnitude larger. And, as a result, correspondingly more intelligent and powerful.

The simulation began to zoom in on one section of the network, offering Marc a much closer look at its contents. Soon he was immersed in the cloud. The nearby blobs looked huge now, their cores blazing in brilliant colors with exorbitant amounts of energy. A closer look at the blobs, however, revealed something startling. They were hard at work, generating little things. These things came flying out of the blobs in masses into the expanse of the cloud, and they were soon everywhere he could point his eyes to. These things were none other than crystals, no different than the one crystal accompanying him and Alisha, no different than the one that had telepathically merged its mind with his and was offering him this trip down its very own memory lane. This entire cloud, this energy network of blobs, was their creator.

It was beautiful. Marc was witnessing the creation of life, of an entire species of living creatures. And yet, it was also frightening. This cloud, whatever it was, was powerful, and seemingly the only one of its kind. It was, in a sense, nothing less than the "god" of this universe. It had created lifeforms shaped in its own image but infinitesimally smaller, each with its own set of blobs and connections between them. Fortunately this "god" seemed benign.

The little crystals sped off in all directions into the depths of space, perhaps to explore their universe and to study it. Every now and then, some would return to the cloud to report their findings to the larger blobs from where they had emerged, while others would head out into the dark expanse. This cycle continued for eons.

Time passed. Marc remained still in the simulation, quietly waiting for whatever would happen next. This being seemed content with its existence and its status quo. The population of crystals seemed content too, busily exploring, learning and increasing the knowledge of their creator. All was well.

But then it happened. A brilliant flash appeared from nowhere, far to the left of Marc's view. It seemed to be a tunnel from another dimension, its path clearly visible as it bore its way like a rapidly growing, slithering worm toward the living cloud. Before he had any time to react, he watched the tunnel crash into the heart of the enormous network of blobs, triggering a mighty explosion that caused the entire structure to crumble. Fragments of the blobs and their connections flew off every which way, as did all the tiny crystals.

The tunnel, impervious to the calamity it had caused, continued to twist, turn and slide away into the depths of space until it eventually disappeared from view.

"Holy crap" were the only words that found their way into Marc's thoughts. This tunnel had to be a consar, that one consar that he and his companions had traveled through all those years ago. The consar had drilled through other dimensions the travelers weren't aware of and didn't care about. Unbeknownst to them, that one consar had destroyed everything in another universe. The consar had destroyed an entire being that had taken ages to form, the only lifeform of its kind. And, while some of its creation would likely go on to survive, the creator would forever be gone.

As the dust settled, the surviving crystals continued to spread far and wide into space, left to live without a purpose, unsure what to do without their powerful master. The shattered cloud, meanwhile, began to condense into far smaller individual clouds, thousands of them spread all across Marc's entire field of vision. And within those clouds explosions began taking place. The process of blob creation was once again underway.

Except these blobs were different. Instead of connecting, they began crashing into each other, getting consumed in the process and growing larger. This process of crashing and absorbing continued until only a fraction of blobs remained, each one now easily the size of a small planet. It seemed they had reached an optimal size and energy level, beyond which they could no longer grow.

The simulation zoomed in on one of them and exposed what Marc had already begun to fear. These were no longer blobs - they were the dreaded anomalies. Glaring red, pulsating in rage, they were giant sacks of energy hellbent on revenge. They didn't have the knowledge or the means to recreate the natural, living wonder from whose ashes they had emerged, but they most certainly hadn't forgotten how it had been destroyed. The sole reason for their existence would now be to make those responsible for that fateful tunnel appearance pay for the havoc they had wreaked. The benignity of the original lifeform had been replaced by the cruelty of its descendants.

The anomalies began to gather and, it seemed, to communicate. How they were communicating was a mystery, but the fact that they were left little room for doubt. They were plotting and planning, and the actions soon followed. In coordination, they began moving about, evidently trying to find the trajectory of the consar. But it was long gone, its path no more visible to Marc's eyes or whatever senses these beings had. They seemed to remember the approximate location where it had crashed with their parent lifeform, but that was as far as they could get with their efforts. As powerful as they were, these anomalies evidently didn't have the skills or the refinement to work on intricate tasks.

Frustrated, they amassed back at their original meeting point before spreading out again across space. As they did this time, each anomaly grew arms, hundreds of them. The arms swerved about the body, and Marc had to squint his eyes to see what they were doing. It became clearer when the simulation zoomed in on a single anomaly to reveal the details. The arms were collecting crystals, wherever they could find them. They were literally sucking up the little creatures like giant vacuum cleaners and storing them in their bodies. Eventually the anomalies returned to the meeting point, where they spit out the little crystals back into the space between them and surrounded them from all sides.

The captured crystals seemed frightened, unsure what kind of fate lay in store for them. They huddled together and tried to comfort each other, while those monstrous balls of fire angrily stared them down no matter which way they looked. These beings were their new masters, and they wouldn't be nearly as benevolent as their earlier master had been.

Indeed, the anomalies pushed and prodded the crystals about, forcing them to move to the consar crash point. Any crystal that disobeyed or tried to break free was punished. More specifically, it was zapped to nothingness by a blazing ray emanating from one of the anomalies. And every time a crystal was obliterated, the others grew more terrified and succumbed all the more to the demands of their overbearing overlords.

At the crash point, the crystals were forced to work, to study and analyze, to find the consar trajectory. They worked feverishly in fear of deadly punishment, and, as soon became evident, their technical knowledge, finesse and speed of operation were way higher than those of the anomalies. They eventually found a way to recreate the consar's path, presumably by identifying and revealing its bulk energy signatures, Marc guessed. They raced back and forth at an amazingly fast pace, and soon had a hollow outline of the entire trajectory completed – from the depths of space where it had emerged, through the crash point and all the way beyond to its eventual disappearance.

Next, the crystals began analyzing the interior of the consar. Marc realized what they were after – the source and destination universe of the consar, as well as the bulk energy signatures of those who had traveled through it. Finally, they reported their findings back to the anomalies.

The anomalies then demanded something new of the crystals. For whatever reason, even with the death threat looming over them, the crystals refused to comply. The anomalies grabbed a whole bunch of them and obliterated them, but the rest of them, cowering in fear, still refused to budge. Marc wasn't sure what was so onerous about this latest order that the crystals were willing to sacrifice their lives for it, but he already had a hunch.

The anomalies grabbed the rest of the crystals, sucked them back into their bodies, and after some time spit them out again. Only this time each crystal came out larger, as if several of them had been merged into one, and in its midst was a bright red core.

And so it begins, Marc thought, the conversion of these intelligent beings to externally controlled, mindless machines. The larger crystals now began working in unison and without any resistance to the demands of their masters. Using the information they had obtained from analyzing the consar, they swirled around in a wide circle to build a gateway entrance, a gigantic one large enough to allow an entire anomaly to pass through.

A gateway to my universe, Marc thought. His hunch had been right. The little crystals had refused to build one, probably because they were smart enough to know the perils of interfering with other universes in dimensions not of their own. They had seen the evidence of it firsthand with the destruction of their creator, and they were not about to do the same to the beings of the universe that had just done this to them. They were not vengeful.

The anomalies, however, were restricted by no such ethics. Vengeance was obviously their highest priority. Somehow all the negative sentiments of the original creator, that majestic living being, had manifested themselves in these brutish, powerful anomalies, while the positive ones had found their way into the more advanced but far smaller, far meeker crystals.

Once the gateway was complete, the crystals turned it on. Soon after, the anomalies began passing into it, one by one. They accelerated and disappeared from view into another dimension.

Into my universe, Marc thought. Ready to wreak all the havoc and destruction they ended up causing.

At this point, the simulation zoomed out to reveal a larger section of this strange universe, only to zoom in on another section far away from the gateway and the anomalies. Marc began making out little objects floating in space as the image around him sharpened. And, as it zoomed in further, he noticed they were the crystals, the little ones without the red cores. There were lots of them, wandering aimlessly through empty space. Evidently, not all of them had been converted to mindless robots. Perhaps all hope for these creatures was not lost.

And then, just like that, the larger-than-life simulation around him faded away.

Chapter 24

It was the fifth probe. The fifth probe was finally the one that didn't blow up. Mendoken Commander Maginder and his crew had already opened the gateway four times prior to launch a probe, only to see it blow up into tiny bits every time. The gateway had never opened up into the other universe as it was supposed to. Instead, it had led the probe to an unpassable wall, leaving no room for it to reassemble itself after initiating the subatomic transformation process. The probe had completely disintegrated, its molecules fully disbursed into nothingness.

But this time, Maginder had followed the new instructions provided by the Imgoerin. The probe was to enter the gateway but to not initiate the subatomic transformation. Instead, it was to hold its position after reaching a fair distance inside and simply wait.

"The trajectory is holding, Commander," Hansa announced as she carefully watched the screen readouts on her station, on the control deck of the Kril-4 ship. "But it has stopped growing."

"The gateway remains open and stable," Sautal added as he sifted through the screens on his own neighboring station.

Maginder floated between his two prized officers. "And the probe?" he asked.

"It has stopped moving near the edge of the trajectory, as instructed," Hansa replied. "It remains intact – no transformation was initiated."

Maginder hummed in acknowledgment. "Then all we can do is wait." With that, he floated away and descended to the lower level of the control deck, where he approached another group of crewmembers intensely scrutinizing an array of screens.

One of them, an officer by the name of Paxia, addressed him as he came closer. "Commander, our Kril-7 vessel has arrived in front of the planet Earth. It is still cloaked from view by the planet's inhabitants. The captain is awaiting your instructions on whether to engage them."

"What is the status on the surface?" Maginder asked.

"The humans appear to be increasingly engaged in hostilities with each other," Paxia replied. "With the military power of the once dominant nation destroyed by the anomaly attack, other nations are taking advantage of the situation to expand their spheres of influence and to settle their grievances with that single nation."

"The United States of America."

"Yes."

Paxia then swept her fingers along a few of the screens in front of her. They began displaying disturbing videos of current events on Earth, including battle scenes, nuclear explosions, and scores of dead and wounded people littering the streets of destroyed cities.

Maginder watched the scenes with disappointment, but as always maintained his robotic composure. "They are moving backwards in the advancement of their society," he remarked. "With the erosion of the United States of America's dominance, the balance of power that kept the planet in check for the past 75 Earth years has tipped beyond the ability to self-recover. The humans are now headed for another global war."

"Should we intervene, Commander?" Paxia asked.

Maginder eyed the events more closely and remained quiet for a while. "No," he finally said.

"This is no longer about our policy of non-interference," Paxia said. "The planet has been directly affected by events beyond the silupsal filter, which is no longer even functioning. They are now in trouble and need help."

"Help they need, yes. But we are not in a position to offer them any right now that they will actually be able to benefit from."

"A single Kril-7 vessel has the capability to drop fighter ships across the entire planet's surface, and to end every military conflict between warring human nations," Paxia replied. "We can deploy ground forces as well, with no risk of harm to any Mendoken. No human weaponry poses a threat to our body shielding."

"This is not about military superiority," Maginder hummed. "It is about how we will be perceived if we intervene. We will be seen as an invading force, an occupying power. Neither side of each conflict will trust us and will suspect we are in cahoots with the other side. Worse yet, they may think we have our own selfish goals to subdue all humans and take over the planet. They have no reason to think we are any different from the anomaly that destroyed much of their world. They may even believe we are the ones who sent the anomaly in the first place.

"Given all they have recently endured, as well as the humbling realizations about their place in the universe with the first ever alien attack on them and the collapsing silupsal filter, they will be on their guard against anything alien. If we attempt to help them right now, they will rise up in arms against us. It will backfire on both us and them."

"Your logic is sound, Commander," Paxia said. "But it is hard to watch them slaughter themselves and do nothing about it, especially when we can easily stop it."

"Agreed, but we can only intervene if we are accompanied by someone both we and the humans will trust. It has to be one of their own, yet someone who can speak for us. Unfortunately there is only one such individual, and not only do we have no knowledge of his time of return, we have no knowledge of his fate at all."

*   *   *

The Mendoken Imgoerin stood still and stared at the screen in front of him, pondering the contents of the latest bosian transmission from his commander at the edge of the Mendo-Biesel star system, at the site of the newly constructed gateway to the other universe.

The door to his office opened, and Autamrin, the old leader of the Aftaran Dominion, walked in. His owl-like eyes were droopy and tired, a clear sign of worry and lack of sleep. "Please have news," he said quietly.

The Imgoerin floated toward him. "Commander Maginder has decided not to engage the inhabitants of the planet Earth. He says the timing is wrong, and that we will be seen as invaders rather than helpers. He suggests we wait until the Earth human Marc Zemin returns."

"You know that's not what I'm asking about. I want to know when we'll get my son back."

"Our best scientists are working on it."

"You keep saying that."

"It is not an easy problem to solve."

"So where's all that Mendoken prowess now? The days that have passed – I've lost count."

The Imgoerin wasn't offended. Mendoken rarely were, about anything. "You are under duress, Autamrin. Why not seek solace in your religion? That is what your people always do."

The Aftaran leader let his large, round eyes droop further. "My religion... it has been awfully, painfully silent through all of this."

"Your scriptures – did they not warn that this could happen?"

"Warn, yes. But that's where it ends. No predictions, no prophecies, no solutions. A first in our entire history of existence. I always used to think our scriptures offered us a complete way of life, a code by which to live and to deal with all kinds of situations. Now... I'm not so sure anymore."

"What about your High Clerics?"

"They are awfully silent too. They have no answers, no unique interpretations of the scriptures that could give us anything to cling onto.

My people... we are at a loss, a dead end. The only hope we have left now... is you. You with all your innovations, devices, systems, all your logical, methodical analyses and scientific reasoning. Above all, your advanced technology. You Mendoken must find a way where we Aftarans have failed. I need to believe that. I need to have faith in that. Otherwise..."

The Imgoerin was silent for a moment. "Come with me," he finally said, and with that he floated through the open door and out of his office.

The Aftaran leader, startled at first, soon hurried after him. "Where... where are we going?"

"To help get you some answers. I was about to go there anyway, as I hear some progress has been made."

"Seriously? Couldn't you just have started the conversation with that?"

They entered an elevator with transparent walls, offering clear views of the outside. From their vantage point, they had a spectacular view of Lind's urban skyline. The giant Mendo-Zueger sun was about to set behind the endless rows of tall, black towers that covered almost the entirety of the planet's flatlands. The normally blue sky was awash with a range of red and orange colors. It was a beautiful sight.

The Imgoerin hummed an order to the elevator's controls. Then, without warning, the elevator closed its doors and shot down at high speed toward the ground floor. The anti-gravity stabilizers, a standard inclusion in all forms of transport used by the Mendoken, worked flawlessly. Air pressure was also kept at a constant level, regardless of altitude. To the occupants, it simply felt like they were standing still.

The elevator did not stop as it reached ground level, nor did it slow down. Instead, it sped on into the depths of the planet's crust. The transparent walls turned dark, now surrounded by thick rock. The elevator was traveling through a long shaft.

"What is this?" Autamrin asked, dumbfounded.

"You are about to see what no non-Mendoken has ever seen before," the Imgoerin replied. "It is highly confidential, for security reasons."

The Aftaran leader's beak widened to manage a smile. "I'm honored."

"This is not about honor, but necessity. But I do trust you more than any leader of any other civilization. We have a good..."

"Chemistry?"

"Working relationship."

The smile widened. "Thank you, Franzek. I've always considered you a good friend."

The shaft eventually gave way, to a view that caused Autamrin's smiling beak to open wider in astonishment.

"We Mendoken have always believed in the concept of redundancy," the Imgoerin said as he watched Autamrin utter a short prayer, presumably to ensure he wasn't dreaming. "To secure the survival of our species and all our knowledge during even the harshest of adversity. It has never paid off more than in recent days, with the destruction of so much of our infrastructure by the anomalies. In our home star system alone, the moon Ailen, our most advanced hub of scientific research and technology in the Republic, was reduced to ruins. Fortunately we duplicated much of its labs and research centers here, deep underground in the crust of our home planet."

"Some duplication," Autamrin whispered, visibly struck by the grandeur of what he was witnessing.

It was indeed a sight for sore eyes. And as far as such eyes could see, much of the planet's crust was hollowed out to make way for an entire city. There were many levels, with evenly spaced walls made out of planetary rock holding them up. Each level had rows and rows of massive buildings. There were buildings carved right into the walls too – no space was left unused. Bright lights littered the walls and the floors of each level, providing the necessary luminosity for visibility in what would otherwise have been pitch dark surroundings.

As with any other Mendoken city, thousands of vehicles were flying every which way. They followed no distinguishable traffic pattern, yet no vehicle crashed into any other. There was an unwritten order about everything, a wholesome neatness that just couldn't be pinpointed to any one source or cause. It was an underground city, though perhaps it was as big as a country back on Earth, and perhaps it spanned around the entire globe just as its more visible, more publicly known sister city of black towers did on the surface of the planet. And it was all functioning with a level of perfection and precision that only the Mendoken could create and sustain.

The elevator, now free of the confines of the shaft, began moving like an independent vehicle among all the other vehicles. Fully equipped with auto-pilot functionality, it needed no manual assistance as it maneuvered itself through heavy traffic and descended multiple levels toward its destination.

And what a destination it was. It came into view from miles away. A gigantic sphere-shaped structure, so big that many of the levels had to come to a circular stop around it to give it the room it needed.

"What is that?" Autamrin asked.

"A replicator," the Imgoerin replied.

"Of what?"

"Anything we want to replicate."

"That really clarifies things."

"It will become clearer once we are inside."

As the elevator-turned-vehicle approached the colossal structure, a gate opened up in its outer wall. The vehicle glided right in and continued to float down a passage or, to be more precise, a long platform. To the left and right were rows and rows of control stations, similar in formation and appearance to those on a Mendoken Euma or Kril interstellar ship. There were numerous Mendoken scientists and engineers manning the stations.

The vehicle stopped in front of one station and opened its door, allowing one of the Mendoken scientists to float onboard. Then it shut the door and kept on moving down the passage.

"This is Leita Geissen 65313459," the Imgoerin said. "She is the lead scientist working on the current replication."

"Pleased to meet you," Autamrin said.

Leita bowed slightly but remained silent.

After a while the control decks ended, after which there was nothing but darkness on all sides. The only light came from regularly spaced lamps along the passage floor.

"Not to worry," the Imgoerin said, sensing Autamrin's slight apprehension. "We are surrounded by a thick, impenetrable wall. You cannot see it, but it is there."

"Good to know."

"We use replicators to perform theoretical scientific experiments, ones that cannot be conducted using actual physical things. These experiments help us better understand the nature of our universe, how it came into existence and how things might have been different if the set of conditions were different."

"You mean by tweaking the laws of physics? Changing the values of constants and variables in formulas?"

"For example. We could determine how different a universe the Big Bang might have led to if gravity was a stronger force."

"Why can't you just run a simulation on a computer? On one of your three dimensional screens?"

Leita spoke for the first time. "This is not a virtual rendition. We recreate the actual physical conditions of a scenario, and then let it play itself out in a controlled environment. We have found this approach leads to much more accurate results."

Autamrin's eyes widened in surprise. "So you can recreate an actual Big Bang?"

"Not of the same magnitude, naturally, or we would all be dead," the Imgoerin said. "But significantly scaled down in size and energy level, yes."

The vehicle kept gliding, as if it knew exactly where it was going. Eventually it came to a stop. They were at the very end of the passage, and it was completely dark on all sides.

"I can't see anything," Autamrin said.

"The wall is covered at the moment," Leita said. "That will change shortly."

"What are we going to see?" the Aftaran leader asked.

"We have taken all the data uncovered from the neutrino oscillations at the anomaly attack site, where the Selcher-44328 space station disappeared," Leita replied. "We have deciphered as much of it as we could. We extrapolated all the information about how to adapt matter in our brane to the other brane where the anomalies come from, to determine the dimensions that universe exists in and what its laws of physics are. We have built an entire replication to recreate such a universe. Highly compressed, of course, to fit inside the replicator. We also took the information retrieved about the energy composition of the anomalies and fed that into the replication."

"I have not seen the results myself yet," the Imgoerin added. "I just received word that the work was done when you arrived in my office."

"How can we see it if it's in different dimensions from ours?" Autamrin asked, puzzled.

"It is a rendition of those dimensions," Leita replied. "We have a translation algorithm that takes the characteristics of those dimensions and visually maps them to ours. We obtained the idea from the Volonan Virtual Translation Grid."

"Granted the Volona use their Grid differently than what we are doing," the Imgoerin said. "They map virtual experiences to real life actions. But the principle of translation still applies."

"Interesting. And we'll be safe inside this elevator?"

"The exterior of the vehicle is getting reinforced as speak," Leita said. "It will be able to handle impacts well beyond the amount of energy generated in the replication."

"In that case, I can't wait."

Chapter 25

"Venture not into the depths of others, never awaken forces you do not understand, against which you have no power, for naught shall save you from their terrible wrath."

"What are you babbling about?" Alisha asked.

She was holding Marc as he uttered these words, slowly opening his eyes after letting go of the crystal. He was in a daze, his mind filled with a whirlwind of images and memories, as if he had just lived firsthand through the entire lifespan of a universe that wasn't his own.

"The Aftaran prophecy," he said slowly, sighing. "It was right. We should not have meddled with consars."

"What did you see?"

He tried to steady himself and regain his balance, but he felt dizzy and had to hold onto Alisha. "We... destroyed an entire lifeform with that consar. A huge living cloud, one that took eons to form and evolve. And it created these..." He pointed at the crystal in front of them, standing quietly and staring at them. "Millions of them."

"So all this is their... revenge?"

Marc shook his head. "Not theirs. Their masters."

"The anomalies?"

"Yes. They were created after the giant lifeform was destroyed. And they took these creatures hostage and made them their slaves, killing many of them just to make a point. Forced them to work for them, made them figure out how to get to our universe and find us. But these crystals, they just want to be left alone. They didn't, they still don't want to help the anomalies. That's why the anomalies began controlling them with those red cores."

"Then why is this crystal helping us? Why does it care?"

"I don't know. My guess is it thinks we can help it and its fellow beings. Apparently it's not the only one left without a red core. There are others, out there in space."

"They help us get out of here, and in turn we help free them from their masters. That's why it wants you to finish this series of punishments so eagerly."

"Yeah, but why it thinks we can help them is a mystery. At least we've figured out a way to communicate, though. It seems to be able to share its thoughts with me by just touching my head. That's something, I guess. But we're still completely powerless in this universe, against those anomalies."

She put her arm around him. "We may think we're powerless, but these crystals obviously know a lot more about this universe than we do. And, with that knowledge, they've still put their trust in us. In you, specifically. So if we're to have any hope of ever getting out of here and back home, I suggest we don't let them down."

He let his head rest on her arm. "Yeah. I just wish I knew how. I can't even get us out of these dratted punishments."

"And yet you got us out of the last one."

"Only to lead us to another. And now we're stuck."

"I have an idea. I was thinking about it while you were in the crystal's simulation."

Marc lifted his eyes to look into hers. "You?"

"Yes. Surprised?"

"No, I, uh, didn't mean to suggest that you..."

"Don't have the brains? For God's sake, Marc."

"No, no, to the contrary. So far, every piece of advice you've given me has been spot on. Without your support – emotional, mental, physical, all of it – I would already be dead several times over. I..."

"It's ok. I've had to deal with a great many chauvinists in my life, and you're definitely not one of them. Trust me."

"Ok, uh, good to know."

She looked him in the eyes. "You are, in fact, the kindest, smartest, most selfless and most courageous man I have ever met."

He felt a tingle of warmth in his chest. It spread quickly throughout his body. "And you," he began, "you..."

But the words gave way to actions. Gone was all the doubt, all the fear of rejection or failure. In an instant, his mind dropped its guard and took a backseat to his heart. Without hesitation, he simply touched her chin and lifted her face, and kissed her on the lips. She was caught by surprise at first, but she did not resist. She gave in completely, closing her eyes and resting her hands on his arms. And she didn't let go.

Nor did he. It was a sweet kiss. It was warm and soft, and it opened up sensations in his head and across his body that he hadn't felt in years. He was kissing an unbelievably gorgeous woman, inside and out, a unique blend of unmatched physical beauty and an insightful, supportive personality. With all the horrible things that had happened to him of late, he was still the luckiest person alive. He didn't want it to end.

But end it had to, for reality was all around them and it desperately needed their attention. The crystal, quietly standing and waiting all this time, was starting to lose patience. It began swaying its arms about and flashing its nodes in different colors. Neither of them noticed it at first – they were too busily engaged in their moist embrace. It took a hard slap on both of their behinds by one of the its swaying arms for them to be startled enough into letting go of each other and turning to face the crystal.

"What the...!" Marc began, feeling the sharp tinge of pain on his butt.

"I, uh... it wants you to get back to the task," Alisha said, rubbing her own backside and trying to regain her composure.

"Yes, ok. You were saying. You had an idea."

"Did I ever tell you why I left home?"

"Huh?"

"Why I left my home in the slums, in Mumbai," she said.

"No, you just told me about the hard life you had growing up."

"Or how I made it from that life to my Bollywood career? You think it was easy?"

"Of course not. You must have worked incredibly hard and fought all kinds of obstacles. So... you just want me to try harder to overcome my fears?"

She shook her head. "There's a lot more to it than just trying. I left home because..." Then she stopped.

"What is it?" Marc asked.

"It's just... it's hard to talk about, even just to remember. My stepfather..."

"What about him?"

She choked. "He used to abuse me."

"What?! Your stepdad?"

"Yes. He did it for years."

"Like... hit you?"

"Worse. Much worse. When I had barely reached puberty."

"Oh, my God."

"First he did it in secret, when nobody else was around. He threatened to throw me out if I told anyone. So I didn't. Eventually my mother found out anyway – she caught him in the act once. She tried to stop him, but he beat her. So badly that she suffered multiple injuries and almost bled to death. He threatened to hurt her even worse next time, and to make me suffer even more if she ever tried to stop him again."

"I am so sorry. What kind of a man would do something like that?" He placed his hands on her face and tried to wipe away the single tear trickling down her cheek. "I suppose it's silly to ask if she or you could have gone to the police, or asked someone else for help."

"In the slums? Are you kidding? It's every man for himself. And every woman and girl for whoever is the man in the family. There was nobody to turn to, nowhere to go to seek refuge." Sobbing, she let her head drop onto Marc's chest.

He tried his best to comfort her, but he thought it best to say nothing.

After a while, she lifted her head again. "Anyway, the reason I'm telling you this is that... the only way I was able to live through that pain, that humiliation, that ultimate betrayal, was by getting back at him in the only way I could."

"Which was?"

"To not give him the satisfaction that he so sought by exerting control over me. He wanted to make me suffer, to try to resist him and to squeal in pain because I was powerless against him. It was that power over me that excited him more than the sexual desire itself."

"What a bastard."

"So I pretended like I was enjoying it, every time he ravaged me. It took me a while to gain the courage and apathy to put on such an act, but believe it or not it helped. It took him by surprise at first, but gradually he came to me less often once he realized he wasn't really raping me 'against my will' anymore."

Marc shook his head in disgust. "This is so sick. Did he stop altogether?"

"No, not completely. But the frequency went down with time. Once I was older, I ran away from home. And I never went back."

"Did he try to find you?"

"He tried, but I kept my traces hidden. Only years later, after I made it as an actress was he able to track me down. But I refused to ever see him. I took my mother and had her move in with me. I finally freed her from his clenches and made sure he could never bother or harm her again."

"You didn't...?"

"What, kill him? No, of course not. I just had some thugs I paid threaten him repeatedly, until he got the message loud and clear. He never came back after that. That's how you get things done in India."

"And that's how you found your calling to acting?"

She nodded. "That's how I knew I was good at it. And that's how I made it to where I finally got. I acted my way through every obstacle that

life threw my way. My stepfather wasn't the only horrible man in my life.
I met many along the way. In fact, I only met horrible men, every one of
them trying to use me for his own ends. I paid the price repeatedly in the
beginning, but over time I learned how to use them for my own benefit
instead to get ahead."

"Wait, you didn't...?"

"Prostitute myself?" She looked at him incredulously. "What are you
thinking?"

"No, no, I mean, uh..."

"Unbelievable."

"I'm sorry, I really didn't mean that."

"I did learn how to use my looks to charm people into helping me out,
that much is true. I had to learn it the hard way, in order to survive."

"And survive you did."

She shrugged. "It wasn't easy."

"I'm sure. You... never had a real father figure in your life."

"I never had a real man at all in my life. One abusive, selfish son-of-a-
bitch after another. Until..." She looked up at him, and her eyes
moistened once more. "You may be one hell of a crazy guy, and you've
gotten me into an incredible mess. But one thing you are not is selfish.
You have looked out for me like nobody else ever has. I wasn't joking
when I said I feel safe around you."

"You're not just trying to charm me to get something from me, are
you?"

Smiling, she placed her hand on his chest. "I think your heart knows
the answer to that way better than that cautious mind of yours does."

Then she put her arms around him and kissed him again.

Marc stared past the crystal at the tunnel entrance behind that it was still
pointing to. He felt energized, reinvigorated, and ready to take on the
challenge. He knew it wouldn't be easy, but he had overcome seemingly
impossible hurdles in the last punishment. He could do so again this

time if he tried hard enough, and now he was armed with both the motivation after learning of the crystals' suffering and an idea from Alisha on how to do it. His recent romantic breakthrough had only compounded this sudden rise in self-confidence.

Simply put, he would try to act. His phobias, as he knew, were purely psychological, but somehow they had been extracted from his mind and were manifesting themselves as physical reality in those tunnels. The more afraid he was of those physical manifestations, the more fear he showed, the more those manifestations gained strength and vigor to frighten him. It was a vicious cycle. Instead, if he showed that he just didn't care and rather enjoyed their presence, then the manifestations would shrink and wither away.

At least, that was Alisha's reasoning, and to him it made sense. But, as he soon found out, acting in general, let alone in front of things that made him want to get away at the speed of light, wasn't nearly as easy as it sounded in theory.

When he treaded back into the tunnel to the left, he didn't get much further than he had the first time around. As soon as the giant spider appeared, he turned and raced back into the opening where Alisha and the crystal were waiting. A collection of tubes appeared again, carrying more of the pink paste.

The attempts continued like this, for what felt like days. Marc and Alisha were continuously nourished by the tubes of paste, and sleep they had to make do with on the floors of the tunnel. It was anything but pleasant, but there was no other option available.

"I can't do this," he said one day, panting after yet another attempt. "It gets even bigger and uglier every time."

"Yes, you can," she replied. "Remember what I keep telling you – put a smile on your face. Look as carefree as possible. The less you seem to care, the less effect the spider will have on you. It will become more fearful of you than you of it. Trust me."

"How do you know?"

"This punishment, or test rather, is different than the last one. I've been thinking about it, and I think I've figured it out now. That one was about your mind winning over your body. As the crystals struck at you, your mind had to find a way to overcome the intense pain, to gain enough strength and courage to strike back. This one seems to be about your body winning over your mind. Your mind is terrified of your phobia, but your body has to find a way to trudge through and come out strong."

He slurped up the tasteless paste from a couple of the tubes, closed his eyes to gather his thoughts and wits, and reentered the tunnel to the left. What Alisha had just said made complete sense, and it added to his vigor to overcome his fear.

This time, he finally held out longer. He tried to face the spider, to stand in front of it. It was taken aback at first, but then kept on trying to attack. In the end, he stuck to his default behavior – he turned and ran back, chased by the monster until he reached the clearing where Alisha and the crystal were waiting.

But this time he didn't run back into her arms. This time, he was determined to keep trying until he succeeded. Catching his breath, he turned and entered the tunnel again.

He got further this time. He even took a few strides forward as the spider lashed its hairy legs out at him. He tried to smile and couldn't, but at least he looked less fearful. It worked. The spider stopped dead in its tracks and stepped back as he edged forward. It seemed to shrink a little. It took everything in him to keep his wits together, to resist the overwhelming urge to turn and run again.

He took another step forward, and another. The spider shrank more. It stopped lashing its legs about and lowered its eyes. Then it began retreating, slowly at first, but as he gained confidence and moved toward it, it began hurrying away. Eventually it sped off into the distance, withering to the size of an actual spider before it finally disappeared in the depths of the tunnel.

Marc felt an overwhelming sense of triumph. He strode forward proudly through the rest of the tunnel. When he reached the end, he saw Alisha and the crystal already waiting there. She was smiling, and the crystal was beaming.

"Wait, how did you...?" he asked, dumbfounded.

She hugged him. "Get here? Don't forget – I can't see the tunnels. For me, it's all open space. We were by your side the whole time, following you step by step on the other side of the tunnel wall."

"Huh. Wow."

"You did it. Finally."

"Thanks to you," he replied.

A new collection of tubes appeared, only this time there were more of them and with an assortment of colors of paste. He tried a blue one – it tasted much better and sweeter than the standard pink one. He handed another blue one to Alisha, who gulped it down eagerly.

The reward for winning, he thought. Alisha had been right again – evidently this whole thing was as much as a test as it was a punishment. The big question, though, still remained – why?

Chapter 26

The second bomb exploded exactly a week after the first. Another very heavy two-stage thermonuclear device, again planted on a boat in a harbor, again in the middle of the night. But a far better known harbor of a far better known city, in a country already reeling from the devastation of the first explosion 200 miles to the northeast.

This city had had its share of terror attacks. Given its significance in the psyche of American society and the world at large, mostly for reasons it had earned as the largest and most famous city in the United States, it had always been a target of terrorists trying to bring the world's greatest power to its knees. This attack, however, dwarfed all others past on this city by many orders of magnitude.

Lower Manhattan was torn asunder, its towering skyscrapers shattered to clouds of dust and debris. The mighty Wall Street, the pinnacle of Western capitalism, was no more. The new One World Trade Center, the tallest building in the Western Hemisphere, built as a shining example of resilience against those who had once attacked the very tenets of American identity on Sept 11, 2001, had in part crumbled to the ground and in part spread as ash into the air.

The mushroom cloud, glowing brilliantly in the backdrop of a dark sky, spread swiftly across all five boroughs of this imposing metropolis, wreaking unfathomable mayhem and destruction on every block it touched. Millions of people poured into the streets in panic, trying to escape the approaching wave of death. But the vast majority didn't make it very far. Those closer to the waterfront were blown apart instantly by the shockwave, while those further uptown fell victim to the thermal radiation as it literally burned their bodies to charred, disfigured carcasses.

President Tucker was woken unceremoniously with a loud phone ring, just like the last time. Only this time he was in a bunker, deep below the East Wing of the White House. With his wife and two children, he had been camped here for days in a single makeshift bedroom.

"What?" he croaked into the mouthpiece.

"Sorry to wake you, Sir," said a voice. "It's happened again. New York City."

He got up and stepped hurriedly to the emergency operations center next door, a small, cozy room with an oval conference table. Margaret Whisman, his Chief of Staff, was already there. The TV was on, with CNN reporting live from New Jersey. The scene was absolute chaos. Thousands were on foot, scrambling to escape the city over the bridges and through the tunnels. Some were crushed in the stampedes, others pushed over the bridges to the depths of the Hudson River. The mighty skyline of Manhattan was in ruins, ablaze in a wash of red, orange and yellow. It was dwarfed only by the white cloud above, still spreading outward in all directions as fast as the laws of physics would allow.

Tucker cringed in horror. "So much for all the extra measures we took. These terrorists still did it without detection."

"There's only so much we could have done with our surveillance systems still mostly down and our inter-bureau communication in disarray," Whisman said. "They were able to operate freely without being detected. They're taking full advantage of our current plight."

"Everyone is."

"Short of rounding up and detaining all foreigners from certain parts of the world..."

"Current manpower issues aside, collective punishment of millions of innocents? Nothing justifies that, not even this." The President nodded at the TV screen. "We're better than that, and always will be."

"Millions are dying."

"We have to find ways to bring these terrorists down, the right way and the smart way. But if we start rounding up all Middle Easterners, the terrorists will simply go into hiding and continue to evade us. All we'll end up doing is stirring up a lot of additional, unnecessary hysteria, not to mention betraying the very fundamentals of our Constitution and all we stand for as a nation."

"So what is the right way and smart way?"

"We work around the clock to bring our surveillance systems back online and to get the FBI, CIA, NSA and all the other agencies to start sharing information again among themselves and with the military. Leverage the contacts we have in local ethnic communities to spot and report unusual, suspicious activities by people they know or are aware of. This war can only be won with the cooperation of those communities, not by alienating them and pushing them to the fringe. The vast majority of those people are innocent, the vast majority hate the terrorists more than we do. Many of them have come from countries ravaged by those same terror groups."

Abu Hashem, the leader of ISIS, could be seen on CNN now, gloating about the latest attack on the embattled United States. "Let the whole world take notice, believers and unbelievers alike," he said softly, his eyes glowing with triumph and the satisfaction of revenge. "Let them see the great devil of this Earth fall to its knees and perish. None can stand up to the power of the Almighty, none can turn away from the one true path to salvation, none can subdue others and rule them forever with tyranny and godlessness. Their time has come. With God's help, we shall level their cities to the ground, one by one, from north to south, east to west. The greatest sinners on Earth shall have no place to hide from God's wrath. The great devil of this Earth shall be no more."

The image faded and returned to the scenes of chaos in New York City. Things were looking even worse, with more fallen buildings and overcrowding on the bridges out of Manhattan.

"If what he says is true, then DC will likely be next," Tucker said.

"Evacuate the city?"

"Immediately."

"That includes you too, and your family. The time for heroics is over."

"I know."

Two green-and-white Sikorsky SH-3 helicopters lifted from the White House lawn in the dusk hours of the day following the horrific nuclear attack on New York City. In one sat a very grim-faced President Tucker, huddled with his wife and children. A Secret Service agent was also on board. In the other were the White House Chief of Staff Margaret Whisman, her husband, one of the Deputy Chiefs of Staff and another agent. Per protocol, the Vice President and his family were leaving the city by other means not disclosed, as were the Speaker of the House, all the members of both Houses of Congress and the Supreme Court. All government agency headquarters in the city were shut down and their staff ordered to evacuate.

With his protective arms around his 11 year old daughter and 7 year old son, the President stared out the window as the chopper rose into the sky, its rotors whirring loudly as it began its course westwards toward the Mount Weather Emergency Operations Center in Virginia. From there, the President and his family would take an as-yet undisclosed form of transportation to an as-yet undisclosed secure hideout.

All the bridges over the Potomac River were already jammed with traffic. Highways 395 and 66 looked like parking lots, at least westwards out of the city. The other side was mostly bare, occupied only by remnants of the National Guard rolling in to set up posts and lay some order to the evacuation process. Police and fire brigade lights could be seen flashing all over the city, particularly at major intersections and in front of important buildings.

Good call, Tucker thought. His administration had done the right thing in ordering the city to evacuate. And, from what he could see, people were wasting no time in heeding it and making their way out.

His gaze shifted back to his kids. His son had fallen asleep again, but his daughter was wide eyed and staring back at him. Her expression said it all, her face aghast, filled with fear and uncertainty. The same kid who looked up to him as the one who always had the right answer, as the one who always knew what to do no matter how tough the obstacle or circumstance, as the one who always knew just what to say to make her feel better, as the one who had risen from humble beginnings to become the most powerful person in the most powerful nation on this planet... the same kid was now looking at a man on whose watch that same nation had lost all its might, on whose watch that nation was now being pounded and torn apart from all sides. And now it could very well cost her and the rest of the family their lives, and the lives of everyone she knew and had ever known.

For the first time in his life, Tucker felt truly helpless. For the first time in his life, he had no answer for his daughter, no words of reassurance or comfort. In this very trying time for her, in this incredibly impressionable age where every single thing she was witnessing would place a permanent scar in her mind and affect her personality for life, there was absolutely nothing he could offer that would make her feel better. He had not only failed as president and leader of the country, he had failed as a father. He had failed to adequately take care of his own children. And it took all the might left in his own mind to not break down, to not burst into tears and scream out in agony.

He looked out the window again, with a sense of shame and defeat. The choppers had already crossed the Potomac and were now flying over the city of Arlington. To the left, he could see the National Cemetery and the ruins of what had once been the massive Pentagon. The trademark of America's military power had been obliterated in the alien attack, as had parts of the US Capitol Building and parts of the National Mall. Miraculously, the White House had evaded any major damage.

How the tables have turned, he thought. All the enemies this great country had created over past decades, all the societies it had attempted to subdue and control with its sheer economic and military might, all the communities it had bombed and people it had killed with its technological sophistication and tactical superiority – they were now taking full advantage of its newly found vulnerability to strike back as hard as they could. And they were succeeding.

The sun was rising behind them, its light slowly trickling over the sky and illuminating the surroundings. The President had a better view of the ground below now, giving him a chance to see things with more scrutinizing eyes. Major roads here were crowded too, with all the traffic flowing away from DC. But then he saw a convoy of vehicles heading the other way. Further out, he saw more of them, heading in the direction of the city on other roads.

"What are those?" the First Lady asked, her soft voice barely audible above the sound of the helicopter's whirring rotors.

He was surprised at first, thinking she had been asleep all this time. Turning to face her, he said, "I don't know. I thought they might be National Guard, but they don't look like military vehicles. They're pickup trucks and SUV's. Some of them seem to be carrying heavy guns on the back. Whoa... mobile missile launchers too. And lots of flags – American and... wait a minute." He squinted his eyes to get a better look as the helicopter flew right over one of the convoys.

"What?"

"There are Confederate flags there too. And Swastikas. What the hell?" And then he saw the most dreaded flag of all on some of the vehicles – a white cross inside a red circle. "The Aryan Nation," he said. "White supremacists."

"Oh God. What are they doing?"

"Coming to take over the capital."

"Are they nuts? Why now?"

"No better time. This is their chance. The federal government is shutting down and the city is evacuating. The National Guard is too busy overseeing the evacuation. These people want anarchy, they want all to have to fend for themselves. Their collective blood is boiling because a black man is their president, and minorities and people of color are increasingly in positions of authority in this country. They feel entitled, that somehow this country belongs more to them than to us. Their plan is to take this country back a hundred years, to a time when white men ruled and everyone else either served them or wasn't here at all. They've conveniently forgotten just how much the minorities have contributed to the success and prosperity of this country, how they've actually created so many of the jobs these white supremacists now hold. And now, these same individuals want to make toast of people like us, of all minorities. Just because they feel they can."

"Aren't they afraid of a nuclear attack on the city?"

"They probably think they can take on the terrorists themselves. Who knows? They're all crazy. This country is being destroyed by crazy fanatics from all sides."

Mrs. Tucker shook her head in horror. "How will we ever protect them?" she said, nodding toward their two children.

"It will get better. It has to get better. We will find a way. This country has an amazing ability to bounce back from the worst of circumstances."

"Always?"

"Even if not, help always comes from the most unexpected sources and when you least expect it. You'll see."

"Who on Earth will help us? Who can?"

He didn't know, of course. And he didn't have time to give an answer either, because the conversation abruptly ended when an incredibly loud bang shook the helicopter and caused it to swerve. Instinctively he grabbed his wife and jumped over his two children to protect them, and only then did he turn to determine what had happened. The helicopter was still intact, but the pilot was desperately trying to bring it under control and resume a normal trajectory.

"What happened?" he yelled.

"The other chopper, Sir," the Secret Service agent onboard said as he tried to steady up the President. "It blew up."

"What do you mean?"

"It was hit."

Tucker frantically looked out the window. There was smoke everywhere, with debris flying off in all directions. "No," he said, aghast with horror. "No. Margaret..."

"I'm sorry, Sir."

His closest staff member and good friend was dead. "These... these helicopters are supposed to be bulletproof," he stammered.

"Bullet proof, yes. I don't think that was a bullet."

"The pilot's voice crackled over a speaker above their heads. "They are shooting missiles at us, Mr. President. Hang tight. I will try my best to evade and get as close to the ground as I can."

"Those Aryan bastards – they've spotted us," Tucker said.

"It seems so," the Secret Service agent said.

Racist shits, Tucker thought. He should have listened to his staff and gotten his family out of DC days ago. He had underestimated the danger these hooligans posed.

A missile flew by in a whiff of smoke, followed by another. The pilot was very skillful, reacting quickly to avoid getting hit. The very next thing he did was to take the helicopter on a nose dive, in the hopes of getting as close to the ground as possible in case it was hit. He surely knew there was only so much he could do to avoid heat seeking missiles. They would turn around and come back, attracted to the warmest body in their vicinity.

And they did, this time headed straight for the helicopter's nose.

Tucker could feel the sense of inevitability. Time began to slow down. He looked at his wife, staring back at him with tear-strewn eyes. Help, it seemed, would not come for them after all. He looked down at his kids – fortunately his son was still sound asleep. At least he wouldn't have to consciously experience the horror of death. His daughter was holding onto him tightly, her head buried in his chest. He could feel her sobs, her tears wetting his shirt.

Looking out the window again, the very last thing he saw was that bright red head of a missile striking the front of the helicopter. Then there was a brilliant burst of light, after which everything went dark.

Chapter 27

The labyrinth didn't end for Marc, even after overcoming the fear of the giant spider and making it out of the tunnel in one piece. Another split tunnel entrance was waiting, and again the little crystal made no secret of pointing out which tunnel he had to enter. The right tunnel would show him nice memories of his past, but he would simply end up back at the point where he had started without making any progress. Progress, if he had the guts to face whatever obstacles lay for him along the way, would only be made through the left tunnel.

"What this time?" Marc asked the crystal, frustrated. "Huh? Another bug? How many more of these are there?"

The crystal didn't answer, of course. It patiently continued to point one of its long limbs at the tunnel entrance.

"Go, Marc," Alisha said. "We'll be right there with you, on the other side of the tunnel wall."

"Easy for you to say. You don't have to..."

"You've just shown you can do this," she replied, cutting him off. "Stop wasting time."

And so he went, with a sense of confidence due to his recent accomplishment intertwined with a fear of what to expect next. It would almost certainly be something different.

At first, it wasn't. The same dark passage, the same path ahead leading to nothingness. He expected to hear the thuds of the approaching arachnid, insect or some other monster at any moment. Instead, he began to hear the faint sound of gurgling water. The sound grew louder and louder as he kept walking, until it became a deafening roar.

It's all in your head, he thought repeatedly, forcing himself to keep going.

Ahead, he saw light. An opening, perhaps a chance for something nice. He hurried forward, hoping for the best. The sound of rushing water kept growing louder. But when he reached the opening, his hopes quickly faded.

Beyond lay a beautiful sight, that much was for sure. The narrow confines of the tunnel walls had given way to open space. It was like a picture taken straight out of an Earth Natural Sights calendar. A waterfall the size of Niagara, forcing thousands of tons of water every second over the edge, shooting plumes of vapor into the air as the water crashed into the riverbed far below. On the other side was land, covered with trees and grazing animals.

The part that wasn't nice was that he was at the very edge of a cliff overlooking the waterfall, a sheer drop of hundreds of feet to the rocky gorge below. There was no barrier, no railing - the path had just ended, and there was no other way forward.

He felt an all-too familiar wobbliness in his legs, combined with a surge of panic spreading up from his chest to his head. He stopped in his tracks and cautiously took steps back into the tunnel without turning around. And he didn't stop until he was well inside the tunnel again, far and safe from the opening.

Heights – his other big phobia. Something he fortunately hadn't had to deal with in a long time. Here it was now, however. Once again, his captors had dived into his mind and uncovered the things he most feared.

He sat down and held on to the relative safety of the tunnel floor and walls. The urge to turn and run back to the tunnel entrance was strong, but he forced himself to stay put. No more embarrassment in front of Alisha. He would overcome this somehow, just like he had overcome the spider. He just needed a little time.

He closed his eyes and breathed deeply. He thought of meditating and immersing himself in an alternate consciousness as he had done before in the first punishment, but soon realized it wouldn't help him here. There was no sixth or seventh sense he could use to strike back at an attacking enemy.

No, the only thing that would help was to overcome his fear as he did with the spider. He had to believe that no physical harm would come to him if he stepped past the edge of the tunnel into the abyss of the waterfall. He would not fall, he would not get hurt or die. It was all in his head. But that drop, that sheer drop of hundreds of feet... His legs wobbled again, and he shuddered just thinking about it.

He sat and thought. He pondered how he had gotten here, the sequence of unbelievable events that had brought him to this unbelievable situation. He remembered how so many were depending on him to get to the end of these punishments or tests or whatever they were. It wasn't just all the individuals from his own universe, it was also these strange crystals who so desperately wanted their freedom from enslavement and tyranny. He thought about his friends Sibular, Dumyan and Zorina, and wondered how far along they had gotten in this maze of tunnels. They would all have to get through, and if he got through first then maybe he could help them get to the end of their treks as well. And lastly he thought about Alisha, this amazing woman who had guided him through so much already and who needed him to keep going. For her alone, he would do this. For her alone, he would have to.

Determined and emboldened, he got up. He began walking toward the entrance. The walking turned to jogging, the jogging to running. And as he reached the end of the tunnel and the opening to the waterfall, he closed his eyes and jumped with all his might.

It felt like eons, but he didn't fall. He flew forward through the air, and eventually landed on his feet. When he opened his eyes, he saw that gorgeous face staring at him proudly.

"You did it," Alisha said, grabbing his hands and hugging him.

"I did."

The crystal was there, standing quietly as always. On the ground lay a collection of tubes of different colors, rewarding him for his accomplishment. He gladly helped himself to some nourishment and passed some to Alisha who downed it as well.

He then noticed that he was in yet another clearing between tunnels. Behind him lay the exit to the tunnel he had just come out of, and ahead lay the entrances to two more.

For God's sake, he thought. It still wasn't over. Again, the crystal was pointing to the left tunnel.

The third tunnel proved to be easier, much easier. It was another phobia of Marc's, but one that was only buried in his memory and for years now no longer haunted him. He had once been afraid of death, when he still had people and things to live for. But after the loss of both his mother and the love of his life, that fear was long gone. He had since found himself in many precarious situations, some voluntarily and some not, with not so much as a tiny rise in his heartbeat.

A knight in shining armor came galloping on a horse, brandishing a long, shiny sword. As the sharp blade swung toward his neck, Marc didn't flinch. He knew it wasn't real, for one. For another, he no longer had an irrational fear about this as he still did for arachnids and heights. He did pause for a second to think about Alisha and his growing care for her, but he convinced himself she'd be fine and in good company with his powerful, resourceful friends even if something were to happen to him.

It was like the sword of a ghost. It slid right through his neck with no friction and with no effect. The knight, realizing he had failed in his mission, galloped away and disappeared. Next came a thug with a pistol, firing multiple rounds at Marc. Again, no effect and again the individual walked away in shame. Finally came a soldier with a powerful machine gun, showering him in a sea of with bullets. Same result.

Marc strode along confidently until he reached the end of the tunnel. Ahead were Alisha and the crystal, patiently waiting for him. As soon as he joined them, the tunnel and indeed the entire labyrinth structure behind him withered away and disappeared. It seemed he had finally reached the end of this punishment, far quicker than he had with the first one. The first one had felt like months, yet this one had just taken days. The punishments were either designed that way, or he was just getting better at tackling them. Perhaps both.

Then the ground began to shift again as it had done in the very beginning of this punishment. But this time, it was converging instead of pulling everyone apart. Nonetheless, the three of them took no chances and held on to each other as the movement under them continued. The space was shrinking. In the growing ambient light, Marc was soon able to make out silhouettes in the distance. As they came closer, it was clear that they were friendly – Mendoken, Aftarans and a few Volonans, all the spectators along for the ride because they just happened to have been on that space station during the anomaly attack. He, Alisha and the crystal were being brought back to the central location where all the others were.

Marc was relieved to find Sibular and Zorina among them, and he hugged them both. They had passed this punishment successfully too, as had the select six Mendoken troopers. Colored food tubes were scattered everywhere, enough to ensure everyone was fed.

"Easy for me," Zorina remarked. "Every phobia that came toward me – I just pretended I was someone else, doing something else. Just like living in a virtual world."

"Acting comes naturally to you Volonans," Marc said.

Zorina bobbed her head up and down in acknowledgment.

"Nothing appeared in the tunnels I went through," Sibular said.

"Nothing at all?" Marc asked, surprised.

"He has no fears," Zorina said. "He's Mendoken. All logic. Nothing to fear if the object of fear isn't really there. He just strode through."

"Where's Dumyan? And the six Aftaran soldiers?"

"They do not appear to have made it out of their tunnels yet," Sibular said. "We have looked for them, but all we see is emptiness no matter which way we turn or go."

"My guess is their space will converge on ours once they make it out, just like yours did," Zorina added.

"If they make it out," Marc replied. "Not surprising. The Aftarans – they have the biggest fear of all. The Creator. It's what drives their faith and their way of life. They don't know how to overcome it, however the fear is manifesting itself in their imaginations."

"We have to find and help them," Alisha said.

Marc squinted his eyes to peer into the distance in the dim light. Like Sibular had said, there was literally nothing but empty space no matter which way he looked.

"Has this, uh, entity been helpful?" Zorina asked, pointing her long trunk at the crystal standing beside Marc.

"Extremely. It's guided us every step of the way. And, we've learned to communicate. Somewhat."

Marc went on to summarize everything he had learned about this universe from the crystal, including the original creation that had given birth to these crystals, how it had been destroyed by the consar and how that had given rise to the vengeful anomalies that had wreaked so much havoc on their own universe and brought all of them here. He also explained how these crystals were being held hostage by the anomalies and forced to do the dirty work against their will.

Zorina was stunned and flapped her ears violently.

"That explains a lot," Sibular said.

Marc nodded. "For sure. There are more of them that are free, out there in space. They're looking for a way to free the rest of their kinsfolk from the tyranny of the anomalies. And for whatever reason they seem to think we can help them."

"Given our circumstances, that faith may be misplaced," Sibular said.

"We'll see. Somehow I can't help thinking these creatures are a lot smarter and more knowledgeable than we might be tempted to give them credit for."

"I still don't get why we have to pass all these obstacles," Zorina said, flapping her ears. "If the goal is to punish us, why not just torture us to death or something?"

"Tests," Marc said. "Alisha thinks they're tests of some sort. I have to agree."

"Why?"

"Beats me."

"Well, if these groups of interlinked blobs are as smart as you say are, perhaps you can ask this one here," Zorina said, pointing her trunk at the crystal again. "While you're at it, ask it where the heck the missing Aftarans are too."

Marc eyed the crystal, gesturing to it that he wanted to communicate. In the past, the crystal had somehow known what it was he wanted to learn and had readily given him that information when they connected. He could only hope it would do the same this time around.

But the crystal didn't come forward to connect. Marc wasn't sure why, so he moved closer to the creature and reached out with his hands to touch the glowing nodes. The crystal seemed to hesitate, but then gave in. Next, Marc leaned forward and touched another node with his forehead.

Talk to me, he thought, closing his eyes. Surely this intelligent being would know exactly what he wanted to hear and would readily pass on all the relevant information.

Silence. No visions, no immersion. Just darkness. He waited, hoping things would change. But they didn't. Eventually he pulled out and tried again, but the result was the same.

"Well?" Zorina asked.

"I... I don't understand. It's not saying anything." He stared at the creature, but it just stood still with no reaction.

"Not so smart anymore, eh?"

He shook his head. "It's not that. I think it only communicates when it feels the need to." At least, he hoped that was the case.

"Well, can you make it understand that we need to find our Aftaran friends?"

"It might not know where they are. Or even if it does, it doesn't know how to tell me. Our communication obviously isn't perfect yet."

Zorina flapped her ears again in annoyance. "Fantastic."

"I... wait a minute. I have an idea." Marc's eyes lit up. He stepped away from the others and sprinted into the vastness of the empty grounds surrounding them.

"Where are you going?" Alisha yelled after him.

Marc turned back and motioned to her to stay quiet. Then he turned forward and kept moving. "Are you here?" he called out.

No answer. He moved this way and that, trying to cover as much distance as possible. "Are you here?" he called out again.

He tried for what felt like hours, circling several times around the region where all the others were amassed, but he found nothing. Dejected, he was about to give up and head back to the others when he heard a faint rustle behind him.

Turning around, he felt highly relieved. He could see the faint stretches of white cloud formations rising from the ground, slowly amassing into a giant gaseous lifeform.

"Jinser-Shosa," he whispered. "Never been happier to see you."

The Phyrax's faceless head and body took shape, looming over the much smaller human that had summoned it.

"What do you want?" it rasped. "I'm trying to stay hidden."

"I know," Marc said. "And you should to avoid detection. But I... we need your help."

"I've helped you already. I pushed you to get a move on when you were sitting on your behind. We all need to get home."

"And thank you for that. I've been moving since. But we're stuck in this punishment until everyone gets through. Dumyan and his Aftaran soldiers are missing."

"What do you need me for?"

"To fly."

Chapter 28

The Mendoken Imgoerin, the Aftaran leader Autamrin and the Mendoken scientist Leita stood in darkness, inside a tiny vehicle at the end of the passage in the heart of the massive replicator, deep in the hollowed-out crust of the Mendoken planet Lind. They were about to witness the replication of the alien universe.

As promised, the shroud around them abruptly vaporized. The entire cover simply crumbled into pieces that quickly shrank and disappeared into oblivion, leaving a crystal clear, jaw dropping view all around. It felt as if the three individuals were suspended in empty space, right in the middle of this gaping expanse.

And what an expanse. It was like getting a close-up, compressed view of the night sky, except it didn't remotely resemble the night sky either the Mendoken or Aftaran leader was used to. There were no stars, planets or galaxies, just a dark sky filled with a uniform haze everywhere that made it hard to see through. In the distance, cloud formations could barely be made out, spread far and wide.

"This universe is different from ours," Leita announced.

"A true understatement," Autamrin replied, his owl-like eyes wide open in wonder. "It's incredible."

"Every universe, every brane in the higher dimensional bulk has its own characteristics and laws of physics," Leita continued, unfazed by the Aftaran leader's bewilderment. "Just a slight discrepancy in one physical property or force can result in a completely different environment. Only a handful of branes out of the uncountable number in the bulk host the conditions for life to eventually form. The vast majority do not. In this universe, for example, the force of gravity is significantly weaker than in ours, making it much harder for matter to coalesce into anything."

"Is there any matter at all?" Autamrin asked. "All I see is haze."

"That is the matter," Leita replied. "High energy plasma, similar to the conditions in our own universe shortly after the Big Bang. Except our universe cooled as it expanded, causing the free-flowing electrons and protons in the plasma to combine and form atoms. That cleared up the haze. Hydrogen and other gases came into existence, and under the force of gravity they came together to form the abundance of galaxies, stars and planets we have around us today.

"This universe, however, not only does not have enough gravity to bring atoms together, it never cooled down enough for most of the plasma to break down into atoms in the first place."

"Why not?"

"Now that is the truly unique thing about this universe, not the low force of gravity. Low gravity is actually quite common in other branes. What is unique about this brane is that it has an exceptionally high concentration of bulk energy, not only higher than anything we have ever replicated, it is higher than anything we could ever have contemplated replicating."

"Bulk energy?"

"The energy that keeps all the branes in the wider bulk in peaceful coexistence, controlling their rates of expansion and contraction."

"I know what it is," Autamrin replied. "Conceptually anyway."

"What is your question, then?"

"Do you know why it's so high?"

"No. Possibly just by chance. With all the branes in the bulk, there are bound to be all kinds of levels and combinations represented across them. And each one presents its own characteristics."

"How high is it?" the Imgoerin asked.

"Per unit of space, compared to our universe, over a trillion times higher," Leita replied.

Autamrin closed his eyes and uttered a short prayer.

"This universe appears to have never evolved from its state of infancy," the Imgoerin observed. "The conditions for life never came into being, as atoms could not form."

"Actually, it has evolved, and life did form," Leita said. "Just not any kind of life as we know it."

"Due to the high bulk energy?"

"Yes, together with the high energy plasma. A unique combination, leading to many strands of complex energy not found in our universe. Watch." Leita used two of her hands to open up a virtual screen in front of her and swept through the controls it displayed of the replication.

The vehicle began moving. Slowly at first, but rapidly gaining speed as it made its way into the expanse of this bizarre replication. Given the size of the replicator and the distance they were covering, it took a while. The view outside didn't change much, except for slight variations in the density of the opaqueness. Their destination – the cloud formations in the distance.

As they came closer, the Imgoerin noticed how the clouds were anything but stagnant. They were constantly moving and changing shape. More importantly, though, there were flashes of light constantly appearing across the span of the clouds.

"What are those?" he asked.

"Everything in this replication is significantly accelerated compared to the time it would take in the actual universe," Leita said. "Otherwise we would reach the end of our lives without observing anything. So you are seeing things happening more quickly and frequently than they should."

"Yes, but what are we seeing?"

"The creation of life. Every one of those explosions is the generation of a lifeform. A lifeform based primarily on energy, not matter."

"How is that even possible?" Autamrin asked, visibly dumbfounded.

"It is possible in theory," Leita said. "We have just never observed it before. In the end, energy and mass are the same thing. One is just a different state representation of the other."

"But what about the body? What about the heart, lungs, and the brain? What about the individual's thoughts and consciousness? And... the soul?"

"The soul we cannot speak to," the Imgoerin said. "That is for you religious folk to sort out. But thoughts and consciousness – thoughts are nothing but energy. Think about it, Autamrin. Your body, made of matter. When it dies, your thoughts and memories are all gone. Because all the energy in your body dissipates. Thoughts are nothing more than energy, and without thoughts there is no conscious life. What is the matter in your body without its energy? It is lifeless."

"But, conversely, how can energy create life without any matter?"

"I did not say no matter at all," Leita interjected. "There is matter, but no complex atoms or molecules, and certainly nothing organic. The lack of complex matter is countered by the presence of abundant, complex energy. The end result is the same – life. Just of a different kind."

The vehicle moved in closer to one of the clouds, allowing the three individuals to get a far better glimpse of what those flashes of light were about. Every flash signified the creation of a blob of some sort, awash in different colors. They were forming at an incredibly fast rate. The blobs adjacent to each other grew limbs to connect and build a larger entity. This process continued until a large-scale structure had formed.

"Lifeforms?" Autamrin asked, gazing in wonder at the spectacle ahead.

Leita hummed in acknowledgment. "Advanced neural networks, naturally created by the combination of concentrated bulk energy with high energy plasma in this universe. We have never witnessed this before, not in our universe or in any of the replications we have done of other universes."

"Neural networks. But don't they need billions of neurons, not... what hundreds or thousands, whatever I'm seeing here?"

"Each blob is not a single neuron – each blob is its own collection of neural networks, containing trillions of connected neurons. Different blobs, in a sense, have different characteristics."

"How?"

"Because the blobs seem to be born with neurons connected in slightly different ways, depending on the environmental conditions in which they are created. These slight differences in connection can lead to very different kinds of neural networks."

"And how do these characteristics manifest themselves?" the Imgoerin asked.

"The ones you see here are generally collaborative and constructive, based largely on convolutional neural networks," Leita replied. "They connect with each other to form a community, where each blob has equal power, both contributing to and benefiting from the wellbeing of the larger lifeform."

Leita then directed the vehicle toward another cloud nearby.

"We adjusted the levels of bulk energy concentration between the different clouds, but within the norm of what is possible in this universe," she said. "The one we are going to now only has a two percent higher concentration, well within the variations that may occur due to natural phenomena. But, surprisingly, this leads the blobs to behave very differently."

Indeed, when they arrived, what they saw was markedly different. There were no structures of connected blobs. Instead, blobs were constantly crashing into each other. In each collision, one always came out the winner, fully consuming and absorbing the strength and energy of the other, and correspondingly growing in size. The end result – out of thousands of blobs, only a few remained. They had become huge, and they looked awfully similar to...

"Anomalies," Autamrin whispered.

The Imgoerin hummed in agreement.

"Their neural configuration is recursive in nature, leading to authoritative and destructive traits," Leita said. "And, due to the recursive configuration, whatever traits they harbor seem to get amplified with every collision and resulting absorption."

"Until they become absolute monstrosities," Autamrin concluded.

"Have you analyzed their composition?" the Imgoerin asked. "We need to understand where they get their power from."

Leita hummed in acknowledgment, opened a screen in front of her and pointed to the images displayed. They showed close-up renditions of an anomaly's surface.

"There is something else you need to first understand about the bulk energy composition in this universe," she said. "As you know, bulk energy is usually either expansive or contractive within a brane. In our own universe, it is currently expansive, meaning it is causing the universe to grow. Eventually it will turn contractive, fortunately not for billions of years, but when it does it will force the universe to shrink over time. Until it reaches a singularity and explodes in a big bang all over again. This is how branes in the bulk are kept in check and from crashing into each other, allowing one to grow larger while the other grows smaller.

"But in this other universe that we are observing, the bulk energy is currently stagnant – neither expansive nor contractive. It was surely expansive during the initial period of inflation, but for whatever reason has stopped being so. This may be one of the reasons for the high concentration of bulk energy here. In a sense, this universe has reached a finite size and is no longer growing. We believe this steady state is critical to the creation and sustenance of these lifeforms."

Leita zoomed in on the anomaly's surface, until it reached the elementary particle level. The particles were bouncing around at high velocities, colliding into each other and releasing bursts of energy. The bursts of energy led to the creation of new particles, and this cycle continued indefinitely.

"What is this?" Autamrin asked, dumbfounded.

"These are quarks, what protons and neutrons are made of," Leita replied. "But even protons and neutrons cannot form here – the high, stagnant bulk energy keeps them apart. So the quarks keep colliding with each other, their short-lived mass converting to energy, and then the energy settling back into individual quarks. As this process continues, plasma is absorbed from the surrounding space. This perpetual cycle powers the neural networks that keep these beings alive."

"A unique, highly unusual combination of physical properties that creates and sustains this kind of life," the Imgoerin observed.

"And also gives them their destructive capability," Leita added. "The absorbed electrons from the plasma can react with the high bulk energy and quarks trapped in their bodies, resulting in a catastrophic chain reaction that generates far more energy than anything we can generate with all of our technology. It appears they are able to keep the plasma, bulk energy and quarks separate in their bodies, and combine them whenever they want to destroy something."

"How do you know?"

"We ran some experiments to stimulate an anomaly into reacting." Leita showed a video on the screen of a Mendoken probe getting awfully close to one of the anomalies. It tried to provoke the anomaly by spraying it with debris. At first the anomaly ignored it, but eventually it shot a bright ray toward the probe and blew it up.

"We tracked the nuclear reactions inside the anomaly as it sent out the ray," Leita went on, zooming in to the anomaly's surface on another screen that she opened up. It showed the quarks and electrons exploding and releasing pure energy at the point where the ray shot out toward the probe.

"That explains why none of our weapons worked on the anomalies," the Imgoerin said. "They just absorbed all the destructive energy into their bodies and became stronger."

Leita hummed in agreement.

"Is it something we can replicate?" the Imgoerin asked.

"Yes, and we did, but only within the confines of this universe replication. Due to the unique physical properties here."

"Then how did the anomalies cause so much destruction in our universe?" Autamrin asked.

"Especially given the lower concentration and expansive properties of bulk energy in ours," the Imgoerin added. "I would expect that much of the concentrated bulk energy stored in their bodies would dissipate into space whenever they traveled to our universe. The same would be true for their supply of plasma."

"That may be why they kept appearing and disappearing whenever they came to our universe to attack," Leita said. "They had to keep going back to their universe to replenish and exceed their usual stock of bulk energy and plasma, before building up enough to strike."

"It begs the question why they did not just strike in one blow for each attack, instead of taking the time to travel back and forth in different trajectories," the Imgoerin said.

Autamrin's eyes widened. "But weren't they doing all those strange trajectories to give us the message of what they wanted? That's how we figured out they wanted the individuals who had traveled on that one consar. It was a form of communication."

"Very true," the Imgoerin said, and paused before adding, "And very interesting."

"What is?" Autamrin asked.

"I think we may have just figured out how to fight them."

Chapter 29

Marc strode onto the short slope that Jinser-Shosa had created from its own mass, allowing him to climb up its tall body. He was pleasantly surprised to find that the Phyrax's versatile, cloudy mass was easily able to support his weight. Apparently being made of gas was no detriment to carrying a solid body. It just depended on the kind of gas, and this kind of gas felt more like a soft, mushy solid than an actual gas.

That same kind of gas, however, led to one temperamental personality, something the Phyrax as a species were generally notorious for.

"Hurry up!" Jinser-Shosa said gruffly. "Haven't got all day."

"You don't?" Marc asked, puffing as he climbed to the top of the tall creature's body.

"What did you say?" The rising anger in the raspy voice was quite evident.

"Nothing, nothing," Marc replied quickly as he sat down on the Phyrax's shoulder, next to its faceless head. "Sorry to offend you, intentionally or not."

Jinser-Shosa grumbled a few swear words.

"Can we, uh, go now?" Marc asked. "Please?"

"I'm not helping you if you fall off."

"Got it." Marc dug his hands into the spongy mass and closed his eyes. Fear of heights here was warranted – this was going to be real, not imagined. Regardless, it was something he knew he had to do, and his recent exposure to and overcoming of the fear in the tunnels would hopefully help.

He felt a surge of force pulling him down, the air blasting against his face. He had to gulp to breathe. Only when it finally stopped did he dare open his eyes again, and when he did he had to grasp extra hard onto the Phyrax's shoulder to offset the wobbliness spreading across his body.

"Holy crap," he whispered, surveying his surroundings in awe.

Jinser-Shosa had shot straight up from the ground, all the way up to the roof of the massive structure they were in. It had to be a couple of hundred feet up, at least. Marc tried not to look down, but up and to the side instead. He noticed there were windows spread across the ceiling, giving a glimpse of what lay beyond. He could see the center of the massive structure these crystals had created out of the remnants of the Mendoken space station they had brought with them from his own universe. They had, in essence, recreated a space station of their own, in a shape and configuration of their choosing. Or the anomalies' choosing, rather.

The center was a bright sphere, with beams reaching out to the wide ring that surrounded it. The station was rotating, generating the centrifugal force needed to create the gravity Marc and everyone else in the ring were benefiting from. This hall they were all in, as big as it was, took up just one section of the ring, its floor facing the outside. As he could see through the ceiling windows, there were more halls stretching along the circumference of the ring. Two more, to be precise, separated by a wall that was visible through the windows on the other side. One hall appeared to be dark and empty. In the other, he could see activity – lots of crystals moving around, likely all being controlled through red cores. He had no idea what they were doing.

He wondered if the three halls corresponded to three punishments, in which case it would explain why one of them was dark – that housed the first punishment he and the others had already passed. And, as he painstakingly realized, it also meant there had to be one more punishment left after the current one, and it was still in the process of being set up. What was to happen after that remained a mystery.

Beyond the ring, out in space, he could see a large, bright red object. An anomaly, without a doubt. It remained still, perhaps keenly monitoring all the activity inside the space station. There was no doubt as to who was boss, who was pulling all the strings here.

Marc knew well, however, that continuing to look outside would do nothing to address the reason he had risen so high from the ground with the help of his gaseous companion. Gathering his wits, he finally dared to look down.

Far below in the dim light, he could see the ground. He could barely make out the crowd of individuals he had left behind, with Alisha, Sibular, Zorina and the little crystal surely among them. From his vantage point, they looked like nothing more than specks of light dust sprinkled atop a dark backdrop. Many of them were likely looking up, trying to keep track of him and the far larger Phyrax that was accompanying him.

The rest of the ground below looked bare. Marc squinted his eyes to search for the missing Aftarans. Left, right, forward, behind. Nothing.

"Do you see anything?" he asked.

"Now I have to look too?" Jinser-Shosa rasped. "What exactly are you good for?"

"Please."

"Bah! Useless." The Phyrax raised its head from the rest of its versatile body, letting its neck grow. Then it spread its head out in different directions, in an 8-spoke star shape. The ends of the star drooped a little to survey the ground far below, covering the entire visible surface in one swoop.

Marc wondered how Jinser-Shosa could even see, given that it had no visible eyes. Or talk for that matter, since it had no mouth. But it could do both, and well. Its vision was certainly better than that of any human.

"Found them!" it announced proudly. "No thanks to you."

"Where?"

One of the head spokes pointed downward. "There."

Marc looked down in that direction, and only after much squinting was he able to make out a few faint specs on the ground. They were way on the other side of the structure, and given the vast distance he was no longer surprised why nobody on the ground had been able to find them even after much searching.

"Let's head down th...," he began to say, but before he could finish he was flung away with one shove from the Phyrax.

"Hahhhh!" he yelled, gasping for air as he tumbled toward the ground. He didn't know what was going on, nor could he gather his thoughts on anything in time. All he knew was that he was dropping quickly toward imminent death.

Within seconds, however, he was lifted up again by the same creature and roughly placed on its shoulder again.

"That will teach you," Jinser-Shosa growled, its eight-spoked head now shrunk back to one. "Never order me around!"

"Huh?" Marc asked, bewildered and trying his best to recover quickly from the shock. "Uh, ok." He breathed deeply. "Can we, uh, please head down there?"

"Much better."

They reached the ground as quickly as they had ascended to the ceiling. Marc found the seven Aftarans, Dumyan among them, not far from each other. They couldn't see each other, or Marc or Jinser-Shosa. They were all in a state of disarray and confusion, running back and forth in tunnels visible only to them. To Marc, it appeared as if the Aftarans were blind, treading carefully and avoiding non-existent obstacles across an open, empty, flat surface.

"They look so silly," Jinser-Shosa chuckled.

They do indeed, Marc thought. He realized how silly he must have appeared to Alisha when he was trudging through his own imaginary tunnels. How considerate of her to have supported me nonetheless, he thought. Now, he realized, he would have to help the Aftarans in the same way that Alisha had helped him make it out of the tunnels.

"Would you, uh, mind if I try to help them through this, since I've been through it myself?" Marc asked the Phyrax, choosing his words carefully.

"Be my guest. My work here is done." With that, Jinser-Shosa allowed its body to spread apart and vaporize. Within seconds, it had completely disappeared.

Marc heaved a sigh of relief. Approaching Dumyan, he spoke softly. "Dumyan, it's me, Marc."

"Huh? What? Marc? Where are you?" The tall Aftaran stopped in his tracks and began frantically looking around, his large, round eyes filled with fright.

"It's ok, I'm here, on the other side of the wall," Marc replied. "You can hear me because this... well, this wall isn't real. It's all in your head."

"In my head?"

"Yes, in your head. I had to go through the same thing." Marc went on to describe his own experience and how he had gotten out with the help of Alisha and the crystal.

Dumyan sat down on the ground and let his head drop to his hands. "How can this be? It's so... real."

"What is? What's so real? What do you see?"

"The same thing. Every time. The horror of..." His words trailed off and became inaudible.

"Of what?"

"The Creator's wrath. The Creator's displeasure with me. My complete and utter failing as an Aftaran to follow the code of our holy scriptures." Dumyan sobbed.

"How does this wrath manifest itself?"

"The big fire."

"Fire?"

"Reserved for those who fail and disappoint the Creator. Eternal pain and suffering after death, instead of eternal bliss as a pious Aftaran is always promised."

"You mean hell?

"Hell, fire, same thing. The worst fear of any Aftaran – we're indoctrinated with it since birth. We've all seen images, holograms, virtual renditions. But this, this is so vivid and lifelike. Every time I see it, I can hear it, smell it, feel it. I get paralyzed. I can't proceed."

"But it isn't real. That's what you have to convince yourself. The faith in the Creator that generates this fear in you, that very same faith you have to put in the Creator that you can overcome and pass through this fire unharmed."

Dumyan sighed. "It isn't just the fire, Marc. It's this overwhelming feeling of having disappointed the Creator. For an Aftaran there is no bigger failure in life than having failed in his or her faith."

"But you haven't failed," Marc replied, shaking his head. "Again, this is all in your mind, in your own imagination."

"My imagination or not, the Creator is watching. The Creator wants me to feel this way. Surely for a reason. If it isn't because I have failed the Creator, what then?"

Marc was silent for a moment. "You say the Creator is watching, that the Creator knows everything, right?"

"Everything that happened and everything that ever will happen."

"How do you know?"

"The Scriptures. They reveal everything."

"Everything?"

"Everything. So many truths, so many facts, so much understood only after we reached a certain level of scientific and technological advancement. So many prophecies. They warned us about playing with consars, didn't they? Look what happened because we did."

"But what did they say about what we'd find on the other side? About other universes, their properties, their lifeforms, their fates?"

Dumyan opened his beak to reply, but he stumped.

"They don't say anything about this, do they?" Marc suggested. "As comprehensive as your Scriptures may be, they don't have the answer for everything."

Dumyan closed his eyes and stayed silent.

"You have prayed to the Creator here, haven't you?" Marc asked. "You have asked for your powers to reveal themselves."

"Yes," Dumyan said softly.

"Have you gotten any response?"

"No."

"Isn't the Creator supposed to be omnipotent and omnipresent?" Marc asked. "Shouldn't the Creator be here as well, across all universes, hearing your prayers?"

"I don't know, Marc. Since we came here, I've felt this hollowness like I never did before. I don't feel the security or even the presence of the Creator, watching over me and guiding me every step of the way. It's so incredibly disconcerting. I pray, but I feel nothing. No powers, no strength, just emptiness."

"Perhaps it's worth considering the possibility that whatever form the Creator actually has and what the Creator wants from all of us, if anything at all, may not exactly match what religion has been hammering into us for generations."

Dumyan opened his eyes slowly. "Hard for me to acknowledge, but... perhaps, just perhaps you might be right."

"'Perhaps' is all the doubt you need right now to overcome your fear and get out of these tunnels. You know what to do, my pious friend. Remember, it's all in your head."

Chapter 30

Dumyan did know what he had to do. It took a few tries, but he eventually overcame his fears, faced the fire and got out of his tunnels. Then he helped the other Aftarans get out of theirs, using the same logic that Marc had used on him. It wasn't quite as smooth every time, as a couple of the Aftaran soldiers were die-hard followers of their faith. But Dumyan, a born leader and well known for his excellent oratory skills, successfully used his powers of persuasion in all cases.

Once the last Aftaran had emerged from the tunnels, the ground began to move automatically. Just as it had expanded in the beginning of this punishment, pulling everyone apart from each other, the reverse was now under way. The space in the hall was shrinking. Marc, Dumyan and the Aftaran soldiers didn't have to move at all. Within minutes, they caught sight of everyone else in the distance, and soon after they were all reunited.

Marc found Alisha and gave her a tight hug. He hadn't been gone for long, and yet it felt like ages. Feelings – feelings he was developing for her, feelings he thought he had locked up for good with the passing of the love of his life. And yet, here they were anyway. Somewhere deep inside he felt a pang of guilt toward Iman, but he tried his best to brush it off.

Enough time had passed and enough crazy things had happened. He was in a totally different universe in different dimensions, for crying out loud, and the chances of ever making it out of here or of survival at all were extremely slim at best.

The time for rejoicing, however, was cut short by a row of crystals with red cores that appeared from the far end of the hall, racing toward the crowd at high speed. The ends of their limbs were locked onto each other, leaving no room for escape between them.

Just like the last time, Marc thought. Everyone would be shoved into the third and final hall for the last punishment, willingly or not.

The little crystal tugged at Marc and Alisha, pointing in the opposite direction of the rapidly approaching barricade. Marc turned his head to look. Just like the last time, there was a wall ahead.

"We have to go through it?" Marc asked the crystal.

The crystal simply grabbed both him and Alisha by the hand and pulled them along as it sped toward the wall. This time, however, Marc wasn't worried about crashing into it.

Been there, done that, he thought. This little crystal knew what it was doing, that much was for sure.

He beckoned to everyone he passed to follow him into the wall. Having been through it once before, and the urgency all the higher now with the barricade of limb-thrashing crystals with angry red cores coming ever closer, they all willingly obliged.

Everyone passed through the wall unhindered, in the nick of time as the barricade reached the last of them. On the other side, the hall they had entered seemed identical to the one they had just left behind. It was dark and completely bare.

"Wonder what they have in store for us this time," Alisha said fearfully.

Marc shrugged. He was ready for anything at this point. He glanced at the little crystal, standing right next to them. It remained still and offered no responsive gesture, as if it didn't really know itself what to expect. He gazed at others nearby, at Dumyan, Sibular and Zorina mingling in the crowd. Everyone was exchanging nervous glances with each other, unaware of what would happen next. They didn't, however, have to wait long to find out.

The darkness gave way to light. Marc couldn't tell at first where the light was coming from, but soon noticed a brightening haze illuminating the ground beneath him. He bent his head downwards to look, only to gasp in shock. The floor had somehow turned transparent, and what he could see beyond it was the largest crystal of them all, filling up much of the view from one end of the hall to the other. It had to be the sum of thousands of individual crystals, all connected via their nodes and limbs, all operating in unison at the whim of a huge, pulsating red core in the center. Worse yet, the crystal was approaching the floor from below at high speed.

"Holy crap," Marc whispered, instinctively grabbing Alisha and pulling her toward him. "Holy crap."

The shrieks of shock and surprise were manifold in the crowd, with only the Mendoken remaining silent. There was no time to react, nor was there anywhere to escape to.

The floor gave way. It just vaporized and disappeared, in an instant. Marc lost his footing, of course, and he felt like he was falling. Not for long, though, because the collision with the monstrous entity followed soon after.

He heard a loud, screeching bang, followed by the feeling of a tremendous force pushing him up into the air. He lost his grip on Alisha, and out of the corner of his eye saw her being flung up and away. In the distance, he saw more bodies being scattered every which way, the little crystal among them. The large creature, having accomplished its task, broke up into many smaller crystals, each inheriting its own red core. They sped off in different directions, chasing the individuals they had just hurled into the air.

Out of the corner of his eye, Marc could see the floor taking shape again, and it was no longer transparent. He expected to come crashing back down onto it, but instead he stayed afloat and kept moving up. He was also spinning like a rotating planet. Angular momentum at its best, he realized as he tried his best to control the rising nausea and urge to throw up. Gravity had evidently just vanished, possibly because the space station's own rotation had come to a grinding halt. He was completely helpless, and unable to stop moving. There wasn't any surface nearby that he could collide with or bounce off to change course. Not that he had much experience with motion in a gravity-less environment anyway.

In between his rotations, he could see that everybody else was moving further away from him, no matter which way he looked. They were all spreading apart into the space of the vast hall, each one followed by a crystal with a red core. Before long, everyone disappeared from his view. He was alone, except for the crystal that was following him. It came closer and reached out with one of its limbs to touch him. He winced and closed his eyes, expecting to be struck hard. Instead, the crystal simply grabbed his leg and steadied his motion. He stopped rotating and moving forward, and he came to a full standstill.

He opened his eyes and stared at the creature in front of him, with its balls of bright, colorful light and long, wavy limbs. The one thing he couldn't get his eyes off was that dratted pulsating red core in the center, the entity that was directing this otherwise benign being to engage in such malignant behavior. He longed to strike at the creature as he had in the first punishment, to break the limbs around the core and free the crystal from mental captivity.

It was obvious, however, that in a gravity-less environment he had no thrust whatsoever to propel his arms and legs forward with. These crystals could clearly move without gravity, but he had never done it before and frankly had no idea how. He was, in effect, completely helpless. And that was very possibly why the crystals had chosen to stop the gravity in this punishment to start with – to avoid a repeat of the results of the first punishment. He was also completely alone this time. No friends, no Alisha or coreless little crystal to help or guide him. He could only hope she was alright, that they were all alright.

Once it had steadied him, the crystal sped off into the distance, leaving him to wonder with increasing concern what lay in store for him.

He didn't have to wait long. It returned promptly, and not alone. On one side it was holding a Mendoken, its limb wrapped around the individual's body to render him completely motionless. On the other side it held an Aftaran with her face unveiled, held in a similar way. Marc didn't recognize either of them – they had to be two of the countless others in the crowd, the innocent bystanders who had had the misfortune of being on the Mendoken space station when the anomaly struck.

Oh no, was all Marc could say to himself. This time others would get punished. Individuals who were innocent, individuals who had already suffered way more than they ever should have, individuals whose suffering he was already very much responsible for. And, if his hunch was right, that responsibility was about to rise to a whole new level and in a far more direct way.

The crystal first pushed the Mendoken closer to Marc. Marc stared at him – he looked as emotionless and expressionless as all Mendoken did. Marc opened his mouth to speak, but no words came out. Somehow his vocal chords had been compromised in this hall – these crystals had put something in the air, perhaps. They clearly didn't want any communication to happen between individuals in this punishment. All he could do was look into the Mendoken's single, head encompassing eye with an attempt to appear reassuring. Not that it mattered – the Mendoken offered no acknowledgment whatsoever.

The crystal pulled the Mendoken back and brought the Aftaran forward. Marc studied her face and her large owl-like eyes. She definitely looked fearful, but also seemed to have a level of resigned serenity about her. The advantage of having faith, he thought. She needed none of the measly consolation that he could offer – she had the reassurance of a much higher power that everything would turn out ok for her, in life or in death. Whether this higher power actually existed or not was perhaps immaterial – in a situation like this, faith was often all that mattered to survive and pull through.

The Aftaran was also pulled back, and then the crystal waited. And it waited. Marc wasn't sure what to do and waited as well. The minutes passed. Eventually the crystal used one of its free limbs to give Marc a stinging slap in the face.

It was painful. He opened his mouth to let out a yell, but no sound came out. Clearly it wanted him to do something. Again, it presented the Mendoken to him first, followed by the Aftaran.

It wants me to make a choice, he thought, between the two of them. For what, though? To punish or spare one of them? And why? It wasn't like he could ask the crystal, so the only option available seemed to be to just pick one. But which one? Assuming the one he picked was the one to be spared punishment, should he base his decision on who he liked more? He didn't know either of them personally, so it would have to be based on his preference for one species over the other. He didn't have one, given his endearing emotions for both. Or should he base it on who would be able to endure the punishment with less suffering? He had no idea which one would – both species had their unique strengths and weaknesses.

Without daring to look either in the face, he pointed to his left. He had picked the Mendoken. Almost instantaneously, the crystal let the Mendoken go. Then it turned its attention to the Aftaran and began shocking her with some kind of high energy blast emanating from its limbs. Her whole body shook violently. Her beak opened wide as she tried to scream in pain, but as with Marc no sound came out. The expression of pain in her round eyes, however, said it all.

Marc felt terrible, helplessly watching her suffer in such agony. He tried his best to move toward her, to do something, anything. But he could hardly budge an inch. If only he had some kind of surface to bounce off of, but he was surrounded by empty space.

After what felt like a long, long time, the ordeal ended. Marc heaved a sigh of relief, only to discover relief was nowhere to be found. The crystal let go of the Aftaran, came forward toward him and began zapping him with the same energy blast.

To call it extremely painful would be like suggesting the sun was a lukewarm ball of docile gas. The fire seared through his body from head to toe, treating it like nothing more than fuel to burn. It was unbearable.

In hindsight, this torment was manifold worse than the physical blows he had received in the first punishment.

It ended eventually, but not until it felt as if every last ounce of energy had been sucked out of his body. The crystal let him go, allowing him to float freely. Whatever strength he had left he used to try to recover from the shock and wonder how he could possibly have made such a wrong choice. It made no sense.

Food? He opened his eyes to look around, but he saw no tubes of paste floating around anywhere. He could certainly have used some now to replenish even a little bit of strength. Rest? He wouldn't get any. The crystal grabbed hold of the Mendoken and Aftaran again, and steadied Marc back to an upright position. Then it did the same thing as before – first presented him with the Mendoken, followed by the Aftaran.

What the hell, Marc thought. Pick the Aftaran? Why was that the better choice? He didn't know, but it seemed the only option given the previous outcome. He hesitated again, only to be served another stinging slap. After that, he pointed to the Aftaran.

The crystal let the Aftaran go and began shocking the Mendoken with that same high energy blast. His body shook just like the Aftaran's had earlier, and no sound emanated from his mouth either.

Marc didn't understand what was going on or why. Once again, he tried to move to help, but he couldn't. And, after the Mendoken's ordeal was over, he once again became the recipient of the same energy blast. It was just as painful, just as unbearable. More so, perhaps, as he was already plenty weakened by the first dose.

After the crystal finally let him go, he was barely conscious anymore. Everything seemed so distant, and faint. Perhaps he was dead. He certainly wished he was. Yet he was still awake, still aware of his surroundings, his mind somehow still barely functioning. He floated helplessly in the gravity-less environment, unable to move or steady himself. All he could sense was that lasting pain radiating through every inch of his body.

There was no nourishment anywhere this time either to help him regain at least a little strength. The crystal eventually steadied him, and once again he was presented with the Mendoken on one side, the Aftaran on the other. Only this time, as he peered closer at the faces, he realized it was a different Aftaran and one he knew personally. Those round brown eyes were hard to forget, the same eyes he had once stared into all those years ago in an Aftaran arena at the very moment he had expected to die. His executioner had turned out to be his savior in disguise, none other than Raiha.

This time, she was the one in trouble. She looked worried, clearly, but like a true Aftaran had that air of confidence about her, that the Creator would see her through thick and thin.

Now what, he thought. Creator or not, there was no way he could let Raiha face so gruesome a punishment. He would have to pick her every time, much to the nameless Mendoken's misfortune. And so, with whatever energy he had left in his body, he lifted his hand to point to her.

As expected, the crystal let go of Raiha and struck the Mendoken. As bad as he felt about the Mendoken's agony, Marc could only hope that this time he had finally gotten it right. It seemed the crystal wanted him to choose based on some kind of logical thought process. He could only hope, therefore, that saving the one he knew was something the crystal would perceive as the better choice, and this vicious cycle of violence would finally come to an end.

To his chagrin, however, the crystal came after him again as soon as it was done with the Mendoken. It struck him hard, with another dose of lethal energy. The shock, while familiar by now, was still insufferable. And with every strike he was growing considerably weaker.

When the crystal steadied him again, he couldn't even keep his eyes open. His breathing was shallow, and hoarse. The only thought crossing his now barely functioning mind was that if he didn't get it right this time around, he would soon be dead. Perhaps that was the objective of this last punishment anyway. He certainly couldn't imagine that he and his friends would be allowed to stay alive after this was all over.

The crystal prodded him repeatedly until he opened his eyes. This time, he saw Raiha again on one side, and a group of Aftarans on the other. They were roped together by the crystal's long limbs, confined and unable to break free. Every one of them looked worried, unsure of what to expect next, and unable to say anything like Marc and Raiha.

Again, he didn't know what to do. Saving Raiha hadn't been the better choice. Nothing had been the better choice. Whichever one he had picked, the other got punished and he got punished as well, every time. He was beginning to wonder if there was any right answer here at all – perhaps this was all meant to be a slow draining of his life until he was zapped of all energy and pronounced dead. The third and last punishment would also be his own end, and likely that of the other fifteen. What would happen to all the other prisoners after that was anyone's guess – perhaps they would all be killed off too, or turned into slaves. If for any reason their lives were spared, they certainly wouldn't have lives worth living.

Perhaps, just perhaps he'd get it right this time. It had to be the better choice to save a group of individuals instead of one, even if that one was someone who mattered. Surely this damn crystal would see that. So, as horrible as he felt about it, he avoided looking at Raiha directly and pointed at the group.

No avail. The crystal punished Raiha as expected, but then zapped Marc right after. As the raging pain seeped through his weakened body once again, he felt helpless and at a loss. And he gave up. He gave up the little strength he had left in his mind and body, and fainted.

When he awoke, it was only because the crystal was sharply prodding him, repeatedly. And when he finally came to his senses, the choice he saw before him this time caused him to gasp in horror.

Chapter 31

The surroundings were blurry and gray. President Tucker couldn't make anything out. His eyes just wouldn't focus. But he was alive, that much he knew. He could hear the sounds of fire crackling, even an explosion or two in the distance. The air smelled of heavy smoke.

His head hurt, badly. So did his arm and back. One of his legs he couldn't feel. He could hardly move, but he tried his best to sit up. He felt a wave of dizziness, but it subsided after a minute. And then the focus in his eyes slowly began returning. He could see again.

He remembered now. He and his family had been in a helicopter. First the other helicopter had blown up after getting hit by a missile, then the one he had been in. Somehow, miraculously, he had survived the explosion and the crash. Instinct kicked in next. Where were his wife and children? He looked around, but he couldn't see much in the dense smoke. He tried to stand up, but he couldn't. His right leg wouldn't move. He couldn't even feel it anymore. Then he noticed it was under a large slab of metal, a piece of the helicopter's body.

He called out their names. "Jocelyn! Where are you? Jocelyn? Leticia! Travis!" Silence. "Anybody? Answer me!"

More silence. Then he heard a faint voice in the distance. "Daddy?"

"Le... Leticia? Is it you? Are you ok?"

"Help me, Daddy. Please."

With all his might, he tried to lift the metal object from his leg. It wouldn't budge, at first. But the protective parental instinct in him forced the adrenalin to rush through his body. One more heave, then another, and his leg broke free. He still couldn't feel any sensation in the leg, but at least he could move his body now. Dragging the paralyzed leg, he pulled himself up and crawled toward the direction his daughter's voice was coming from.

The smoke was hanging low around him, delivering a thick haze that made it hard to see very far. There was rubble everywhere too, remnants of the chopper that only made it harder to move about.

"Leticia, where are you?" he called.

"Here, Daddy, here!"

He found her eventually, buried under what was left of one of the back seats of the helicopter. She was cowering in fear and pain, but the expression of relief on her face was very visible as soon as she saw him.

"Hold on, baby, I'll get you out," Tucker said. "Does anything hurt?"

"Everything does."

"But is anything unbearable?

"No."

"Do you feel any part of the seat under you?"

"Huh?"

"Is anything stuck under you, or are you touching the ground only?"

"The ground only, I think."

"Ok, good."

He rose slowly and stood on his working leg. Trying to keep the balance, he gently lifted one edge of the seat.

"Slither out," he puffed. The seat was heavy.

She tried. "I can't... move."

He had to lower the seat to give his arms a break. "Yes, you can, kid. Come on. Try again. Here you go."

He lifted it again. This time, she dragged herself out, slowly, yelping in pain as she did. Once she was out, he let the seat go. It fell to the ground with a thud.

Tucker knelt and hugged his daughter tightly. It was a miracle that she was alive and unhurt. "Are you ok?"

"I'm ok," she whispered, holding onto him and letting the tears flow out of her eyes. "Thank you."

"Where's Travis? Your Mom? Have you seen them?"

"Travis is over there." She pointed to her right. "Mom, I don't know."

Tucker crawled over in that direction, and soon found his son lying on the ground. He wasn't stuck under anything, but his eyes were closed and he wasn't moving. Tucker quickly felt his pulse and heaved a sigh of relief. He was alive, but unconscious. He had bruises on his face and legs, but otherwise he seemed unharmed. Tucker lifted the boy's head and softly rubbed his face. Slowly he came to.

"Dad?" he croaked.

"Yes, son. It's ok. You'll be fine."

Leticia had gotten up and joined them, and she clutched tightly on to both of them. Tucker couldn't keep his own tears from trickling out of his eyes. Both of his kids were safe. Nothing in the world mattered more than that. He cherished that moment, as long as it did last.

"Where's Mom?" Travis asked, slowly sitting up.

"I'm going to look," Tucker replied. "Stay here."

"I'm coming with you," Leticia said.

"No, stay with your brother."

The smoke was starting to clear, just a little. Tucker could see further now, and he wasted no time in surveying the surroundings. Amidst the wreckage, he noticed a body lying on the ground. Fearing the worst, he crawled over.

Thankfully, it wasn't his wife – it was the pilot, and he was dead. To the right, Tucker noticed another body. It was the secret service agent who had accompanied them on the chopper. Also dead. Tucker closed his eyes for a moment to try to come to terms with the losses. These men had given their lives to protect him and his family, as so many countless others in the government and armed forces would have done. If he ever made it out of here alive, he would make personal visits to the families of these fallen heroes to pay his respects. For certain.

He crawled toward the main part of the helicopter's fuselage, now nothing more than a charred, twisted array of metal and debris. There was someone lying there. Could it be Jocelyn? Maybe it was.

"Jocelyn!" He hurried forward, as fast as his paralyzed leg would allow. "Jocelyn!"

The long, straightened brown hair, as ruffled as it now was, was unmistakable. As was the blue dress she had been wearing. It was undoubtedly her.

"Oh no," he whispered, his hands shaking as he tried to revive her. Her face was bloody and bruised, her eyes closed. "Jocelyn, wake up! Jocelyn!"

Fearing the worst, he felt the pulse on her neck. Nothing. Then he placed his ear on her chest. Still nothing. Feeling desperate, he tried to shake her. But there was no reaction.

The truth sank in slowly, though shock had already overwhelmed any other sensation or emotion. But there was no mistaking it. Jocelyn, his wife of eighteen years, his best friend and lover in one, was dead.

Tucker buried his face in her chest and let the tears roll. The sobs turned to cries, the cries to howls. It wasn't long before both his children found him, and once they caught wind of the situation they shrieked in shock. Together they huddled over the fallen body and, united in grief and sorrow, wept their hearts out.

The sound of a car moving startled Tucker and his kids. All this time, not a single soul had come by. The helicopter had crashed in the middle of nowhere, an open field in the depths of rural Virginia. There was no road nearby, no farmhouse, no sign of human presence. And yet, the car was coming ever closer.

Actually, it wasn't a car. It was a truck – the engine sound was deep and rattling. Most definitely a diesel. There was more than one – several, perhaps. They were coming closer. Through the clearing haze, he could see them now.

Help at last, he thought. He felt relieved, and he was about to tell his kids to stand up and start waving to draw attention. But the relief was short-lived, once he noticed the flags atop a couple of the vehicles. A white cross inside a red circle. Unmistakable, and unmistakably dreadful – the Aryan Nation.

He heard the sounds of doors opening, people getting out and shouting orders at each other, followed by rapid footsteps.

"Travis, Leticia, run," he said quietly.

"Huh?" his daughter asked.

"Run for your lives."

"But... Dad, you can't move," Travis said.

"Leave me. I mean it. Run... now!"

"Who are they?" Leticia asked, terrified.

"The ones who shot us down," Tucker said. "Go!"

"We're not leaving you," Leticia said. "Travis, help me."

She grabbed her dad's left arm, while Travis grabbed the right. Together, they lifted him up, at least high enough so that he could limp. With his arms swung around their shoulders, they began moving, dragging him away from the trucks as fast as they could. Their destination was the line of trees in the distance, perhaps the only place in the vicinity where they might be able to hide. Their speed of movement, however, was anything but satisfactory.

"This is insane," Tucker said after a few minutes of painfully slow progress. He could hear the loud panting, he could see the expressions of pain on the innocent faces of his two little kids. "You have to go without me. Otherwise you'll never make it."

"Never," Travis huffed.

"Stop being stubborn! It's your life!"

But the kids refused to leave him. He and his wife had raised them to live by principle above practicality and all else, and it was showing. Were it not for the current circumstances, he would have felt great pride as a father.

Tucker turned back to look. He could see the shadows of several figures now, quickly closing the gap. They were beginning to fan out on both sides to form a circle. There was no mistaking it – he and his kids were already trapped. It was too late.

The last straw hit when he tripped over a stone and fell, his sheer weight taking both kids down with him. They crashed onto the ground, the only solace being that the ground was covered with lush grass and soft soil. While they sustained no more injuries, the pain of the existing wounds was only exacerbated by the impact of the fall. They certainly wouldn't be getting up by themselves anymore. Especially not with a horde of heavily armed, angry looking men surrounding them within seconds and staring them down.

They were mostly dressed in dark clothes. Some of them wore leather jackets and caps, others t-shirts with swastikas and crosses surrounded by circles blazoned all over. Some had long, unkempt hair and beards, while others had shaved and shiny bald heads. Ugly tattoos covered much of their exposed skin. The one thing they all had in common – every single one was carrying some kind of firearm, be it a pistol, rifle or machine gun. And one more commonality, of course, given the nature of their cause – they were all white.

Tucker stared up at them, shifting his gaze from one individual to the next. They looked roughed up and tired. Individually they must have traveled from all corners of the country to gather here to take advantage of this tumultuous time, to take up the fight against the federal government while it was at its weakest in its entire history. Yet, regardless how tired they were, every one of them had a fiery expression in his face, in his eyes. An expression of zeal, of uncompromising anger and hate, of unwavering conviction that their time had finally come and that they would make the most of it. It was a sight that would make anybody who wasn't one of them feel a sense of fear and distress, of uncertainty how much these people might choose to harm him or her.

Tucker, a man of military background who had endured conditions far worse than this in battlefields galore, wasn't worried about himself. His wife – well, he wouldn't even get the chance to mourn her death right now. If he survived this somehow, the time for that would come. His only concern at that very moment was the safety of his kids. He beckoned to them, and both grabbed on to him as the ringleader came forward.

"Mr. President himself," the man jeered, his long hair and beard fluttering in the wind. The accent was unmistakably southern. "Alive, but not so, heh, well I see. It's a pleasure, dear sir, to see you finally put in your place."

Several of the others snickered and egged him on.

The President remained quiet, trying his best to refrain from bursting out in anger. This individual was responsible for the death of his wife and several of his best staff members, and for placing his kids in harm's way. It took his mind a few seconds to register who this man was. The face was unmistakable from all the photos on the reports he'd seen of the Aryan Nation on his Oval Office desk. Steven Bane, the much feared, much hated, racist, xenophobic, hate-mongering leader of the Aryan Nation.

"We were expecting you to be dead, but no matter," Bane continued. "This actually works out even better." He waved his hand at the men beside him. "Fellas?"

A few of them came forward to grab Tucker and his kids.

"Daddy!" Leticia cried.

"My kids!" Tucker begged. "Leave them out of it."

"Oh no," Bane replied. "We wouldn't separate them from you. What kind of people do you take us for?"

Before he could say anything more, Tucker felt a sharp blow on the back of his head and blacked out.

Chapter 32

Marc was conscious again, but he certainly wished he wasn't. If he could only somehow disappear, if he could cease to exist to avoid this level of agony on himself and those he was affecting with the choices he was being forced to make. And this time, the choice was beyond horrible.

On the right side was Raiha again, visibly weakened after her zapping by the crystal. And on the left, none other than Alisha.

Marc closed and opened his eyes several times, hoping that beautiful face would vanish and magically be replaced by a nameless other. But no such luck. She looked terrified, her eyes locked onto his, with the faintest glimmer of hope that somehow the man she was falling for would find a way to protect her.

For him, of course, it was no contest. As bad as he felt about it, he did not hesitate to pick her over Raiha. The crystal zapped Raiha once again, followed by the standard zapping he had to endure. Unsurprisingly, given how weak he now was, he fainted again.

Awakened once more by a vigorous shaking, he was faced with Alisha again on the left side, and on the right by a larger group of both Mendoken and Aftarans. The group was so large, in fact, that it was spread across the clutches of multiple crystals. A number of them had arrived in the meantime, and they had all amassed to the right behind the crystal holding Alisha.

One against hundreds, he thought as he forced himself to open his eyes and resist the overwhelming urge to drift off to endless stupor. There easily were hundreds of prisoners there, all innocent, all to face a harsh agony if he chose the one individual over all of them. But it was the one individual that mattered. He noticed Alisha shake her head and nudge toward the other side, likely in an effort to persuade him to sacrifice her for the sake of so many others.

He would get zapped again no matter which side he picked, that much was clear. There was no escaping his eventual demise through this ongoing torment. If he could at least protect the one person who mattered the most to him from suffering until then, that was probably the last useful thing he'd be able to do before breathing his last breath. What happened after that, well, he would have no control over that.

So he picked her again, and watched in horror as the hundreds of prisoners had to endure what for many of them was likely the most painful experience in their entire lives. Then, as was routine, it was his turn after which he passed out.

The next time, the gathering of Mendoken and Aftaran prisoners was even larger. And the next time even larger.

This must be a numbers game, he began thinking. What if he did pick the large group over Alisha? It hadn't worked earlier when it was Raiha pitted against a group, but that had been a group far smaller, by multiple orders of magnitude. Perhaps he just needed to cross a certain numerical threshold, where the crystals found it logical to sacrifice one individual for the many, even if that one individual was someone who mattered.

He stared at Alisha, his eyes remorseful and sorry. She looked back at him approvingly, nodding and signaling that it was high time for him to make this sacrifice.

Brave woman, he thought. He admired her even more at that very moment. Closing his eyes, he pointed at the crowd. He kept his eyes closed, unable to bear the sight of her being zapped by the crystal. He could only hope that she would pull through and wouldn't have to endure it again, that this choice of his would finally end the ordeal.

But it didn't. He got zapped next, and when he finally awoke he saw her still in the crystal's clutches, pitted against an even larger crowd of prisoners. At least she was alive and conscious, thankfully.

He shook his head in dismay. He was so feeble now, so helpless, so out of answers. He couldn't think straight at all anymore, but think is precisely what he needed to do. And he needed the time for it. Between the slaps prodding him to choose and the increasingly longer periods of unconsciousness from one zap to another, however, he wasn't getting any. The growing weakness was also causing him to hallucinate, and he wasn't even sure anymore what was real and what wasn't.

But if there was any even remotely possible way to get out of this and to save everyone from endless punishment, he needed time to think and strategize. He had, after all, successfully gotten out of the first two punishments. Granted, those had been with help and support from others. This time he had no such luxury – he was on his own.

The next time around, as he eyed Alisha on the one side and the large gathering of Mendoken and Aftaran prisoners on the other, he decided to endure the slaps from the alien as it tried to get him to choose. The slaps weren't nearly as painful as the zapping that followed anyway, even though they did get progressively more forceful the longer he procrastinated.

He closed his eyes and began thinking between the slaps. He wondered what this punishment might really be about. The first punishment or test had clearly been about physical pain, getting the mind to overcome the body's sensation of that pain and finding a way to fight back against the perpetrator of the pain. The second one had been about exposure to fear and phobias, getting the body to overcome the mind's sensation of fear and trudge through no matter what.

The first two had therefore been about mind and body, and the tight relationship between them. So what about this one? It involved physical pain for sure, but it wasn't about overcoming that pain. It was about making choices, choices based on... well, he didn't know. Clearly every choice he had made so far hadn't helped or ended the suffering, and every choice he had made was based on either logical or emotional thinking. Perhaps there was no right choice. That this was meant to be his last punishment was quite clear. He wasn't even allowed to communicate with anyone, lest they try to influence his choices. The crystals wanted him to die a very slow and painful death. They didn't expect him to "pass" this one, and by design. But what did passing even mean here?

He realized he simply wasn't making the right choices. This test wasn't about mind or body, but something else. Something perhaps the crystals either lacked or expected him to lack. It could only be the third thing that organic intelligent life comprised or was believed by humans at least to comprise – the soul. The soul had a conscience, a sense of morality. It was higher in standing than both the mind and body. He had to make the moral choice here, the moral choice, not the logical or emotional choice.

In a moral world, he discerned, it wouldn't be a choice about whose life was more important or how many lives of one type were equivalent to just one of another. In a moral world, every life would count just the same, because every life mattered.

The crystal slapped him again, harder than the last time. It was growing increasingly impatient with his inaction. He opened his eyes and viewed the choices. One individual who mattered against an entire population of those who didn't. But they all mattered – maybe not as much to him, but they all mattered the same. There was no right choice, they were all right choices. And so, raising his hands, he took the chance and simultaneously pointed at both sides.

The crystal didn't react at first. It seemed dumbfounded, taken aback. Eventually it let go of both Alisha and the group of prisoners it was holding on the other side. All the other crystals behind also let go of their prisoners, who began dispersing in all directions in the gravity-less space. It was like watching a large collection of balloons spreading into the sky after being released.

Marc tried to move, but he couldn't. He wanted to get closer to Alisha, who was involuntarily floating away from him. Neither could speak, so calling out wasn't an option either. He didn't know what was going on. Had he somehow "passed?" What now? The crystal was motionless, with only the edges of its limbs swaying just a little. The other crystals behind started coming closer together, eventually connecting at the edges. They also connected with the crystal in front. The red cores began shooting streaks of light at each other – they were syncing somehow. All of the crystals were morphing into one large creature. It was a scary sight.

The newly formed giant crystal began surrounding him, by shapeshifting and stretching out around him to form a hollow sphere. The only thing inside – him. He was completely trapped. Then the sphere began shrinking the size of its inner wall, reducing the space for him to move about. This creature was, in effect, going to crush him to death.

Marc began frantically moving his arms and legs about, useless as it was to do so. Without the force of gravity to aid him, there was no way he could strike hard enough at the crystals' limbs to break their bodies apart. What could he possibly do? After all he had been through, what a horrible way to die. Those bright nodes and limbs in between were coming at him from all sides. Their energy blasts would vaporize his body to shreds. Soon he was confined to a space the size of a cocoon, just big enough to hold his body.

He thought of closing his eyes and letting the memories flow as death overtook him, but at that very moment his eyes came into focus on the nearest node, a bright green one just inches from his face. He recalled how he had communicated earlier with the little friendly crystal, and wondered if, just by chance...

At this point, what did he have to lose? He lifted his hands and touched the node. Immediately he could feel the hot energy seeping up his arms and into his body. Rolling his head back just a little, he thrust it forward until his face smashed into the node.

* * *

Marc's surroundings turned into a blurry haze. Just like the last time he had done this with the little crystal, he felt a flurry of emotions. But the emotions were different this time. It wasn't pain and suffering, it was anger and hate. Downright scorn, from a collective consciousness, and it was all directed at him. It was intense and overwhelming. But he remembered how he had coped with the intensity of the emotions last time, and he forced himself to stay above it all. The emotions eventually gave way to blurry visions, and the visions slowly became clearer.

He found himself immersed in some kind of virtual reality, like the last time. The environment this time, however, wasn't a simulation of the creation of a universe or of lifeforms. Rather, it seemed to be the same surroundings he was physically in. The only difference he noticed right away – gone was the entire giant crystalline structure that had engulfed him. Gone were the nodes and their mesh of intertwined limbs. Instead, all he could see were the red cores and the direct connections between them. It was like looking at an x-ray image of a body, where all the muscles, tissue and organs were rendered invisible, while the bones buried deep within could clearly be seen.

It's the red cores, the sophisticated remote-control mechanism that's preventing these otherwise benign crystals from being themselves, Marc thought. Now that so many of them had merged to form a larger being, their red cores were behaving as one. Flashes were constantly passing from one to the other, ensuring the whole creature remained in full compliance with whatever orders were coming from above.

And, speaking of above, he could now see a direct link that led from the central red core up and away, well beyond the creature. Following its path, he noticed the link reached far beyond the confines of the space station. The walls of the space station, in fact, were no longer visible at all. He could see empty space beyond, but even so the standard haze and distant cloud formations of this universe weren't visible either. The only thing that was visible in the distance lay at the tail end of the link – a bright red, blazing anomaly. This link, therefore, was clearly virtual, likely based on some kind of energy flow that easily passed through anything material.

Gazing around, he noticed other anomalies spread apart across space. They were all connected to each other via more links, and each of those anomalies in turn were connected back to other giant crystals back inside the space station. The central red cores of the giant crystals were also connected to each other.

Marc realized he could see the entire virtual network connecting the anomalies with each other and with the crystals they were controlling. It was a gigantic mesh of links, heading every which way no matter which direction he looked. More importantly, though, he realized this was all he could see because he was now connected directly to the minds of the anomalies themselves and not to the individual crystal that had engulfed him. If there had ever been any shadow of doubt whether the crystals were being controlled by the anomalies via the red cores, it was now fully lifted.

Marc could essentially now see the entire "brains" of the anomalies. It seemed they hadn't yet noticed that he had plugged in to their collective consciousness, because he wasn't facing any obstruction or pushback.

In between the anomalies in the distance, images came into focus. At first, he couldn't make out what they were showing, but it soon became clear. They were moving images, like video replays. He was actually "seeing" the thoughts of the anomalies. At least, he had no other explanation of what was unfolding before him. All this time, the crystals and anomalies had been watching him, tracking his thoughts and using them against him. Now, for the first time, he was seeing their thoughts. This proved one very important thing – these anomalies weren't invulnerable. If he could only hold out long enough and finally use this to his advantage. If only.

Some images were showing more space stations, and they looked much larger than the one he was on. Many of them were completed, others still in construction. He could also see an opening to another gateway, like the one he had traveled on to get to this universe. A steady stream of solid stuff was coming out of the gateway at a constant rate. It wasn't clear what the "stuff" was, but it appeared to be rocky material of some kind.

They're transferring matter from our universe, he thought, likely from some other galaxy without advanced civilizations to evade detection. To build all those space stations, probably. But why? Surely they weren't planning on bringing more individuals over to imprison and punish them?

He didn't know, and he found it all very bizarre. And why not planets instead of space stations? They were clearly bringing enough matter over. Then it dawned on him – the much lower gravitational pull in this universe. It would be hard to build a rocky planet large enough to hold all its matter together given the low gravity. The matter on the surface would just keep flying off. A ring-shaped space station, however, could compensate for the low gravity by spinning around faster, thereby generating the centrifugal force necessary to feel sufficient gravity along the ring's outer wall.

In addition to their hell-bent determination for revenge, these anomalies were clearly extremely intelligent and capable. It was equally clear they were experimenting with complex matter and gravity, both of which they had very little of in their own universe. If only he knew why.

He noticed an anomaly right next to every space station, reaching out with limbs it had shaped on the fly which attached themselves to the station's outer ring. He was hoping one of the images would zoom in so he could see in better detail what was happening, and given enough time perhaps that would have happened. It was, however, only going to be a matter of time before his connection to the collective mind of the anomalies got noticed, and get noticed it did. And as soon as it did, everything around him instantly blacked out.

What followed was agony, extreme agony. He didn't know what it was – it certainly wasn't physical pain or suffering, just immense mental discomfort. And it came very suddenly. He was getting bombarded with powerful negative emotions, way more than his one mind could handle. He wanted to shut it all out, but he had no idea how to it.

It was so incredibly overwhelming, and his physical weakness from all that zapping earlier certainly wasn't helping. He found himself drowning in sorrow, and he wished he could just die. That was no doubt the intent anyway. The crystal that had surrounded him hadn't been able to physically kill him, so now that he was connected to its mind its masters would do it mentally from a distance.

He had to fight back, somehow. He didn't know how to pull his head and hands out of the crystal node he was connected to. He was so deep in this virtual realm that he couldn't sense his physical body anymore at all. No, the only way was to resist the mental pressure itself. Gathering whatever strength he had left, he tried to calm his mind down. He tried to convince himself that all these negative emotions weren't real, that they could have no real effect on him. He reminded himself of how he had overcome dealing with physical pain in the first punishment and his phobias in the second. If he put his mind to it, he could overcome any obstacle no matter the severity.

Meditation. He needed to meditate, he realized, just like in the first punishment. He had to apply his years of kung fu training once more to shut out all external influences and concentrate his mind on just one thing – fighting back.

He let his mind sink slowly into a meditative state, a task made all the harder with the barrage of negative energy coming at him from all sides. But he did it. And then, he began training his mind to throw the energy right back to where it was coming from. Every sentiment, every painful thought that came – he refused to let it enter and pushed it right out of his mind. The more he did this, the more he noticed the sheer darkness around him slowly lifting.

Before long, he could see things again. He saw the crystal's network of red cores first, then the anomalies in the distance, and then he could even see a visual manifestation of the barrage of negative energy being sent toward him from the nearby red cores. They looked like streaks of lightning, one after the other. He was successfully fending them off and sending them back to their sources.

Every time a streak struck back at the core it originated from, that core seemed to suffer a blow and a setback. It weakened just a little, and the next streak it sent was just a tad lower in intensity. As soon as Marc noticed that, he felt increasingly confident that his actions were working.

He kept up the resistance. Before long, the nearest red core withered away and let go of its connections to its neighbors. The next one followed suit soon after. Then he noticed something even more interesting. Far away, he saw other cores shrinking and dying too, no matter which way he looked. What was going on?

That couldn't have been due to his actions – there hadn't been any direct interaction between him and the cores in the distance. It could only mean that... yes, others were doing the same thing he was, connecting to the crystal in different parts of its body and fighting it mentally.

Others – who could they be? It didn't matter. Given the circumstances, all help was welcome, regardless of the source.

In front of him, red cores all across the large crystal body began to disintegrate and disappear, taking their connections to other cores along with them. Then the connections to the anomalies in the distance began to fade as well. As this continued, his vision returned ever so slowly to that of real life. The crystal body, with all its nodes and limbs, was starting to become visible again, as were the boundaries of the space station. The sensations of his physical body began to resurface – he could feel his arms and legs, and his head.

As soon as he was able, he pulled his head back right away from the node he had attached himself to, and his hands followed suit. Then, just like that, he was back in the real world. And what he could now see surprised him at first, but then it began to make sense.

Chapter 33

Commander Maginder of the 357th Mendoken Armada stood still on the third level of the massive control deck of his lead Kril-4 ship, waiting patiently. He was expecting the arrival of a fleet of ships from the Mendo-Lairel system, the site of the nearest primary ship manufacturing center inside the Mendoken Republic that had not been attacked by the anomalies from the other universe.

The Mendoken had been hard at work for many days now, building entirely new ships and retrofitting existing ones with new weapons. All of this new weaponry had been ordered by the Imgoerin himself, after scientists on the planet Lind in the Mendo-Zueger system had uncovered the composition of the anomalies and from where they got their mighty destructive power. The new weapons, Maginder had been told, were the only thing that had any chance of harming the anomalies and reducing their destructiveness.

The Mendoken, of course, were not exactly known for their boastfulness or tendency to exaggerate things. Quite the opposite, in fact. He could only hope, therefore, that the weapons would be able to do a lot more to the anomalies than just reduce their destructiveness.

Maginder floated over to his most trusted officers, Sautal and Hansa. They were both busily monitoring things on screens at nearby stations, two of many scores of Mendoken on this one level of the control deck alone.

"Anything yet?" he hummed.

"No, Commander," Sautal replied. "Do we know how many ships to expect?"

"They have kept it secret. For security reasons, in case the anomalies somehow find out and try to attack the convoy en route."

"Did you receive any information on the technology of the weapons, Commander?" Hansa asked.

"No," Maginder said. "For the same reasons."

They waited silently. Maginder stared through the wide transparent walls of the control deck at the monstrous ring beyond. The gateway to the other universe within it was still open, a huge gaping hole awash in different colors that narrowed into a cone the further it led into the other realm. The end, of course, wasn't visible. It just faded away into the distance.

"Surprising that the gateway has remained open all this time," Hansa commented. "With our last probe in there still steady and holding position at the edge." She pointed at a screen showing a pictorial rendering, recreated from signals sent back by the probe, of the end of the path.

Maginder hummed in agreement. "Thankfully. The edge of the gateway has not moved at all. Whoever is controlling the other side is still waiting for something, or just is not yet ready to let us pass."

"Just as well," Sautal added. "We were not quite ready either."

"That is about to change," another Mendoken officer said, floating over. "The fleet is approaching and slowing down."

"How many ships and which types?" Maginder asked.

"We cannot read that information," the officer replied. "They have cloaked the convoy. For..."

"Security reasons, yes. We will have to wait till visual contact."

They didn't have to wait much longer. A blip appeared on one of the screens at Sautal's station, showing a zoomed-in section of space outside. Sautal immediately pointed toward one side of the transparent wall.

"The fleet is coming from there," he announced.

Everyone shifted their gaze in that direction. Indeed, a flash of light appeared in the distance. As it came closer, already out of its bosian layer and slowed down to a speed where its movement could be tracked by the naked eye, its shape became evident.

"A Kril-8 battlecruiser," Hansa observed.

Maginder hummed in acknowledgment. "A battlecruiser makes sense, and the Kril-8 is the most powerful. And the next one?"

Sautal studied his screens. "I do not see any."

"I do not understand," Hansa said.

Maginder was puzzled too. "Just one ship? How do they expect to fight with just one ship?" He was about to move away and send a message to central command on Lind to ask what was going on, but something caught one part of his head-encompassing eye. It was another flash of light behind the approaching vessel. It looked like a new star that had appeared out of nowhere.

Then, without any warning, that entire side of the sky lit up with countless lights. It was as if one whole side of the already dense Glaessan galaxy had suddenly doubled its concentration of stars.

"What... is this?" Maginder asked, bewildered. At least, as bewildered as a Mendoken could be.

"There are hundreds of them," Hansa observed.

"Of what?"

Sautal had no answer – his screens were registering nothing. "They have completely cloaked themselves from any form of identification."

As the lights came closer, they began to appear blue in color. And, closer still, their shapes became clearer. They looked like sunflower heads, with deep navy petal-like extensions around centers of a light blue hue.

"They are much larger than conventional ships," Hansa said.

"Planet destroyers," Maginder said. "I have never seen so many of them together before."

"They are traveling in parallel, spread apart," Sautal observed. "To speed up the journey."

"The Imgoerin is leaving nothing to chance with this mission," Hansa said. "He has amassed the most powerful armada ever in the history of the Republic."

"Given all the damage these anomalies have caused us, he wants to quash this threat once and for all," Maginder said. "In addition to the fact that the abduction of the space station, carrying not just Mendoken but individuals from the other major civilizations in our galaxy, happened on our watch. It is our responsibility to try to bring them back with all the means at our disposal."

The approaching planet destroyers, now much closer and blocking out much of the view of space beyond, looked like a wide, symmetrically spaced collection of blue sunflowers rising from a dark meadow. It was an incredible sight, revealing nothing short of the sheer magnitude of Mendoken military power. Were beings of any race less robotic than the Mendoken present to witness the scale of this technological marvel, they would surely gasp in astonishment.

"Will they even fit through the gateway ring?" Hansa wondered.

Sautal performed some calculations. "Barely."

"The engineers must have taken that into account already," Maginder said.

"Communication channel opening from the approaching Kril-8 ship," another Mendoken officer nearby announced.

Another screen opened up in thin air in front of Maginder. The moving image of a Mendoken head appeared.

"Commander Maginder, this is Commander Soldara Graenzen 45329874 of the 507th Armada," she said. "We are ready to travel through the gateway."

Maginder wondered how someone he had never met or heard of before had been given the charge to run so critical a mission for the Republic. Then again, it was a big Republic with lots of Mendoken, and perhaps he had spent too much of his life here in the fringes instead of being physically nearer to the seat of power. No regrets, though. Like most Mendoken, he didn't believe in having an ego or raw ambition for the sake of individual career advancement when it wasn't deserved or necessary. It was all about the collective good of the entire civilization.

"Commander Soldara, we are at your service. The other side of the gateway still has not opened, however. The probe we sent in remains in a state of limbo at the edge."

"We have it on good authority that once we enter the gateway the other side will open."

"How so?"

"The Aftarans are convinced that whoever is controlling the other side is waiting for us to be ready to pass through. Granted their reasoning is not logical and hence why we may not understand it, but it worked for us when you sent in the last probe. The Imgoerin is asking us to trust what the Aftaran leader is saying."

Maginder was confused. "The Aftarans were saying that the other side would open only when whoever was controlling it was ready for us, not us for them."

"They have since adjusted their view, and now feel it may be both."

"So entering with an armada of battle-ready ships will somehow signal the other side that we are ready?"

"Not the battle-ready ships themselves, but what they are carrying."

"How will the other side even know?"

"That is where our logic reaches its limits and the Aftarans' faith comes in."

Maginder had no idea what to say to that. "Why do you need planet destroyers?" he asked instead.

"Because of the size of the anomalies and the required firepower to strike at them. Nothing in our arsenal has more firepower than the planet destroyer."

"Nothing in the entire galaxy has more. But we have tried using them before against the anomalies. It did not work. The anomalies simply absorbed all of the energy from the blasts and only grew stronger."

"That was before we understood the composition of the anomalies," Soldara said. "All of the planet destroyers in this fleet have been retrofitted."

"With what?"

"A taste of our universe."

"Please explain, Commander," Maginder requested.

"The anomalies gain their power from the combination of high energy plasma and the high concentration of stagnant bulk energy in their universe. Take one of them away, and they will lose their destructiveness."

"How can we do that?"

"Our universe has a much lower concentration of bulk energy, and here it is expansive in nature. Imposing the laws of physics of our universe on the anomalies for an extended period of time should cause the bulk energy enclosed in their bodies to spread out and dissipate, putting an end to the continuous chain reaction that gives them their power. That is the theory."

"So...?"

"So all we have to do is replace the conditions of their universe with those of ours, at least within a confined space that we enforce upon each anomaly."

"Like a shell?" Maginder asked.

"That is one way of putting it."

"This theory - has it been tested?"

"Yes."

"In replication, on Lind?"

"Yes. More evidence in the fact that these anomalies rarely stayed for long at a time when they came here to our universe. Before any attack, they kept disappearing and reappearing."

"You believe it is because...?"

"To replenish energy, yes. Because they were losing it so rapidly in our universe whenever they showed up. The patterns by which they appeared and reappeared may initially have been to confuse us, but later on the patterns took on a distinctive meaning – a message to us explaining what they wanted."

"I remember," Maginder said. "That would also actually explain their destructiveness here. In essence they dissipated their own internal energy in each attack because they could not keep it together anyway. They just chose to channel it in specific directions for maximum impact."

"Correct."

"Are all vessels prepared for subatomic transformation as they pass through the gateway?" Maginder asked.

"Yes, Commander," Soldara replied, her posture and tone of voice remaining constant throughout. "Any more questions?"

"Just one. What if the other side of the gateway does not open?"

"And what if it does? Would you want to miss that chance?"

The fleet of planet destroyers had traveled in multiple parallel paths from the Mendo-Lairel system to reach Mendo-Biesel in the shortest time possible. Now that they were here, the ships had to change formation into a single line behind the entrance to the gateway. Given the sheer number of ships and the colossal size of each, this was going to be no trivial task.

The unique organizational skills of the Mendoken, however, would ensure that this undertaking got done in a fraction of the time it would have taken any other advanced civilization such as the Aftar, Volona or Phyrax. An accomplishment even more noteworthy when considering that none of those other civilizations had ships even a fraction of the size of the planet destroyers.

A single line of hundreds of planet destroyers, with a single Kril battlecruiser in the middle carrying Commander Soldara. Her ship was purposely placed in the middle to protect the chain of command in the journey through the gateway and on to whatever threats lay in wait for them on the other side, provided they ever got there.

"Why not just have the Commander onboard one of the much larger planet destroyers?" Hansa wondered aloud, watching the spectacle unfold before her from the safety of her own ship. "Why have a battlecruiser at all? It is a single point of failure."

"That is precisely why," Maginder countered. "When the enemy sees a horde of charging giants, the last thing they will worry about is the small speck in between them. It is actually a sound strategy."

"Albeit risky."

Maginder couldn't disagree with that. He was just thankful that he and his fleet of ships had not been assigned to travel through the gateway with the attack force. His role was to stay put – to monitor and ensure the stability of the entrance to the gateway for the duration of the entire operation. If the operation was successful, it would be the only way back home for Commander Soldara and her army, along with any survivors from the abducted space station they may just happen to rescue.

"The first destroyer is ready, Commander," Sautal announced.

"Are we ready on our side?"

"We are."

"Give them the go ahead, then."

Subatomic-level conversion of something as large as a planet destroyer was a massive undertaking. If anyone could muster the technology to do it, however, it was the Mendoken. The conversion of the first destroyer happened flawlessly, all the way from the initial breakup of the entire structure into smaller and smaller pieces until they eventually reached the subatomic level, then reformatting every particle to obey the physical laws of the other universe, followed by re-amassing the entire ship and its contents into the same shape and function that it originally had.

As the second destroyer entered the gateway and began its conversion process, the first one reached the end of the trajectory, right behind the probe that was still patiently waiting at the very edge.

"Anything?" Maginder asked, peering over the screens that Sautal, Hansa and a number of other Mendoken officers were actively monitoring on the control deck of his ship.

"Not so far, Commander," Sautal replied.

They waited. The second destroyer finished the conversion and reached the edge behind the first one. The third one entered the gateway.

Maginder turned to the screen showing Soldara's face. "Nothing is happening, Commander."

Soldara's face was as expressionless as ever. "Patience, Commander. We need to reach critical mass to get noticed, to demonstrate that we are ready to fight. The Aftaran leader predicted this."

"You mean more of these large destroyers? Do you not consider it risky to have so many of them in this narrow gateway at the same time, unable to move ahead?"

"A risk we have to take."

More ships began entering, one by one, and each went through conversion. They were lining up at the edge.

Maginder was beginning to think this was a hopeless task, and even thought of floating away for a bit to contemplate other options. But at that very moment, a number of screens began lighting up and notification sounds went off across the control deck.

"Something is happening, Commander," Hansa announced.

"What?"

"The edge of the gateway trajectory – it is opening."

Chapter 34

Marc was back in the real world. A strange universe still, no doubt, but it was physically real. The crystal that had engulfed and attempted to crush him to death was no more a single being. Its red cores destroyed and gone, it was broken up into hundreds of little crystals scattered every which way in the gravity-less environment, little crystals just like the one that had helped him and Alisha through so much of these punishments.

Between the little crystals, he could see Mendoken and Aftarans, hundreds of them. They were the helpers, they had come to his aid. Seeing what he was doing, they must have followed suit and attached themselves to other nodes around the giant crystal's body to mentally fight it. They had somehow succeeded, and very thankfully so. Their intervention had helped destroy the red cores and break the creature apart.

His voice still gone, all Marc could do was nod to them in a show of gratitude. Several of the Aftarans nodded back and smiled, Raiha among them. As always, the Mendoken showed no reaction.

Having lost the link to the remotely controlled red cores, the little crystals were no longer a threat. They were moving about, flying in different directions and touching each other with their nodes. It was almost as if they were affectionately greeting each other, like old friends or family members that were coming together again after a very long time.

They're free and happy, Marc thought. He wondered how long it would last this time before an anomaly came close to set them straight again. This time he and all the other Mendoken and Aftarans would have to work extra hard to hold them back from the influence of those dratted anomalies.

But he was so weak, so tired, so hungry, so spent. He didn't know how he'd be able to muster the strength to even move about and so something useful, and that too without gravity. Frankly, it was a miracle he was still alive. The Aftarans were helpless just like him. They couldn't move without the assistance of gravity or a way to exert thrust in a particular direction.

The Mendoken, however, had one major advantage here – their metal-encased bodies were used to floating above ground, thanks to a levitation mechanism powered by electric motors. They could use the same motors to generate thrust in any direction of their choice, pushing their bodies wherever they wanted to go. With the more powerful remote-controlled crystals now no longer a threat, they were free to roam about as they pleased.

And they did. They began steadying the Aftarans in their midst, and one of them also came for Marc. He didn't recognize her personally, but he nodded to her to express his gratitude. Holding his hand, she pulled him toward a gathering in the distance. From his vantage point, it was an amazing sight, looking awfully similar to the structure of a monstrous atom. The gathering was the nucleus, while around it were many, many of the little crystals whizzing about like electrons.

As he came closer, he could make out more details of the gathering. It comprised what he suspected – all the thousands of Mendoken, Aftarans and others from the space station. Closer still, he began looking for familiar faces and, of course, for the one familiar face that mattered the most. Mendoken, Mendoken, more Mendoken, many Aftarans, a few Volonans, no matter which way he looked. Nobody he knew.

The Mendoken pulling him along let him go as he entered the crowd. Seeing no familiar faces, he began bouncing off one individual at a time to float ahead through the crowd. Still no luck. Gazing outwards, he saw more individuals being pulled in by Mendoken from the depths of the hall. Among them, he finally recognized one individual – Zorina. It was easy, given how she stood out as a Volonan among all the non-Volonans. He waited to see where she entered the crowd, then began bouncing toward her location.

Reaching her eventually, he wasn't surprised to see her tired and worn out, just like him. They hugged each other and tried to speak, but the sound from their voices remained elusive. Using hand gestures, Marc tried to explain how he had endured and survived this last punishment, and she responded by showing similar gestures with her large elephant-like trunk and ears. She had been through the same thing, and she had gotten out just like he had with the help of others.

Marc gestured with his hands that he wanted to find their friends, and Zorina bobbed her head up and down in agreement. Holding on to each other, they began bouncing off others to keep moving through the crowd. They found Sibular after much searching, just as he entered the crowd. Soon after they found Dumyan, already in the crowd, looking dazed and weak like Marc and Zorina. Sibular, on the other hand, whose hybrid Mendoken body continuously obtained nourishment from the radiation surrounding him, seemed in relatively decent shape despite the ordeal he must have just gone through.

Marc's friends had successfully made it out of this punishment. They had seen through the moral dilemma posed by the crystals, perhaps more easily than he had. Not surprising, he thought, given how they came from civilizations far more advanced than his own. Their morality was superior to that of these anomalies, that much was for sure. The anomalies hadn't expected anyone to pass this last punishment, most likely because they thought everyone was as selfish and narrow minded as they were.

But they were mistaken, not just about the morality but also about the subsequent mental anguish they had used the crystals to put Marc and his friends through. Sibular, Dumyan and Zorina had learned their lessons from the first punishment, just like Marc had, and they had successfully used meditation to fight back once again.

Still, Alisha was nowhere to be found. Holding on to his friends, Marc continued to bounce through the crowd, hoping she would appear somehow, somewhere. They trudged through most of it, without finding so much as a trace of her. At the very end of his remaining strength and energy, Marc could feel despair and hopelessness sinking in. He felt like closing his eyes and letting it all go.

He was about to do just that, when he felt a nudge on his arm. It was Dumyan – he was pointing away from the crowd toward the depths of the hall. Marc's eyes were nowhere near as sharp as the large owl-like ones of an Aftaran, so he had to squint to look and focus. First he could only see dark, empty space in the direction Dumyan was pointing. Then he saw a small number of node-like lights appearing in the distance. It was a little crystal, with no more than five linked nodes spread apart in a pentagram-like formation.

That color combination – blue, green, red, blue, yellow – it could only be... Yes, it had to be that same little crystal that had helped him before. And it wasn't alone – it was pulling somebody along with it. As they came closer, his hopes grew. The silhouette could only be human, and the only other human here with him was her.

His eyes met hers, and they both smiled with relief. He bounced off Sibular to float toward her, holding out his arms to catch her as she arrived. They embraced and hugged, and a kiss soon followed. Marc forgot all his woes, his exhaustion and hunger. None of it mattered anymore. Not being able to speak didn't matter either, just being able to hold each other was good enough.

Eventually Marc loosened his grip of her and turned to face the crystal. He bowed slightly in a show of gratitude, and Alisha followed suit. The crystal lowered its upper nodes toward them in a show of acknowledgment. Marc then pointed to his mouth and his legs, trying to indicate that the lack of gravity and speech were problems that somehow needed to be solved. He also put a hand on his stomach to show that he was hungry.

Without hesitation, the crystal spread out its limbs and motioned to Marc, Alisha, Sibular, Dumyan and Zorina to each grab onto one of them. It seemed unconcerned by the additional weight it would have to pull, and it soon became clear why. Once each of them had a grabbed a limb, it sped off into the depths of the hall without as much as a whimper. This creature had way more strength than met the eye.

The wind blowing in his face as they headed for a destination unknown, Marc could only hope the crystal had understood what he had meant and knew how to help. He exchanged glances with Alisha and the others, but they were as clueless as he was. They had no choice but to place their complete trust in this creature carrying them away.

They reached the top of the hall. The ceiling, of course, was narrower than the floor, given that it was a circular space station. The ceiling had transparent sections that gave a view of the central sphere in the distance around which the ring was built, along with three massive beams that connected the ring to the sphere. Marc deduced that there was one beam for each of the three halls spanning the full circumference of the ring.

The little crystal, still pulling the five individuals, kept moving along the ceiling toward the edge of the nearest beam. Once they reached the beam, Marc noticed an opening in the ceiling – the entrance to a passage right into the beam. It likely led all the way into the central sphere.

Into the passage they went. It was dark, cold and deserted, but at least there was breathable air. Marc wouldn't have been able to see a thing were it not for the brilliant light emanating from the nodes of the crystal. The passage was like the inside of a wide, hollow cylinder. It went on for a while, but after everything he had been through, Marc knew to simply hold on to his patience. By now, he had also built more than enough trust in this simple little creature to know that it wasn't leading him and his friends into some kind of trap.

At the very end of the passage was the opening to the central sphere. As they passed through it, what Marc saw before him was something he couldn't have remotely imagined, and that too given all the crazy things he had already seen in this crazy universe.

It was extremely bright, and it took his eyes some time to adjust. There was a golden haze all around, and lots of empty space. It took him longer still to make out the microscopic pathways in the distance that went every which way. More pathways emanated from those, and more still from those. It was a gigantic mesh of tiny pathways, and where every pathway met another there was a tiny node-like lump. These lumps flashed as streaks of light passed through them and made their way up and down the paths.

These pathways and lumps were many orders of magnitude smaller than the limbs and nodes of a crystal, as there were many orders of magnitude more of them within a comparable volume of space. This was not a crystal, Marc surmised. The only thing he could imagine was that this was something similar to the interior of a single node of a crystal. Much larger, though. Taking up much of the core of the central sphere, in size it was comparable to a structure clumping all of the crystals in this space station together.

Regardless of size, this thing was clearly some kind of advanced neural network. It had intelligence, perhaps not in the same conscious way that the crystals and anomalies did, and perhaps the crystals were just using it as a machine or computer of sorts. This was, in effect, likely the control center of the space station.

The little crystal kept moving, pulling everyone along with it, until they reached the very edge of the massive structure. Letting them go, the crystal reached out with one of its nodes and touched the nearest collection of lumps in the neural network. The lumps immediately lit up and began sending many messages along the pathways across the rest of the structure.

A wave of something, Marc wasn't sure what, spread outwards from the structure soon after, passing through him and everyone else, out of the sphere and toward the ring of the space stations. He didn't feel anything other than a whiff of air as it hit him, but its effect soon became evident. His throat began rumbling as it cleared some buildup, and the sound came out of his mouth soon after.

"Hmmm," he uttered. "Ahhh. I, uh, this is working. My voice is working." He couldn't resist a weak smile.

Zorina bobbed her head up and down in delight. "Finally!" she exclaimed. "That was like having a gag shoved into my mouth." She went on to utter a series of profanities.

"Thanks to the Creator for ending it," Dumyan said, whispering a short prayer right after.

"Gratitude would be better served if directed at this crystal," Sibular added quietly, nodding at the little creature.

The crystal, however, paid no attention to him. It was still busily communicating with the giant neural net. More of the millions of pathways lit up, more messages were getting sent.

There was a noise – a loud, creaking noise.

"What's that?" Zorina asked, startled.

Marc's gaze turned away from the neural network and toward the surface of the sphere. "It's turning," he observed, noticing the movement of the solid, inner wall.

"Gravity," Sibular said. "The station has started turning again. But we will not feel the effects here. Only on the outer floor of the ring."

"Things are returning to normal," Dumyan remarked with relief. "Now we just need food."

The crystal and the neural network must have read their thoughts or heard their conversation, because within seconds stacks of tubes filled with paste appeared around them. Marc, Alisha, Dumyan and Zorina grabbed as many as they could and gulped their contents down, one after the other. Sibular, of course, needed none, but he sipped some paste from a single tube anyway to fill his reserves.

The horrid taste aside, it was much needed nourishment, and in the nick of time. Marc felt replenished, both the extreme hunger and thirst soon subsiding as he consumed the nutrient-rich paste of a dozen or more tubes.

He put his arm around Alisha. "Feeling better?"

She nodded. "Just when I thought things couldn't get any weirder."

"You've got that right."

"We should head back to the ring," Zorina said, her expression visibly more at ease after filling up on food. "Enjoy the gravity, as long as we can."

"As long as we can," Dumyan repeated. "Only so long before the anomalies strike back."

"But the punishments appear to be over," Sibular retorted. "Which begs the question – what is next?"

"You saw the images when you were surrounded by the big crystals with the red cores, right?" Marc asked the others. "When you touched their nodes?"

"Yes," Sibular replied. "More space stations under construction, and matter being transported from our universe."

"Those were the thoughts of the anomalies," Dumyan said. "We were reading their thoughts. All this time, they've been reading ours and using it against us. Finally we got a chance to see theirs."

"Exactly," Marc said. "But we still don't know why they're doing all of this, or what they really wanted from us. I doubt it was all just to give us a really hard time. I wonder..." He turned to look at the gigantic neural net, blocking most of their view to one side, above and below.

"This big thing?" Zorina asked.

"It's clearly the control center of this space station," Marc pointed out.

"Likely just following orders from the anomalies," Dumyan said.

"But it should at least have some useful information," Sibular retorted. "One of us needs to connect to it. Perhaps with the help of the crystal."

Marc's eyes lit up. He looked at the little crystal inquisitively. It was still holding on to some of the lumps at the edge of the neural net.

"No," Alisha said immediately.

"I have to," he replied.

"Why?"

"Because I'm the only one this crystal seems to have a connection to."

"It may not be safe, Marc," Dumyan said.

"Not because of security controls," Sibular said. "I doubt this structure has any. Its creators had no expectation that we would ever make it this deep into the heart of the space station. We were all supposed to be dead by now. It may, however, be unsafe for other reasons."

But after all that nourishment, Marc was re-energized. "Only one way to find out." He paused, before adding with a smile, "And perhaps the only way for us to find a way out."

"Let me have a go instead," Zorina said.

"Why you?"

Zorina flapped her ears. "I was able to connect with these crystals too. I went through the same experience in this punishment like all of you did." Then she pointed her trunk at Alisha. "Besides, you now have someone to live for, unlike me."

Chapter 35

"What happened?" Marc asked. Both he and Sibular grabbed Zorina and tried to steady her.

She looked flustered, her heart beating fast and her breaths rapid. Tears were rolling from her eyes, and her ears flapped uncontrollably. She had just pulled her head and hands away from the giant neural network, a connection the little alien had helped her make. She had remained connected for several minutes at least.

At least she's alive and conscious, Marc thought.

She didn't speak at first. It took more urging by everyone around her before she finally opened her mouth.

"We... we have to rush," she quivered.

"Where to?" Sibular asked.

"Back to the outer ring. Now!"

"Why?"

"I'll explain along the way."

Marc gestured accordingly to the little crystal. It grabbed hold of them, one with each limb, and sped off, away from the giant neural network and out of the central sphere.

"We have to warn everyone else," Zorina said rapidly as they flew up the same corridor they had earlier come down. "They're coming."

"Who's coming?" Marc and Dumyan asked in unison, trying to keep their voices audible above the wind noise.

She just flapped her ears again.

"Zorina, what did you see?" Sibular asked.

"That big structure in the sphere's a control center alright," she finally said. "And a lot more. It's kept record of everything that's been going on here. I saw snapshots of every single punishment we went through, along with numbers and charts in languages I couldn't read, analyzing every single reaction each of us had, every movement we made, even every thought we had. There were detailed depictions of our anatomies, our cell structures, brains, everything."

"So they were studying both our physiologies and our behavior," Marc said. "Seems you were right, Dumyan."

"It wasn't all just punishments or a form of revenge," Zorina went on. "They were testing us too. Each punishment tested different things – the first our bodies' endurance of physical pain and the ability of our minds to overcome it, the second our minds' endurance of mental anguish and the ability of our bodies to overcome it, and the last the pain of both our bodies and minds together, with the ability of our souls, or our conscience, to overcome it. They didn't expect us to survive the last one. In the end, it was all to understand how physical beings with all three things actually work – body, mind and soul."

"Any information on why the punishments seemed to get progressively shorter in time duration?" Sibular asked.

"No," Zorina replied. "Though if I were to guess, it shows the relative priority the anomalies placed on each test. The mind controlling the body was probably most important to them. The last one was probably just to make us suffer a little more before killing us. I don't think they had any real interest in the soul or conscience."

"Interesting," Marc observed. "Certainly makes sense."

"Regardless, that thing measured everything and fed all the information into a master design," Zorina added.

"For what?" Dumyan asked.

"A lifeform."

Marc's eyes widened. "A lifeform? What kind?"

"Based on complex matter. Not sure if it's organic or not. But its consciousness comes from the anomalies themselves - they pass it on, via some kind of direct connection, like breathing life into them or something."

"It would explain why they scanned our bodies with such detail," Sibular observed.

"It makes sense now," Dumyan said. "The anomalies originally came to our universe to find and punish us. But when they saw the physical attributes of our universe, all the matter and all the life it contains, they wanted the same for themselves. They wanted more out of their own lives than just flying around aimlessly in empty space. Now they're trying to play the role of a creator. By passing on some of their own consciousness to these new creatures, they can live new lives in parallel."

"They studied us while punishing us, and they planned to kill us off in the end once they got all the information they needed," Marc said, shaking his head. "Sneaky."

Zorina tried to flap her ears in the wind. "And cruel. But I think the worst is yet to come."

"What do you mean?" the others asked in unison.

"The first lifeforms have already been created. And they're coming here now. Another space station is docking with this one. That's what I saw - the neural net was preparing this station for the dock."

"What do these lifeforms look like?" Alisha asked, her long hair fluttering in the wind.

"I'm not sure," Zorina replied. "I pulled out before I could get to see those images."

"They are probably optimized to live and operate in the conditions of these space stations," Sibular remarked.

"Whatever their appearance, I doubt they're coming here to socialize with us," Dumyan added.

"No, they're coming here to complete what the crystals failed to do," Marc said anxiously. "To finish us all off."

Zorina agreed. "Which is why we have to rush back to the hall where we came from. To warn everyone else."

The hall was in chaos. Gravity was back at least, thanks to the rotation of the ring underway again. The floor of the hall, which of course rested on the outer surface of the ring, was once again the supporting ground for everyone's feet. But that was the only semblance of order Marc could detect amidst the scene before him, as he and his companions exited the beam and began their descent from the top of the hall to the floor.

Everyone was rushing about and coming back together in panic, looking for ways of escape but finding none – the Aftarans and select few Volonans, and even the otherwise usually stable Mendoken. Jinser-Shosa and any other Phyrax who happened to be around were, as usual, nowhere to be seen, likely dispersed and spread thin across the air in the wide hall to avoid detection. The crystals were whizzing about everywhere, with no apparent sense of purpose or control.

There was good reason for the despair. Through the transparent sections of the hall's walls, Marc could see that a number of anomalies had appeared in the distance, and they were spreading out to surround the space station. More were coming. That in and of itself was not the issue - it was that another station had indeed docked with this one, as Zorina had predicted. Another station of the same shape and size, clamped perfectly with this one. The two rings were touching each other all along their respective circumferences, like a giant double bracelet. The central spheres were also touching each other, likely allowing the two neural networks to merge in some way.

Even that was not a reason to panic, nor was it the multiple gates that had sprung open along the wall touching the other station. The cause of panic was what was coming out of those gates.

"Holy crap," was all Marc could say. He glanced at Alisha, who looked terrified.

"There they are," Zorina said. "Told you. We've got to get down there and help the others."

"If we can," Sibular added.

Dumyan closed his eyes and uttered a short prayer.

As they came closer to the ground, Marc was able to make out the silhouettes of these new creatures. They were big, many times larger than a human, but not huge – no bigger than the combined crystals with the red cores. The size, however, was not the part that made him shudder at their sight. It was the speed with which they moved as they entered the hall, the skeleton-like shapes of their bodies and, above all, the monster-sized wings on their backs that enabled them to jump and instantly fly across swathes of air-filled space.

Sibular was right, Marc thought. The physiques of these creatures were indeed optimized for their local surroundings. They would thus be all the harder to combat. He eyed one of them more closely. The body consisted mostly of very muscular legs, and there were a lot of them. Eight to ten on each side, perhaps. Strong legs, attached to a central spine and curving outwards until they reached the ground. From a distance, it kind of had the basic shape of a human rib cage, but with very large wings jutting out from the back of the spine.

There were no arms, which Marc at first found a little strange. If you had the option of designing a physical creature from scratch, why would you only give it legs and no arms? But when he noticed the head jutting out from a long neck attached to the edge of the spine, he realized why. It was big and wide, shaped somewhat like a hammerhead. It swooped downward, as if to stare down whatever prey had the misfortune of crossing its path. Given the length and flexibility of the neck, however, the head could turn in any direction it wanted.

At each edge, facing forward, to the side and even to the back, was a bright, gleaming red eye. It looked like a short, fat line. Together, the eyes looked menacing, but not nearly as menacing as what lay right below them – an open mouth that stretched across the width of the head, spraying shimmering rays of energy every which way. This creature looked truly frightening, and extremely ugly to boot.

The rays were just as effective as hands, Marc realized, and then some. Hence why no arms were needed – the rays had the power to move matter around. Any time a ray hit an object or individual, it tossed it aside as if it was nothing more than a dust mite. Mendoken, Aftarans, even the crystals – it didn't matter. These monsters didn't distinguish between friend or foe, or perhaps to them everyone was now a foe. None of the crystals had red cores anymore controlling their actions, so perhaps that wasn't surprising. Either way, the monsters clearly had superior power and strength to all others. But that wasn't even the worst.

"Oh, no," Marc whispered slowly. He could hear shrieks from Zorina, Alisha and Dumyan. Some of the monsters were shooting different kinds of rays now, and their effect was far more devastating.

"They're... killing them!" Alisha exclaimed.

Whoever these rays hit - Mendoken or Aftaran – was literally being vaporized into thin air. The molecules of their bodies were somehow being converted into a blast of energy, and, worse yet, the energy was then sucked into the gaping mouth of the monster that had shot out the deadly rays. Upon consuming the energy blast, the monster seemed to grow just a little bigger and stronger.

"We have to stop this," Marc said, horrified. "Where's Raiha?" He searched frantically in the crowds to make sure she was ok, but there were too many individuals no matter which way he looked to spot her.

"I see her," Dumyan said, pointing down and to the right. "She's far from any of the monsters at the moment."

But likely not for long. They were everywhere already, having spread out quickly around the hall with their high velocity of movement. They could gallop with their strong legs and even fly with their wings. Nobody was safe. And that sound, oh that rumbling, piercing sound every time one of them released a ray – that thunder-like racket was deafening.

Marc and his friends were close to ground level now. "We need a plan to...," he began to say, but that sentence would never be finished. His attention was desperately needed elsewhere, for a monster had just jumped up from the ground, spread its wings and left very little doubt that it was heading straight for them.

There was, however, no time to react – to run or fly away. There wasn't even any time to say something or make a facial expression. These monsters were just too fast. Time, it seemed, came to a standstill for those five individuals holding on to that one little crystal that was whisking them through the air. All they could do was stare at the rapidly approaching beast as its mouth lit up with a deadly ray aimed squarely at them.

Marc instinctively closed his eyes and squeezed Alisha's hand. He could feel her squeezing his back. The crackling sound of the ray made it to his ears as well, just as he felt a tremendous push on his body. The push, however, was in a direction perpendicular to that of the ray's motion.

He opened his eyes in bewilderment, in time to see the ray blasting through the very spot in which he'd just been. The others – Alisha, Dumyan, Sibular and Zorina – had been flung away in the nick of time as well. But by whom?

As he fell to the ground with a thud and a pang of pain on his butt, he saw the monster moving on without turning back. It had likely noticed other prey ahead to target instead.

Short attention span, he thought. He also realized one individual was missing – the crystal that had been holding them together. He feared the worst that the ray had struck the crystal and destroyed it. But then he noticed something out of the corner of his eye – a small, glowing sphere hovering in the air, barely wide of the ray's trajectory. And, as the ray dispersed and evaporated, the sphere opened up and grew rapidly back to its original shape and size. It was the crystal.

What an amazing creature, Marc thought. The crystal had both immense strength, which he already knew, and superfast reflexes. It had thrown all five of them out of harm's way in the blink of an eye. Plus it had the ability to curl itself up into a tiny object in the face of imminent danger.

He got up and ran toward Alisha, helping her up. Then the two of them ran to gather with Dumyan, Sibular and Zorina. Chaos was still all around, with monsters blasting out rays that caught and killed innocent members of the crowd. But, at least for the moment, the spot where these five individuals stood was not in the crossfire.

"I have an idea," Dumyan said as he glanced at the crystal that had just saved their lives, hovering in the air above.

"How to fight them?" Zorina asked.

"Yes. But it'll be very risky."

Chapter 36

"It's their necks," Dumyan said. "Their necks."

"Huh?" was the unanimous response from Marc, Alisha and Zorina. Sibular stayed quiet, other than emitting a faint, inquisitive hum.

"Their necks. It's the one part of their bodies they can't protect. You see how they can turn their heads to shoot a ray in any direction? Because of their long necks." Dumyan pointed at the nearest monster. "The one place they can't strike is on the backs of their necks. Flexible they may be, but even that flexibility has limits."

Zorina flapped her ears. "Are you actually suggesting we jump onto them?"

"None of us can outrun them," Dumyan said. "Not even the Mendoken with their floating bodies. So, in a word, yes."

"How would we get on?" Zorina asked.

"That's where the crystals come in," Dumyan replied, pointing at the crystal still hovering above them. "They can catapult us up onto the monsters."

"Are you nuts?" Marc exclaimed, dumbfounded.

"We just witnessed how strong this crystal is."

"Even assuming that works, then what? Strangle them? I doubt they even breathe or need to."

"No, but perhaps we can cut their heads off," Sibular said calmly. "Then the one weapon they have will be rendered useless. Even if the head can function without the body, it will not be able to move anywhere to inflict any more damage."

Alisha looked both disgusted and puzzled. "What with? I really don't think their necks will be as easy to snap as the limbs of the crystals. They're so much thicker."

"Something so gruesome isn't quite what I had in mind," Dumyan replied.

But before he could get to any further explanation, they noticed a monster galloping toward them. "Quick, Marc," he said. "Tell the crystal. It only listens to you."

"Tell? Oh, I get it." Marc looked up at his crystal friend and motioned to it to fling Dumyan at the approaching monster. The crystal didn't seem to understand, for it wouldn't budge.

"Marc? We're running out of time!" Dumyan said nervously, eyeing the rapidly approaching monster, about to shoot its first ray at them.

Marc reached out, grabbed the nearest node of the crystal and pulled it down to touch his forehead. The crystal had passed its thoughts and memories on to him before, so he could only hope that if he concentrated hard enough with his thoughts, he would be able to reverse the flow of energy.

Concentrating amidst the impending threat of extermination was no easy feat, but it worked. The crystal abruptly cut off the connection, lunged at Dumyan, curled all of its nodes together to cover his body and heaved him up with a mighty push.

Dumyan's body rotated like a soccer ball as he steered through the air in a curve toward the monster, avoiding contact with its straight-shooting rays that way. He landed on the back of its neck, but not without almost falling off. His long, strong arms caught on in the nick of time and helped settle his body onto it.

The monster, sensing his unwanted presence, screeched and immediately began thrashing about, trying to yank him off its body. It sprayed rays in random directions, but, as predicted, none of them could reach Dumyan. Nor did they reach anyone else – most of them shot right up into the air. He continued holding on with all his might, wrapping his arms and legs around the neck to stay secure in position.

"What's he doing?" Zorina wondered aloud.

Rodeo, Marc thought. The scene reminded him of a rodeo. Dumyan was riding on this monster like a cowboy on a wild horse. Except, as he now realized, Dumyan's ultimate goal here was slightly different.

"He's distracting the monster," he said. "That's all he's doing. The longer it's distracted, the fewer rays it shoots at targets and the fewer individuals die." He looked around – so many of the other monsters were still chasing down Mendoken, Aftarans and Volonans, who were trying so desperately to flee from the rays' deadly trajectories. But there was nowhere to go in this wide, empty hall, nowhere to hide where the monsters couldn't get to them.

"We've got to do the same thing," Marc added. "We've all got to do it, to as many of the monsters as possible."

"Are you sure?" Alisha asked. "To what end and for how long?"

"As long as it takes. Perhaps we can tire them out."

"Highly unlikely, but I see no alternative," Sibular said. "We have to save lives, for as long as we can."

Marc turned toward his crystal, and quickly touched one of the nodes with his forehead again. This time, he asked it to spread the word to all the other crystals the hall, in whatever way they communicated with each other. Then he positioned himself in front of the crystal, motioning to it to catapult him toward the nearest monster.

The crystal understood right away and shoved him off. He closed his eyes initially at the sensation of sudden acceleration through the air, but he opened them quickly again in order to aim correctly for his destination. Following a curved path while constantly rotating his body was no easy or pleasant feat, especially for someone as prone to motion sickness as he was.

He landed on the back of the monster, at the very bottom of the neck. He almost fell off at impact, but he was able to steady himself by grabbing onto the shaft of the neck and wrapping his arms around it. Then he rotated his body around the neck so that he was on its upper side.

As expected, the monster stopped dead in its tracks and began thrashing about. Marc held on for as long as he could, but as a human he didn't have anything close to the physical strength or stamina of an Aftaran. To him it felt like an eternity, but he likely lasted no longer than a minute. It eventually threw him off like a fly, sending him off to crash on the ground several feet away.

Bruised and shaken, he raised his head to see the furious monster charging at him, its eyes glowing red and mouth lighting up with rays to be shot right at him.

There was no time to get up and run. Fortunately his crystal saved him again, pushing him away with a hard shove. It shrank to a tiny size right after, barely avoiding the impact of the deadly ray itself.

Marc got up and quickly surveyed the scene, knowing he only had seconds before the monster charged at him again. Thankfully the message had spread. Crystals everywhere were catapulting Mendoken, Aftarans and Volonans onto the backs of monsters. Some lasted seconds before being thrown off, others minutes. Some absolutely refused to let go no matter how hard it got. But regardless how many times they fell, they got right back up and had the nearest crystal send them off again. The net result – life was getting much more difficult for the monsters, and they were no longer able to inflict nearly as much death and destruction as before.

He motioned to his crystal, which had regrown to its original size in the meantime, to send him off again as the same monster he had climbed onto earlier came attacking once more. The same thing repeated itself, although this time he was able to stay on a little longer. Then again, and again. A few times he was able to stay on for up to a minute, other times no more than a handful of seconds. The only issue – the monster seemed to be losing no energy or drive to destroy him. He, on the other hand, was getting hurt with every fall and growing increasingly tired.

He came across Alisha at one point, just as she was recovering from one of her own falls.

"Are you ok?" he asked.

She looked far from happy. "I don't understand the point of this. We're not winning," she said, rubbing her bruised arm. "We're just delaying the inevitable."

Marc didn't know what to say. He knew she was right. "What I don't understand is why they're killing and consuming everyone in one shot. Wouldn't it make more sense to ration us?"

"We may not be their only source of nutrition. They probably just want to do away with us altogether before we become any kind of threat to them. They're getting their nourishment and quickly getting rid of us at the same time."

"You may very well be right."

As he gazed around to take stock of the situation, he realized things were about to get much worse. "These monsters are changing tactics."

Alisha agreed. "They're helping each other out."

Indeed they were. Having realized that they were being played, they were now amassing into groups of two or three and attacking together. If anyone landed on the back of one of them, then one of the others would use its head to knock that individual off right away. And, after that, all three would fire rays on him or her. The chances of the nearest crystal being able to push that individual out of danger in time had just dramatically reduced themselves.

"Oh no," was all Marc could say, as he watched the killing begin again. About a third of the Mendoken, Aftarans and Volonans in the hall had probably already perished, fed off as energy to the monsters. He searched frantically for Sibular, Dumyan, Zorina and Raiha, and he sighed with relief as he spotted them one by one. They were all still alive. Zorina was nearby, but she was lying on the ground – she seemed hurt.

Marc and Alisha darted as quickly as they could toward the Volonan.

"Zorina, are you ok?" Alisha asked her as they arrived.

"My leg," she stammered, pointing at it. "I can't stand, or even move it."

Marc inspected her left leg. "Does this hurt?" he asked, touching a protrusion in her knee.

She howled in pain. "Stop!"

"Sorry." Even with his limited knowledge of Volonan anatomy, it was quite obvious to Marc that the leg was broken. As if things aren't bad enough, he thought. There was literally nothing he could do for her at the moment. Then he remembered the crystal's healing powers and turned to look for it. It had followed them here and was only a few meters away.

"Marc!" Alisha shrieked.

"What is it?" He turned the other way to see three monsters galloping right toward them. Zorina's healing would have to wait. Instead, he motioned to the crystal to send him off toward one of the monsters. But the crystal wouldn't budge. He began frantically waving with his arms, but it refused to cooperate.

"It's no use," Alisha said. "The crystal knows it's futile. We're... done."

"Sorry, Marc," Zorina said feebly. "Nothing I can do to help anymore."

Marc and Alisha faced the approaching creatures, holding onto each other.

This is it, he thought. All the time spent in this strange universe, all those endured punishments and tests, all for naught. What a way for it all to end. He watched as all three of them lit up their mouths in unison, getting ready to blast the seething rays that would instantly vaporize him and the woman he had fallen in love with, as well as a dear, wounded friend. At least their deaths would be together and instantaneous.

Just as the rays were about to hit them, however, a white cloud appeared from nowhere and shot across in front of them like a moving wall. It blocked the rays from progressing any further, somehow absorbing them into its mass without blowing up.

"Jinser-Shosa!" Marc exclaimed.

The Phyrax proceeded to completely engulf Marc, Alisha, Zorina and the crystal, forming a protective hemispherical shell around them with its gaseous body.

"How did you...?" Marc began.

Jinser-Shosa's head came into shape inside the shell. "Hah!" it rasped. "Nothing a Phyrax can't handle."

The monsters, however, weren't stopping. They were standing right outside now, and taking shot after shot at the cloud, trying to break it up. Other monsters had seen the spectacle and were joining in the effort. The Phyrax was completely surrounded and getting relentlessly pounded from all sides.

"What are you doing?" Marc shouted, trying to make himself heard above all the commotion of the repeated blasts. "You'll never survive this!"

"Do you dare challenge me?" Jinser-Shosa's voice was starting to sound hoarse, and it was breaking up. "I do whatever I want."

"But why?" Zorina asked, sounding quite hoarse herself. "At least you can stay hidden. You're sacrificing yourself for nothing."

"It's not for nothing." Jinser-Shosa was sounding fainter by the second. The cloud cover was also starting to grow thinner. The damage the rays were inflicting on its body was real.

Zorina flapped her ears ever so faintly. "What's it for, then?"

"Call it our strict sense of loyalty if you like, for old friends."

Marc recalled the long friendship between Zorina and Jinser-Shosa, and especially how he had accompanied Zorina into the Phyrax Federation to seek out Jinser-Shosa's help in fighting the Starguzzlers. The only reason Jinser-Shosa had agreed to help was because of Zorina's friendship, and that help had been instrumental in the eventual victory over the powerful Starguzzlers.

"I'm as good as dead already," Zorina retorted. "I'm wounded. And there's no way out for any of us. Don't do this, Jinser-Shosa, please. Save yourself."

"There's still hope, for you and the rest of this lot that's still alive. I promised this friend of yours here that I'd help get all of you home," Jinser-Shosa replied, nodding at Marc. It also had to pause briefly to regain enough energy to keep talking. "We Phyrax, call us rowdy and hot tempered, but we never lie to or betray anyone. We stick to our word.

Death? I'm not afraid of it, or of anything else for that matter. But I'll fulfill my promise yet. I just need to make sure you stay alive long enough."

"Long enough for what?" Marc asked.

Jinser-Shosa's gaseous body faded away completely as it feebly uttered the last words it would ever say. "Look outside."

Chapter 37

Jinser-Shosa was gone. Vanished, vaporized. The mighty, crazy Phyrax was dead, but there was no time to mourn. Marc expected to die right after, as the rays from the monsters would now hit him and his friends uninhibited.

But he didn't, because the monsters had stopped firing. They had, in fact, moved away. They were all moving away and amassing in an area from where they could gaze unhindered through a transparent section of one of the hall's walls at what was happening in space beyond.

"Look outside" were Jinser-Shosa's last words, so Marc followed its advice. He set his gaze in the same direction that the monsters were looking, but given how far he was from that window and especially given that the monsters had crowded around it blocking much of the view, it was hard to make out what was going on outside.

At first, all he noticed were the many anomalies out there, surrounding the space station. Evidently they had gathered to witness the final destruction of the prisoners they had transported from the other universe, the final destruction of individuals they harbored so much anger and hatred toward that they first had to punish them mentally and physically in such painful ways for so long a period of time before killing them off.

"Oh, my!" Alisha exclaimed.

"What?" Marc asked.

"Over there." She pointed at a gap between two distant, adjacent anomalies.

Marc squinted and focused his eyes, and then saw it. There was a hole opening up. It looked like a black hole at first, but as it grew in size its interior was awash with all the colors of the rainbow.

"A consar opening?" she suggested.

Marc thought so too. But the hole continued to grow beyond the typical size of a consar, well beyond. Its diameter was soon larger than that of an anomaly, many times larger. This thing was, simply put, enormous. And it seemed to be stable.

"That's no consar," Zorina said meekly, still lying down but propped up on one side with her elbow to get a better view. "That's a full-blown gateway, similar to the one that brought us here to this universe."

"And they seem surprised," Marc added, nodding at the monsters and the anomalies outside. "It's not one of theirs. Which can only mean..."

He didn't have to finish that sentence, for at that moment a gigantic shadow appeared and came out of the opening. The shadow was shaped like the head of a sunflower, and as it drew closer its light blue core and deep navy petal-like extensions became visible.

"A... planet destroyer!" Marc called out.

"A what?" Alisha asked.

"A Mendoken planet destroyer. Their biggest warship and weapon. It's here. They're coming!" He grinned excitedly.

The planet destroyer was soon followed by another, and another. Many more came, and as they did they fanned out quickly across space, surrounding the anomalies that were surrounding the space station.

The anomalies, clearly surprised at this unexpected intrusion into their realm, initially seemed unsure how to react. But it didn't take long for one of them to blast a flash of annihilative energy toward the nearest destroyer, the same kind of energy flash that had wreaked so much havoc on Earth and other worlds in Marc's home universe. It looked like a red fireball, large enough to engulf a whole city and more, and bright enough to outshine a nearby sun.

The destroyer reacted right away, firing a shot of its own from the depths of its sunflower-like core. This shot was a white streak, and as it neared the approaching fireball it spread out like a cloud, engulfing it quickly and slowing it down. The cloud thickened and brightened. The surface began pulling on the fireball from all sides, forcing it to expand quickly. Then the unimaginable happened – the fireball vaporized in a puff of smoke, fully contained within the confines of the cloud. Soon after, the cloud dissipated into space and disappeared. That unstoppable flash of deadly energy was gone.

"They've figured out how to fight the anomalies," Alisha said, visibly relieved. "I wonder how."

"Mendoken genius," Marc replied. "They must have determined the energy composition of the anomalies and identified a way to break that energy apart."

The anomalies began firing a barrage of flashes at the Mendoken destroyers, in all directions. The sky lit up as if a dazzling combination of laser and fireworks shows was going on. The destroyers shot back with their new weapon, catching and pulverizing every flash in the nick of time. There were a small number of cases, however, where the shot from the destroyer barely missed the target or didn't completely vaporize the incoming flash, and the flash managed to hit the destroyer. The result – a badly damaged ship, and a couple even blew up.

Casualties of war, Marc thought sadly. The Mendoken had come here to rescue them, but they were giving up lives of their own in the process.

Fortunately more planet destroyers were still coming through the gateway. By now, there had to be hundreds of them that had already arrived. While a good many stayed to join the battle against the anomalies surrounding the space station, a greater number were venturing into the depths of space to look for others. Marc assumed they were also going to try to destroy all the other space stations that had been built and shut down the gateways that had been opened.

"They've come prepared," Zorina said, bobbing her head up and down in delight. "With enough resources to finish off the anomalies in this universe, once and for all."

After all the setbacks he'd recently been through, Marc was a little more cautious. "One can only hope," he said.

The anomalies began moving about, trying to get between the planet destroyers and to fire at them from different angles. Some also tried to escape. The destroyers, however, would have none of that. They chased them down, wherever they went. Not only did they continue to react to the energy flashes that were raining down on them, they began shooting streaks directly at the anomalies too.

These streaks that were fired directly were bigger and brighter, each one gaining its size and power from multiple streaks from individual planet destroyers. This step required careful coordination between the destroyers to fire exactly in unison at specific angles, so that the streaks could combine in the right way before heading together to their target.

When one of these combined streaks reached an anomaly, it spread quickly over the entire colossus, engulfing it and forcing it to expand. It didn't take long after that for the whole anomaly to crumble and dissipate, following the same fate as the flashes it had just fired at the unwelcome invaders.

The anomalies had finally met their match, and no matter where they flew off to, they fell one by one. The Mendoken did have casualties, but few in comparison to the sheer number of vessels and crew they had brought with them. And they didn't give up until the very last anomaly within visible distance was eliminated.

Marc felt a staggering sense of relief. All the pain, all the anguish, all the physical and mental suffering he and so many others had endured for so long, all the helplessness he had felt at the overpowering hands of these evil beings, all the devastation they had caused across so many worlds in his universe – justice was finally getting served.

He looked around the hall. Everyone was standing still, mostly huddled in areas where they had a view of the outside through transparent sections of the wall. They were fixated on the battle unfolding before them, be they Mendoken, Aftarans, Volonans or crystals.

Marc then eyed the monsters in the distance, still crouched around the area with the best view. They seemed fixated as well, every now and then casting nervous glances at each other.

"They're confused," Alisha said. "Unsure what to do."

"Not surprising," Marc replied. "This is not at all how they expected things to unfold. They were supposed to be masters of their own destiny, created from the consciousness of and given free reign by anomalies that were supposed to be all-powerful. Now those all-powerful beings are being exterminated like pests."

"Then they'll hopefully leave us alone," Alisha said.

"For now anyway. The question is, what do we do now?"

The answer to that came soon after. A single ship was approaching the space station. Nobody had noticed it earlier, since it was dwarfed by the gigantic planet destroyers on either side. But as it came closer, its large size became clear in its own right. It was, in fact, as large as a whole city.

"A Mendoken battlecruiser," Marc said. "Kril class, I'd say." The wide, inverted mushroom shape with the many extensions was unmistakable.

"Kril-8," Zorina added. "Their most advanced battlecruiser."

The ship drew ever closer, unhindered and unengaged. All the anomalies out there had, after all, either been destroyed or were about to be.

The smooth, gray surface of the battlecruiser began to take up the view of everything outside. Lights were gleaming all over the ship, signifying lots of life and activity onboard.

"Feels great," Marc said, grinning again. "Our own kind, from *our* universe. *We're* in the majority now."

The Mendoken battlecruiser slowed down and came to a standstill as its lower body aligned itself with the rings of the two space stations joined together. Then came the gangways – a number of them shot out from the hull of the ship, hitting the outer edge of each of the space stations' rings within seconds. Marc could feel the loud thuds under his feet, and soon after came the louder explosions as sections of the floor caved in and disappeared.

The monsters were in panic, staring at the gaping holes and periodically casting nervous glances at each other. They had every reason to be, and even more so as a deep, whooshing sound could be heard emanating from the holes. Even more so still as the first floating vehicle popped out of one of the holes, followed by another and another, and many more that came out all the holes.

Each of the egg-shaped vehicles was populated by a Mendoken, with weapons at the ready. They wasted no time in identifying the villains and went straight after them. The monsters spread out and galloped for their lives, some spreading their wings and flying up into the air. Others turned back and shot rays at the approaching vehicles. A few of the vehicles received direct hits and blew up, but some were able to fire back in time, causing the monsters to explode in a colorful display of fireworks. The vehicles sped off to all corners of the hall, looking for monsters and engaging them in battle until they were destroyed.

Marc couldn't help yelling with joy as he watched the spectacle, and Zorina bobbed her head up and down with delight.

Alisha yelled too, but for a different reason. "Marc!"

"What?" Marc turned around to face her. She was staring at a Mendoken vehicle hovering right above them, its weapon pointing at a crystal next to her. At *the* crystal, more precisely, the same crystal that had that had accompanied and saved them so many times. The crystal stood motionless, unsure of what to do.

"Whoa, wait!" Marc exclaimed, waving frantically at the vehicle. "They're not the enemy! Leave them alone!"

The Mendoken driver of the vehicle appeared not to notice, as its gun remained pointed at the crystal and began lighting up.

Marc lunged forward and placed himself between the crystal and the vehicle. "No!" he shouted, gesturing to the driver to back off.

This time the driver took note, lowering the gun and turning away. Marc noticed other vehicles also turning away from crystals – the message had evidently been received and immediately transmitted to all the other drivers.

The crystal lowered one of its nodes before Marc in a show of gratitude, which he reciprocated with his own short bow.

"That was close," Alisha said.

Marc nodded. They watched as the last monster in the hall fell and exploded in the distance. Soon after, the vehicles began landing everywhere across the hall. Their doors opened up and the drivers got out to help the prisoners onboard. Each vehicle could take no more six or seven individuals, so it would take many vehicles and multiple trips to get everyone – all Mendoken, Aftarans, Volonans and even the couple of Phyrax still left –
transported to the Kril-8 battlecruiser.

A vehicle soon came for Marc, Alisha and Zorina. The Mendoken driver helped a wounded Zorina onboard, and then Alisha. When he came for Marc, Marc hesitated.

"What is it?" the driver asked.

Marc looked back at the crystal, standing still. "What about them?"

"We cannot take them," the driver replied.

"But... we can help them."

"Those are not my orders. We need to go now, to be on schedule to reenter the gateway and return home."

Marc got onboard reluctantly. As the vehicle sped off and sank into one of the holes leading to the ship, he felt a sinking sensation in his heart as well. Catching his last glimpse of the crystals spread across the hall, he couldn't prevent all his relief and gratitude for finally being rescued from being overshadowed by both guilt and regret at leaving them behind like that, leaderless and without cause.

Chapter 38

The Mendoken Kril-8 battlecruiser entered the gateway and began the process of matter conversion as it headed back through the bulk to its home brane. It was one in a series of ships, in between all the planet destroyers making their way back. Their mission accomplished, there was no official reason for them to remain any longer in this forsaken, matter-less universe.

Marc, Alisha and everyone else who had been rescued had to wait for care and treatment until after the conversion. They were separated into different rooms by species onboard the ship to increase the efficiency with which care could be administered, in true Mendoken style.

Marc sat in a seat next to Alisha, alone in a small room, as the conversion process began. It was a room along the outer rim of the lower part of the ship, with a window on one side giving a view of the wide tunnel they were passing through. The space in the tunnel was dark and empty, but its walls were filled with random outlines of different colors that constantly changed shape and size.

"We'll lose consciousness," he said, gently squeezing her hand.

"I know," she replied. "This had better be the last time we ever have to go through this, though."

Marc said nothing.

"How will this work without the crystals here to break everything up, convert it and put it back together?" she asked.

"Supposedly the Mendoken have figured out how to do the subatomic transformation by themselves. A wave of some sort."

The wave came soon enough. It passed right through the entire ship, through the room they were in and through their bodies. Marc felt a momentary sensation of heat as the wave flowed through him, followed by a numbing of his senses. He was no longer able to move or feel anything, but his vision was still intact.

Then came the breaking up of everything. The walls of the room around him, the seat, Alisha's body and his. The feet came first, followed by the legs and all the way up to his head. Every single part came loose and broke up into tiny bits, and those in turn into even smaller bits, and into even smaller ones until they were too small to see. As the process reached his head, he blacked out.

When Marc came to, he was still seated in the same room. Alisha, still next to him, was waking up as well. When he gazed through the window, he noticed they were still in the same tunnel.

Did it not work? he wondered, lifting his hands and staring at them. The pain he felt all over his body, along with the strong, overbearing feeling of nausea, however, soon convinced him otherwise. It was the same way he had felt when he had involuntarily traveled through the gateway the first time.

"The good news is that it means the conversion worked," he said to Alisha. "The pain and nausea will soon subside."

Instead of responding, she threw up on the floor.

Or not, he thought. He got up and held her head as she barfed some more.

"I hate this," she whispered as she finished. "I'm sorry, this is so embarrassing."

"It's ok," he replied. "You've been through a hell of a lot."

"Never again, hopefully."

The door to the room slid open and two Mendoken floated in. Without a word, they cleaned up the mess with some kind of machine one of them was carrying and began examining the two humans with numerous other devices. They also offered them nourishment of some sort to sip up through straws. It tasted good and refreshing, much better than all that soggy paste they had been consuming for an uncountable number of days.

"Finally some proper food," Alisha said. She looked much better after downing some of it.

Marc felt better too, and he smiled as he noticed the end of the tunnel ahead. The ship seemed to speed up as it approached, and, just like that, it broke free of the gateway and re-entered regular space. The canvas of countless stars dotting space every way he looked was a very welcome sight.

"We made it," Alisha said softly.

"Thanks to our friends here," he said, nodding at the Mendoken crewmembers tending to them.

"And your Phyrax friend for sacrificing its life to keep us alive long enough."

"Very true."

There was a row of planet destroyers in front and behind. More were coming out of the gateway, now a gaping hole quickly fading into the backdrop of space. Ahead, an armada of Mendoken vessels was amassed toward which all ships seemed to be heading. All ships, that was, except for this one. This one began speeding up and veering course in a different direction.

"What's going on?" Marc asked the crewmember just as he finished tending to him. "Why aren't we stopping like the others?"

"The good news, Mr. Zemin, other than a collection of bruises and chronic malnourishment, is that you both appear to be fine," he replied. "The bad news is that there is no time for rest."

The door to the room slid open, the crewmembers ushered Marc and Alisha up from their seats, and then led them through a couple of corridors to the end of the building where a floating vehicle was waiting. The two humans were asked to enter the vehicle, after which it closed its door and sped off through the bowels of the ship on autopilot, leaving the crewmembers behind.

Minutes later, the vehicle landed on the fifth level of the ship's control deck. As with all Mendoken ships, the deck had a clear view of space in all directions, as if there was no wall or barrier there at all. The lower half of the inverted mushroom shaped ship jutted out below for what looked like miles.

Zorina, Dumyan and Raiha were standing nearby, on the same level. Zorina's wounded leg was healed, it seemed, thanks to Mendoken medical prowess. Marc and Alisha joined them.

"I'm so sorry about Jinser-Shosa," Marc said to Zorina.

Zorina flapped her ears in sadness. "A bizarre, rowdy character for sure. But one heck of a trooper and a great friend to the very end."

"Jinser-Shosa will never be forgotten," Dumyan said, closing his eyes to utter a short prayer. "I have never seen such courage in one individual in all my life."

"We should also pay tribute to all the innocent prisoners who died from the rays of those monsters, as well as all the Mendoken who died trying to save us," Marc said.

Everyone agreed, and a moment of silence followed.

"Where's Sibular?" Marc finally asked.

"He and she were waiting for you to show up," Zorina replied.

"She?"

Zorina pointed with her trunk to the left. Sure enough, a little further away, Sibular was standing, communicating with another Mendoken. When he noticed Marc and Alisha, he floated over with his companion.

"This is Commander Soldara Graenzen 45329874 of the 507th Armada," he announced. "She led the fleet."

"Ah, well, thank you for rescuing us," Marc said. "Our condolences for all the Mendoken who died in the process."

The others followed suit with their own words of gratitude.

Commander Soldara hummed in acknowledgment.

"Where are we headed now?" Dumyan asked.

"Mr. Zemin's home planet, Earth."

Marc was surprised. "We're in the Mendo-Biesel system?"

Soldara hummed again. "We came out of the gateway in the same place where we entered, and where you left this universe too when the anomaly struck and captured you. At the Selcher-44328 station, where it used to be. The silupsal filter has significantly disintegrated in the meantime."

"How... long have we been gone?" Alisha asked.

"In your time units, 35 days."

"Huh?"

"But... we've been gone for months," Marc said, surprised. "It feels like months."

"It was months for us," Sibular said. "But not for everyone here. Time passes differently in other universes. We should just be thankful that the difference was no greater."

"True," Marc agreed. "Why the rush to return though? We should have stayed to help the crystals. They were prisoners too, of the anomalies."

"We destroyed all the anomalies," Soldara replied. "Your crystals are free again."

"But spread and scattered," Dumyan said. "They weren't like that before. We are actually the reason they became that way, as much as we are the reason that the anomalies formed to begin with. It was all one gigantic lifeform that we inadvertently broke apart during one of our consar journeys."

"Those crystals – they wanted, they needed our help," Marc added.

"Regardless, whatever the reasons and causes, we cannot go back," Soldara said. "It is too risky. Too many lives have been lost already. We do not want any more dangers from that universe coming our way. Our orders were to bring you back and then to close the gateway for good. From the Imgoerin himself."

Marc was uncertain what to say, his thoughts and feelings torn. "Tell me," he said eventually, "how did you come after us? How did you build the gateway and how did you figure out how to convert matter to adapt to the other universe and back?"

"We found instructions," Soldara replied.

"Instructions?"

"Yes. At Selcher-44328, where the anomaly attacked and took all of you. They were encoded in the neutrino patterns left behind by the gateway that the anomaly used to get away."

"Instructions from whom?" Marc and Alisha asked in unison.

"We do not know," Soldara replied. "There was no trace of identity anywhere. The instructions were just there."

"That didn't strike you as odd?" Dumyan asked.

"Our mission was clear," Soldara said simply. "Not to waste time questioning the methods used to ensure our success."

A very Mendoken way of looking at things, Marc thought. But the questions still remained. Still, he knew better than to show the slightest bit of ingratitude for so daring a mission undertaken by these advanced, robotic beings to save his life and those of everyone he cared about, and the sacrifices many of them had made with their lives for this mission. Perhaps best to drop the subject for now.

"Why the rush now to get to Earth?" he asked instead.

"Your planet is in bad shape," Soldara said. "Bad enough that we even contemplated interfering now that the silupsal filter has disintegrated anyway, but we decided to wait until we got you back."

"Why?"

"Because interference by aliens will inherently be seen with suspicious eyes by anyone indigenous. Especially after all the destruction wrought on your planet by the anomalies, your people are unlikely to be able to distinguish between good and bad aliens. Whereas if we are accompanied by someone of their own kind, it will go a lot more smoothly."

"How bad are things exactly?"

"Things are really out of hand and reaching a critical juncture. We will not even have time to transfer you to a smaller ship for atmospheric entry. We will have to go straight down."

"Can a ship this size fend off the gravitational pull of the planet?"

Commander Soldara hummed. "We are Mendoken, Mr. Zemin."

"Right." No need to probe further on that, Marc surmised. "Can you at least explain to me what's been going on?"

"I cannot, I lack the knowledge and am just following orders. But I will open a communication link to another Commander who is more familiar with what is happening on your planet."

"What's the name?"

"Maginder Kloiden 52110984. He is waiting there with his armada of ships, all cloaked to evade detection. Do you know him?"

"I do indeed."

"Good, then you can skip the formalities of introductions, as there are only 43 Earth minutes left to bring you up to speed before we arrive."

Chapter 39

US President Alan Tucker was jolted awake by a splash of cold water on his face.

"What... who?" he blubbered.

As his senses slowly came back into focus, he began to feel the sharp pain in his right leg again. It was the same pain from the chopper crash, but it wasn't the only pain. The back of his head hurt too, likely from the blow he had received earlier to knock him out. The memory of that strike came back with a thud, as did the memory of the crash, the death of his wife and the arrival of the Aryan Nation bastards. His children had survived, thankfully, but he didn't know where they were now. He could only hope they were still ok.

The other pain he could feel, however, was in both of his arms. And, when he opened his eyes, he realized why. They were stretched up and out, thanks to chains wrapped around his wrists that reached out to hooks on the wall on either side. He was down on his knees on the floor and he couldn't move. To say that the position was extremely uncomfortable and painful, especially given his injured leg, was a huge understatement.

Once his vision had cleared a little more, he noticed that he was in a small room. There was a window on the left wall letting in a bit of sunlight, and a door on the wall ahead. The amount of light in the room was high though, mostly due to a powerful lamp hanging from the ceiling. In front, a video camera was perched on a stand. Beside it was a flat screen TV that was turned off, and on the other side was a chair on which a man was quietly seated – the very same, very loathsome Steven Bane, leader of the much reviled Aryan Nation. Behind him stood two of his henchmen, one on either side of him, their rifles at the ready. One of them was also holding a half-empty bucket of water – clearly the one who had so unceremoniously splashed water on the President's face.

"Wakey wakey, Mr. President," Bane said in his gruff voice.

Tucker shook his head to try to clear it, but all it did was worsen the pain. "Where... are my kids?"

"They're fine, don't worry. For the moment anyway."

"What do you want from me?"

"Justice, retribution."

"What have I done to you?"

Bane chuckled. "What haven't you done?"

"I don't understand."

"You, sir, are a summary of all that's gone wrong. This was once a great country. Heck, it was the greatest nation in the world. We were a nation of principles, of work ethics, of purity, of kindness to each other, of tradition and real patriotism, all based on unshakable faith in our Lord. Then those damn libtards took over and let in all the colored vermin from all corners of the Earth, with all their blasphemous, pagan religions, savage cultures, moronic customs and perverted sexual deviations."

Tucker sighed and shook his head. He was so flabbergasted by what he had just heard that he didn't even know what to say. As weak as he was, however, there was only so long he could stay silent to such insane commentary. "I was born here, like you," he said eventually. "I'm a Christian, like you. My ancestors were brought here by force by your ancestors, as slaves. They helped your ancestors build this country. Now we're free, as American as you, and as proud as you to be living in this free country based on a constitution that treats *all* people as equal."

Bane sneered. "Now, see here, that's where you've got it all wrong," he said in his strong southern accent. "You were brought here as slaves because that's all you lot are good for. If you black folks were runnin' this country, we'd be faring no better than the rest of that dump of a continent y'all came from. Thankfully that never happened, till now, and thankfully it won't happen again."

"Don't you know that all humans came from Africa, and that Africa was once the cradle of peaceful civilization? It's the colonial powers from Europe, with all their weapons of war, that destroyed it all."

"Good riddance, I say."

Tucker fumed quietly.

"Let me ask you something," Bane said. "Was Jesus black?"

Tucker was startled by the question. "Huh? No, but he wasn't white either."

"Oh yes he was, as white as me here," Bane replied, pointing at his own face. "And there's a reason for that. See, God came to this Earth as a white man, not a black, yellow or a damned brown man. A white man."

"Jesus was brown skinned, he had brown hair and brown eyes."

"What the hell you talkin' about? You seen all the pictures of Jesus? Blond and blue eyed."

"Pictures? For God's sake, those are all make believe paintings, painted by white people in Europe and America. That doesn't make it real. He was a Middle Eastern Jew. Have you seen what Middle Eastern people look like?"

"Jesus was God, the Son of God, not a Jew."

Tucker felt exasperated. "Whether he was the Son of God or not, Jesus was born a Jew, in a Jewish household, in a Jewish land and to a Jewish mother. Know your history, man."

"I know what Jews look like – they're as white as me." Bane pointed at himself again.

"Many Jews in this country, yes, because they've lived in the west for generations. But Jews of the Middle East – many of them look no different than their Arab cousins. Have you ever been to Israel? Jesus was a Middle Eastern Jew. But why does it matter? If you believe in Jesus, the first thing you're taught in church is that he was sent for all people – black, white, brown, yellow. It doesn't matter what his race was."

Bane looked angry. "Arabs? Trust a black man to speak fondly of that filth of a race."

"What are you talking about?"

"Bunch of terrorist ragheads, every one of 'em. We should have nuked them all off the face of this Earth decades ago."

Tucker shook his head again in disgust. "You do know that Western civilization is forever indebted to the Arabs, especially for all they taught us about math and science?"

Bane got up and turned on the TV. "Enough time wasted on chit chat. I ain't listenin' to or reasonin' with no black man. Now, you're goin' to read aloud what it says on this screen, we're gonna record it and we'll broadcast it over all news channels nationwide. Those channels which are still functioning, that is."

Tucker lifted his head to peer at the screen. It took only a few seconds for him to guffaw in disbelief. "There's no way I'm going to say any of that, no matter what torture you have planned for me."

His remark was answered with a hard punch in his stomach by one of the henchmen. He cringed in pain as his breaths grew shallow, his body dangling almost lifelessly by his chained arms.

"I have no doubt," Bane said. "I'm well aware of your military experience. But, heh, it wasn't you I was plannin' on hurtin'." He motioned to the other henchman, who opened the door, stepped out of the room and returned promptly with two little individuals. He shoved them forward roughly, so that Tucker could see them in plain view – his kids Travis and Leticia.

They looked frightened, and when they saw their dad in the position he was in, both yelped and tried to rush forward to help him. They were, however, abruptly halted by the henchmen and held back.

"Let... us go!" Leticia yelled, only to have her mouth clamped shut with a rough hand. Travis had the same done to him before he could even say anything.

Tucker's mouth fell open in shock and dismay. As horrible an individual as he knew Bane to be, the idea that he would be willing to stoop so low to hurt children to get what he wanted was just beyond unfathomable.

"No, please don't," Tucker pleaded. "They're little, they're innocent."

"Then read what's on the screen. Aloud."

"Please don't do this. Please."

Bane motioned to the man holding Tucker's daughter, who brought her forward under the light, in clear view for the President to see. He began squeezing his big hand around her neck, making her choke. She tried to pull the hand off, but she wasn't strong enough. All she could do was make wheezing noises as the air pipe through her throat closed to the point of suffocation.

"Now!" Bane roared. "If you want her to live."

"Ok, ok, I will!" Tucker said, defeated. "Please, just let her go."

The man let Leticia go, after which she fell to the ground and breathed heavily to regain her composure. Her brother tried to reach her to help, but his captor wouldn't let him go.

Tucker pulled on the chains to try to get up and help her, but he was roughly shoved back into position by Bane. Bane then pointed at the camera and, without another word stepped behind it and pressed a button.

Tucker noticed a red light on the video camera turn on, which meant it had begun recording. Exhausted out of all other options, he cleared his throat and began reading aloud in a shaky voice:

"I, Alan Tucker, hereby resign from my post as President of the United States of America on October 19, 2014, effective immediately. The Vice President will be taking over all my responsibilities until the next presidential election, at which time a president will be elected who is representative of the real America. I hereby also solemnly apologize to the American people for misleading them into electing a charlatan like me, someone who isn't a true American, of a racial background that is not deserving of the highest office of this greatest of all countries. Indeed, it is but certain that all the calamities that have befallen this nation of late are due to God's wrath on all of us. And it's all because of me and the likes of me, for daring to assume authority and power over which I as an inferior, sinful being have no right. The right to govern this great nation should be left to those who deserve it, to those who have built it, not to those who pollute it and bring shame upon it. The right to rule is reserved for those to whom God has bestowed that right, not those whom He in His infinite wisdom has condemned to be ruled."

Tucker tried his best to hold back the tears and the urge to belch as he read the last couple of sentences. "For all my transgressions, I bear full responsibility and ask for forgiveness from God and from the American people. And, as I fully accept the justice that both I and my family are now due for my inexcusable crimes, with justice served this country will surely see much better days ahead under the watchful eye of the one and only true Lord Jesus Christ. Now that I am no longer your president, may God truly bless you, and may God bless the United States of America."

The red light on the camera didn't go off. The recording continued as Bane put on a mask over his head, as did the other two henchmen. They shoved the children in front of the camera beside their father, and then wrapped chains around the necks of all three of them. Bane stood behind the President, while the other two men took one child each, all in plain view of the camera's lens.

Tucker couldn't believe it. This was going to be a modern-day lynching, not too different from the fate so many of his ancestors had suffered. "Wait, what happened to letting the children go?" he cried.

There was no answer.

"You can't do this!" he went on. "I am begging you. Please, they are chil..."

He was abruptly cut off by a gag that was shoved into his mouth and tied around his head. The same was done to his two whimpering kids.

"In the name of the Lord, let justice be served!" the men cried in unison, muffling their voices to avoid recognition on camera. Then they began tightening the chains around the three individuals' necks, to choke them to death.

Tucker could feel the rising pain in his neck and pressure on his throat. His breathing came to a standstill, and as his body involuntarily thrashed about he could feel whatever strength was left in his body slowly withering away. He tried to turn his head to look at his kids – if there was only just some way that he could help them and get them to safety. But he couldn't even see them, let alone help them. They were beyond his field of vision. The only thing he could see was the window in the wall to the left, and he thought he noticed a sudden reduction in the light coming in from outside, accompanied by a deep rumbling noise that shook the ground ever so slightly. Perhaps a thunderstorm had arrived, or perhaps it was just the life draining out of him. Either way, he could feel his eyes closing for the last time as his body let go.

Then, just as his eyelids reached the very last millimeter before shutting completely, an immensely bright light flashed in front and all around him. It was followed by the sound of a deafening explosion, the blast of which somehow forced the chains around his neck and his wrists to shatter into dust. The shockwave further sent him, his children and his captors flying toward the back wall of the room.

Lying on the ground and still barely conscious, he thought he could see flashes of what looked like lasers shooting every which way above and around him. Soon after, all fell quiet, and soon after that a hand grabbed onto his and began pulling gently.

"Mr. President?" a voice said. "Here, let me help you up."

Tucker reacted defensively, raising his other arm with his eyes half shut. He was still in complete shock, unsure what had just happened or who this was.

"It's ok," the voice continued, sounding calm and reassuring. "You're safe now, and so are your kids."

Tucker opened his eyes further. The light in front was blinding, and once his eyes had adjusted just a little he realized why. The wall in front was blown asunder, as was much of the rest of the house. The sun was shining right through, although its radiance was partially blocked by a huge, dark cloud in the sky. Closer to him was something else blocking the view – the man who had helped him. He looked strangely familiar, but Tucker couldn't place how or why.

"My kids?" he asked, as the man helped him stand up.

"They're right here."

Both Leticia and Travis rushed to their father and hugged him tightly. Tucker felt overjoyed and broke down in tears, as did both his kids.

"Thank you," he said between sobs. "Our captors?" He surveyed the floor around him for any bodies, but he saw none.

"They won't ever cause you any grief again, don't worry."

"Who are you?"

"My name is Marc Zemin," the man said.

"Marc Zemin? Wait, that name..."

"It seems we got here in the nick of time."

"We?"

"Yes. This is Alisha. Alisha Bedi. She's with me."

Tucker noticed another individual beside Marc Zemin for the first time, an attractive woman, likely of South Asian descent. She looked familiar too, but he couldn't recall from where. TV perhaps. Everything felt like a whirlwind at the moment, so he wasn't sure whether to trust his memories or not.

"It's a pleasure to meet you, Mr. President," the woman called Alisha said. Her accent was definitely South Asian.

Tucker was confused. "The two of you just took down a group of heavily armed Aryan Nation men?"

"We, uh, had some help," Marc replied.

"From?"

"Come step outside, please, but brace your eyes and ears."

"After all I've been through lately, nothing can surprise me anymore."

Marc smiled. "It will be more surprising if this doesn't."

Chapter 40

President Tucker was not only surprised, he was positively shocked. Having stepped out of the house that had held him and his children captive, he was surveying his surroundings with utter disbelief. He had first noticed the normal stuff he had been expecting – he was in the middle of nowhere, with nothing but empty land no matter which way he looked. The house where he and his kids had been held captive was a farmhouse, with its entire frontside now blown away. His kids were there with him, one on each side, helping him stand with his injured leg. The two individuals Marc and Alisha were a little further ahead.

That, however, was where the normalcy ended. The dark shadow covering much of the view of the blue afternoon sky above was no thunderstorm. It was a huge, monstrous, enormous structure, easily the size of an entire city. It could only be one thing – a spaceship, and it was floating in the sky with nothing holding it up. It looked like an inverted mushroom, although most of what he could see was just the underside. Gray in color, it had lights gleaming all across its surface.

Gates all around the ship were open, and smaller ships were coming out of them and fanning out in all directions. Some seemed to be heading east toward the capital, others north, south and west. They were of different shapes and sizes – some looked like fighters, others like basic transporters. A couple of the smaller ships had already landed and were parked nearby.

Tucker's mouth dropped in amazement, as did those of his kids. Even more so as he noticed a group of individuals behind Marc and Alisha. They were not humans. They almost looked like robots with their metal bodies and arms which, amazingly, were floating above the ground with no support. But their heads seemed organic – dark, leathery skin with a single gleaming eye going all around the head. On every head was a hat, and the hats had different colors. There were probably around ten of them, and some of them were carrying what looked like weapons. They floated toward him together with the two humans.

"Mr. President, meet the Mendoken," Marc said. "The most technologically advanced civilization in our galaxy. We live in a part of the galaxy controlled by them."

Tucker was so shell shocked that he didn't know what to say. "They, uh... ok. Well, can they understand us?"

"We can," one of the aliens said in a male, slightly robotic voice. "My name is Maginder Kloiden 52110984, and I am one of the Commanders here on site. It is a pleasure to make first official contact. I have watched over your star system and your planet for many years."

Tucker remained stunned, awestruck by these bizarre creatures, the way they looked and the size of that thing in the sky. He recalled images he had seen of the spaceship that had appeared over LA during the alien attack, but this one was way, way bigger. And then, as he turned his gaze toward Marc, he finally remembered.

"You, you, you are the one with the aliens," he said. "I thought you looked familiar. I've seen your picture before. You were apprehended by the Air Force, weren't you? But you escaped."

"I did," Marc said.

"These aliens, they're not the ones who attacked us?"

"No, they're not. As cliché as it sounds, there are good aliens and there are bad aliens. These are the good aliens. And, believe it or not, they have secretly kept an eye on and protected us and our world since long before we humans even existed."

"What's your role in all this, then?"

"I will explain. But let's have the Mendoken take a look at you and your kids first. You need medical attention."

"What will they know about human anatomy?"

"They know a hell of a lot more about us than just our anatomy, trust me."

Tucker and his kids were onboard the Mendoken spaceship floating in the sky. They had been tended to and fed, and they were feeling much better. Travis and Leticia were excitedly darting from level to level in the control deck of the ship, checking out all the stations and watching the crew going about their business. Tucker himself, meanwhile, was in a room on the outer edge of the deck, with a magnificent view of the lower part of the ship and miles of land beyond. From this vantage point, he could even see the buildings of Washington DC in the distance.

He had been engaged in a long conversation with Marc and Alisha. He had also been introduced to Sibular, Dumyan, Raiha and Zorina, had learned about the other major civilizations in the galaxy and been given a brief rundown of galactic history. This included the silupsal filter, the wars that had been fought and how Marc had gotten pulled into all of it.

It would have been an enormous amount of information for any normal person to digest, let alone a man that had just lost his dear, beloved wife and his kids' mother, one who bore the burden of the recent deaths of so many millions of people in Boston and New York, and one who had on his conscience all the devastation caused across this country in recent weeks. But Tucker was no ordinary person. He was not president of the United States for no reason. He took it all in stride and let the information sink in. The time for mourning would come, but for now it would have to wait.

"The Mendoken, what do they want?" he finally asked, now alone in the room with Marc.

"Nothing from us, to be honest," Marc said. "There's nothing we have or can offer that's of any value to them. And even if there was, they could just take it without asking for our permission. Heck, they could blow this entire planet up in a second if they wanted to."

"That doesn't sound very reassuring."

"They're here to help us, not harm us. To help us rebuild after all the devastation. That's why they're spreading out across this continent already as we speak. Other ships like this one are already descending over other cities."

"Why?"

"A good question for a human like you or me to ask. But they don't operate that way. They aren't selfish like we are. They feel responsible for us, one because our solar system falls under their jurisdiction, and two because they know they're partly, albeit indirectly, responsible for the anomaly attack on Earth. Specifically on the United States and parts of Canada and Mexico. Because of that attack, there has been much devastation and the human race has been catapulted in an unexpected direction that all but ensures its self-destruction within a few years.

"Now that the filter surrounding us is gone and real space has prematurely been exposed to us, they've taken the unusual step of engaging with a species that isn't yet developed enough in their eyes for first contact. Just to help us get out of the rut we're in, to give us another chance at survival."

"So they're just going to take over and rule us, make us do things their way?"

"No, not at all. They will leave us alone once we're back on our own feet again."

"What then?"

"The Mendoken will help the United States rebuild its destroyed infrastructure, and they will do the same for the affected areas in Canada and Mexico. They will help return the world to the balance of the power it had before the anomaly attack. They won't help you fight those who are trying to harm you, though. You should be able to do that just fine on your own once you have your power back."

"Really?"

"Yes, and then the Mendoken will leave. But they'll do it all only under one condition. This country must find ways to work better with other countries to solve humanity's problems as a whole, to help humanity advance as a whole. We have to especially find a way to collaborate with China, a country that will continue to grow in dominance on the world stage.

"We have to protect the planet we call our home, and we have to protect each other no matter what our race, religion, nationality, geographic location or economic state. Only then will we ever have a chance of reaching a level considered high enough to join the galactic community of civilizations. This message will be given to all nations on this planet, not just us."

Tucker shook his head as he smiled. "All great in theory. Not like it hasn't been tried before. Never worked. We humans are inherently selfish creatures. At the end of the day it's every nation for itself, every human for him or herself."

"True, and we can't change human nature, I get that. At least not overnight. But as leaders we can change the way we rule and govern, the way we engage with other nations, the way we exert power on others with fewer means than us, others less fortunate than us. We can show a hell of a lot more empathy toward each other and be less selfish. Every nation should count, no matter how small or how poor. The same goes for every human being. There will always be inequality – it's in our DNA, although we can certainly work to reduce it. At the end of the day, however, every individual should matter, every individual should be able to live with dignity and have basic rights, no matter if it's the richest and most powerful person on Earth or the poorest beggar on the street."

"What exactly are you proposing?"

"We have an alien civilization way more powerful than us backing us up. Let's use it to our advantage. We'll convince Congress first, which should be the easy part. Then we'll use the UN – we'll turn it into what it was envisioned to be when it was founded but has never quite become. You, me and the Mendoken – we'll call the General Assembly to order and we'll present a vision for the human race and our planet that nobody will be able to say no to. It's the only shot we have of one day making it into the galactic community, and we have to make that very clear to the entire human race."

"Why me?"

"Two reasons. You are the president of the one nation that was still considered the leader of this planet before the anomaly attack. Granted other countries were catching up, and China in particular was projected to overtake us economically in the next several years. But the United States still had more political, military and economic clout than any other nation. It will return to that state with Mendoken help."

"And the other?"

"From what I know, Mr. President, you are actually a good man, something that often goes missing in political leaders. There is no better person than you to be in the driver's seat on the world stage at the moment."

Tucker smiled. "I appreciate that. But how do we get people to trust each other, to trust us and follow us like that? People aren't going to change centuries-old ways of doing things overnight."

"When they see the amazing things the Mendoken can teach us, the things they can give us to build a better world for ourselves and for all other living things on this planet, believe me, they will all want a piece of the action. Nobody will want to be left behind."

Chapter 41

Getting the backing of Congress was indeed easy for the President. For all the senators and representatives, it was a no brainer to get help from friendly aliens to rebuild the heavily damaged US infrastructure. The UN meeting then went ahead as planned. An emergency session was called to order within a few days after both houses of Congress passed the bills to support the President. The only catch – it had to be held in Geneva, Switzerland in the second largest of the world's four major UN office sites. The reason was that the largest site, the one where the UN General Assembly usually met, had been destroyed in the second nuclear bomb attack on US soil by ISIS on Lower Manhattan.

Marc, President Tucker and Commander Maginder addressed the General Assembly and laid out their grand vision for how the world's nations would have to come together and reshape human society the right way. Initially, the Mendoken offer to help with the reshaping effort was met with cautious euphoria by most world leaders, but as the conditions for help were laid down the skepticism grew consistently. By the end, some of the leaders were ready to get up and leave in protest. However, as Marc had predicted, once they witnessed demonstrations of the scientific and technological prowess at the disposal of the Mendoken, they came back readily with their eyes lit.

Amongst others, some of the highlights included the tapping of unlimited energy from solar and all electromagnetic radiation in general, the ability to produce quality food from high yield agricultural crops at a fraction of current costs and a fraction of the land, the ability to quickly remove harmful pollutants and greenhouse gases in the atmosphere, to clean up the planet's water supply and even to begin modifying the weather to avert natural disasters such as hurricanes, floods and droughts. Enhancements to computers, electronics and robotics were a given, with safeguards in place that the Mendoken had already mastered to avert the rise of artificial intelligence to reach any kind of singularity.

In the meantime, the Mendoken began helping the American, Canadian and Mexican governments rebuild their damaged infrastructure. Their large Euma and Kril vessels moved back up into orbital distance around the planet, while the smaller scout and fighter ships carrying crewmembers spread out across the three countries to offer aid in reconstruction. At the same time, the Mendoken placed themselves right in the middle of conflict zones around the globe, standing by the oppressed and persecuted, and forcing the aggressors and occupiers to disarm and fall back. They also came to the aid of the poorest, most malnourished of people, offering them food and aid in whatever shape or form they needed. Anywhere where people desperately needed help and protection, in any shape or form, the Mendoken were there. This was not in order to take over and run things, but to show national governments on Earth how they needed to take care of their own if they wanted Mendoken help in scientific and technological advancement.

The Mendoken generally didn't mingle much with humans, nor did they stay for any lengthy stretches of time on the Earth's surface. They always came down for missions or meetings, and then went back up to their ships. Again, this was to demonstrate that they weren't interested in invading or taking over the planet, just to help as needed.

It was truly a dream come true, and a real chance for human society to be reborn. For so long, it was exactly what Marc had wished for – for humans to finally unite and turn into a single civilized, compassionate society. For so long he had hoped that humans would turn the corner by themselves, for so long he had tried to convince people that this was something worth doing. The hope had, however, been in vain. Now they were only doing so with external support, sure, but better to do so with support than not to do it at all.

Indeed, Marc should have been the happiest person in the world. Even more so because he was actively involved in planning things out and making it happen together with the Mendoken and world leaders. And more so beyond that because he was doing all this with his beautiful, kind, friendly and supportive new girlfriend by his side.

And yet, he was surprised to discover that he was far from happy. The dissatisfaction, in fact, was growing day by day. At first, he wasn't sure why. All the wonderful things happening around him, to humanity in general, were amazing. All the help from the Mendoken was beyond any form of generosity he had ever known. But none of it seemed to matter anymore. Alisha tried to talk to him and comfort him, but to no avail. He was falling into a deep state of discontent.

Then came the nightmares. For a number of nights, he relived the deaths of his mother, wife and stillborn daughter, just like he had been forced to do so many times while imprisoned in the other universe. Over time, the nightmares evolved to the death and destruction caused by the Starguzzlers and Unghans in his first adventure out to space eleven years earlier. Then things moved to that one fateful consar trip he had been on that had destroyed the giant lifeform in the other universe, giving rise to the creation of the anomalies and all the death and destruction that had followed back in his own universe. Jinser-Shosa's sacrifice came crashing down on him too, a courageous individual who had no fault in any of this but had to give up its own life to save his. The same went for the deaths of all the Mendoken, Aftaran and Volonan prisoners, as well as all the Mendoken who had given up their lives to rescue him and the rest of the surviving prisoners. He had a big responsibility in all of it, he began to realize, and the guilt was insurmountable.

Guilt – that was the key. He felt guilt, tons of it. That was why he wasn't happy. And when on one night after many restless ones he awoke with the sharpest jolt of all, so much so that it awoke the person lying next to him in bed as well, it all became clear.

"Wha... what the hell?" Alisha said groggily. "What is it?"

Marc was already sitting upright. His head and back were drenched in sweat, and his heart was palpitating.

"What's wrong?" she said, her eyes slowly opening.

"It's... the crystals," he whispered. "I just saw them."

"What do you mean?"

"It felt so real, like I was there. Back in the other universe. I could see dead crystals everywhere, floating aimlessly in space." He shook his head.

"Seriously? Now you want to have this conversation? In the middle of the night?"

"I can't help it. It was a nightmare. But it felt like I was really there. We left them behind to die, to wither away into extinction."

She got up and faced him. "Yes, we did. We had no choice. The Mendoken gave us none."

"But they needed our help."

"How could we have helped them?"

"I don't know. They placed their trust in us. That's why they – that little crystal –

helped us escape. That's why they left behind a trail here for the Mendoken to pick up, to figure out how to travel through the gateway to their universe, to figure out how to fight and destroy the anomalies. It's got to all be connected somehow, and there must have been a reason for it. It can't all have been out of pure selflessness."

"Ok, let's discuss this later. In the morning. In daylight hours like everybody else does." Alisha sighed, lay back down and closed her eyes.

Instead of listening to her, Marc got up, walked to the window and stared into the night. It was raining outside over the streets of

Washington DC. He and Alisha were staying at the Sofitel in Lafayette Square, one of the nearest hotels to the White House. His proximity to President Tucker and much of the federal government was vital during this critical time when the United States was trying to stand back up on its own feet with the help of a way more advanced alien civilization whose loyalty and friendship only he had the privilege of holding.

He stood silently for a long while. Alisha eventually got up and came to him.

"Marc, come back to bed please," she said.

He wouldn't budge. "I need to go back," he finally said.

"What?"

"This whole thing – it's unresolved. That's why I'm not feeling normal. I have to help those crystals."

She looked startled and dumbfounded. "Are you nuts? Even if there was a way to go back, how could you even do anything to help them? Didn't you just say they're dead already?"

"I don't know how to explain it. It's like a... longing. It's been building up every day, getting stronger and stronger. And after tonight's dream, I feel like it all makes sense. Something is pulling me back there. I had a connection with them, especially with that one crystal. Whenever we came into contact, I could see, hear and feel its thoughts and memories." He paused. "They may be dormant, but they're not dead. I know it, I can feel it. They can be brought back to life."

"Oh, my God," she said in exasperation. "You can't possibly know that. You don't know what's happening in that other universe. Look, together we're rebuilding humanity according to the vision you've always had. And we have all the help, resources and knowhow we could ever have asked for. You need to fight this, whatever you're going through. It's a miracle we returned at all. You should be thanking your lucky stars, not wanting to go back to that hellhole of a place. What if the anomalies imprison you again? Actually this time they'll just kill you."

"The anomalies are all destroyed," he replied. "So are those monsters they created. Look, I don't expect you to understand. I lost my mother because I couldn't help her. I lost my wife and unborn child because I took her on a stupid trip to the desert when she was seven months pregnant. To Death Valley. Death Valley! Who takes his pregnant wife, a pregnancy rife with complications, to a place called Death Valley?"

His eyes welled up as he went on. "I was responsible for a consar trip that destroyed a sentient, intelligent being that ruled over its own universe. The ending of so many billions of lives across thousands of star systems as a result of that you well know. And now, I once again am responsible for the deaths of those very beings whose parent we destroyed, and who helped us survive and escape from that hellhole as you call it."

He shook his head and sobbed. "No more, Alisha, no more. No more guilt. This time, I have to fix it before it's too late."

Alisha's expression of annoyance was slowly turning to one of concern. "Don't do this, Marc. Don't let yourself be overridden with guilt. It's not your fault. There was nothing you could have done to help those crystals when we left. There's nothing you can do now for them either. Listen to me. Your place is here, on Earth, with me."

"I'm sorry. Your place is definitely here on Earth, and you can carry on the work that we've been doing together with the US government and the UN. But my place is out there." He pointed at the sky.

"Have you forgotten that we're a couple now? You know what that means, right? We're supposed to discuss things and make decisions together. Not me just following and accepting whatever you decide."

He let out a deep, heavy sigh. "Well, maybe we shouldn't be one anymore."

She stepped back, her facial expression now shifting to anger. "Are you serious?"

"My life will always be full of risk and danger," he said. "You've seen it yourself."

"I've faced all that risk and danger with you. I stood by you through thick and thin. This is how you thank me?"

"I got you back to Earth, as promised. You're safe now. But for me, it isn't over yet. He pointed at the sky again. "It's become my fate now."

She threw up her hands in frustration. "I don't recognize you anymore."

"It's all me," he insisted. "I'm just realizing certain things, now that I'm back here. You shouldn't have to be with someone whose life is like mine. With your looks and fame you can literally have anybody you want."

"What about feelings? Don't they count?"

"Of course they do, but we have to be practical as well."

"Why are you pushing me away like this?"

"I'm afraid for your safety."

"We are safe, damn it! This is our chance to build a life together. Why are you throwing it all away?"

"Because you deserve better than me."

"I don't want better than you." She was quiet for a moment. "Do you have any idea how many men come after me all the time?"

"I'm well aware of that. Hence why I just said…"

"What is this really about? Are you worried I'll follow your wife's fate? Or your mom's?"

Marc snorted. "No, of course not. I…"

"History doesn't need to repeat itself. We can choose our own fate."

"Sometimes we can't."

"All this for one stupid dream? You're being an idiot."

"Maybe, but I'm seeing things more clearly than I have in a long time."

A single tear came out of one her eyes. "Go to hell, Marc."

He avoided her gaze. "I'm sorry, but it's for your own good."

Chapter 42

The lobby of the Lafayette Sofitel was empty at 3am, save for the lone individual behind the reception desk. She barely noticed Marc as he walked past and offered him nothing more than a faint smile.

For his part, Marc didn't notice her at all. His mind was a mess, deep in confused, conflicted thought. He had just broken up with someone he had been through a lot with, someone he had truly gotten to like and possibly already loved. He wasn't even sure why he had done it. Her reasoning made total sense - he should be staying with her, building a life together and helping human society rebuild itself the right way with Mendoken help. He was needed here more than ever. And yet he just felt he had to do this – for her sake and for his.

As he stepped out into the cool, rainy night, he didn't even know where he was going or what he was going to do. The only thing he knew for sure was that he had to go. His guilt demanded it of him, it was consuming him.

He began walking, hoping it would give him time to think and figure out which course of action to take. The fact that he was getting wet in the light rain was of no consequence. He had much more important things to worry about.

He walked down a deserted 15th St NW in the direction of the National Mall, past the White House and the South Lawn. He then began cutting across to the Ellipse, a large park with an elliptically shaped path around its edge, positioned right between the White House and the National Monument. As he trudged toward its center, he began to have an eerie feeling that he was being followed. There wasn't a soul anywhere ahead or to either side, and although the only sound he could hear was the continuous, pitter-patter sound of raindrops hitting the ground, he could still sense that something was there.

The feeling grew steadily, but he felt no fear – just a shot of adrenalin pumping through his body as his heartbeat rose. He slowly came to a standstill at the very heart of the Ellipse, adopted a defensive Wing Chun position and abruptly jumped around to catch his pursuer off guard.

His intuition had not been wrong. Except it wasn't one follower but three, and he recognized them immediately. Their silhouettes were unmistakable – a floating, robotic body with a hat on the head, a tall, lanky creature in a loose robe, and a short, chubby individual with an elephant-like trunk and flappy ears.

"Huh?" he began. "Didn't you already go home to your worlds? Didn't we say goodbye on the ship?"

"Goodbye, yes," Dumyan replied. "But we never left. My father keeps asking why I haven't yet returned home. Raiha is already back on Meenjaza."

"So why haven't you?"

"None of us have had any desire to," Zorina said. "We've been staying onboard one of the Mendoken ships out in orbit. The same Kril-8 that brought us back from the other universe."

"Well, it's good to see you, trust me."

"We have been experiencing unnatural emotions," Sibular said. "All three of us."

"What kind?"

"Zorina and I have been having the same kind of unpleasant dreams night after night," Dumyan said. "It's been making us feel very sad and guilty."

"We Mendoken do not sleep, but I have been experiencing the same emotions nonetheless," Sibular added.

"Unbecoming of a Mendoken," Marc pointed out. "What are you feeling sad and guilty about?"

"The crystals, we left them behind when they needed us," Dumyan said. "It was most unethical."

"We came looking for you, to see if you have been experiencing similar issues," Sibular said.

Marc couldn't help smirking. "The guilt is overbearing and unbearable, and nobody else seems to understand."

"Then our theory is correct."

"What theory?"

"We are the ones who had physical contact with the crystals over a prolonged period of time," Sibular explained. "Granted they were being controlled by red cores for most of it, but it is possible that the crystals subconsciously passed some of their innermost thoughts and feelings into our minds without the knowledge of the red cores."

"You, Marc, had a lot of contact with that one free crystal too," Zorina added. "Which may be why your feelings are even stronger than ours."

Marc's eyes widened. "The only way the crystals knew how to communicate with us was through touch and the passing of thoughts. But... does it mean they're controlling how we feel?"

"Controlling may be a bit of a stretch," Dumyan said. "But I do think they passed something onto us that is affecting our thoughts and feelings. I have no idea how."

"It may be related to bulk energy," Sibular posited. "They obviously know how to harness it, and they may have implanted concentrations of it into our brains."

"Regardless, I think they are simply asking for help," Dumyan said. "They want us to come back."

"Your spiritual powers – are they back?" Marc asked.

"They are, now that we've returned to this universe," Dumyan replied. "But I find no consolation or guidance from them for what I've been going through."

"Interesting," Marc said. "We should locate the others as well. The six Mendoken troopers and six Aftaran soldiers who shared our fate."

"It turns out none of them have left either," Sibular said. "All the other survivors who were imprisoned by the anomalies have gone back home, save for us and those twelve individuals. We have already spoken to them and discovered they are experiencing the same thing. None of them want to leave – they are just staying here, waiting."

"Where?"

"In the same Kril-8 ship where we have been staying."

"Sounds like we need to pay them another visit."

At that very moment, a Sil-2 scout ship materialized out of thin air in the center of the Ellipse, right beside where the four of them were standing.

"That's how you came down?" Marc asked, contentedly eyeing the sleek, fighter plane shape of the craft.

"Yes," Sibular said. "We kept it cloaked, for obvious reasons."

The sixteen partners in crime were back together – Marc, Sibular, Dumyan, Zorina, the six Mendoken troopers and six Aftaran soldiers. Unwilling partners in crime, that was, as none of them had voluntarily taken on the designation of being responsible for a consar voyage that had unleashed such a devastating chain of events. Nevertheless, they were back together for a reason – because they were all experiencing the same extreme emotions and feelings of guilt.

They were in a hall onboard the Mendoken Kril-8 ship and had just finished sharing their recent experiences with each other. They had also unanimously reached agreement that they wanted and needed to go back to the other universe to help the crystals, regardless of the dangers that lay ahead and the high likelihood that they might never return. Their sense of guilt was just too strong to entertain any other option as a possible outcome.

The problem, of course, was how to go back. Commander Soldara had already left onboard another ship and was headed back to the heart of the Republic. Commander Maginder had taken over command of this ship and had added it to his armada. Sibular had therefore set up a meeting with Maginder to request permission for the sixteen of them to travel.

Maginder floated into the hall at the appointed time, exactly on the dot as was typical of Mendoken timing etiquette. He found everyone standing in a semi-circle, eagerly awaiting his arrival.

"Yes?" he said.

"We would like to request a scout ship to be at our disposal, Commander," Sibular said, floating forward to meet him.

"For what purpose?"

"To reach the gateway entrance and travel back to the other universe."

"The gateway has been shut down."

"We would like to request permission to have it reopened."

"The Imgoerin's orders are that it should never be reopened. The risks are too high."

"We have a case to go back," Sibular said.

"Is it an emotional one?" Maginder asked, eyeing everyone closely.

"It is also one of conscience, which, being one of our society's core values, is rational for us to address."

"The maximum I can do is send a message to the Imgoerin on your behalf. It is his decision."

The Imgoerin's reply came within several hours. Thanks to the wonders of bosian messaging technology, thousands of light years of distance could be covered within that timespan.

The sixteen were back in the same hall after some rest, anxiously waiting to hear the message. The holographic projection of the Imgoerin's physique opened up in the middle of the room as soon as it arrived, and the recording began playing soon after.

"I have contemplated with much deliberation on the request to re-open the gateway and to let you travel," he said. "My initial reaction was to say no right away. The risks are too high. Time runs more slowly in the other universe, so many things could have happened there in the meantime. The anomalies may have been reborn, or other, new dangers may have come together. We do not want to give them an opportunity to harm you or, worse yet, find an opening to come back to our universe and wreak havoc on us again.

"As leaders, however, we often have to make difficult choices, and we can only do so after weighing all the arguments for and against, all the consequences both short and long term. I have heard your plea, and I realize the sixteen of you may have been mentally affected in a way we do not yet understand. The fact that it has affected Mendoken, Aftaran, Volonan and Mendo-Biesel Earth human alike suggests it is real and should not be overlooked. There may be no remedy for you other than to face whatever it is that is beckoning you to the other side.

"More importantly, though, I agree that this is a moral issue. We Mendoken live our lives by upholding the highest levels of ethics in our society and the choices we make every day. It is what makes us as successful and civilized as we are, more so than our reliance on logic and rational thought. Now that I know more about the crystalline beings, where they originated from, how we inadvertently destroyed their creator, how they helped you escape, that they are likely the ones who left us all this information to come and rescue you, and that from what we know they are now scattered lifeless and without purpose, it behooves us to at least try to help them come back together and rebuild their lives. Whether they can do so I do not know, but we should do our part to facilitate the process for them.

"Finally, and perhaps most importantly, if there is anything I have learned from this entire war with the anomalies, it is that we should not let anything fester or remain forgotten unless we have complete resolution. As logical as it might be to avoid danger by keeping the gateway shut, by doing so we may well be allowing another major problem to brew on the other side that will generate far more danger for us in the future.

"All lives matter, no matter how big or small, how important or irrelevant, how famous or unknown. Our lives matter, and so do those of the crystals. Their creator's life mattered too, and we destroyed it. Not purposely, but we destroyed it. As big a life as it was, it certainly did not justify the taking of so many of our lives by the anomalies in return. The anomalies, however, were cruel and vengeful. We are not.

"Dumyan, I have asked for permission from your father, and after hearing the entire story he has reluctantly agreed to let you go. There is nobody better than the sixteen of you to take on this mission, given the special bond you have clearly established with the crystals due to all the contact you had with them. So, with that, you now have whatever means you require at your disposal to travel. May you return alive and well, and soon."

As the Imgoerin's last words were uttered, the hologram faded away from view.

That's what you call a true leader, Marc thought.

Chapter 43

It was a Sil-5 scout ship, just like the one the same sixteen had used those eleven years ago on that fateful consar journey. It was only fitting that they should travel aboard such a ship back to the other universe.

After having left the mother Kril vessel in stationary orbit around Earth, the ship had arrived at the edge of the solar system an hour later. The silupsal filter surrounding the system was almost completely gone by now, so there was no gate to pass through. The only thing to pass through up ahead was the gateway to the other universe, at the very spot where the Selcher space station used to be.

The Mendoken manning the gateway from a nearby group of ships had already been alerted that it was to be activated again, so by the time the scout ship arrived its ring was already gleaming blue in color. The blue hue was spreading inwards to fill the hollow circle.

The scout ship was piloted by one of the six Mendoken troopers. "No time to stop," she announced from the cockpit as she steered it toward the ring. "The timing is set so that the gateway will be fully operational by the time we reach it."

The cockpit of the ship was a neatly designed, spacious area that took up over a third of the span of the ship. That much was needed for all the sophisticated navigation equipment, computers and screens that were available onboard. It also summarized how Mendoken generally viewed traveling in space. It was all about function and practicality, and had very little to do with comfort, luxury or even accommodation.

The rest of the ship did indeed have some living space, but it was quite sparse as far as creature comforts went. Mendoken didn't lie down or sleep, nor did they sit down, so there wouldn't have been any beds or seats at all were it not for the single human, seven Aftarans and one Volonan onboard. They had been hastily set up with makeshift accommodations before leaving the mother ship, including a lavatorial facility since Mendoken didn't generally use bathrooms either.

The cockpit had a 270 degree, bird's eye view of the outside, thanks to a single, curved window stretching from floor to ceiling that went all around its outward facing perimeter. It was a sight that Marc, Sibular, Zorina and Dumyan were all enjoying from their vantage point behind the pilot.

"How do we know if the other side will open?" Marc asked. "The exit point?"

"The full trajectory of the gateway is now permanently recorded in the bulk energy ripples around it," Sibular said. "Which means that we should just be able to follow the full path to the other side."

"Because the path is already there?"

"Correct. It was created by all the ships that already traversed it. There is no new path to try to create or wait to be created by anyone on the other side."

"You sure?"

"No. But there is only one way to find out."

"The Mendoken equivalent of a reassuring statement," Zorina said as she stretched out her trunk.

The gateway was indeed fully operational by the time they reached it. The giant circle was lit in a brilliant blue haze, with a cone-like shape reaching out from within into the depths of the multi-dimensional sea of the bulk. The walls of the cone were awash with random outlines of different colors that constantly changed shape and size.

Thankfully, the ship passed through the gateway entrance unhindered and continued into the depths of the passage. As expected, after some time the matter conversion process began. A wave passed right through the ship, breaking up everyone and everything into tiny bits before reassembling them again into a form that was compatible with the physical laws of the universe they were about to enter. Marc and everyone else lost consciousness during the conversion, also as expected, and when they came to everything was once again intact.

"It worked," Sibular announced as he looked through the cockpit window. "The exit is opening up ahead."

"Thank goodness," Marc said groggily as he stood up and tried to regain his composure. This was the third time he had gone through the conversion process, and the combination of nausea and body pain afterward was no less unpleasant than the first time.

The ship passed unhindered through the exit point and broke free into regular space. Marc turned his gaze to a side window to look back at the huge, gaping hole, now slowly falling behind against a far larger backdrop of dark emptiness as they sped away from it.

"How long will it stay open?" he asked.

"We have 15 hours, but that is time in this brane," Sibular replied. "Back in our brane, that translates to no more than 5 hours. That is how much time the Imgoerin gave us, after which a shutdown of the gateway will be initiated from the other side."

"And if we don't reenter within 15 hours?"

"Then we can look forward to building a life for ourselves here."

"Here, in this...?" Marc looked out through the cockpit window. The starless sky, filled with nothing but the trademark, uniform haze no matter which direction he looked, was a sight he had definitely not missed.

"Regrets?" Dumyan asked.

"None," Marc said. "Just worry."

"Join the club. It will be alright."

"Says your Creator?"

Dumyan's beak widened into a smile. "Says I."

"Good to know."

"Now, what's out there? I can't make out anything in the haze."

"The ship's sensors can," Sibular said.

They all shifted their eyes to one of the screens in the cockpit. It showed a wheel shaped structure, or at least what had once been one. Now it was broken up into multiple sections, and the connections to the central core were also gone.

"The space station," Marc said. "The one we were on?"

"It appears so," Sibular replied.

"It hasn't fared so well," Dumyan observed. "I suppose it was badly damaged when the Mendoken attacked it."

"For us, it's only been a couple of Earth months," Zorina said. "But here almost a year has passed since we left. It's easy for a damaged space station to disintegrate over time when there's nobody left to run or maintain it."

"Especially in a universe that was never made to sustain the kind of matter the station was made of," Sibular said.

"That's what comes of trying to build things in an environment for which they were never naturally intended," Dumyan added.

The ruins of the station began appearing through the haze. The pilot carefully maneuvered the scout ship between the big, dark blocks of floating debris. It was an eerie, morbid sight for the occupants of the ship. It almost felt as if they were surrounded by giant tombstones.

"I guess the same is true for the monsters," Marc said. "The crystals should still be here, though. They were naturally created in this universe."

"There." Sibular pointed with one of his four robotic hands toward a region between two neighboring blocks of debris. A section of the cockpit window automatically zoomed in on that area, rendering a highly magnified view of numerous shapes floating aimlessly in space.

"You're right," Marc said. The physiques were unmistakable – long, slender bodies with many limbs and nodes connecting them. The nodes were dim, though – colorless and lifeless.

"Are they... dead?" Zorina asked.

"Hard to say," Sibular said. "We need to get closer."

The pilot began slowing the ship down and brought it to a standstill in front of the flock of crystals. There were hundreds of them, perhaps thousands. Not one of them seemed to exhibit any signs of life.

"There are more," Sibular said, eyeing one of the screens in the cockpit. "The ship's sensors are picking them up all over now, spread around and beyond the station debris."

"I don't think they're dead," Marc said. "I can... feel it."

"Me too," Dumyan said.

"Same here," Zorina chimed in.

"We need to get out there," Marc said. "Are there spacesuits on board?"

"Yes, but meant only for Mendoken," Sibular replied. "It will be awkward and uncomfortable for you at best."

"Don't care. I'm going. Suit me up."

Marc didn't end up going alone. Zorina, Dumyan and Sibular joined him. They all put on suits and ejected into space through one of the ship's airlocks. It had required some explaining by Sibular how to operate the suits, but he had been right. The suits were designed for Mendoken, and they were extremely uncomfortable to fit into and maneuver in for anyone else. Zorina found it hardest, but Marc didn't fare much better. For Dumyan the suit was too short, but he managed to pull his long legs in to fit. Thankfully the oxygen levels were adequate for everyone.

"What a heap of excrement," Zorina muttered, trying to keep her trunk rolled up and squashing her ears to fit her large head into the tight helmet.

"How does... this thing even work?" Marc asked, trying to figure out the suit's built-in motion controls. His arms barely fit into the two front arm covers, while the two back arm covers just dangled loose. Their voices were audible to each other over the intercom system linking the suits and the ship's cockpit.

"I warned you," Sibular said. "The translator devices you are carrying should translate all the instructions automatically into your respective languages on the helmet screen. Give it a moment, and some practice."

After some trial and error, Marc, Zorina and Dumyan got the basic hang of it. They then followed Sibular into the crystal graveyard. The sight was even more macabre than the earlier view of the space station ruins. The nodes of the crystals were all dark, and their limbs limp and shriveled up. It was like wading through a sea of dead, giant octopi.

"They're not dead, I'm sure of it," Marc said. "I wonder if..." He reached out and touched one of the nodes of the nearest crystal.

The reaction was instantaneous. The node lit up into a brilliant orange and passed energy through its connected limbs to its other nodes. Before long, the entire creature was alive and awake. It lowered its top node toward him in a show of gratitude.

"Told you so," Marc said. "They were waiting for us."

The others followed suit, touching the nodes of the crystals they were nearest to. The crystals all came alive in the same way.

"It's got to be something they passed onto us during all those physical punishments," Zorina said.

"Yes," Dumyan agreed. "I'd bet that even though the red cores were in control of the crystals' bodies when they were punishing us, the crystals created a connection with us on a much deeper level. They could control thoughts and feelings with their ability to manipulate their own energy and the bulk energy around them. It's how they communicated with us before, especially that one crystal with you, Marc."

"That's it!" Marc exclaimed. "They created a deep mental connection with us for their own protection. Even though the red cores were controlling their bodies, the crystals still had their own minds somewhere in those nodes. They planned this, don't you see? They knew they were in trouble ever since their creator got destroyed and the anomalies took over and enslaved them. They knew they needed help if they were to ever be free again, so they took advantage of the anomalies' desire to punish us to connect with us without the anomalies even realizing it. They also knew that since we were brought here by force, we would possibly end up getting rescued one day. So they hedged their bets. Either when we got rescued we would destroy the anomalies and save them, or we would get rescued without saving them. But if we got rescued without saving them, then the mental connection they created with us would ensure that we'd feel guilty enough to come back and save them."

"You really think these crystals are that smart?" Zorina asked, her voice muffled thanks to her big head finding no space in her helmet. "What about all the instructions that were sent back to our universe when the anomaly attacked the Mendoken space station, explaining how to create the gateway and the composition of the anomalies? How could the crystals have done that?"

"I don't know," Marc replied. "They were smart enough to figure out how to travel to our universe, remember? They did all the analyzing for the anomalies and opened the gateways for them."

"Then why do they need saving?" Zorina went on. "They were already safe once the anomalies and monsters were destroyed. Couldn't they just have continued living their lives?"

"My guess is there's more they want than just staying alive," Marc said. "They were waiting for us to return for a reason."

"There is only one way to find out," Sibular said. "Let us finish what we started. We need everyone. Those of you back on the ship, put on your suits and join us. We need to awaken all of the crystals."

It took time, but what made it quicker was that the awakened crystals in turn were able to awaken other crystals by themselves. It set off a chain reaction that eventually reached the many thousands of crystals around and beyond the debris.

The entire space around Marc and his companions was lit up now, with the familiar, multi-colored glow of crystal nodes. It was beautiful, and it reminded Marc of winter holiday decorations in the downtown areas of some European cities. Except this was way, way larger and more spread out.

"It's not stopping," Zorina observed. "Look! There's many more crystals out there in space."

Indeed, thousands was an understatement. It was more like millions. No matter which way they looked, more and more lights were popping up in the distance. It was almost starting to look like the starry sky of their own universe, except the stars were of different colors and amidst that ever-present hazy backdrop.

"Amazing," Marc whispered. "Where have they all come from?"

"They were probably always there, scattered in space," Sibular said. "They just stayed hidden during the era of the anomalies to avoid being recruited and controlled by them. Maybe some of them played a part in sending the information back to our universe in secret when the anomaly attacked our space station."

"Marc, behind you." That was Dumyan's voice.

Marc turned to look and was astonished. It was the crystal, *his* crystal, floating right there in front of him. There was no doubt, it just had to be. The five nodes with that unique color combination – blue, green, red, blue, yellow. Besides, no other crystal would have come forward to meet him like that after being awakened.

Marc felt exhilarated, overjoyed. It was like finding a lost loved one after a long, long time. If he could, he would have given it a big hug. Instead, he bowed his head as best as he could in the gravity-less environment, and the crystal lowered its top node toward him right away in response. It was gleaming brightly, perhaps its way of showing satisfaction that all the effort and mental connection it had invested in Marc was finally showing signs of paying off. Or perhaps it was just glad to see him.

"Ask it, Marc," Dumyan said. "Ask it what it wants. What all these crystals want. Why they wanted us to come back."

Marc maneuvered his suit to edge closer to the crystal. Then he stretched out with both his hands and touched its top node. Pulling the node toward him, he brought it into as close contact as he could with his head. The helmet was in the way, of course, but he could only hope that it would still work.

The crystal, however, didn't seem concerned. A part of the node passed seamlessly through the helmet as if it wasn't there at all, and it came into physical contact with his forehead. The connection was made.

Chapter 44

"Well, what did you see?" Zorina asked.

The crystal had pulled back from Marc's head and out of his helmet. The connection had lasted quite a while.

Dumyan floated toward Marc. "Are you awake?"

Marc was quiet and kept his eyes closed. His mind was bursting with intense, conflicting emotions, and if he could he would have yelled out at the top of his lungs to let some of it out. Not a good idea in a space suit, he had to remind himself. Instead, he breathed deeply a few times to calm down and gather his thoughts.

"Our theory was right," he eventually said. "They were waiting for us. They stayed dormant to save their energy until we came back. But it wasn't just about protecting them from the anomalies."

"What then?" Sibular asked.

"They needed the gateway to be reopened, and they couldn't do it from their side alone."

"So they want to travel to our universe," Zorina said.

"No, there's something hidden inside the gateway," Marc explained. "And they want it to come out."

"What is it?"

"They don't seem to know anymore. Whatever memory they have of it, they buried it deep inside our minds when they connected with us. And then they erased it from their own. They're all connected to each other mentally – they think collectively like one being. It's amazing – I could feel millions of them communicating with me, not just this one crystal."

"To prevent the anomalies and monsters from finding out about it," Sibular observed. "Makes sense. Even if they were brought to heel with red cores implanted into them again, their lack of knowledge would prevent them from ever revealing anything."

"But they have knowledge of gateways," Zorina said. "Why couldn't they have opened it themselves?"

"They seem to have erased that from their memories too," Marc replied. "They didn't want to ever get taken advantage of again to cause harm for our universe or any other. What's more, they buried different parts of all the knowledge among the sixteen of us. It requires all of us to bring it back together, so they can put together the whole story and do what they need to after that."

"Do you sense any danger?" Dumyan asked.

"Not at all."

"So what do we need to do?"

"Form a circle and allow the crystals to come between us."

The circle was wide, with the sixteen spread all around its circumference. In between each of them were a number of crystals. Then other crystals came forward and placed themselves above the circle. Yet others placed themselves above those crystals, and more above them. This process continued until a glistening path of crystals was formed for many, many miles – all the way from the circle to the edge of the gateway.

"Alright, here goes," Marc said. "You all ready?"

Dumyan, Sibular, Zorina and the twelve others voiced their unanimous consent.

Marc reached out and touched the nearest node of his crystal friend with his right hand, positioned to his right in the circle. With his other hand, he touched the nearest node of the crystal to his immediate left. Those crystals, in turn, touched their neighboring crystals with their nodes.

The others did the same, until the circle was fully connected. Then the crystals in the circle connected with the ones above, and so on until all the crystals were connected in the long path to the gateway.

Marc closed his eyes in anticipation of the next thing. It came within seconds, as the crystal above him lowered one of its nodes onto his helmet and connected with his head. He felt a lunge of warm energy searing through his head and across his body. His mind began bursting with intense emotions again, and once again came the urge to yell out in anguish.

Thankfully the mental pain soon plateaued and subsided, and it was slowly overtaken by a feeling of peace, of comfort and contentment. He felt lighter and more agile, as if a heavy burden was being lifted from his shoulders. The feelings of guilt and shame that he had been carrying since the return to his universe were fading away. He was connected with the other fifteen, and with all the crystals. Thoughts were being shared, knowledge being retrieved from the depths of minds including his own, complete pictures being painted. He felt good, and he could sense that the others did too. It was invigorating.

The emotions gave way to visions, just as they had done in his previous communications with the crystals. The blurry images that were starting to take shape around him soon grew into a full three-dimensional simulation. He was taken back to the time of the original, monstrous lifeform, the creator of these crystals, that had once ruled this universe. It looked as magnificent as ever, with its wide network of blobs spread across its central, round bright core and millions of colorful spikes sticking out in all directions.

The magnificence, however, was not to last. He was once again taken through the painful memory of the consar tunnel that appeared out of nowhere, broke its way into the heart of this gigantic being and caused the entire structure to crumble. That consar that he and his friends had traveled on, the accursed consar that had set off a chain reaction of calamitous, irrevocable events that had caused so much devastation and suffering both in this universe and his own.

Yet, this time, the simulation focused on something else he hadn't seen before. As the consar burrowed its way through the core section of the lifeform, causing it to collapse and dissipate, the very central part of the core fell into the consar's trajectory and disappeared. And, just like that, it all became clear to Marc.

The main, central intelligence of the original lifeform had not been destroyed. It had fallen into a realm of alternate dimensions in the bulk, thanks to the consar that had passed through it. Now that the conditions were safe in this universe, the crystals were trying to re-open this gateway so that they could access those same alternate dimensions and retrieve the central part of their creator's core.

Brilliant, Marc thought. Absolutely brilliant. He could only hope their plan would work. The chances that this gateway would open up to the same dimensions that consar had traveled through all those years ago were, while not zero, low at best. Then again, these crystals had clearly done their homework and had studied that consar in depth, and for all he knew they had passed instructions to the Mendoken to create this gateway to travel through the very same dimensions to reach this universe.

The simulation faded away. Marc opened his eyes as the node connected to his head pulled away. He looked up, in time to see the entire path of crystals to the gateway lit up in brilliant light. From the very top of the path, a ray shot out toward the gateway entrance and passed into it.

It was probably only moments that passed, but to Marc it felt much longer. Eventually, the ray stopped emanating. Then, something began coming out of the gateway. It looked like streaks of mist, and it just kept coming. It filled up the space around the gateway entrance and began spreading out in all directions. It came down the path of crystals toward the circle, soon encompassing Marc and the other fifteen as well. As it passed over and around him, Marc felt far from unsafe. This mist was benign, he knew it wouldn't harm him.

And it didn't. It left him and his friends untouched, but it took all the crystals. They let go of each other and let the mist simply carry them away like feathers in the wind. The mist began moving away with the crystals from Marc and his friends, who were left to float in empty space beside their ship. Still visible through the haze, Marc could see the mist coalesce into a dense cloud, together with all the millions of crystals it was carrying with it. The crystals merged into groups and began looking awfully similar to the blobs he remembered in his visions of the original lifeform.

As the cloud coalesced further, a series of explosions could be seen across its surface and within its interior. But they weren't violent explosions, nor did they have any impact on the sixteen observers. It was more of a metamorphosis. And, as things cleared, Marc could make out a central brilliant core forming, with colorful spikes reaching out every which way. It looked awfully similar to images Marc had seen of supernovas, except that it wasn't momentary or blinding to his eyes. This phenomenon was here to stay. Blobs were spread across the body, all connected to each other. While significantly larger than an anomaly, it was still many orders of magnitude smaller than the original being that had once ruled this universe. But it was quite clearly that same lifeform. It had been recreated, and with time it would perhaps grow to its original size again.

"Incredible," Marc whispered. It was all he could say.

The lifeform looked truly beautiful, like a work of art. Even with its sheer size, it didn't come across as scary or menacing, a true contrast from the raging, pulsating bodies of anomalies. Out of one of its blobs a crystal came flying and headed straight for Marc. As it came closer, the color combination of its nodes was once again unmistakable. It was his friend.

The crystal came forward and lowered its top node toward Marc, who touched it with both his hands and bowed before it. He couldn't hold back the tears, but thankfully they were tears of joy. He and this crystal had been through a lot together, and all for the better in the end.

He let go of the node, and he sighed with a tremendous sense of relief and satisfaction as the crystal speed off back to the lifeform.

"We did it," Zorina said, trying to bob her head up and down in the tight helmet.

"No, they did it," Sibular corrected her. "They have restored life in this universe back to its natural state. That bulk energy could give rise to such intelligent, rational beings that can communicate and control minds with the same energy they are made of, we Mendoken could never have imagined. There is still clearly much for us to learn about the diversity of life."

"As for us Aftarans," Dumyan said. "Lots that our Scriptures and pious way of life never taught us."

Dark energy is not so dark, Marc thought. Humans had lots more to learn about it than anyone else, and they would have to pick up the term that everyone else in the galaxy used for it – bulk energy.

"I would not be surprised if it was this lifeform that sent us all the instructions about opening the gateway and how to fight the anomalies," Sibular said. "It may not have been the crystals themselves. This lifeform clearly has a bigger intelligence, and it may have secretly been monitoring everything from the other dimensions. It was communicating with and directing things in both universes, in both branes from somewhere in the bulk."

"Which would also explain why this side of the gateway remained closed until things reached a certain point," Marc deduced. "The Mendoken were only able to come through with their planet destroyers once the anomalies had reached their end game. This lifeform was watching things inside the gateway too, and as a result literally controlling everyone's fate with the decisions it made."

"Why was it waiting for us to come back, then, if it's so smart and powerful?" Zorina asked. "Couldn't it just have opened the gateway and come out here by itself to rejoin the crystals once the anomalies were destroyed?"

"My guess is it was somehow stuck in the alternate dimensions and needed help getting out," Marc said. "It may have been able to pull strings and communicate with the universes on both sides of the gateway, but it wasn't able to get out by itself."

"Perhaps," Dumyan replied. "Or perhaps it was all controlled by another, higher power. We may never know the real answer. The only thing we do know is that the anomalies were caught by surprise, which means they had no idea that information about them and this universe was passed back to ours. They were not expecting any retaliation."

"I'm just glad we didn't give up on the crystals," Marc said. "I feel free now, all the feelings of guilt are gone."

Dumyan's large, round eyes narrowed. "It's unimaginable. These crystals, the lowest in the hierarchy of living things in this universe – slapped around, used and abused by other creatures far more powerful than them. And yet, they prevailed in the end while the others perished. They were much smarter than everyone and everything else, us included."

"All lives matter, as the Imgoerin said."

"Couldn't be more true, at least the lives of those who don't maliciously take away or harm the lives of others."

"Right," Zorina agreed. "But now I think it's time for us to go home. More importantly, I need to get out of this suit."

The journey back through the gateway was uneventful, and well within the time boundary the Imgoerin had placed on keeping the gateway open. They had been given 15 hours in the time scale of the universe they were leaving behind, and they had only used up 5. The gateway was closing up behind them as they passed back through it, closing up for good this time as the Mendoken had vowed to destroy the entry ring once this scout ship returned safely through it.

The matter conversion occurred without a hitch and, true to promise, as soon as they exited the gateway they witnessed the crumbling of the ring behind them. There would never again be any contact with that other universe.

The scout ship docked with the armada of Mendoken ships ever present in the vicinity of the ring, right where the Selcher-44328 space station used to be. There, it was time for the sixteen to part ways. Sibular would head home to the heart of the Mendoken Republic, Dumyan to the planet Meenjaza in the Aftaran Dominion to reunite with his father and his wife Birshat, and Zorina to the Volonan Empire. The six Mendoken troopers would disperse to their homes within the Republic, while the six Aftaran soldiers would return with Dumyan to the Dominion and then head to their homes. Long vacations and periods of rest amidst much recognition and praise awaited all of them, as promised by their leaders.

The scout ship was left just for Marc, who was given a crash course on how to operate and take care of it. It would stay with him on Earth, to use at his discretion and as needed. Never again would he be left without a means to contact or reach the Mendoken or any of the other advanced civilizations in the galaxy. Nobody knew what kind of situations might arise in the future where such contact was needed, as this whole anomaly adventure had shown. And now that humans knew about the Mendoken and his relationship to them, there would no longer be a need to hide the ship's existence either.

On a landing deck aboard one of the Mendoken Euma ships, the four friends bid each other goodbye. It was emotional, of course, especially the moment when they paid tribute to Jinser-Shosa together. But overall Marc felt much better about it this time, because he now had a way to stay in contact with the others if needed. He just had this feeling that he'd be seeing them again someday.

The hug with Dumyan was long and heartfelt, and the warmth of his thick brown robe very comforting.

"Your spiritual powers are back?" Marc asked.

"Yes," Dumyan replied. "I have learned a thing or two, though, about religion and the extent of its place in our lives."

"Don't forget to spread that message to others."

Dumyan smiled. "I won't."

The hug with Sibular was, as expected, a lot shorter and more awkward. He didn't understand its purpose or why it was necessary.

"Your moon Ailen, was it completely destroyed by the anomalies?" Marc asked him.

"Almost, but it has since been rebuilt. The research centers are even better and more modern than before, from what I hear."

"A heaven for you, then."

"It will be an improvement."

And, finally, Zorina spread her wide ears around Marc's body and squeezed him tightly.

"Take care of yourself, Marc," she said. "I'll really miss you."

"As I you," he said. "Will things be ok with your sister?"

"We'll be fine. We already have been. I just need to find another partner for myself now. Speaking of which, don't give up on Alisha. Go back to her and spend the rest of your life with her."

"I'm not sure she'll take me back. I wasn't very nice to her when I left."

"You were under a foreign influence. You can explain that to her. Besides, if she's even a fraction of the amazing individual I believe she is, she will forgive you in a heartbeat."

"I hope you're right."

"You need to let go of your past, Marc. It's been long enough."

"The punishments I faced at the hands of the anomalies and the crystals they were controlling made that very clear."

"Ironically it wasn't at all what the anomalies intended, but all the suffering they put us through has actually made us stronger. It's given us clarity on what's important to us and what isn't. History really doesn't need to repeat itself, especially once you let go of the tragedies in your past, overcome your fears and make the right choices."

Marc nodded. "Yeah."

"Nature does have a weird way of replacing or substituting what it once took away from you, you know," Zorina said.

"Hardly for everyone."

"True. But often enough, and sometimes from corners you'd least expect."

"We'll see. Time will tell."

With that, the four friends parted ways and headed to their own ships.

Chapter 45

Dharavi, the most well-known slum in Mumbai, India, had a population of about 700,000 crammed into less than a square mile, giving it the distinguished standing of being one of the world's densest areas in addition to being one of its biggest slums. In existence for more than a century, it had suffered numerous epidemics and other disasters thanks to its poor sanitation and lack of adequate basic infrastructure. On the flip side, however, it housed people from all religions and races in India, making it a truly diverse settlement where all inhabitants had learned to co-exist due to their one common, shared predicament – extreme poverty.

With the arrival of the Mendoken, things were looking up for Dharavi, as they were for poor people across Mumbai, across India and indeed around the world. While the Mendoken were purposely not directly interfering or doing things for individual people, they were providing national governments with both advanced knowhow and physical resources to enhance the quality of life for all of their citizens. Within days of their arrival, Dharavi was seeing plans put in place by the Indian government for the construction of tall apartment buildings to house its inhabitants, the spread of sophisticated sewage systems, as well as the supply of electricity, food and fresh water to all of its corners. The inhabitants themselves were being employed to help build up their township and serve their community, so that over time they could reach complete self-sufficiency and independence. No longer would they be taken advantage of by the wealthy, powerful and corrupt.

That said, there were still so many people in the crowded slums who lacked hope and had nowhere to go. So many homeless orphans, so many sick and disabled people, so many elderly with nobody to fend for them. City officials, now equipped with funds and direction from the national government thanks to Mendoken insistence, were already setting up kiosks across Dharavi's dense network of narrow, dirty roads to register the neediest people and get them help. Orphans would be adopted by people around the country, the sick taken to newly constructed hospitals and the elderly to retirement homes.

It was on one of these very narrow roads in Dharavi that Marc was carefully treading, trying to avoid stepping into any puddle of water or heap of garbage. It was his first time in a slum, and he was horror-stricken by the conditions under which people were living day in and day out. He looked completely out of place with his skin complexion, facial appearance and clean clothes, and he tried his best to avoid the curious gaze of all the individuals he passed, young and old.

It had been a number of days since his return from the other universe. He had needed the time to touch base with Commander Maginder and the rest of the Mendoken contingent still at Earth, to discuss how things were progressing on the planet's surface. As it turned out, things were going quite well overall, and if it continued along the current trend then the Mendoken would be able to leave quite soon and just keep a watchful eye from a distance like they used to before. He had further taken the time to meet with US President Tucker and other world leaders to ensure things were going smoothly from their perspective. He was a well-known figure around the world now, and he had to act accordingly. It was also important for him to ensure that he wasn't needed anywhere to address any diplomatic issue between the Mendoken and humanity. Fortunately he wasn't. Then he had taken care of some loose ends as far as his home and belongings in Palo Alto, California were concerned, and he had resigned from his post as a sociology professor at Stanford University.

Now, here in the maze of paths of this mega shantytown, he kept turning one corner after the next, following the guidance of the portable locator device he had found in the Sil-5 scout ship that was now his to keep.

Then, after one more turn he finally found what he was looking for. Up ahead, there was a kiosk with a line of people queued up in front of it – mostly children and disabled people. Around them was a large crowd, watching the scene with much curiosity and interest. Behind it, he saw a couple of doctors and nurses attending to individuals. And there between them, talking to each person and typing information into a laptop with that warm smile he had so missed, was the reason for the crowd. It was likely the closest any of them had ever gotten to a Bollywood movie actress, and that too one of such immense fame and beauty. The fact that she was raised in Dharavi was all the more alluring for the many individuals present, a sign of hope that a product of this slum could indeed conquer all obstacles to make it to such towering heights.

He stopped and stood for a long while, admiring her and the way she was working. She was so full of life, of radiance, of positivity and encouragement. It didn't seem to matter how dire the situation was, she seemed to find a way to make every person feel better and offer him or her hope.

He couldn't help smiling, he couldn't help thinking how lucky he was to have met and fallen in love with such an amazing individual, how lucky he was to have caught her attention, her love and affection. He had been a fool to throw it all away – granted he had been under the influence of the crystals, but some of it also had to do with his own fears and experiences. He had been selfish to make the decisions for her about her safety and protection. It should have been her choice to make, not his. He had lost loved ones in his life, sure, but that didn't mean he had to project that onto her. There was no reason for history to keep repeating itself.

Now, here in front of her, he could only hope she would find it in her heart to forgive him and take him back.

At some point, in between tending to people in the queue, she looked up past the crowd and noticed him standing there. At first she seemed to think she was imagining things, looking away again quickly. But then her gaze returned. She looked surprised, and then she looked relieved. But then, within a few moments her expression slowly turned angry.

Not a good start, he thought. As he walked through the crowd toward her, she kept her eyes fixated on him. He passed the line and came to a stop right in front of her.

"Hey," he said.

"Hey," she replied tersely.

"I am sorry, so very sorry. I was wrong. You were right. I was stupid. A total idiot."

She said nothing.

"If I tell you all the reasons why I behaved the way I did, you won't even believe it," he went on.

Still silence.

"I've missed you, a lot," he added.

People in the line began speaking up, asking him to move out of the way and let the registration process continue. The Mendoken translator device he was carrying was happily translating all of their insults from Marathi and Hindi into English for him, but he ignored them.

"I'm working," she finally said.

"Can I, uh, ask you to please forgive me?"

Silence again.

"Please?" he added.

She glared at him. "What, you think it's that easy?"

"What do you mean?"

"You broke my heart, Marc."

"I know, I'm really sorry. But you have to believe me, I was not myself."

"That's one of the lamest excuses I've ever heard."

"It's true. Those crystals, they had a hold on me. It wasn't just me, the same happened to Sibular, Dumyan, Zorina and the others who were on that consar voyage with me. You can ask them if you don't believe me."

"Ok, let me talk to them then."

"Uh, they aren't here anymore. They went home."

"Isn't that convenient," she sneered.

Marc looked around. People were yelling at him now to leave, and a few came forward.

"Alisha, I'm serious," he said, realizing that he was out of time. "You have to believe me. I would never do that to you in any sane state of mind."

"Why not?" she asked, watching contentedly as some of the people pushed and prodded him away.

"You know me," he called out, now barely audible amidst all the uproar as he kept getting pushed further away. "You've gotten to know me inside and out. You know I fell in love with you. I still love you. My love for you has only grown. Please, just give me a chance to explain what happened."

He began receiving blows to his head and body by people in the crowd. But he refused to run away. Instead, he tried to push his way back toward Alisha. Eventually he tripped and fell, and people began beating him from all sides.

"Enough!" she finally called out.

The crowd fell silent immediately.

"Let him go," she said.

The people surrounding Marc moved away and let a path form between him and Alisha. Marc immediately got up and hobbled toward her.

"I've missed you too," she finally said as he reached her. "But I really got hurt."

"I will never do that to you again, I swear by all that I believe in and ever cared about. I was possessed by the crystals, not too different from the way they were once possessed through the red cores by the anomalies. But I'm not anymore. It's all done and my conscience is clear now."

"For you, perhaps. For me, it isn't so simple anymore."

"What do you mean?"

She motioned to someone behind her. A little Indian girl came forward and stood beside her. She looked five years old, perhaps, but malnourished as she was, she was possibly a little older. She was wearing a clean dress, though, one she probably only obtained recently as a donation. Her hair was tied neatly into two pigtails. She was cute, and she had a very sweet, innocent look about her.

"This is Riya," Alisha said, gently placing her hand on the child's head. "She's an orphan from here, and I've just adopted her. I'm her mother now."

Marc was taken aback at first, but his eyes lit up as soon as he recalled Zorina's parting words. He dropped down to his knees and raised his hands to touch Riya's. "Hi, Riya, I'm Marc, it's nice to meet you," he said, letting the translator do its work.

"Are you the man from space?" Riya asked, pointing up to the sky. "I've seen you on TV."

Marc smiled. "I guess you could say that."

"I want to live on Mars one day," she said. "Under a red sky."

"Really?" Marc said. "Did you know that Mars has blue sunsets?"

Riya shook her head.

"Would you like to see it?"

She grinned and nodded.

"What are you doing?" Alisha asked.

"I'm trying to make an impression," he replied. "May I?"

"Why?"

"To try to win her heart, and yours. How else will we ever be a family?"

"Who says we're going to be a family?"

"I don't know if we will. All I ask is for a fighting chance to prove to you why I should earn your love and trust again so that we hopefully can."

"You think I love you?" she asked.

"I know you do. That's why you got so hurt by my actions. And again, for that I am so very deeply sorry."

Alisha looked down, deep in thought. A faint smile eventually spread across her lips, but she tried her best to hide it. Then she stood up and faced him. "Never abandon me again," she said sternly.

"Never." He put his arms around her and kissed her on the spot. It felt as nice and warm as the first time they had kissed, and it lasted for many a second.

When he finally let her go, her face was blushing, likely from embarrassment at her public display of intimacy. After all, such behavior was far from the cultural norm in the heart of an Indian slum. The crowd around them, however, seemed to feel otherwise. The loud cheers coming from every direction made that very clear. Gone was all the anger that they had held toward Marc just moments earlier.

"Also, I'm staying here to help these people," she said. "I've finally found my true calling."

"That makes two of us," he replied.

"Really?"

"Yeah. To help the poor and needy, and to be wherever you are. But first, let's take a short break."

"Huh?"

He lifted his hand, and immediately a shadow materialized in the air above their heads. Gasps of shock and surprise quickly followed from the crowd. It was his Sil-5 scout ship, hovering quietly in the air. A door opened on the side and a metal ladder descended to the very spot where he was standing.

"Wow!" Riya exclaimed. "A spaceship!"

Marc stretched out his hands and picked her up. "Come on, kid, let's go pay your red planet a little visit. We'll be back in time for dinner."

Riya's face was beaming with excitement.

Alisha shook her head and laughed. "You're crazy, Mr. Zemin."

"True that."

"So are you really going to tell me what happened out there?" she asked as she began climbing the ladder.

Marc followed in her footsteps, holding the ladder with one hand and Riya with the other. "No secrets between us, Alisha," he said. "Not now and not ever."

After they had climbed aboard, the ship raised the ladder automatically and closed the door. Seconds later, it sped off into the sky.

ABOUT THE AUTHOR

S.W. (Sajjad Waiz) Ahmed is an American science fiction writer of Bangladeshi origin. He grew up in Austria and moved to the United States at the age of 18, where he studied electrical engineering and pursued a career in computer software. A keen follower of science and an avid reader of science fiction since childhood, he now writes his own sci-fi stories as a hobby. He currently resides in the San Francisco Bay Area. *Dark Energy* is his second novel and a sequel to his first novel *Dark Matter*.